Full Circle

Books by Donya Lynne

Strong Karma Series
Good Karma
Coming Back To You
Full Circle

All the King's Men Series
Rise of the Fallen
Heart of the Warrior
Micah's Calling
Rebel Obsession
Return of the Assassin
All the King's Men - The Beginning
All the King's Men Collection - books 1-3
All the King's Men Collection - books 4-6

Single Titles
Finding Lacey Moon
Winter's Fire

Full Circle

Donya Lynne

Full Circle

Donya Lynne

Copyright © 2015 Donya Lynne

ISBN: 1938991125

ISBN 13: 9781938991127

Cover art by Reese Dante.

Dedication

To you and your happy ending.

Acknowledgements

Mark and Karma's story came to me back in 2013, during the peak of popularity of my All the King's Men Series. So, I would first like to acknowledge both my AKM characters and my fans of that series. Anyone who relies on creativity understands the concept of inspiration striking. And Mark and Karma definitely struck me, shutting down everything else. So thank you for your patience as Mark and Karma took over my brain.

Thank you also to my wonderful beta readers. As always, your feedback made this book better than I could have made it on my own. Every author needs a tough group of readers who aren't afraid to say, "Hey, this isn't working." Thank you for being mine. And a special thanks to Sue for the four-hour brainstorming "consults." You have no idea how much they helped.

And to my readers, thank you for investing your time with my books and me. Every word I write is with you in mind. I hope you enjoy the final installment of the Strong Karma Trilogy.

In the end, only three things matter. How much you loved, how gently you lived, and how gracefully you let go of things not meant for you.
-Gautama Buddha

Part I

Happiness is like those palaces in fairy tales whose gates are guarded by dragons. We must fight in order to conquer it.
-Alexandre Dumas

Chapter 1

I feel a new beginning coming toward me, and I'm running to it with open arms.
-Author Unknown

Karma stared at the blank sheet of paper on the table.

Well, it wasn't exactly blank. She'd gotten as far as writing *Resolutions* in the top margin, along with the number one below it. After that... nada. She couldn't think of a single New Year's resolution. Probably because she already had everything she wanted. Mark was back. She'd just started a new job. She was happy.

Still, a new year didn't feel complete without at least one resolution. After all, resolutions were a symbol of hope, and hope fed the dreams for the future. Surely she could dig up at least one aspiration... one dream. Something to carry her forward.

This time last year, there had been no shortage of dreams *or* hope. The summer before, after spending four life-changing months with Mark Strong—four months in which she tumbled head over heels in love with him—he'd left her to return to Chicago, leaving her shattered heart in his wake. Which meant last December, her resolutions had centered around the hope her pain would end, she could find a way to forget him, or—dream of all dreams—he would come back to her.

And her dream came true.

He *had* come back.

Because he'd fallen in love with her, too.

She'd known in her heart he had, but it took him an hour too long to admit it to himself or he never would have left in the first place.

But now all that was behind them.

Not that the past was forgotten. The past still hovered in the background like a disconnected shadow.

But a new year brought fresh ambition. And resolutions carried that ambition forward.

All the more reason to come up with one.

"Hey, stranger."

Karma glanced up from her notepad as her best friend Lisa joined her at the window table inside Greek Tony's, their favorite pizza place.

"Hey you."

When she and Lisa worked together, they'd seen each other every day, chitchatted every morning, and went to lunch together at least twice a week. But since leaving Solar a couple weeks ago, Karma hadn't seen Lisa, so she was suffering major friendship withdrawal.

Lisa leaned in and gave her a one-armed hug. "You look good."

"Thanks. So do you."

Lisa slung her coat over the back of the chair next to Karma's. "I'm starved. I sort of missed lunch today."

"How do you 'sort of' miss lunch?"

"Your precious boyfriend is keeping me busy." She slid onto the chair across from her.

"Mark?" Karma's brow bunched as her mouth twisted into a crooked smirk.

"Yeah, Mark. He's seriously interfering with my professional sanity, as well as my lunch schedule, so . . ." She pinched her lips together then huffed. "But hey, I ate some yogurt and granola earlier, so I'm not completely famished."

Karma gestured toward Greek Tony's order counter. "I wish I'd known. I would have ordered a deep dish or breadsticks or something. I just got our normal."

Their normal was a thin and crispy garden veggie pizza. Not the kind of meal that quenched starvation, but damn near the best pizza in town when you were watching your figure.

Lisa waved her hand through the air in a don't-worry-about-it motion. "I'll live." She peered at Karma's notepad. "What's that? Resolutions?" She blew out an amused huff. "Wow. Do you think you have enough?"

"Hush." Karma glanced at the blank page before closing her notebook and smugly stuffing it in her leather briefcase. "I've got Mark, so I don't need resolutions."

Lisa laughed. "You might not have him much longer if he keeps finding new customers at a record pace, making my life hell as I try to find new personnel to fill all the positions he's creating. I might have to kill him just to catch a break."

Karma laughed. "He can't help being good at his job."

Lisa sipped at the soft drink Karma had ordered for her. "Yeah, well, he's overachieving." She took another drink then gestured toward Karma's briefcase and the abandoned notebook. "You ready for the new job?"

After getting back together with Mark in November, it had become clear Karma could no longer work at Solar, so she'd contacted Dr. Whitman, one of her college professors, who made a few phone calls on her behalf and found her a position as a junior editor for Winstrom Press, a Chicago publisher.

It was a ground-floor position, but at least it was in her field of study, unlike the executive assistant job at Solar.

"I'm a little nervous, but I'm ready."

"You'll be great." Lisa threw her a playful scowl. "But we'll never get to see each other anymore. I still can't believe you left Solar. Traitor." She lightly smacked Karma's hand, teasing her.

"We'll still see each other."

But carving out time to see Lisa was already a challenge. What would happen once she officially started her new job in a couple of weeks and her days were filled with manuscripts and classes? Who would she turn to, to help her get through the days? Lisa had been a daily source of moral support and friendly motivation just a flight of stairs and a few offices away. Now Karma would be working from her lonely, quiet apartment. Talk about a major shift.

"I know, but I'm used to you being there every day. It's weird walking upstairs and not seeing you at your desk, sipping your tea, making moon eyes at Mark's office."

"Moon eyes. Right."

Lisa giggled and twirled her straw in her drink, then sobered and leaned forward. "Seriously, though, I'm really happy for you. I mean, sure, I miss you like crazy at the office, but this is a good move for you."

"It's a lucky break is what it is."

She'd originally been slated for a position in St. Louis that would have required her to move. Thank goodness Dr. Whitman had been able to find her the Winstrom job, which allowed her to work from home. She would miss seeing Lisa every day at the office, but at least she could stay in Indiana.

"It's a sign." Lisa's eyes opened wide as she said it. "One door closes, and a better one opens. It means you're on the right path."

Karma laughed. "You and your signs."

"Hey, don't knock signs and the power of the universe. After all, those are the things that brought Mark back to you."

Mark had made no secret that he had let the universe guide him in his journey back to her last summer. He'd told her for the year they were apart, he'd waited for a sign they were meant to be together. When he was offered the job at Solar, he knew his time had come.

But his plan had almost backfired. If he had waited only a few months longer, she might have been married to Brad. Thank God that hadn't happened. She counted her blessings every day that Mark had returned when he did, because he'd made her see how wrong Brad was for her. How she'd simply been using Brad as a fill-in. She should have known nobody could ever fill Mark's larger-than-life shoes.

Oh, sure, she had been angry with Mark at first, but she knew now that was only because she'd been fighting how much she still loved him. Once she gave in to her feelings, falling into his arms had been as natural as breathing.

"Mark's faith in signs saved me, didn't they?" She grinned like a damn schoolgirl as she glanced out the window.

Surely, she couldn't live the rest of her life in such a cosmic state of bliss. Could she? Heck, maybe she could. Maybe life would now be an endless smile. A never-ending stream of joy.

Lisa shook her head. "You've got it so bad."

Karma pretended to be affronted. "What do you mean?" She struggled not to giggle like a love-struck adolescent.

"You are too ridiculously happy for your own good."

"Is it that obvious?"

Lisa sardonically tilted her head. "Oh, not at all. Everyone walks around with goofy smiles on their faces and eyes shaped like hearts. This whole cupid-in-love look you're working is perfectly normal. Totally."

Karma giggled and flitted her fingers over one of the paper

napkins she'd pulled from the dispenser. "You're right. I *am* ridiculously happy. Everything finally seems to be falling into place." She glanced at the classy, dark-brown Coach briefcase beside her. It had been a gift from Mark. He'd told her she needed a serious briefcase now that she was a serious editor. "I mean, what more could I want right now?"

Lisa grinned as if Karma had just made a poignant observation.

"What?" Karma said. "Why are you looking at me like that?"

"What do you mean?" Lisa tried to disguise her amusement by shrugging and sipping her drink. When she set her cup down, she looked far too innocent to actually *be* innocent.

"That face you just made." Karma arched an eyebrow at her. "What did I say that was so funny?"

Lisa shook her head and tried to give her the brush-off. "Nothing. I'm just . . . you know   happy to see you so happy." She fumbled with her drink cup again, almost knocking it over.

"You're up to something."

"Who? Me?" Lisa glanced toward the counter. "When's our pizza gonna get here. I'm about to eat my arm."

Karma rolled her eyes. "Quit changing the subject."

"I'm not changing the subject. I'm hungry."

"Yeah, sure."

"I am." Then Lisa snickered. "But don't worry. You'll find out soon enough."

"So you *are* up to something."

Lisa shrugged nonchalantly then said, "I'll never tell."

"Ugh. You're so mean."

Lisa fought back a mischievous smile, clearly in on some joke Karma wasn't privy to. "So, tell me again when you start your new job?"

Fine. Let her have her secrets.

Karma pushed aside the napkin she'd been picking at. "January seventh."

"And you're doing okay financially?"

"Yes, Mom." She smirked. "I've been a good little penny-pincher and have a nice amount saved to hold me over until I get my first paycheck." And since she took a payout on her remaining vacation days, that also helped.

"Okay, good. I just wanted to make sure you're covered."

"I'm fine. No worries there. I mean, the pay at my new job is less than at Solar, but I'll be okay. I've already worked out a new budget and everything."

She glanced up at the TV hanging in the corner. According to the headline, the talking heads were chattering about the playoffs.

Playoffs. Something she and her dad had always enjoyed together in the past. Not so this year. They hadn't said more than two words to each other since Thanksgiving, when she'd shown up with Mark for dinner. Her dad had been furious. Harsh words had been said, deep lines drawn in the proverbial sand, and she and Mark ended up leaving to celebrate the holiday alone.

Even a month later, her dad still reeled over Mark being back in her life.

In less than a month, she and her dad had become more like strangers than family.

"Hey, you okay?" Lisa reached across the table and touched her hand.

Snapping out of her miserable thoughts, Karma forced a smile. "Yes. I was just thinking about my dad."

Maybe she could somehow turn this Dad versus Mark issue into a resolution. After all, it was the one thing in her life she would like to improve.

"He still hasn't come around?"

"No, and I'm beginning to think he never will."

Before Lisa could respond, Andrew approached and set their pizza on the table. "There you go, ladies. Enjoy." He smiled then returned behind the counter to take another customer's order.

Karma gingerly pulled a hot slice from the platter and dropped it on her plate while Lisa dug in, not even bothering to wait for hers to cool.

Chomping a huge bite, Lisa winced and fought not to spit out the hot morsel, panting and fanning her mouth with her free hand.

"Hungry much?" Karma laughed at her.

Lisa made a noise that was part curse, part growl, and sounded a little like, "Bite me."

After she managed down the bite of food, Lisa said, "What about Christmas? Did your dad even invite you over?"

Karma shrugged and blew on her slice of pizza. "Not really. He went through Mom to invite *me*, but it was clear Mark wasn't welcome."

And that shit didn't fly. She and Mark came as a package deal now. Until her dad got down with that program, she wouldn't be making any trips — holiday or otherwise — to her parents' house.

"Damn. That's harsh."

Karma picked a mushroom off her pizza and popped it in her mouth. "It is what it is. But I dropped off gifts yesterday, and Mom gave me a couple she and dad bought for me."

"And . . . ?"

"And what? My dad could barely look me in the eye." She huffed and took a bite. "I wish he would just get over it and accept that I'm happy. This is my life, not his, and it would be nice if he would support my decision."

"Maybe he feels bad about how he acted and doesn't know how to make amends and still save face. Your dad can be pretty stubborn, you know."

"I know." Karma licked pizza sauce off her finger. "It just sucks. Do you realize this will be the first Christmas I haven't spent with him."

"Give him time," Lisa said. "He'll come around eventually. The separation has to be hurting him as much as it's hurting you. You two are so close. He's got to be feeling it." Lisa paused. "And maybe you can look at the bright side."

"What bright side?"

Lisa offered a sheepish grin. "That you and Mark can spend your first holiday together, just the two of you." Her voice lilted like she was making a suggestion. "Knowing Mark, he'll make Christmas extra special for you." There was that mischievous grin again. Whatever Lisa was hiding from her, Mark was somehow involved.

"Have you two been conspiring behind my back?"

Lisa's eyes shot wide and her mouth fell open as if she were affronted.

"I knew it." Karma dropped her pizza on her plate and leaned forward. "What are you two up to?"

Lisa shook her head, averting her gaze as she nibbled her bottom lip. "Nothing." But her resolve appeared to be cracking.

"Uh-huh." Karma wasn't buying it, but at least she wasn't as depressed about her dad shunning her, anymore. Now she was distracted trying to figure out what Lisa and Mark had up their sleeves. "If you were really my friend, you'd tell me."

Lisa huffed and tossed Karma a plaintive look. "I'm sworn to secrecy, so stop tempting me. He would kill me if I let something slip, and unlike you, I still have to work with him. Just know that it's killing me not to tell you. You already know more than you should, anyway." She was about to fidget out of her seat. From excitement or guilt, Karma wasn't sure.

Karma shot her a dramatic glare. "I'm not sure I like leaving you two alone together at Solar. Especially if it means you're going to gang up on me like this."

Lisa rolled her eyes. "You make us sound so devious. We're not ganging up on you."

Stewing over the great void of not knowing what awaited her at some unforeseen future moment, Karma grumbled as she picked at her pizza. "Just remember paybacks are a bitch, Lisa. Maybe I'll return your Christmas present."

"You already gave it to me." Lisa smiled smugly then sank her teeth into another bite of pizza.

Karma sneered at her then grinned. "Your birthday present then."

"Oh, calm down." Lisa giggled conspiratorially. "And oh my God, Karma, you're going to love it. You'll thank me later for keeping it a secret."

"We'll see."

But she knew from experience that whatever Mark had planned, she would, most definitely, love it. Without even making an effort, Mark possessed an uncanny ability to make the mundane spectacular, the boring riveting, and the everyday extraordinary.

"Well, since you're dead set on not telling me about whatever it is you and Mark are planning"—she narrowed her eyes in a fake glare—"at least fill me in on how the search for my replacement is coming along."

"Slow but steady. Mark's pretty picky, but I think we'll eventually find what he needs."

What he needs.

As far as Karma was concerned, *she* was what he needed. For as long as they'd known one another, she'd been his assistant. That had been her identifier and what, ultimately, had brought them together. Now she worked elsewhere. The connection that had defined so much of their relationship was now fading into the past.

They no longer needed to hide their relationship from the public. They no longer needed to maintain secrecy. For the first time, they were free and clear to be openly together.

Which was a tiny bit scary, because now they needed to find where they fit with one another when work didn't dominate so much of their relationship. When she'd worked with him, she'd seen him almost every day at the office. Now, he still worked at Solar. She didn't. And even though she had no reason to doubt his feelings, a tiny niggle of insecurity fed the paranoia just waiting to launch an all-out assault on her emotions.

Okay, confession time. She was jealous of his new assistant. There, she'd admitted it.

She dropped her gaze to her fingers, picking at the corner of her paper napkin again. "You know, this really kind of sucks. I miss working with him. What if—"

"Stop." Lisa held up her hand. "Just stop right there, sweetie. Because I've known you too long not to know what you're thinking." Lisa sighed and shook her head. "Honey, you are the apple of Mark's eye, and no one's *ever* going to replace you. And that's coming from him, not me."

Karma perked up. "What do you mean? Did he say that?" An unexpected thrill shot through her.

"No, but he might as well have." Lisa washed down a bite of pizza then plunked her cup on the table. "That man is as bad as your father, Karma. So damn stubborn. Do you realize we've brought in six temps, and Mark has found something wrong with every single one of them?" She rolled her eyes. "That man is the damn pickiest man I've ever met. He wants another you, but I can't make him realize you were an exception. Most of these gals don't have the level of education you do, nor do they have the experience. And you think differently than the typical administrative assistant. You think more like a manager." She sighed, her eyebrows raised. "But Mark is looking for that needle in the haystack. And he is getting seriously frustrated we can't find it. And as a result, he's seriously frustrating *me*." She planted her open palm in the center of her chest.

Karma giggled then forced herself to stop when she saw the irritated expression on Lisa's face. "I'm sorry, Leese. I don't mean to laugh, but you have to admit, this is a bit of an ego boost." The thought that Mark couldn't find a suitable new assistant secretly elated her. It shouldn't have, but it did.

Lisa leaned across the table. "Karma, I like Mark, but if he doesn't find his new assistant—and I mean soon, ego boost or not—you could end up with a eunuch for a boyfriend."

Karma laughed. "Don't you dare touch my man's manly parts."

"I can't make any promises. I mean, really, Karma. I'm about to hurt him. Seriously." Lisa's eyes opened wide, emphasizing her frustration over the situation.

Karma understood. After all, she'd worked for the guy and dated him for five nonconsecutive months. If anyone knew how particular Mark was, she did.

"I'm sorry, Leese." But she liked knowing she was irreplaceable. "Maybe things will turn around soon."

Lisa huffed. "Do you realize he's in my office within a day of a new temp starting, complaining about how this one isn't proficient enough in PowerPoint or Excel, and then the next one isn't assertive enough. The one we dismissed Tuesday was too gossipy."

"Mark detests gossip. You know that." Karma sat a little higher, her ego inflating by the second.

"Exactly." Lisa calmed as if a moment of Zen had come over her. "Hopefully, the gal we brought in yesterday will work out. Mark hasn't complained about her yet, so there's reason to hope."

"Oh?" Karma's bubble deflated, her shoulders slumping.

Lisa gave her a suspicious sidelong glance. "I saw that. You like that he's having so much trouble finding a new assistant, aren't you? You little sadist." She tore off another slice of pizza and held it in front of her mouth, her eyes never wavering from Karma's. "Tell me I'm wrong."

Karma sighed and wrinkled her nose as if she'd smelled a rotten egg. Sometimes it sucked that Lisa knew her so well. "Fine. I'm secretly happy he's having so much trouble finding a new me."

Lisa laughed. "I knew it."

"What can I say? I'm possessive."

Lisa's eyebrows bunched. "You've never been possessive before."

She shrugged. "Maybe I was and just didn't know it until now. After all, Mark *is* my first real boyfriend." She didn't count the guy from high school, who'd been more of a friend. And she didn't count the jerk she'd spent a few weeks with in college, who ditched her the day after she slept with him. And Mark had come along before Brad, who she'd never felt a strong connection to. "Maybe I'm learning that I'm more possessive than I thought."

"And Mark *is* all about teaching you new things, right?" Lisa narrowed her eyes knowingly.

Karma had told Lisa all about the sex lessons Mark had given her during their four-month affair two summers ago. He'd been a brilliant teacher, too, helping Karma feel things she'd only read about in books or seen in movies.

"Something tells me jealousy and possessiveness weren't what he had in mind," she said.

Lisa wiped a dab of tomato sauce from the corner of her mouth. "Hey, it comes with the territory, sweetie."

"Yeah, well, I don't want to be *that* girl."

"Please." Lisa waved her off. "You will never be *that* girl. Besides, it's perfectly normal to feel a little territorial and hate the idea of someone else stomping around on your turf. And don't forget I know how you put Jolene in her place a time or two, as well. You have a possessive streak in you, missy. Admit it."

Jolene. Karma simply wanted to forget that bitch had ever existed.

"It's just that he and I worked so well together."

One of Lisa's eyebrows shot up, and she acerbically lowered her chin. "Girl, I think everyone knows just how well you two worked together." She sucked cola through her straw, innocently batting her eyelashes, before adding, "And that, my dear, is why you no longer work for the company."

Karma rolled her eyes to glance out the window at the fat, lazy snowflakes drifting to the ground, where they melted on contact. "Quit reminding me." She was happy with her new job, but sometimes she missed working with Mark to the point of distraction. Once she was up to her ears in manuscripts, she had a feeling she'd get used to the new situation, but for now, putting the past in the past proved challenging.

Without missing a beat, Lisa added, "I can only imagine what could have gone on in your private meetings had you stayed." She snickered as she set down her cup. Lisa knew what had gone on between her and Mark at the office, right down to the wicked conference room sex against the wall two summers ago.

Karma kept no secrets from Lisa.

"Okay, fine. So Mark and I have a disease called we-can't-keep-our-hands-off-each-other. Sue me."

Lisa's loud laughter broke through the other conversations in the dining room, making several nearby diners turn their way.

"But . . ." Karma raised her index finger. "We always got our work done."

"Uh-huh. I'm sure you did."

Karma sneered at her. "We did." Deciding to get back on topic, she asked, "So, who's this *scag* you've brought in to try and fill my very unfillable shoes?" She pushed her empty plate aside and crossed her forearms on the table.

"Scag." She laughed. "Noooo, you're not even the teensiest bit jealous. Not at all."

Karma gave her a chagrined smile. "Just tell me what she's like."

Lisa grew more serious. "She's nice. Professional. Seems put together."

"How old is she?"

Lisa thought a moment as if trying to determine her age from her appearance. "Maybe thirty."

Karma was only twenty-six. This chick was closer to Mark's age. That didn't sit well.

"Is she pretty?"

Lisa smiled patiently. "Kit's attractive, but not amazing or breathtaking or anything like that. I mean, she's not going to grace any *Sports Illustrated* covers, if that's what you're asking."

"Funny. Har har."

Lisa blew out an impatient breath. "You know what I mean."

Karma had never been considered amazing or breathtaking,

either. And yet Mark thought she was the most beautiful woman he'd ever met. What if he ended up deciding his new assistant was the most beautiful woman he'd ever met instead? It could happen.

And what kind of name was Kit? That was a Playboy Bunny's name if she ever heard one.

"So, is this Kit chick married?"

Lisa tilted her head and raised her eyebrows. "Honey, you do *not* need to worry about her. The only woman in Mark's heart is you. Don't you know that by now?"

"Well, yes, but..." Old insecurities and that bastard named Paranoia reared inside her mind.

She had gained so much confidence in the last twenty months, but sometimes the previous twenty-four years still haunted her. She'd been bullied ruthlessly as a child and had carried a mountain of self-doubt and esteem issues into adulthood. It wasn't until she met Mark that she began to see herself in a more positive light. He'd been a major confidence booster, but she couldn't expect to be totally cured in less than two years when she'd lived with those damn naysaying voices for twenty-four.

And she couldn't expect never to falter and fall back into those destructive thought patterns at some point, either. Not that they would completely overtake her, but she wasn't so delusional to think her past insecurity would never sweep her back into its grasp, especially at times of change, when fear and doubt came in high supply.

Like now.

This was a huge change for her. For them. Her and Mark. They were no longer secret lovers. He was no longer going to leave her on some predefined end date. He was no longer her teacher, and she was no longer his student. And they no longer worked together.

For the first time in their tumultuous almost-two-year, on-and-off-and-back-on-again relationship, they were a bona fide couple. And to hear Mark talk, he wanted to spend his life with her.

But they'd only just gotten back together. What if things didn't work out? What if, now that he was back, he realized she wasn't all he expected? What if she discovered the same about him? He could tire of her, or they could tire of each other and break up. Couples broke up all the time, even after professing undying love.

So yeah, everything could still fall apart. Nothing was secure, and any little thing could destroy the fragile newness of *them*.

Which was why doubt prickled Karma's sense of security. A new woman was entering Mark's life in a capacity that, until recently, had been dominated entirely by her from their inception. A little territorial insecurity was bound to haunt her.

"I'm just..." A troubled, almost sad sensation stirred inside her chest. She didn't like this feeling of being replaced. Of losing this one simple connection. Even though she possessed Mark in the most important way, it still felt like loss.

Lisa reached across the table and took her hand. "Honey, listen to me. You have nothing to worry about. Mark is head over heels for you. He loves you. He's all but asked you to marry him."

"But he hasn't." She waved her free hand as if dispelling a mist. "And it's too soon for that, anyway."

"The hell it is. It's been almost two years since you met each other. You spent four incredible months together. Four months that burned themselves on Mark's brain and heart so deeply that he tattooed your name on his chest. Four months that made him realize the two of you were meant to be together. And now look at you. You *are* together. Right where you belong." Her eyes warmed. "Karma, what I'm trying to say is sometimes you just know. And something tells me Mark just knows with you."

Lisa always knew what to say to make her feel better.

"Thanks, Lisa. I needed that. I just get so—hey, look at this." She pointed out the window at a black Cadillac limousine pulling up to the restaurant. "Fancy bling for a place like Greek Tony's, don't you think?"

Lisa followed her gaze then straightened when she saw the limo. She checked her watch in such a way it seemed she'd known the limo was coming and had lost track of the time.

Karma frowned at her. Was this part of her and Mark's scheming?

The driver exited the vehicle and strode purposefully toward the entrance. Once inside, he stopped and scanned the dining room. When his eyes met hers, he smiled and approached.

Lisa cleared her throat and leaned back in her chair as if to give the man room.

He stopped beside their table. "Miss Karma Mason?"

She looked from the driver to Lisa, who had her lips pressed together as if forcing herself to look innocent.

She glanced back up at the driver. "Yes."

"Would you mind coming with me, please?" He held out his hand as if to help her from her chair.

Everyone in the dining room was staring at them.

She turned her gaze back to Lisa, who bit her bottom lip harder to keep from smiling and bobbed her head toward the driver's outstretched hand as if to remind Karma it was there. "Go on, Karma. Go with him."

"What did you and Mark do?"

Lisa giggled then turned an invisible key over her lips.

Karma reluctantly met the driver's eyes "Where are we going?"

The man's smile could have melted butter. "I've been instructed not to say."

"By whom?" But she could guess. This had Mark's MO stamped all over it.

His gaze sparkled with intrigue. "I'm not allowed to say that, either."

"Uh-huh, I see." She arched one eyebrow at Lisa. "You were in on this, weren't you?"

Her cheeks turned rosy as she guiltily—but playfully—bowed her head. "Maybe."

"Ma'am?" The driver nodded toward his outstretched hand. "I apologize, but I have to insist we not delay. We're on a bit of a timetable."

With a resigned sigh, she placed her palm in his but narrowed her eyes on Lisa. "I'll get you back for keeping this from me."

Lisa laughed. "You're going to love it. I promise."

"I'm still going to get you back. Just wait." She began to pick up her briefcase, but the driver easily plucked it from her hand.

Okay, fine. He could carry it for her.

He took a step back as she slipped on her coat.

"Wait. What about my car?" She couldn't just leave her car there.

Lisa giggled and pulled her spare car key from her purse. What the hell? How had Lisa gotten her spare key? Oh wait. Mark. He must have stolen it from her purse the last time he'd spent the night.

Sneaky bastard.

"Daniel's waiting for me to call him so he can come and meet me," Lisa said. "He's going to drive your car back to your apartment. Then I'll take him home."

So, Daniel was involved in this plot, too? Just how many of her friends had Mark enlisted to pull this off?

"How long have you and Mark been planning this?"

"About two weeks."

Karma gasped and smacked Lisa's arm. "I can't believe you kept this from me for two weeks!" She straightened and raised her chin. "I'm revoking your best friend status." She snagged her purse, slung the strap over her shoulder, and stepped beside the driver.

Lisa laughed.

Sucking her tongue between her teeth, Karma nodded toward her car's spare key in Lisa's hand. "Tell Daniel he'd better not scratch the paint."

"Just make sure you text me and tell me all about..." Lisa trailed off as if she didn't want to give away too much of Mark's plans. "Just text me."

"We'll see." With that, and with Lisa's giggles teasing her, she turned and followed the driver out the door to the limousine.

He opened the rear door for her, and she peered inside.

And there he was. The man she was madly, deeply, and irrevocably in love with.

Mark Strong. The captain of her heart.

Lounging on plush, cream-colored leather, he wore a black knit sweater, black slacks, and a sexy-as-hell smile under bedroom eyes. Just...God.

In the dictionary, beside the word luscious, there had to be a picture of Mark wearing this outfit and that expression. There just had to be. With dark hair, dark eyes, strong jaw, straight nose, and angular lips that did such naughty, wicked things to her anatomy, he was the epitome of sex appeal.

He took her hand and drew her onto the bench seat beside him. A moment later, the door closed, leaving them alone.

"What are you doing here?" she said. "I thought you were flying to South Carolina today."

At least that's what he'd told her when they spent the night together Monday. He'd said he was meeting with a potential client and wouldn't be back until the weekend. It was only Thursday. Apparently, his story had been a ruse to throw her off.

Mark wrapped his hand around her inner thigh and tugged her closer. He cupped her face in his other hand as he leaned toward her. "I lied."

His face was barely an inch from hers. "I sort of figured that out," she whispered.

The way the outer corners of his eyes crinkled as he grinned tugged at her heart. "I'm kidnapping you instead."

"Kidnapping me?"

He pushed her hair away from her neck and softly pressed his lips against the subtle dip below her ear, sending shivers down her spine.

"Yes, kidnapping," he whispered, as the car pulled away. "You're my prisoner now." His warm breath washed over her skin before he kissed her again, lower. Then again and again, burning a trail down the side of her neck. As he inched downward, he nuzzled her flesh and gently pushed her collar down her shoulder with his lightly scruffy chin while his lips continued feasting on the tender curve of skin where her neck and shoulder met.

"Where are you taking me?" It was hard to focus when he was seducing her so exquisitely.

He straightened and smiled. "This wouldn't be much of a kidnapping if I told you, would it?"

She glanced around at the limousine's luxurious interior. The leather was soft as velvet, and the silver accents gleamed without a smudge of fingerprints.

"It's not much of a kidnapping at all, if you ask me. I'm not blindfolded. My hands aren't bound. In fact, I feel completely safe."

"Mmmm, you do tempt me, don't you?" His heated gaze slid down her body then back to her face. "The blindfold and handcuffs can come later. Does that ease your mind about the seemingly gentle nature of your kidnapper?"

She nibbled her bottom lip and ran her hand across his hard abdomen as she leaned into him, eyes lowered. He could still make her feel so shy. "Something tells me my kidnapper isn't as gentle as he lets on. I think he has a darker side. A *much* darker side." Sex had grown both more intimate and more debauched since they'd gotten back together. As if now that they were a legitimate couple, he felt more comfortable showing her a more abandoned, brazen side to his sexuality while still worshipping her body like it was his own private temple.

And, God, the sex was good. All he had to do was give her *The Look,* and she was ready for him. Hot, wet, and ready. They could be lounging casually on the couch, watching a movie and sharing a bowl of popcorn, and out of nowhere he would glance at her, one eyebrow slightly higher than the other, eyes smoky, eyelids heavy, his head turned a fraction away from her so he was looking at her out of the corner of his eye, with a modest smirk curling his lips. Instantly, moist warmth flooded her core. Within minutes, the movie and popcorn were forgotten.

The Look worked even better when he was wearing a button-up shirt unbuttoned far enough to reveal some of the hair on his chest, as she had found out Monday night.

What an evening. It had taken her until Wednesday afternoon before she could think about what they'd done to each other without going completely weak kneed and slick between the legs.

He cupped her cheek and drew her face toward his shoulder as he dipped his nose into her hair. "Your kidnapper *does* have a darker side." He spoke softly, his voice low, which heightened his proclamation and sent shivers down her spine. "But only because he loves you so much and feels safe enough to share that side of himself with you."

She smiled to herself as he confirmed her suspicions. "I thought so."

"You did, did you?" She heard the pleased smile in his voice.

She nodded and lifted her face so she could look into his dark, grey-green eyes. "Yes."

He brushed the backs of his fingers down her cheek. "Rest assured, my beautiful *kidnappee.* There are things he hasn't shown you yet."

"Why not?"

His gaze fell briefly as his mouth tightened. He took a breath and met her gaze again. "Maybe he doesn't want to scare you."

"He won't."

"Maybe he wants to make sure you're ready."

"I am."

He grinned, but the gesture appeared tense. "Well, maybe he just wants to save something for later."

She got the feeling there was something he wasn't saying, but this was Mark. There was always something he didn't say. It was part of what made him so exciting.

"You're evil."

He chuckled then gazed into her eyes for several seconds before asking, "Do you know what today is?"

It was the twentieth of December. Thursday. But she knew he wasn't interested in what any old someone off the street could simply pull off a calendar.

"We've been back together for one month."

His grin widened, and a spark lit in his eyes as if he were delighted she already knew the answer. As if she could forget.

"Yes, it's our one-month anniversary." His arms tightened around her, and he kissed her temple. "One month. One month with you again, when a year ago, I feared I'd lost you forever." He sighed, tipping his forehead against hers. "I'm so grateful I got this chance again. So grateful to have you back in my life. After a month together, it feels so perfect."

"Perfect except for the fact my dad is still being an ass."

His posture slumped slightly. "I know. I'm sorry. That's part of the reason why I've planned this little getaway." He leaned back and gestured toward the inside of the limousine.

"Trying to make me forget about my family's crappy behavior?"

He nodded. "Now that I'm your man, it's my job to keep you happy."

She shook her head. "You do make me happy, but it's not your job."

He broke away and opened a small refrigerator beside them. "Well, I think of it as my job. After hurting you so badly two summers ago, I have a lot to make up for."

He reached inside the fridge then pulled out a bundle of ornate chocolate rosebuds on white lollipop sticks that looked like stems. Some of the rosebuds were made of dark chocolate, some were white, and some were a combination of both. But the colors and delicately curled petals blended seamlessly, as if they were real.

"What's this?" She'd never seen such a beautiful treat.

He shut the refrigerator door and turned toward her. "The short answer is chocolate-covered strawberries."

There were strawberries inside all that sculpted chocolate?

"Okay, so what's the *long* answer?" She took the one he held out to her as if he were handing her an actual flower. And just like a real rosebud, the texture was smooth and silky, almost fragile, curving like a woman's hips from the bottom, narrowing in the middle like a corseted waist, and arcing outward at the top as if to accommodate a full bosom.

Pride softened his expression. "The long answer is that they are tokens of my affection, handmade with love, so I could show you how much you mean to me."

"Wait, what?" She turned unbelieving eyes to the masterpiece in her hand, then to the eleven he was still holding. "Are you saying you made these?"

He'd made her a dozen chocolate strawberry roses? With his own hands? They were exquisite enough to be made by a professional chocolatier, not a sexy businessman who dabbled with food as a hobby.

He placed the remaining roses in a small vase secured in the console then took the one he'd given her. "My dad makes these for my mom every year on Valentine's Day, and then again on their wedding anniversary and her birthday." He gently tugged the berry from the stem, which he discarded, then held the treat toward her over his palm, tempting her to take a bite. "He taught me how to make them when I was a kid. And now I'm carrying on the tradition by making them for you."

"But it's not Valentine's Day or my birthday." She didn't mention the whole wedding anniversary thing, though. She knew how Mark got when he heard the word *wedding*. After what had happened to him eight years ago, he couldn't even think the word without having a mini nervous breakdown.

"But it's our one-month anniversary, which is just as good. Take a bite." He tilted his head toward the rosebud as he lifted it to her mouth.

She sank her teeth into the treat. Sweet strawberry juice burst over her tongue, and the thin chocolate petals melted in her mouth. The flavor was exquisite, with hints of orange, vanilla, and almond, as if he'd melted the chocolate and added flavored extracts before letting it solidify again.

Mark's culinary abilities never ceased to amaze her. His homemade meatballs and marinara sauce were swoon worthy, and without his help, she still wouldn't be able to make a decent truffle. And now here he was presenting her with handmade chocolate-covered strawberries that looked like actual rosebuds. If he ever decided to leave his life in the corporate world to open a restaurant, it was sure to be a hit.

"How long did it take to make these?" She swiped the last bite of rosebud from his hand and set it on her tongue so she could savor it a moment before chewing.

"That's not what matters." He picked up another one and plucked the bud off the stem. "What matters is that I made them for you, so that I could take pride in watching you smile as you eat them."

"Well, you need to have a taste of what you created. These are incredible." She took the treat from his fingers and lifted it to his mouth.

Without argument, he slowly sank his teeth into it, holding her gaze in a way that made her wish she were the strawberry sliding over his tongue.

"I love you." She took the rest into her mouth.

"You're easy," he said with a slick wink.

"Easy?" She arched one eyebrow.

He nodded, brushing back her hair as he rested his head on the back of the seat, which only served to make him look even sexier as his eyelids slid halfway closed. "All it takes is a dozen chocolate-covered strawberries to win your heart."

She took another from the vase and bit off the end before feeding him the rest. "Trust me, it takes a lot more than chocolate and strawberries, Mark. But that's a good start."

"I'll keep that in mind."

"I think we're well on our way, don't you?"

He licked a piece of chocolate from his lip. "What do you mean?"

She peeled a white petal from another rosebud and slid it into her mouth. "Haven't you noticed how chocolate seems to follow us into each phase of our relationship?"

He grinned and scooped her onto his lap so she straddled his thighs. His hands rested on her hips, his fingers drumming her bottom through her jeans. "Please explain."

His amused, playful grin, combined with the way he tilted his head to one side, made her heart skip.

She nibbled on another rosebud. "Well, for starters, when we met, you used a chocolate chunk brownie and a piece of Dove chocolate to teach me about orgasms."

He chuckled and dropped his head against the cream-colored leather again. "That's right. I did, didn't I?"

"Mm-hm. Then on Thanksgiving, right after we got back together, you helped me make my first batch of perfect chocolate truffles."

His eyelids lowered and one brow lifted slightly, putting him halfway to *The Look*. "Mmmm, I think my favorite part was when we let the ganache set."

"I think that was my favorite part, too." They'd ended up in bed having some of the most intense sex they'd had to date.

She lifted the rosebud in her hand. "And now you're wooing me yet again with more chocolate. I'm beginning to think this is part of some chocolate conspiracy."

His hands eased around her rump and he pulled her farther up his lap. He was hard, and all that hardness pressed against her in the most lascivious way. "I just know how much you like chocolate."

"Uh-huh," she said doubtfully.

He grinned, but the gesture did nothing to make him appear amused. Steam-up-the-windows sexy, though? Yeah. He definitely looked like he was one degree shy of boiling.

His gaze dropped to her mouth as she teased her lips with another strawberry.

"Have I mentioned chocolate is an aphrodisiac?" he said.

"Isn't that just a rumor?"

"Absolutely not. It's a bona fide fact."

"Who says?"

He smirked, eyes narrowing. "Let me ask, are you sexually

aroused right now?"

"Is this a trick question?"

One thick, dark eyebrow rose contemptuously even as his smirk evolved into a smile. "Yes or no? Are you aroused?"

She sighed, sinking more fully onto his lap. "Yes, but I think that has more to do with you than the chocolate."

"I rest my case."

She gasped. "What do you mean? That does not prove that chocolate is an aphrodisiac."

"Of course it does. You're aroused. Chocolate is an aphrodisiac. Case closed."

Sharply drawing in her breath, she smacked his shoulder, making him cringe and laugh. "The case is *not* closed. Your logic is seriously flawed here, Mr. Strong. I'm aroused, yes, but not because you're feeding me chocolate. I'm aroused because you're the damn sexiest man I've ever met. You just look at me and I get turned on. And that has nothing to do with chocolate unless you melt it, pour it over my naked body, and lick it off."

"Mmm, now there's an idea." His hands skimmed firmly up her back, pulling her forward. "Melted chocolate instead of wax. Nice."

Warmth filled her cheeks, and she hid her face against his shoulder, realizing she'd gotten a little carried away.

He made an affectionate noise deep in his throat then kissed her cheek. "You do the same for me, you know."

She lifted her head and drew away a few inches so she could look at him. "What do you mean?"

His eyes searched hers, skipping back and forth. "Just that you walk into the room, and I get excited. You look at me, and my heart stops. And sometimes when you touch me, I'm not sure I can contain myself enough not to scare you." He took a long, deep breath, his gaze raking her body. "Because, baby, now that you're mine, I want to claim you in every way imaginable. And when I say every way imaginable, I mean it." He paused, letting the gravity of his words fill the empty space. "You say you're ready for all of me, but are you really? Do you really know what you're saying you're ready for? Because sometimes I'm not even sure *I'm* ready." His body shivered, and he quickly pulled her against him, tucking his face against her neck. "You make me want things I haven't wanted in a long, long time, Karma."

They'd gone from playful to profound in less than a minute. But this was how Mark was. He was a study in extremes. He could shift gears faster than a racecar driver.

For Karma, the personality fluctuations were invigorating. She felt they were part of Mark's spiritual evolution, as if the more he vacillated from one extreme to another, the more it meant he was finding his way back to who he really was. To the man he'd been before Carol left him at the altar all those years ago.

She took comfort in the sharp turns his moods took. As long as it meant he was, indeed, finding himself, she was more than fine to endure his severe swings.

And, clearly, he was still finding himself. She wasn't sure what he meant when he said that sometimes he wasn't even sure he was ready, but, obviously, there were still things he hadn't shared with her. Things that, for whatever reason, he still withheld.

"We'll get there together," she whispered, combing her fingers through his short, thick hair. "There's no rush. But when you're ready, I'm ready."

"And that's why you have my heart." His lips brushed her skin as he spoke. "You don't push." A gentle breath escaped his mouth as his cheek rose against the bottom of her jaw, so she knew he was smiling. "You take me as I am and make me stronger without expecting me to open up too fast." He pulled back so she could see his eyes. "Which makes me want to open up more. So, I have to wonder if it's you and not me engaging in some kind of conspiracy. Some kind of magic that makes me addicted to you. Because . . . I am addicted." His gaze danced over her face as if he were looking at a mystical faerie and couldn't quite believe it.

"No conspiracy here, Mr. Kidnapper. I assure you, I'm innocent on all counts."

Unadulterated joy broke over his face, and he leaned back in his seat again, pulling her with him. "You are most certainly not innocent, Miss Mason. If you were, I wouldn't be so captivated by you."

"And here I thought it was my innocence you found captivating."

"It was . . . in the beginning. Now, though . . . ?" He brushed his palm down the side of her face. "Now I'm captivated by the way you make me feel. Just being around you makes me feel . . ." His gaze searched the air past her shoulder as if he could find the word he sought there.

Mark always presented himself so eloquently that to see him floundering for the right word was somewhat amusing. "What?" she teased. "How exactly do I make you feel?"

Their eyes met a split second before he said, "Powerful. You make me feel powerful."

"Powerful?" That wasn't what she'd expected.

The way his eyes narrowed and his mouth quirked thoughtfully made it clear he still wasn't sure that was the right word, either, but he was sticking with it.

"Karma, you make me feel like there's nothing I can't do, as long as you're with me." He frowned. "I've never felt that before. I've never felt like the definition of who I am relied so heavily on another person. It's like I'm rediscovering myself with you." The idea seemed to baffle him. His gaze drifted, and a hint of confusion crossed his expression before he smiled it away and locked gazes with her again.

"Well, you are rediscovering yourself, aren't you? At least, that's the way it sounds to me."

He nodded tightly, gaze lowered. "Yes, I am. You're right." He pulled her down so her head rested on his chest. His heartbeat thumped heavily against her ear.

She closed her eyes and let him hold her like that for several minutes, the two of them silent as the limousine swiftly carried them along the interstate. But she could feel him thinking. She could feel the energy of his mind racing in the air around them.

After some time had passed, Mark kissed the top of her head. When he spoke, his voice was so soft it was almost a whisper. "Yes, I'm rediscovering myself with you, Karma. And while I'm eager to capture this new version of me, I won't lie and say it's all good. Sometimes, I'm scared for where the journey is taking me. Sometimes, I worry how you'll react as you learn who I really am. What I've done. Who I want to be." His entire body shivered as he tightened his embrace, revealing just how vulnerable his words made him feel.

Her heart beat a little harder that he'd trusted her enough to share his fear with her. What he said next, however, made ice flow through her veins.

"But sometimes, Karma, I worry my love won't be enough."

Chapter 2

Very often a change of self is needed more than a change of scene.
-Arthur Christopher Benson

There was still so much Mark hadn't told Karma about his past. Things he hadn't thought about in years, some he hadn't even remembered until the past few weeks.

Something about falling in love and wanting to build a life with Karma forced his tucked-away memories to awaken and leap to the front of his mind. It was as if he'd chosen to not only push what had happened with Carol into the shadows, but also all the affairs he'd sought out afterward to help him forget. And now, his desire to fully share himself made him remember everything. Even those things he simply wanted to let fade into the recesses of oblivion.

But he couldn't undo what had been done. And he couldn't completely stamp out memories that had burned themselves on his mind.

It had been eight years since Carol, and for the first six before he met Karma, he'd engaged in an endless stream of short-term flings. He hadn't been shy about his sexual prowess. He'd pursued women with an unquenchable thirst, at least at first. He'd done things. Tawdry things. Crazy things. Even a couple of disturbing things. All in his quest to forget Carol.

Oh, sure. He'd said he wanted to better understand women and learn how to be an expert lover so he never had to suffer the same heartache again, but those were just excuses to give him a noble purpose. The truth was, all the shit he'd done during those six years had been about one thing, and one thing only. Forgetting Carol. The rest was just gravy.

Then he met Karma. From the moment he saw her tugging self-consciously at the hem of her red dress while sitting at the blackjack table at the fundraiser in Chicago, there hadn't been room for anyone else. What countless women hadn't been able to do for six years, Karma did in one night. He forgot Carol. Not permanently, because Carol's memory still haunted him, but at least for a few hours. Karma had made him feel hope for the first time that night.

Something no other woman had been able to do. Which was ultimately how he knew she was the only woman he'd ever want for the rest of his life, even if it had taken him a while to figure that out.

But he couldn't erase all the shit he'd done in those six years, no matter how badly he wanted to.

He had become so good at his façade — so skilled as a lover — that if he didn't end his affairs within a month or two, the women began expecting more. More time, more intimacy.

More *commitment*.

And commitment was something he hadn't been able to give. After Carol, he'd become almost allergic to the concept. Just hearing the word *wedding* was enough to send him into a panic attack. Actually attending a wedding required a generous dose of Valium or Xanax.

To avoid commitment-centric complications, he'd begun warning women up front that he wasn't interested in long-term relationships. Better to do that from the start rather than risk a misunderstanding later. Unfortunately, doing so had landed him a few women who took his affection to the other extreme. They'd wanted sex, and a lot of it. And sometimes the sex walked the line between socially acceptable and unconventional. Or maybe deviant was a better word. Because things he'd done a time or two had definitely been deviant. At least by the definition he eventually accepted for his own behavior.

But those first two years post-Carol had been a nefarious, perverted time.

Eventually, he developed his own brand of sexual behavior, choosing to focus more on the women he dated than on his own needs. He learned to forsake his own kinks to give women what *they* wanted.

But now, with Karma, he'd found a woman he wanted to explore his own desires with again, not just hers. He wanted to give himself completely to her, and he wanted to unlock the closet of his sexual fantasies again.

But he wasn't sure how Karma would react. He was pretty sure she would be receptive to a couple of things he wanted to do, because they'd already played around with the ideas. But there were a couple she might shy away from. And then there was the one thing he wasn't even sure *he* could do, anymore, simply because he was so fucking damaged. That one wasn't even sexual, and yet it tortured his soul.

He was walking a very thin, extremely delicate line. One that he needed to cautiously guide Karma along. How far was she willing to let him go? How far was she willing to trust him? If he pushed her too far, he risked altering the entire dynamic of their relationship and driving her away. However, if he could take her just to the edge without crossing it, the increased intimacy could vault them to pure euphoria and a depth of trust that would bind them forever. But if he edged her even a millimeter past that line, the trust would be broken and shatter them.

The situation was even trickier because he wanted to marry her. But to marry her, he needed to tell her everything. He needed to confess not just the things he'd done, but also the things he wanted to do. He couldn't do that until he knew how far she was willing to go.

Which put him in a tight place. Because he couldn't know how far she was willing to go until he told her what he wanted to do, and vice versa. Talk about your rocks and hard places. There was no easy way out of this one.

And to make matters worse, he was still trying to overcome his anxiety over the thought of standing at the front of a church, waiting for her to walk around the corner and stride up the aisle on her father's arm.

He was ready to propose. Ready to put the ring on her finger and make their relationship official after only one month back in her life. But he was scared shitless about all the rest.

What the hell was wrong with him? Why couldn't he get past this? He seemed forever stuck in the middle, and that meant she was stuck there with him, neither of them moving forward.

This was getting to be familiar territory in their relationship.

The entire four months they'd been together two summers ago, they had flirted with commitment, but neither had let themselves or the other quite get there.

Middle ground.

Then they'd been apart for a year. But even apart, they'd both held onto hope they'd be together again someday. Hope had prevented either from embracing a life with someone else, even though Karma had tried with Brad.

Again, middle ground.

And here they were once more, finally together, but not *really* together, because he hadn't thoroughly let go of the past and his fears. Something still held him back, despite his absolute belief Karma was *it* for him. The only woman he ever wanted to sleep with, kiss, hold, and love for the rest of his life.

Fucking son of a bitch middle ground. *Still.*

Even after the hell and strife he'd overcome to find his way back into her life, he still clung to shreds of the past, caught in the middle as he strived to reconcile the innocent young man he'd once been — pre-Carol — with the sexually enlightened man he'd become after she jilted him, as well as with the more tempered, balanced man he *wanted* to become with Karma.

This new feeling was both familiar and foreign, like it wanted to take him back to his innocence yet push him toward even greater depths of maturity. The problem was, he was no longer innocent, and yet he wasn't as innocent as he wanted to be. He *had* engaged in some kinky shit on the initially destructive path he'd followed post-Carol, before he'd cleaned up his act with his best friend Rob's help. But some of the perverted things he'd done in those first two years were things he wanted to share with Karma now, while others he simply wanted to let lie in the past, as they had already served their purpose.

And that was one reason for the trip he was taking her on for their one-month anniversary. He wanted to reveal more of himself. More of his past. More of his own desires. This trip wasn't just for celebrating their relationship, or getting her away from the situation with her dad, or even for one very important question he intended to ask her. It was also for testing the waters. In the next week, he planned to share things with Karma he'd never told her — never told *anyone*. Not even Rob.

The limousine slowed, and Karma, who was still positioned on his lap, lifted her head off his shoulder and glanced out the window into the darkening evening.

"Where are we?" Her eyes narrowed as she looked back at him.

"Where do you think we are?"

She tilted her head to the side, giving him her trademark exasperated look. "You simply can't give a straight answer, can you?"

"Not when you're so cute looking at me like that."

She smirked and turned her gaze back to the window. "Is that...?" She squinted into the darkness. He hated how it got dark so early in the winter. "Are we going to the airport?"

Her thighs were slender and firm against his palms. "Yes."

"Why are we going to the airport?"

"Because we can't get to where we're going by driving."

"Oookaaay. So, where are we going?"

He shook his head. "It's a surprise."

She huffed. "Mark, I can't go on a trip right now."

"Yes you can. You don't start your new job for two weeks. We'll be back in plenty of time for that."

"But—"

"It's done. You're going. End of discussion." He grinned at the way her shoulders slumped in defeat even as her eyes lit with curiosity and excitement.

She snuggled closer, nibbling the inside of her bottom lip. "And you're sure you can't tell me where we're going?"

He slid his hands around her hips, resting them on her firm bottom, giving a little squeeze before saying, "Positive."

"Can you give me a hint?"

He thought for a moment, trying to decide just how much he should give away about their destination. "We have to fly over an ocean to get there."

Her eyes flew open wide. "Really? Which ocean?"

He shook his head. "Nope. That's all you're getting. No more hints."

"You're no fun." She giggled as she glanced back out the window, pulling another of the chocolate rosebud strawberries from the vase.

He watched her nibble through the chocolate petals and resisted the urge to lick strawberry juice off her lips as she bit into the center. The scent of strawberries and chocolate mixed so perfectly with the clean fragrance of her skin.

"Okay, I'll tell you one more thing," he said, brushing back her thick, auburn hair. He caressed her cheek with the pad of his thumb. Her pale-green eyes turned toward him expectantly. "We're traveling in style."

Her slim eyebrows sank into a frown. "We're traveling in style? That's it? What the heck does that mean?"

"You'll see."

She growled in frustration. "You're infuriating." She popped the last of the strawberry in her mouth and turned her attention once more out the window as the limousine slowed even more.

He couldn't wait to see her expression when she saw what waited for them next.

* * *

Less than an hour after being kidnapped from Greek Tony's, Karma got out of the car at the airport and shivered against the cold wind. Once again, Mark had outdone himself, and she didn't even know where they were going, yet. What she did know was that he'd taken care of everything, which apparently included chartering a private jet.

She turned toward the Learjet being loaded with their luggage. Wherever they were going, Mark had been right about one thing. They were most definitely traveling in style.

She glanced from Mark to the jet and back again. Watching him give instructions to the steward loading their luggage, a passing thought stuttered to a stop in her mind. Just how big was Mark's bank account? She'd never thought about that before, but now, with a private jet and a trip over an ocean to God-knew-where in her immediate future, and an expensive limousine ride behind her, his financial position seemed a bit more interesting. Not in a gold digger kind of way, but a why-haven't-I-ever-thought-about-this? way.

He drove a hundred-thousand-dollar car, had lived in a luxury apartment in downtown Chicago before moving to Indianapolis, and wore suits from the top designers. Gold cufflinks, Montblanc pens, Italian shoes. Money never seemed to be an issue for him. And she'd seen a couple of impressive pieces of jewelry in his apartment once, but didn't want to think about that now. The point was, in the face of all that materialism, how had she never pondered the state of his bank account?

Perhaps because it had never seemed important. Or maybe because she'd never seen him spend this kind of money in one pop. The limo ride was one thing, but chartering a private jet went beyond extravagant, especially since he seemed too familiar with how things were done for this to be the first time he'd traveled with his own personal flight crew.

Mark helped load the last of their bags then turned toward her with a smile.

One month with him felt like both a lifetime and a blink. In some ways, the time had blown by, and in others, it passed at a snail's pace.

"You ready?" Mark took her hand.

She took comfort in the warmth his touch provided. "Given I have no idea where we're going and haven't flown in years, I suppose I'm as ready as I'll ever be."

"Come on." He tugged her toward the jet. "Paradise awaits."

Paradise? They had to fly over an ocean to get there? Her heart suddenly froze. "Wait! My passport. I don't—"

"Taken care of."

"But . . ." The last she remembered, her passport was in her files at home. She didn't carry it with her everywhere she went.

Mark swept her toward him, his gaze reassuring and confident as he curled his hand around her neck and ran the pad of his thumb over her cheek. "Don't worry. I have it."

Relaxing, she sighed. "You do?"

He nodded and dipped down for a tender, chaste kiss. "I've taken care of everything."

Taking another deep breath, she nodded then glanced from the limo to the jet. She should have known he wouldn't forget her passport. After all, this was Mark. "You've thought of everything, haven't you?"

"Every last detail." The way he said it sent a ripple of awareness through her blood. Maybe it was the brief pause before he answered, or the quiet way he let the words flow smoothly from his mouth, or perhaps the way the skin around his eyes pinched then softened, but something about this trip was different.

Mark never did anything without a reason. She'd learned that during their sex lessons two summers ago. Every move Mark made had a purpose. And while this was their one-month anniversary, she had a feeling there was more to this trip than just that.

With a frosty wind biting her ears and nose, she followed him up the steps to the jet and was greeted by a pretty, dark-haired flight attendant dressed in a flattering grey suit. The gold tag pinned over her right breast read "Janie."

"Good evening," Janie said, waving her forward.

"Hi." Karma looked from her to the interior of the cabin. There were only four seats—all upholstered in cream-colored leather like the seats in the limo—and each wide enough to comfortably fit a three-hundred-pound defensive lineman.

Janie gestured inside. "Please make yourselves comfortable. We'll be departing shortly."

Mark ushered her toward the two seats on the left, where they sat facing one another.

She glanced around at the light interior. Not only were the seats cream, but the walls were, too. And every panel, every cabinet, and even the ceiling of the cabin was trimmed in gold. The plush leather was a far cry from the uncomfortable, cramped, vomit-hued fabric seats she remembered from her last airplane trip.

This was how the rich and famous traveled, not the everyday common citizen.

"Have you ever flown on a private jet?" Mark crossed his ankle over his knee, eyeing her.

"No. Have you?" But she already knew the answer. And wasn't it apropos that Mark would prefer to travel this way than on a crowded commercial jet? If you had money and means, why settle for less than the best? And it was becoming clearer by the second he had both.

His expression remained even, not giving much away. "When I was a kid, my parents chartered private jets to fly to dance competitions. I traveled quite a bit with them."

So, lots of experience flying on private jets. Noted.

Mark hadn't told her much about his parents. She knew they were professional dancers, instructors, and choreographers, but that was about it.

"Did they win a lot of competitions?"

"Almost every one they went to. They were unbeatable in their day. Now they mostly choreograph and teach, although they still dance in exhibitions, even at their age." He smiled fondly as he glanced absently — maybe even a little forlornly — out the window.

The pilot announced they were preparing for takeoff as she wondered about his reaction. Did he miss dancing?

"Why didn't you follow in their footsteps?" Usually, children professionally followed their parents in families as prestigious as Mark's. At least, that's how it seemed to Karma. You only had to look at football to see the family legacies at work. The Mannings, the Longs, the Montanas. Typically, like father like son. So, how had Mark come to denounce dancing and turn toward business instead, especially when it appeared he still felt a pang of longing to cut a rug?

He fastened himself into his seat with a tense shrug. "Dancing just wasn't in the cards for me."

"There has to be more to it than that." He'd told her that when he was a kid, he'd practically lived in the studio, as well as on the competition circuit with his parents. With all that exposure, it was surprising he hadn't followed in their well-placed footsteps.

Mark looked out the window, the line of his brow tight. "I was good. I trained with them and could have competed if I'd wanted to. But then . . ."

This had to do with Carol. The reason he had walked away from dancing had to do with her, didn't it? Maybe not entirely, but somehow Carol had been the one to clinch the deal and force him off the dance floor for good.

As the jet taxied toward the runway, he tapped his fingers restlessly on his armrests. "For a while I thought I might pursue dancing, but I was never as good as my parents. I knew competing would only be marginally successful for me. So I turned my attention toward earning my business degree. My grandfather was an Italian immigrant who built a fortune as a successful Chicago businessman. His success allowed my mother to follow her dreams of becoming a professional dancer. Between his money and her talent, as well as my dad's, they've built quite an empire, drawing the best dancers from all over the world."

"Like Carol?"

His gaze darted to hers then flicked away as he cleared his throat. "Yes. Like Carol."

"Is she why you stopped dancing?" She might as well get the notion out there.

He cleared his throat again and shifted as if he couldn't get comfortable. Karma knew she was pushing her luck by bringing up Carol. But he never talked about her, even though Karma could tell his ex still haunted his thoughts, even if only occasionally.

If they were going to have a future together, Mark needed to purge that woman from his mind sooner rather than later. Going forward without doing so was like trying to slog through knee-deep mud. It could be done, but it took a lot of work and left you completely drained. Karma didn't want to have to work that hard at trying to overcome Mark's memories of Carol, and she shouldn't have to. No woman should have to compete with her man's past girlfriends, and sometimes that's how Karma felt. Like Carol was still right there, getting in the way.

Seeming a bit flustered, Mark gave a tight shake of his head. "No, she's not the reason why I stopped dancing." His earnest gaze met hers. "Not entirely."

"What do you mean?"

"I knew before she . . ." He paused and pursed his lips as if the words had locked up in his throat. Then he sighed and started again. "I knew before she . . . *left me* . . . that dancing wasn't my future. I had decided I wanted to follow after my grandfather and build a business."

Karma heard something unspoken hanging beyond his words. "But . . . ?"

He heaved a deep sigh. "But I thought I could still dance as a hobby." He rubbed his palm over the lower half of his face. "And I thought Carol and I would take over the studio someday. That my parents' empire would become *our* empire. That I would use my business education to manage the business into the next generation and somehow find a way to still participate as a performer or at least an instructor."

It sounded like he was admitting the truth not just to her for the first time, but also to himself. As if he'd forced himself not to remember the plans and dreams he'd made when he and Carol were together.

"You know," he said with an uneasy sigh, "I don't want to talk about this now. I don't want this trip to be about what happened in the past." His gaze faltered as his eyebrows ticked inward, making it seem as if that was exactly what this trip was about and he just didn't want to admit it. "I want it to be about us. You. Me. Our future. You're what's important to me now. What happened eight years ago isn't significant, anymore, Karma. You are."

But the hard lines of his face remained, and his mouth formed a taut, straight line, and she wondered what he wasn't telling her. Clearly, what had happened eight years ago was more significant than he wanted to admit.

"You're my life now, Karma, and I want this trip to solidify that."

She wanted to believe him, but it was obvious he was hiding something. He said the past was insignificant, but that was a lie. With Mark, the past was everything. The past had kept him from committing to her the first time around. It had nearly destroyed any chance they would be together. And it was still affecting him and their relationship now.

The voice in the back of her head warned that Carol wasn't gone. Not just yet. Carol was still there, filling the tiny gaps where her and Mark's souls hadn't fully melded together, yet. In fact, Carol was the reason *why* their souls weren't yet completely one. Until Mark expelled her from his system for good, Carol would always be there. A third party in what Karma wanted to be an exclusive relationship.

Mark told her he loved her. His actions reinforced his words. But there was still one small door in his mind she wasn't allowed to enter, and every so often she found herself on the outside with no way in. Not often, but once in a while Mark seemed to be on the other side of that door, his mind briefly consumed by whatever fear and pain Carol had planted inside him.

Karma wanted to break that door down, pull Carol out of Mark's memories, and take her rightful place in *all* aspects of his life. She wanted to protect Mark from what Carol had done to him, but she knew she couldn't. Only Mark could pull himself free of his ex's hold. All Karma could do was wait for him to wrestle himself away from his demons.

But for now, on what she was sure Mark intended to be a romantic getaway, she wouldn't push. Mark would deal with his past when he was ready.

She just hoped she wouldn't have to wait too long.

Chapter 3

Peace is the result of retraining your mind to process life as it is, rather than as you think it should be.
-Wayne Dyer

One overnight flight and one refueling stop in Miami later, Karma gazed out the window at the lightening morning sky as she sipped from a mug of tea and wiped sleep from her eyes. She hadn't slept much. Partly because of where she was, and partly because of Mark.

She smiled to herself about what they'd done to each other last night.

The jet had a bed in back.

A giant, round bed.

A bed she and Mark had put to good use to induct her into the Mile High Club.

She couldn't really say the sex was any better up here than on land. Then again, sex with Mark was always great, so did it really matter?

Her smile tightened then faded as she recalled afterward, though. When they'd been cuddling the way they always did after sex.

Their playtime had actually started where she was sitting now, in the public area of the cabin in the plush leather seats, only a few feet from the galley where Janie had disappeared and shut the door after taking away their dinner dishes.

A few minutes later, Mark had enticed her into a sexy game of temptation, seeing who could coerce the other to leave his or her chair first. She'd won, but it had taken removing her blouse and her bra to coax him from his seat.

God, what had she been thinking?

"I can't believe you got me to undress out there," she had said while lying in bed with him, his arms around her. "Janie could have walked in on us." She glanced over her shoulder to see he'd closed his eyes.

He snuggled closer and kissed the back of her shoulder. "I instructed her not to interrupt us after dinner."

Of course he'd instructed her not to interrupt them. He'd already set the stage, right? He had probably prepared this whole scene days ago.

She shifted and turned to face him, head supported on her arm. "Don't you ever do anything spontaneously?"

He rolled to his back and pulled her free arm over his stomach, lacing his fingers around hers. "I like planning things."

"I bet you'd like spontaneity, too, if you'd just give it a try."

"Probably." He grinned, let go of her hand, then tucked her hair behind her ear.

Her palm rested on his pec, and she combed her fingertips through his chest hair. "Then why do you plan everything?"

He shrugged. "Maybe I like being in control." His gaze never left hers.

"If you recall, you enjoyed when I blindfolded you that time at your apartment in Chicago. You weren't in control then."

The corners of his mouth curled introspectively, as if he were fondly remembering that night and what she'd done to him. What they'd done to each other.

"That was different," he said.

"How so?"

"It just was."

Her fingertips played through the soft hair on his chest, sweeping back and forth. "Well, I'm not seeing it."

"Trust me, it was." He averted his gaze toward the ceiling and didn't speak for several seconds. Then he said, "There *are* things you don't know about me, Karma." His voice hitched ever-so-slightly. "Things I've never told you."

Her hand stilled. He'd said something similar in the limo. Was he warning her? Or maybe preparing her? It sure sounded that way. As if he wanted to confess something but couldn't quite get the words out. Then again, this was Mark. A man who'd been locked up tight as a vault full of royal secrets for years. Opening up about his innermost thoughts wasn't his strong suit.

She angled her head and gently kissed the base of his neck. "Then maybe you should tell me." Her intuition told her not to push, though.

His arm around her squeezed, pulling her closer. "In time."

"During our trip?"

"Maybe."

"I hope so."

His chest rose and fell heavily beneath her cheek. "Are you so sure you want to know?"

His heart was beating hard. She could actually feel its accelerated thumping against the side of her face.

She rotated her head and placed her chin on his pectoral. His eyes moved to meet hers, but he didn't say anything. He didn't have to. She could see the solemn concern in his gaze. There was something he wasn't telling her. Something that scared him. Something he desperately wanted to get off his chest. That much was clear. So, why wouldn't he tell her what it was?

She regarded him for several seconds. This was her man. Her lover. Her future. She wanted him to feel comfortable enough to share his most despairing thoughts with her.

"I want to know everything about you, Mark."

"Even the bad stuff?"

What could be so bad to scare her away? She already knew he wasn't a saint. He'd always been honest about that.

"*Especially* the bad stuff." She wrapped her arm around his torso. "It's all part of who you are, and I love *all* of you."

His eyebrows dug into his eyelids, and his mouth set in a firm, grim line. "I love you, too." He searched her face as if she held the answers he needed to exorcise whatever haunted him. Then, with a troubled sigh, he turned his gaze back toward the ceiling.

She wasn't sure what to make of his reaction. Obviously, something was bothering him, but he didn't want to talk about it.

"Mark . . . ?"

He snapped out of whatever funk had taken hold of him. His expression softened, and he forced a smile as he rolled toward her, urging her to turn over so he could spoon her.

"Get some sleep, baby." He pressed his nose into her hair the way he often did, nuzzling her. "Okay?" He pressed his lips against the back of her head. "Let's sleep. It's a big day tomorrow. You should rest."

In other words, he didn't want to talk about whatever was bothering him right now.

Which made her all the more curious about what he was hiding.

And she was still curious this morning.

She broke from her thoughts and glanced into her half-empty teacup then set it on her tray. Mark sat across from her, his tablet in one hand and his coffee in the other. He looked like he was either reading his e-mail or perusing one of the many online newspapers he subscribed to. Two bites of eggs Benedict remained on his abandoned breakfast plate on the tray beside him.

He seemed better this morning, but he hadn't mentioned what had happened last night. Those demons, whatever they were, remained locked away.

The pilot's voice broke through the speakers.

After a good morning greeting and a few polite words about hoping they'd slept well, he said, "Please take your seats and fasten your seatbelts. We're beginning our descent into Saint Lucia. We'll be landing in about twenty minutes."

Her gaze shot to Mark's. "Saint Lucia? So, this is where you're taking me?"

He grinned and gave her a self-satisfied one-shouldered shrug as he handed his coffee mug to Janie then fastened his seatbelt.

Saint Freakin' Lucia!

In the Caribbean.

Sun, warmth, clear blue water, and sand.

Setting aside her concerns about last night, Karma gazed out the window as the jet descended. The water was such a deep, vivid blue it didn't even look real. In the distance, land came into view. As they drew closer, she spied what appeared to be a bustling port to the south. A pair of cruise ships stood out like monoliths against a bevy of smaller boats.

"Saint Lucia is one of my favorite places in the whole world." Mark leaned toward the window, his expression relaxed and content.

"You've been here before?" Surprise, surprise.

He nodded. "When I was younger. It was my mom's favorite place to vacation. She loves the tropics." The right corner of his mouth lifted, making his lone dimple cut into his cheek. "My parents even owned a vacation home here for a while. Sold it about five years ago, though."

The question about how much money Mark had ballooned inside her mind again. "Do your parents own vacation homes elsewhere?"

He nodded absently, craning his neck to look out over the water toward the bay in the distance. "A few."

A few? She did well to afford one small apartment. And his family had "a few" vacation homes splattered around the world? What exactly was she getting into with him?

"Where?"

He casually leaned back in his chair. "Paris." He paused, lifting his eyes to the ceiling as if in thought. "London. And then there's my mom's home in Italy. She'll never sell her villa, though." He spoke as if having homes all over Europe was nothing unusual.

"Your mom has a home in Italy?"

"It's actually my grandparents' home, but my mom inherited it after my grandfather died. My grandmother had already passed, so . . ." A fond, pensive expression crossed his face.

"So, the house was left to your mother."

"Yes."

The way he tipped his head and smiled affectionately spoke volumes about the type of relationship he had with his mom, as well as the one he'd had with his grandparents.

"You were close to them? Your grandparents, I mean."

"Very." He shifted in his seat, uncrossing his legs. "You know, not only was my grandfather a remarkable businessman, he was also a fabulous cook." His dark eyes sparkled with what Karma could tell were happy memories. "Every Sunday, the family got together at his place. He would give the staff the day off and spend the entire day in the kitchen. I often spent the day in there with him, helping, listening to his stories about Italy and business and everything else he'd experienced."

She propped her elbow on the arm of her chair and settled her chin on her fist, adoring this personal glimpse into his past. "Is he where you got your passion for cooking?"

His eyes danced, and blissful contentment washed over his features. "I think he's where I got my passion for everything. Business. Cooking. Even basketball. Grandpa loved watching the Bulls play." He chuckled then sobered. "It's as if he passed on to me what he couldn't pass on to *Mamma*."

Karma loved when he fell into his Italian accent. "Your grandpa wasn't a dancer then?"

He shook his head. "No. Not like *Mamma*. She must have gotten that from my grandmother." He made a wistful noise. "And my mom had no interest in running a company, so when I expressed an interest in business instead of dance, I think Grandpa saw a chance to pass on his legacy, which is why he took such an interest in my education. He's the reason I chose to attend the University of Chicago, and then the Booth School of Business, where I earned my MBA. I wanted to be like him."

"I love the way you talk about him."

"He was a great man."

"And you want to honor his memory."

His gaze fell briefly in a way that bespoke that he felt he would never live up to his grandfather's stature. "I'd like to think that someday I could honor him."

And there it was again. The shadow that had dogged Mark for the past twelve hours. What was troubling him? He'd mentioned twice there were things she still didn't know about him. If only he would tell her what was on his mind so they could get past it.

As the jet continued its approach, she pushed aside her concerns and turned her attention back out the window.

What would it be like to come from a wealthy family? Sure, money didn't solve every problem, but it had to make dealing with life's challenges easier, right?

She glanced at Mark out of the corner of her eye. His gaze was fixed on the dark-blue ocean.

She knew Mark's past. Knew better than anyone the pain he'd endured. And yet money hadn't been enough to keep Mark from falling into a horrible tailspin after finding Carol in bed with her dance partner when she should have been promising to love, honor, and cherish him till death do they part. For all his family's wealth, he had still suffered. Maybe even more deeply than someone who didn't come from privilege. Because people who grew up without unlimited means were used to hearing the word *no*. Used to not always getting their way. Which better prepared them for heartbreak.

Karma imagined that for all the crap Mark had told her he'd endured as a kid, he'd never really known true heartbreak until Carol jilted him so viciously. No wonder he'd developed such a powerful aversion to commitment. He was like a victim of a bad car crash who had suffered brain trauma. On the outside, he looked fine, but on the inside, vital components had been knocked out of place, and he had to figure out a whole new normal.

So maybe she was giving money more credit than it deserved, because Mark clearly had money and it hadn't been enough to make him overcome Carol's actions and the depression that followed.

"I haven't been here since I was eighteen," Mark said quietly. He wore a wistful, content expression. Clearly, Saint Lucia held a special place in his heart.

Her own heart swelled for the courageous man sitting across from her. He'd faced so much emotional adversity and pain, but despite his fears, he'd come back. *For her.* He'd found a way through the wall he'd erected around his heart so he could be with her. He loved her that much.

And that made her love him even more.

"Why have you waited so long to return?"

The smile he turned on her could only be described as love incarnate. "I haven't had a reason to until now."

The air in the cabin bloomed with warmth, tenderness, and something else. Something heady and intoxicating expanded and wrapped itself around Karma like a cashmere sweater, soft and luxurious.

"And I'm your reason?" Her voice sounded so small.

With a gentle nod, he leaned forward and reached for her hand. She teetered toward him and slid her fingers around his.

"Saint Lucia isn't a place you visit alone." His thumb caressed the back of her hand. "It's a place for lovers."

She fought back a smile. "You had a lover at eighteen?"

He narrowed his eyes then smirked. "No. Family vacation. We came here almost every year over Christmas break when I was a kid. But it never felt like the kind of place for family vacations. As I got older, I saw it as a place where lovers escaped so they could forget everything else but each other for a while."

She let the warmth of his words seep in as she stared at his thumb still skimming back and forth on her hand.

"Did you ever bring Carol here?" she asked quietly, hopefully. She didn't want to feel like she was following in Carol's footsteps, treading where *the other woman's* feet had already been.

When she lifted her gaze to his, he slowly shook his head. "No."

A thrill shot through her. She shouldn't have been so happy about Mark's response, but she was. She hated feeling like she was competing with Carol. As if his ex still wriggled around in his heart, which was insane, because she knew Mark would never go back to her. Still, to know Mark had never brought Carol here felt like a small victory.

The jet touched down, jolting her back into the moment, and she let go of Mark's hand.

The airport was the smallest Karma had ever seen. One long stretch of runway, and not much else. The main building was underwhelming, too, but then, while Saint Lucia was a tourist hot spot, travelers probably didn't flock here the way they did to larger locales. According to Mark, Saint Lucia was only twenty-seven miles long and fourteen miles wide. A person could drive around the entire island several times in one day if they wanted to.

After grabbing their luggage and working through customs and picking up their four-wheel drive rental, Mark drove them away from the airport.

The hardest thing to get used to was driving on the left side of the road, but of course, Mark handled it with ease.

"How long are we staying?" she said as they drove south along the coast. She caught glimpses of the sea between the trees and shops dotting the roadside.

"Nine days. We fly back next Sunday."

Over a week in paradise. Nine days of beaches and walking in the surf. Of no one but her and Mark. No work, no tense family Christmas visits.

Was Christmas really only five days away?

And she wasn't spending it with her family.

It saddened her that her dad had drawn such a hard line against Mark, and, consequently, her. Didn't twenty-six years of love, devotion, fishing trips to Peterman Lake, and countless father-daughter nights in front of the TV cheering on their favorite teams count for anything? Her dad had discarded her as if their relationship meant nothing.

Her melancholy must have shown, because Mark reached across the console and closed his hand around hers.

"What's wrong?" he said.

Mark could read her so damn easily. He'd always been able to. An invisible link seemed to connect his mind to hers. She'd never known anyone so attuned to her.

"I was just thinking about my dad."

He squeezed her hand. "He'll come around."

"I'm not so sure." She sighed and dropped her gaze to her lap. "Do you realize this is the first Christmas I won't spend with him and my family?"

Mark's fingers wove more firmly around hers. "I know. It's one reason why I wanted to bring you here. To help take your mind off what's happening between you and your dad." He paused, shooting her a quick glance before turning his eyes back to the road. "And . . . I remembered what you said about that picture in your bedroom. The one of the seascape. You told me that you often lie on your bed, looking at that picture, and imagine yourself on a tropical beach somewhere."

She smiled at their joined hands then admired his profile. "And, now, here I am. You've brought my daydreams to life."

"Something like that." He darted another sideways glance toward her and smiled reassuringly.

He took such good care of her. She had never complained about the coming holiday. Had never mentioned her sadness over not being able to spend Christmas with her dad. But Mark had known. Whatever connection his mind shared with hers had warned him she needed extra TLC right now. And like a knight in shining armor, Mark delivered above and beyond. What better way to take her mind off her sadness than by whisking her away to a tropical island?

When the hustle of Castries lay fifteen minutes behind them and they'd entered a more isolated area, Mark slowed and turned into the driveway of a large villa. Karma nearly choked on her saliva at the enormous size.

"What's this?"

Mark shut off the engine. "This is our home for the next nine days."

Her mouth fell open as she turned her gaze back to the impressive home. "We're not . . . I . . . hold on a second." She raised her hand, feeling like a fairy princess in the middle of a fantasy. "We're not staying in a hotel?"

His eyebrows knotted over the bridge of his nose as his mouth twisted in amusement. "No. Should we be staying in a hotel?"

"I just assumed . . ." She turned wide eyes back to the villa as words failed her.

He had rented them an entire house, complete with an open view of the sea and a crystal blue sky dotted with puffy white clouds. This was so much better than any beach-infused daydream she'd ever conjured while staring at that picture on her bedroom wall.

Mark chuckled and hopped out. "Come on, Alice. Let's explore the rabbit hole."

She pushed open her door and slowly slid off her seat until her feet struck ground. The view . . . the villa. No fantasy did justice to the reality. The air smelled of the sea, fresh and vibrant, and the breeze kicked her hair away from her face in such a refreshing way.

"So . . . do you like it?" Mark glanced at her from across the hood of the SUV.

She took a deep breath and slowly blew it out. "I love it." She walked toward the villa like it was a mirage and would evaporate. Instead, the closer she got, the more real it seemed.

Lush vegetation consumed the landscape around the large covered porch, and as she waited for Mark to unlock the door, she smoothed her fingers down a palm frond the size of an elephant's ear.

Mark took her hand and led her inside, which was just as magnificent as outside. Windows, windows everywhere, letting in the sun and the view. A large, fully-stocked kitchen waited for Mark's culinary skills to breathe life into it, and a high-ceilinged living room opened onto a massive, multi-level deck and sun room.

But the bedroom was the grandest of all. A stone floor cooled her feet after she kicked off her shoes and spun a slow circle. Where to look first? One half of the room housed a sitting area complete with large, cushioned chairs and a polished stone table that felt like cold glass when she touched it. An enormous bed situated in front of a huge picture window dominated the other half of the room. It was covered with a plush, white comforter that looked like a thick layer of pristine snow. Gauze-like curtains hung from a circular runner on the ceiling over the bed. The sheer curtains currently hung open, draping delicately over the ornate, wooden headboard.

As she gaped over the bedroom, Mark meandered to the sliding door facing the sea and slid it open. The breeze wafted in, billowing the airy drapes hanging throughout the room.

"Come here." He waved for her to join him. "Come and see this."

She gasped as she stepped outside and the wind lifted her hair away from her face. Off to one side hung a massive hammock large enough for at least four people. Down one level was a pool, which faced the sea. It was one of those infinity pools that appeared to end against an invisible barrier or simply fall away like a waterfall.

A place for lovers.

This villa was definitely a place for lovers, designed specifically to encourage intimacy.

Only a small section of the deck was wood. The rest was stone, including the steps that led from the upper level to the lower. And beyond was another set of stone stairs that led to the private beach a hundred feet below. Karma hadn't even realized how high up from sea level they were.

"So, what do you want to do first?" Mark eased his arms around her waist from behind.

The question caused her brain to go into lockdown. How could she decide? Everywhere she looked was another wonder to explore.

The sudden rumble of her stomach broke the quiet mood.

She slapped her hand against her abdomen with a giggle. "Um, how about lunch?"

He chuckled and pulled her back inside. "I'll get the luggage if you want to see what's available."

In the kitchen, she found just about everything they could ever want.

Fresh, colorful fruit filled a bowl on the counter. Bananas, mangoes, limes, and a coconut. An actual coconut. Not something you see in your everyday Indiana kitchen like an apple. But here, coconuts were probably commonplace.

She smiled, set the coconut back in the bowl, and started preparing lunch.

*   *   *

Mark made three trips to the SUV, but he eventually hauled all their luggage into the bedroom while Karma busied herself in the kitchen.

Kneeling beside his hunter-green suitcase, he peered over his shoulder, making sure Karma hadn't snuck in behind him. Still alone, he unzipped the flap and dug his hand into his folded clothes until he found the light-blue Tiffany box with the white silk bow around it.

He pulled it out and checked over his shoulder again. He'd made a promise to the universe that if Karma came back to him, he'd fight for her and never leave her again. The diamond engagement ring set in a filigreed, platinum band inside the box was the culmination of that promise.

He grabbed the clothes from his suitcase and piled them into the middle drawer of the dresser before tucking the box underneath a folded stack of briefs. He slid the drawer closed, exhaling a breath of finality.

He still wasn't sure how he would propose, but he knew in his heart that the perfect opportunity would present itself sometime during their trip. By the time he and Karma returned home, she would be wearing that ring. And for the second time in his life — and hopefully the last — he'd be an engaged man.

But there was more to this trip than just proposing. A lot more.

Quelling the sudden stir of panic in his chest, he cleared his throat, took another deep breath, and left the bedroom, ready to help his future wife make lunch.

This would be a vacation neither of them would ever forget.

He just hoped it would be for all the right reasons.

Chapter 4

Everyone comes with baggage. Find someone who loves you enough to help you unpack.
-Author Unknown

They spent their first day in Saint Lucia lazing on the deck, snuggling and dozing away the jet lag.

On Saturday, Karma woke with the sun to find Mark already up. As much as she was a morning person, he was even more-so.

He entered the bedroom with two mugs in his hands. Using his elbow, he brushed aside the filmy curtain hanging around the bed then sat on the edge.

"Good morning." He extended one of the mugs toward her. Tea, no doubt. He knew she didn't drink coffee.

She rubbed her eyes and sat up, letting the comforter fall into her lap. "Good morning." She took the tea and blew over the top before taking a tentative sip.

"Sleep well?" He sipped his coffee.

"Mm-hm." She stretched and glanced out the window. "It wasn't a dream. We're really here."

He chuckled. "Yes, we're really here." He brushed his fingers down her arm. "And we're going to the Latille Gardens today."

"The Latille Gardens? What's that?" She took another drink.

Lifting his leg onto the bed, he shifted so they faced one another. "Waterfalls, tropical flowers, breathtaking scenery. You'll love it."

"And you're going to be my tour guide?"

He leaned toward her, softly brushing the backs of his fingers down the curve of her shoulder. "Yes. I'll be your tour guide."

"My sexy tour guide." She dipped her face into his hand as he cradled her cheek.

They stared at each other for a long moment, and then he gingerly kissed her.

She melted just a little bit at his tenderness.

He kissed her again then stood and slid the white see-through curtains back, officially welcoming the new day. "Make sure you wear a bathing suit under your clothes." He grinned before disappearing into the bathroom.

A moment later, the shower turned on.

As she'd unpacked yesterday, she'd been surprised to find a dozen new bikinis and bathing suits he'd bought for her. Some of the suits were appropriate to wear in public, but a couple were definitely meant for Mark's eyes only. As in, they looked like they would barely cover her naughty bits.

She swung her legs off the bed, pattered barefoot across the stone floor to the dresser, and selected a pair of khaki capris, a T-shirt, and a full-coverage bikini in a tropical print.

After Mark showered, she took over in the bathroom while he fixed breakfast.

Once they'd eaten, they headed out for the eastern side of the island, the sunroof open. Forty-eight hours ago, she'd been huddled against the overcast cold. Now she was in sunny paradise. Talk about surreal.

Mark slowed the SUV as they approached a homemade, hand-painted sign made of what looked like driftwood and stray branches. The word "WELCOME" was painted on flat, connected slabs of wood that reminded Karma of the sticks paint stores gave you to stir your paint, only these were all painted green. They were mounted on straight branches bound together to form a panel. Some of the slabs were thicker than others, some shorter. And the lettering consisted of all hard angles, the *O* shaped like a diamond instead of a circle.

But what did she expect? A big fancy marquee? This was much more charming and fit the island's tropical personality.

Under the welcome sign hung a warped piece of wood with the word "PARKING" stenciled in white. A haphazardly painted green arrow pointed them toward the right.

"Fancy sign." She pointed and giggled as they passed into what looked more like a grassy picnic area than a parking lot.

Mark shot her a humored glance as he pulled to a stop. "Hey now, don't make fun of the locals."

"I'm not making fun. I think it's quaint." The sign actually added to the feeling that they were on a tropical adventure, away from civilized society and drawn into a simpler, more romantic time and place. A place unfettered by commerce, corporations, and the drive to achieve. A place where relaxation and enjoyment reigned.

A dark-skinned attendant wearing a rainbow-colored, hand-knitted slouch cap greeted them. While he and Mark exchanged pleasantries, Karma took in her surroundings. Green. Lots of lush, green vegetation. A few pink flowers scattered the edges.

A dog that looked like a mix between a yellow Lab and a retriever trotted into the opening from somewhere and wagged its tail at Karma as it approached.

"Hi, you." She knelt and raised her hand.

The dog sniffed her fingers, leaned its head into her palm for a quick nuzzle, and then meandered toward Mark and the attendant.

A moment later, the local and the dog headed off, and Mark joined her, taking her hand. "We're the only ones here."

That sounded ominous. "Should I be worried?"

He led her toward a dirt path bordered by a wooden railing that looked as fancy as the welcome sign. "Only if you wore the silver bikini. If you did, I can't make any promises."

She laughed. "Then I'm safe. I didn't wear the silver bikini."

"Damn." He snapped his fingers as they entered the trail. "I guess it's just going to be sightseeing then."

She hugged his arm against her side. "Don't worry. I have a feeling there will be plenty of time for the other stuff."

He raised her hand to his lips and kissed the back as he glanced at her over the top of his sunglasses. "You bet your ass there will be time for the other stuff. I didn't bring you all the way here just to read and play cards. I plan on taking full advantage of having you to myself for nine days." He dipped his chin, drilling his over-the-sunglasses gaze into hers. "Full. Advantage."

Butterflies fluttered in her belly. "Darn. And here I was so looking forward to getting caught up on my reading."

"Always the smart retort from you." He grinned and squeezed her hand.

"Always."

He guided her along the path, taking her deeper into the wilderness.

"So, is that why you brought me here? To take advantage of me?" She swept her gaze around the lush, green canopy as they rounded a bend and descended toward the innards of the gardens.

He grew quiet, and they walked silently for at least thirty seconds before he answered.

"I brought you here because I knew you'd love it. It's a magical, mystical place." He paused, letting his gaze fall to the dirt floor as if he were watching his step. "It's the perfect place to feel safe. To feel like I can tell you anything." The shadow that had followed him for the past two days darkened his expression, and then was gone.

Whatever was troubling him was starting to worry her. If only he would just blurt it out.

She was about to push him to do just that when he led her around a curve and into an opening, revealing a secluded pool. On the opposite side, water flowed down a jagged wall of rock so dark it looked black.

"But for now," he said, "let me show you one of the most breathtaking wonders of the island." He stepped behind her, winding his arms around her waist. "I give you one of the many falls in the Latille Gardens."

For the remainder of the day, she dismissed Mark's secrets. He led her from one falls to the next, up dirt paths enhanced by man-made steps built of fallen branches, down ivy-covered ridges, through vibrantly flowered gardens, stopping to swim in one of the larger ponds and rest under the falling water a while before leading her back to the entrance midafternoon.

Back at the villa, they napped in the hammock after eating a late lunch then lounged by the pool until dinner. Afterward, they took their wine back out to the pool and relaxed.

"So, what did you think of the gardens?" Mark said, his voice quiet.

The sun hung low on the horizon in a cloudless sky. A breeze blew off the ocean, rejuvenating her spirit.

"They were beautiful." Maybe for the islanders, the falls were status quo, but for a Midwesterner like her, where flat farmland was the norm, the falls were like a luxurious mirage, too brilliant to be real.

"Told you."

They fell into silence for a while, staring at the endless ocean and the deepening sunset.

When she was younger, she had often fantasized about faraway lands, wondering what life was like in other parts of the world. To her, everywhere seemed like a happier place than where she was. Maybe that was a product of being bullied, but she had wanted to escape and go somewhere new. Somewhere she could start over.

She smiled to herself as she made the connection to making New Year's resolutions. New beginnings. Forgetting the past. She'd been thinking a lot about both the past two days.

"Have you made your New Year's resolutions, yet?" She turned toward Mark.

He rolled his head on the cushion to look at her. "No. Why? Have you?"

"I started, but couldn't come up with anything."

His gaze drifted back to the clear sky. "I haven't really thought about it. I don't usually make resolutions. I used to, but . . ."

The way he trailed off set Karma's awareness on end. "Why did you stop?"

He sighed and turned back toward her, his expression almost apologetic as guilt shadowed his eyes. "Do you really want me to say it?"

This had to do with Carol. Once again, that woman shot up like a spiked wall between them, interfering, getting in the way. And she'd had enough.

She abruptly sat up. "Yes, Mark, I really want you to say it." Damn him if he didn't just get whatever was bugging him off his chest. She huffed and slapped her hands on her thighs. "You've been hinting for two days that there's something you want to tell me. I wish you'd just come out and say whatever it is, because it's eating me up. It's eating *you* up." She waved her hand toward him. "I hate seeing you like this. This is supposed to be our *romantic vacation*, but whatever's bugging you is mucking it all up. Just when I think it's gone, it comes back and gets in the way." She stood and walked toward the edge of the pool deck, facing the beach below, arms crossed.

A moment later, Mark eased up behind her and traced his palms up her arms to her shoulders. "I know I'm being secretive. I'm sorry. I didn't mean to upset you."

"What aren't you telling me, Mark?"

He let out a heavy exhale and tipped his forehead against the back of her head. "Karma . . . I . . ."

She turned and faced him. "Just tell me." When he didn't answer, she pushed further. "Why won't you talk to me?"

He frowned and looked down with a shake of his head.

"Come on, Mark, what's going on?"

"You don't understand, Karma."

"Then enlighten me." She crossed her arms again. "It can't be that bad, can it?"

He blew out a scornful exhale. "For someone as pure as you, it might—"

"Pure? You think I'm pure? What are you saying? That you're *not*?" She lifted her hands to the sides. "Tell me something I don't know, Mark."

He frowned. "But—"

"And I can assure you, I'm not as pure as you think. Maybe I'm not as experienced as you are, but that doesn't mean my thoughts haven't gone down a wayward trail or two."

"Fantasizing and doing are two different things. One isn't as bad as the other."

"I'll be the judge of that. Oh wait, that's right, you won't let me, because you won't tell me what's going on."

He let out an exasperated growl. "It's not that simple, Karma. What if you don't like what I have to say? What if it changes everything?"

"You think I'm so superficial that I would base my feelings for you on something you did before you even knew me? And what if it *does* change everything? For the better? How is opening up and sharing your most personal fears with me a bad thing if it means it will bring us closer?"

His jaw tightened. "You're making assumptions."

"Because you won't talk to me!"

"You're assuming that what I want to tell you is all about my past and what I've done. What if it's something else. What if . . . ?"

She waited for him to finish, but he didn't. His mouth opened, closed, opened again, but he said nothing further. Only stood there and shook his head as if he couldn't speak.

Couldn't? Or wouldn't?

"Forget it." She pushed past him and took the steps to the upper deck.

If he wasn't going to talk to her, she wasn't going to stick around and argue with him, especially when she was one breath shy of crying.

At times like this, it felt like he would never let her in, and she hated how that felt.

*   *   *

Mark watched her disappear inside then slumped against the railing separating the pool deck from a sharp decline to the beach below.

He was messing up everything. This wasn't how he'd wanted the conversation about his past to go. He'd planned to ease Karma into the discussion, feeding her small bits a little at a time. But then she'd brought it up, and he hadn't known how to respond, and now everything was fucked. She was inside and angry with him, and he was out here alone. An enormous chasm separated them when they should have been enjoying the sunset together.

Maybe he hadn't given her enough credit. She said she loved him and wanted him to tell her everything. Maybe he should put more faith in her. Because if their roles were switched, wouldn't he be forgiving if she revealed her darkest secrets to him? He loved her enough to accept anything and everything about her, no matter how damnable she thought it was.

He needed to unburden himself. Let the chips fall where they may. Maybe it wasn't how he'd wanted this discussion to happen, but he couldn't put it off anymore.

He took the steps two at a time then crossed the upper deck to the open sliding door to the bedroom. The bathroom door was closed, and he heard her soft sobs beneath the sound of the shower.

"Karma?" He knocked.

She quieted.

"Can I come in?"

Silence.

He turned the handle and eased open the door.

The glass panel hid nothing of her slender, beautiful body, but she was turned away from him, shoulders hunched, face hidden.

He quickly undressed then opened the shower door and stepped in behind her, hugging her close as the warm water spilled over them.

"I'm sorry. Okay? I'm so sorry."

"Why won't you talk to me?"

"I will. Now. I promise. I just didn't want to do it this way. I'd planned to—"

"You need to quit planning so much and just *do*." Her tone was chastising but gracious.

"I know. I'll try harder." He turned her toward him and forced a tight smile. "I'll make that one of my New Year's resolutions. See? You helped me find one."

Her eyebrows turned up in the middle a split second before a forgiving smile broke over her face. She wrapped her arms around him and pressed her face against his chest.

He held and rocked her a couple of minutes then ran his palm down her silky, wet hair. "Come on. Let's finish in here so I can . . ." He took a shaky breath and blew it out. "So I can tell you everything I need to tell you."

She lifted her head. "You promise?"

He kissed her. "I promise. This is just hard for me, Karma. These are things I've never told anyone."

"Not even Rob?" Her slim eyebrows scrunched.

"No. Not even Rob."

"And it scares you." Not a question.

He answered anyway. "Yes."

"Why?"

He shifted uncomfortably, not liking how fear felt rolling down his back. "Because what you think of me is important. More important than anything else. I don't want to disappoint you."

She folded her hands around his. "There's nothing you can say that will change how I feel about you. I love you. I've always loved you. The only thing that will disappoint me is if you continue keeping secrets from me."

His gaze dropped to the tiled shower floor. "It's just that I've lived like this for a long time. It's hard for me to open up, even when I know I need to."

She tipped her head back to rinse her hair then looked back up at him. "I'm not going anywhere. You're stuck with me, Strong." She let go of his hands and opened the shower door. "I'll meet you in the bedroom." She pulled a towel from the rack and wrapped it around her then twisted another around her hair before smiling encouragingly over her shoulder at him as she left the bathroom.

Was he really going to confess everything? Right now?

Jesus. His hands were shaking.

He quickly washed, rinsed, and dried off. When he joined her back in the bedroom, she was sitting cross-legged on the bed, wearing the silk, floral-print robe he'd bought her two summers ago. She had a pair of notebooks in her lap.

"I have an idea," she said, lifting one of the notebooks and a pen.

He slipped into his own red, cotton robe and approached the bed. "What's this?" He took the pen and notebook and sat down across from her.

"I thought this might make things easier." She flipped the cover of her own notebook open and turned to a blank page. "You can jot down what you want to tell me, and I'll write down a few things I want to share with you, too. Then we can take turns revealing what we wrote to one another."

"You don't have to do that."

"I want to. It will make it easier for you to share your secrets if I share mine, too." They were sitting in the center of the bed, and she reached behind her to untie the sheer curtains so they fell halfway around them. "This way you'll see I'm not as pure as you think I am."

"I don't think you'll ever prove to me you're not pure." He pulled the drapes closed, sealing them into a cocoon. "But if it makes *you* feel more comfortable, I won't stop you."

"Then it's settled." She set her notebook in her lap. "And writing down what you want to say will help organize your thoughts. Trust me, I know. I used to write in a journal almost every day."

An expectant air hung over them, like a giant balloon just waiting to be popped.

"So . . . just write?" he said, flipping to a blank page.

"Yep. And I'll do the same."

Okay, here goes.

With a trembling hand, he pressed the ballpoint to the paper and scrawled the first item on his list.

1. Cocaine and alcohol.

He didn't need to write more than that. He knew what needed to be said, and he'd already told her about the alcohol. Now he just needed to make her see how bad his post-Carol devastation had really been. How far he'd actually fallen, if only temporarily.

2. Sex addiction. The parties, the clubs, Nina and her hard-core fantasies, group sex.

This point contained too many variables to list, none of them he was proud of. Those first eighteen months following Carol had been filled with shameless hedonism. They'd been a blurry, fucked up hive of depravity. But they were a part of his past, and he needed to own them. It was time.

3. Role-play sex.

Not dressed-up-like-a-French-maid bullshit. He was talking about full-on, intense, highly developed fantasies. His role-play fetish was about so much more than playful sex. He wanted to live the parts. To become the roles and set up elaborate scenes that extended for hours or even days. To him role-play sex wasn't as much about escapism as it was about enhancement. It had been a long time since he'd found a partner he wanted to play such games with. But only because, for him, role-playing opened doors between the players he hadn't wanted to open again until now.

4. Anal play.

So this item was a complicated one. What if, when she learned exactly what he wanted, it made her too uncomfortable? What if she looked at him differently? Because ... yeah, that could easily happen.

He needed Karma to understand his fetish was normal and healthy, not dysfunctional.

5. *Exhibitionist sex.*

Something about getting caught having sex was an incredible turn-on. Even just the threat they could be caught excited him. He had sensed such tendencies in Karma, too, but so far hadn't explored them. He wanted to, but that might mean finding a sex club tame enough not to offend Karma but not so tame that it would be like attending a book club discussion on better sex. At the very least, he would have to get creative about finding places that allowed them enough privacy to play yet put them close to potentially prying eyes.

6. *I want to dance again.*

He stared down at the paper.

There it was.

The big one.

The one item on his list he wasn't even sure he could do, anymore. Yeah, lame, right? But for him, dancing was about so much more than learning a few steps. It was about joy and intimacy, as well as a hundred other little things.

Carol had stolen his joy of dancing. She'd stripped away his desire to sweep a woman into his arms and truly dance with her the way he used to. As if his heart depended on every roll of his hips during a sensual rumba or every commanding snap of his arms during a *paso doble*. As if his soul longed to guide his partner through the dance, his arms and hands caressing, turning, touching.

To him, ballroom dancing wasn't about competition. It was a sharing of hearts, of two bodies so tuned in to one another they flowed seamlessly as one over the dance floor.

It was about true partnership. Complete trust.

And Carol had shattered that. Much in the same way her deception had created an inborn fear of weddings, it had scared him away from the dance floor, as well.

He didn't count slow dancing, though.

No, wait. His eyebrows scrunched inward. That wasn't entirely true.

Until he met Karma at the benefit in Chicago, he hadn't even slow danced in six years. Six whole years. How had he not made that connection before? Of all the women he'd dated during that time period, he hadn't danced with a single one. But within thirty minutes of meeting Karma, he'd had his arms around her, swaying to easy jazz played by a live band. He should have known then just how different she was from all the rest.

But slow dancing wasn't Latin ballroom dancing. And the idea of dancing Latin ballroom style still shackled him with the shakes and a side of cold sweats. But damn it, he wanted to dance like that again. With Karma. And not just dance, but *live*. That's what dancing meant to him. It was foreplay, almost as intimate as making love. As much a part of sexual intimacy as kissing.

But he couldn't expect Karma to fill Carol's shoes. She wasn't a professional Latin ballroom dancer. It wasn't fair to expect her to indulge this side of him simply because he missed it. In fact, he imagined she would be offended—and maybe even intimidated— that he still longed for something that had clearly been a sizable aspect in his and Carol's relationship.

He frowned at his words on the sheet of paper. He was selfish to want that with Karma.

No. Number six had to go.

He slashed a line of black ink through it.

He could deny himself this one point for the sake of their relationship, even though it was the one thing he longed for more than all the others.

But relationships required compromise, and this would be his.

"Are you finished?" Karma asked, capping her pen.

Scanning the first five items, he ignored number six and nodded. "Yes." He handed her his pen.

She set it next to hers on the bedside table. "Okay. I'll go first." She shifted her legs, creeping closer until their knees touched.

He took her hands. "Wasn't this supposed to be about me opening up to you?"

"Yes, but I figured it might make it easier for you if I broke the ice." Her fingers tightened around his reassuringly.

Her compassion never ceased to amaze him. Only a short while ago, she'd been angry with him. Angry enough to walk away and cry.

He'd made her *cry*, for God's sake.

And yet, here she was now, lovingly laying a path for him to follow, trying to make this easier for him. Whether she believed it or not, she was pure. Only a pure soul could give so selflessly.

"Okay." She let go of his hands and clasped hers together. "Here's something I've never told you." The guilty, mischievous sparkle in her eyes made him smile. "Remember when you first came to Solar?"

"How could I forget?"

She bit her lip and grinned shyly. "Well, there were days I was so turned on just sitting so close to you that I had to go to the restroom and... you know..." Her face shaded bright pink, and she squirmed, making her knees rub against his.

He curled his palms encouragingly over her knees. He already knew how her confession ended, but that made him want to hear her say the words even more. He pushed his hands up her inner thighs, his fingers disappearing under the hem of her robe. "Come on, you can say it."

She giggled and closed her eyes, bowing her head. "I masturbated. I couldn't help it. Especially after we started seeing one another." Her face took on a dreamy quality. "I would sit at my desk, remembering how you kissed me... how you looked at me... things you said. And I could barely sit still. So, I'd escape to the ladies room, sometimes two or three times a day."

His fingers gripped her thighs as his mouth dropped open. "Two or three times a day?"

She hid her face behind her hand and giggled. "Yes. You turned me into a nymphomaniac."

He chuckled, recalling a time or two when he'd glanced up from his place at the conference room table to see her returning to her desk, face flushed, unsteady on her feet. Now it all made sense. He leaned toward her and whispered, "I'll let you in on a little secret."

Her gaze met his. "What?"

"I did the same thing."

Her eyes widened. "You did?"

He nodded. "Quite often, in fact. Especially when you wore a pair of sexy shoes. Something I think you did on purpose just to turn me on." Emphasizing his point, he skimmed his palms down her legs and closed them over her bare feet, making a mental note to add foot jobs to his confession list. "And don't deny that wasn't your intent when you dangled one of your sexy shoes from your toes."

She blushed and looked down. "Guilty."

"Uh-huh. I know." He let the tips of his fingers play along her arches as his mind wandered to the time when she surprised him at his apartment in Chicago. She'd used her feet on him for the first time during that trip. Only a little, but enough that he'd almost come just watching her pretty toes curl around his shaft.

He remembered with utter clarity telling her the next time they did that, they would use baby oil. But next time had never come. She'd teased him. She'd played footsy with him. But she'd never come as close to delivering a repeat of one of his greatest fantasies as she had that night.

And tonight, among other things, he was going to reveal that he wanted to. He only hoped Karma would be open to that and all the rest, and that the reason she hadn't put her feet on him again wasn't because she hadn't liked it the first time and didn't want to again.

Clearing his throat, he squeezed her feet and glanced down at the sliver of mattress separating them. "I guess it's my turn, huh?"

He'd never been one to shrink away from difficult discussions. In fact, he considered himself a deeply confident man. But at times like this, he wondered if his confidence wasn't just a mask to hide his fears and insecurities. Hadn't he considered that possibility in the year he and Karma were apart? That he'd assumed such a bold persona more as a defense than as a natural portrayal of who he really was?

She folded her hands over her lap. "Yes. Your turn."

"Okay, well, I might talk a little longer than you did." He had a lot more to say.

She smiled and gave him a shallow, encouraging nod. "That's okay."

He took a deep breath, fidgeting. "I'm not sure how to start. Like I said, I'd planned—"

"Stop planning." She placed her hands over his. "Don't even think about it." Her voice was kind, gentle. Coaxing. "Just start talking, and before you know it, you'll find a rhythm." She pulled her hands away and placed them in her lap again, waiting for him to continue.

The person he'd been two years ago wouldn't have had any trouble opening up. Old him would have seen this coming and would have headed it off at the pass. Which was sort of the point, wasn't it? Because old him would never have even let him get to this point. Old Mark never would have let himself fall in love. He would have walked away that day at the benefit the moment he saw Karma sitting across the room in her incredible red dress if he'd known she would be the one to break through his armor and steal his heart.

But he hadn't walked away. He'd crossed the room and sat down next to her. He'd flirted, did the casual dancing thing with her, and then taken her up to his room. He had intended to make her another of his conquests. But before he could seal the deal, she'd bolted. And that would have been the end of their relationship had he not met her again two days later at Solar in Indianapolis. However, even then, had it not been for that one night in Chicago, he doubted he would have pursued her. By then, his heart had already belonged to her. He just hadn't realized it at the time. But by the end of that summer, he knew he would never be the same man he'd been before they met.

Old Mark had been dealt a fatal blow that night in Chicago. And he'd been dying a slow death ever since, giving way for a new Mark to emerge. A man whose skin he still didn't feel comfortable wearing.

But he was trying.

Taking her advice to just start talking, he closed his eyes, threw out a prayer for strength, and took off.

"After Carol left me, I fell into a really dark place." He released her feet and reached for her hands. She slid her fingers into his palms, giving him an anchor to hold onto.

"I know."

He shook his head. "That's just it, you don't know."

She blinked as her eyebrows furrowed. "But . . . I thought . . . you told me about—"

"I told you only some of what happened, but not everything. And my duplicity wasn't completely intentional. I put a lot of what happened out of my mind. I wanted to forget all the shit I'd done."

He puffed out a derisive exhale. "And I was drinking so much, anyway, everything felt like a dream, making it much easier to forget."

Karma nodded tightly and licked her lips. "Okay, so why now? Why are you remembering everything now?"

"I wish I knew, but . . . I think it has to do with you."

"Me?"

"You've done something to me, Karma." How could he explain it when he didn't fully understand himself? "It's like you woke me up from a six-year nightmare the moment I met you, and now I'm changing. I'm becoming someone else. Not exactly who I once was, but more than who've I've been. And part of this transformation is that all those memories I wanted to forget are pushing to the forefront of my mind. I'm being forced to deal with them now. Deal with the guilt, the shame . . . and the excitement."

Her frowned deepened. "I don't understand."

"I know, and that's why I need to explain, or at least try to. Because for whatever reason, this new person I'm becoming needs you to know. I need you to understand. You're part of whatever is happening to me."

She pulled her bottom lip into her mouth then let out a shaky exhale as if she were finally beginning to see how bad some of what he was about to say could be. "I'm listening."

After another short pause, he continued. "Okay, so I was in a really bad place. I'd just been left at the altar, found my fiancée in bed with another man, and pretty much had my entire world pulled out from under me. I was young. I was stupid. I got a little self-destructive as I tried to find footing again." He closed his eyes at the memories of some of the shit he'd done. "Okay, make that *a lot* self-destructive. I started drinking. Heavily. Somehow—and I don't know how—I was able to keep it hidden from work . . . or maybe I didn't and just think I did. I don't know. All I know is they didn't fire me. But that's not why I'm telling you this. I'm telling you this so you know just how bad it got."

She scooted forward, tightening her grip on his hands. Otherwise, she didn't say a word.

"Karma . . ." He sighed. "It was so much worse than I ever let on. Not even Rob knows how bad I really got. I never told him. Like I said before, you're the first person I've ever admitted any of this to."

He was risking everything. He was putting his heart on the line for the first time in over a decade—maybe even for the first time *ever*—and it scared the holy living shit out of him.

"Hey," she said, running her right hand soothingly up his forearm and back down to his wrist. "It's okay. Take your time. I'm not going anywhere."

She said that now, but after he told her everything, would she still feel the same way?

"Yeah, well, you might want to by the time I finish."

"Give me more credit than that, Mark. I love you. Whatever you have to tell me, we'll get through it."

He certainly hoped so, because now that the memories of that wretched year and a half had pushed their way back into his mind, he wasn't sure he could even live with himself.

"Karma, I did some awful, terrible things. Immoral things." He sighed. "Shameful things." For a moment, he sat silently, sorting through all the shit, deciding what he should reveal first. "Not only did I drink, but I did drugs." Just saying it made him feel like a criminal. Like he was the lowest form of life.

"What kind of drugs?"

"Cocaine." He bowed his head, shaking it. "God, this is hard to talk about."

She let go of his hands and cupped his face. "It's in the past, Mark. Let go of it."

He met her eyes. "I'm trying. That's why I want to tell you this."

Compassion filled her gaze, and she offered a tiny smile of encouragement. "Like I said, I'm not going anywhere." She nodded encouragingly. "So, tell me. How long did you use . . . cocaine?" She said the word softly, hesitantly. As if she didn't like how it felt rolling off her tongue.

"Not long. A few weeks, maybe a month."

"And was cocaine the only drug you used?"

"No. I did try crack once. I guess technically it's cocaine, though, so . . ." He cleared his throat and glanced down. "But I also took a few hits of Molly."

"Molly?"

"It's a designer drug."

"Oh." She bit her bottom lip as her eyes shifted awkwardly.

"I didn't really like how the drugs made me feel, though, so I stopped. But I was hurting. I was looking for any outlet to help me forget. So, I turned to drugs and alcohol. Then it was just alcohol. And then Rob pulled me out of the bottle, and I thought maybe I was going to be okay, but there was still something missing. I was still hurting. That's when . . ." He closed his eyes and lowered his head, giving himself a moment to breathe before going on. He looked back up, met her gaze, and said, "That's when I became addicted to sex."

She pulled back a fraction of an inch and blinked as her eyebrows lifted. Clearly, she hadn't expected him to say that.

"Clinically speaking, I wasn't addicted, but I started going out with a lot of women. I wanted to replace Carol. It's like I had this deep-seated need to find what I'd had with her with someone else, and then it just turned into something ugly."

God, it was a wonder he hadn't caught some disease or gotten some girl pregnant. He'd been so reckless.

Karma deserved so much better than a man like him, but fate had driven them together. Now he needed to come clean so they could go into their future unencumbered by the past. But right now, he wouldn't even be able to look at himself in a mirror, he was so ashamed.

"The things I did, Karma. I was such a hedonist, and not in a good way."

"Like what?" Her voice was barely a whisper. "What did you do?"

"I think a better question is what *didn't* I do?" He shook his head shamefully. "I did it all, Karma. Threesomes. Foursomes. Sex parties. I went to fetish clubs. I even paid a woman to have sex with me. Do you understand what I'm saying? I paid a woman, Karma. What kind of an asshole pays for sex?" He let go of her hands and scooted away. He couldn't stand the thought of defiling her simply by touching her.

She grabbed his wrist and pulled him back, pushing up on her knees and inching forward so she could close the distance between them and prevent him from turning away. "Hey, you were in a bad place, remember? You said so yourself. You weren't thinking clearly. Don't be so hard on yourself, Mark. That was a long time ago, and you're not that person, anymore."

Now it was his turn to frown. Was he in another dimension? He'd just told her he'd done drugs, done unspeakable things, and paid for a night of sex with an escort, and yet she was comforting him. She was putting her arms around him, hugging him, pressing her cheek against his.

This wasn't the reaction he'd expected, but he was grateful for it.

"You deserve better than me," he said, pushing her away so he could stroke his fingers down the side of her face. "I'm not good enough for you."

She cocked her head to the side and arched one eyebrow. "Why don't you let *me* decide what is and isn't good enough for me. I can assure you, if I didn't think you were, I wouldn't be here now. I'd probably still be with Brad."

Just the mention of Brad's name sent prickles up and down Mark's back. "Maybe you should be. Maybe—"

"I didn't love him. I love *you*. You coming back helped me see that before I made a terrible mistake and married him." She stared him down hard, as if she were trying to burn her thoughts into his brain. "He never excited me the way you do." She exhaled sharply. "He didn't excite me *at all*, if I'm being honest. Sex was more like a chore. So what if he seemed like Mr. Perfect? Perfection is boring. There's no character in perfection." She shook her head and rolled her eyes. "Brad never did a foul thing ever in his entire existence. He exercised. He didn't smoke. He didn't do drugs. He worked hard. He ate right. He made good money. He was a decent man. Check, check, and check." She slashed her finger through the air three times as if drawing checkmarks. "He had everything my dad wanted me to find in a man. Everything a lot of women would give anything for. But you know what he didn't have? He didn't have my heart. He didn't touch my soul. He didn't make me feel alive. *You do*."

She pressed closer, her expression stern, eyes intense. "You came into my life, and for the first time, I actually felt alive. You made me see things in myself that I'd never seen. Things I'd taken for granted. You made me see that I *am* a beautiful woman. That I *am* passionate. That I have an inner, sexy vixen who has desires of her own. *You* did that. And you were able to do it because you *aren't* perfect. You've lived hard, Mark. And living hard is sometimes ugly. But that's what makes us who we are, changes us for the better, and gives us a greater understanding not just of life, but of the world and others.

"So, stop beating yourself up thinking I'm going to think less of you, or that I'm going to leave, because I'm not." She stared into his eyes. "Whatever else you have to tell me, just say it. Get it out. All of it. I promise I'll still be here afterward. And I promise you more than deserve me, because, Mark, I'm no angel. I'm not perfect, either. But together, *we* are perfect. Okay? Believe in *that*."

His heart nearly exploded with the love he felt for this incredible woman he'd chosen to make a life with.

"You're amazing. I've never known a woman like you." He'd been sitting across from her hating himself, but all she saw was a man worthy of her love. Learning the truth about his past hadn't pushed her away, it had drawn her closer.

She smiled. "You're not so bad yourself." She sat back and slid her hands around his again. "So, what else do you have to tell me? I want you to tell me everything. It's important that you're honest with me, Mark. More important than any of this other stuff. As long as you're honest, I really don't care what you have to say. Just don't lie to me. Don't hide the truth. That would upset me even more than hearing the truth, no matter how painful."

He took a deep breath. She seemed more than ready to hear what he had to say. Might as well keep ticking down his list and see if she was as forgiving of everything and not just items one and two. "Okay, so what if I told you that even though I'm ashamed of a lot of what I did during that time in my life, there were other things that I really enjoyed? Things I wouldn't mind experimenting with again. With you."

Her shoulders tightened slightly. "Like what?"

"Have you ever heard of role-play sex?"

She tilted her head inquisitively to one side. "You mean, like me dressing up in a schoolgirl outfit or something?"

If only his fantasies were so tame. "Not exactly. I like taking sexual role-play further."

Her fingers twisted together in her lap as she bit her lip. "Are you talking about BDSM? Like whips and chains and pain? Domination and submission?"

He shook his head, and she let out a relieved breath. "I don't take it that far. Think more along the lines of between the two extremes. I'm into acting out darker, more serious fantasies. Fantasies that take a little planning."

She grinned. "Of course."

He raised one eyebrow and cocked his head. "Don't mistake my planning to mean boring or stilted. I plan these fantasies because they require a little forethought."

"Okay . . ." She scooted a couple inches closer. "So what exactly are you talking about here?

He leaned toward her, smoothing his palms reassuringly over her bare thighs. "Let's say your car breaks down on the side of the road." He lifted his gaze to hers. "Maybe your car ran out of gas. You're miles from the nearest gas station, so you're hitchhiking to get there, carrying your one-gallon gas can."

"I would never hitchhike," she said.

He smirked. "In my fantasy, you do."

Her cheeks flushed pink as she glanced down at his hands as the tips of his fingers slipped under the satin hem of her robe. "Okay . . ."

He dragged his hands back down to her knees. "So, as you're hitchhiking, I'd pull up and ask if you needed a ride. Of course, you'd say yes and hop in my car, even though I'm a complete stranger and we've never met before. We'd talk. I'd ask you where you were headed. You'd tell me some story about how you're on your way to Vegas to become a blackjack dealer or something."

She smiled at his obvious reference to how they'd met. "And then what?"

The flirty lilt in her voice reassured him. It meant she liked the idea of his fantasy. "Then the conversation would turn more personal. Maybe I would ask you how you plan to thank me for giving you a ride. Then you'd offer to pay me, and I'd tell you I don't want your money. I'd suggest something more intimate. You might resist at first, but I'd finally wear you down. I'd pull over somewhere, and we'd have sex. Really hard, feverish, on-the-side-of-the-road sex that leaves us both shredded. Then maybe I'd take you to a hotel for the night if I don't feel you've compensated me enough for my kindness. Tie you to the bed. Torture you with sex until I'm satisfied. Afterward, I'd take you to the gas station, return you to your car, help you fill the tank with your one gallon of gas, and then drive away."

"You'd leave me there?"

"That's part of the fantasy."

"Couldn't that be dangerous? I mean, where would we do something like that, and what about—"

"That's what the planning is for."

She gave him a chagrined smile. "Touché."

He winked. "Exactly."

Then he gave her a moment to weigh his words and think about the scene he'd just laid out.

After a few seconds, she said, "Okay, so how did you discover that you liked that sort of thing?"

He cleared his throat and glanced down at the shallow stretch of comforter between them. He was confessing, so he couldn't stop now.

"I got involved with a woman who was very, shall we say, adventurous. Nina was older than I was, and she was bisexual. She introduced me to my first threesome, and then to my first foursome. I discovered sex parties and fetish clubs through her." He cleared his throat again and nervously rubbed his thumbs back and forth over her fingers. "She was into some hard-core stuff and got off on role-playing some pretty intense scenes. At the time, I was so messed up that I didn't have much of a moral compass, so I did some pretty fucked-up shit. But as time passed and I began to reconnect to my moral and ethical side, I grew uncomfortable with some of the extreme shit she wanted me to do to her. I loved the role-playing, but sometimes she took it to a place that was just too dark."

"How dark?"

He shook his head. "Too dark for me to be comfortable saying much more about it. All I'll say is she got off on rape fantasies." He cringed at the stuff Nina had gotten him to do to her. He would never be that man again and was glad he'd gotten out when he did, or he'd be an even bigger fucked-up mess than he already was. "I'll admit that much, but I don't want to talk about it beyond that. It's just too much for me."

"That's okay, I won't make you." She nodded compassionately. "How long were you together?"

"About five months."

"Really? That's a long time for you."

He brushed his thumbs over her knuckles. "It was. But when she hit me up wanting more — wanting a commitment — I couldn't do it. It wasn't just all the hardcore shit she was into. It was me. I couldn't commit."

"Because of Carol."

"Yes, because of Carol." He paused, recalling the sense of desperation and panic he'd felt when Nina suggested they move in together and hinted they'd make the perfect power couple if they got married. "After Nina, I decided I didn't want that kind of relationship. Not the lifestyle she led nor the commitment she wanted. I started looking for nicer women. Women like you." And women like Carol. But admitting that would take his confession too far. It was better to keep some things to himself. "I redirected my energy toward learning what women like you want instead of catering to my own desires. I wanted to become the best me I could. The kind of man every woman wanted."

"Even though you couldn't commit."

"Right. Even though I could no longer commit." He snuffed out a derisive exhale. "I was like a gigolo, only I wasn't. Always with a woman but never really with her. Always giving her what she wanted without really fulfilling my own needs. But I've already told you about all that, haven't I?"

He was covering old territory.

"Yes, but I don't mind. In a way, hearing how everything melds together helps me see how the pieces fit to make you the man you were then and the man you are now."

They sat in silence for a while until Karma spoke again.

"Okay, so, you like role-playing." She shimmied closer as if prompting him to continue. "Would that be kind of like me pretending to be your kidnap victim while you play my kidnapper?" She smiled shyly, almost coquettishly.

He didn't miss the way the air sizzled as her gaze met his expectantly then flicked away.

Could she actually be considering playing the part he'd

fantasized for her when making his seemingly innocent statement in the limousine two days ago? As soon as he'd said he was kidnapping her, he'd wanted to blindfold her, bind her hands, and pretend he really was stealing her away. The whole scene had unfolded in his mind in a matter of seconds, and it had been incredibly arousing. Then again, the scenes he envisioned for his fantasies followed a tamer, forbidden love theme versus the seedier, rougher themes Nina had preferred.

He pushed his hands over her thighs and under the hem of her robe. "That's one possibility."

She lifted on her knees and crawled toward him. "Okay so what else did you discover you liked in your dysfunctional, experimental phase?" She situated herself on his lap.

This conversation had taken a pleasantly surprising turn. One he didn't want to come to an end. The fact she spoke so casually about subject matter he'd been dreading for days encouraged him.

"Foot jobs." He pushed his hands farther up her bare thighs to her hips.

"Foot jobs? What are those?" Then her eyes lit with awareness. "Oh, like blow jobs, only with feet."

"Yes."

She giggled and hid her face against her palm. "I should have known that."

"No, that's okay. It's just . . . you haven't done that to me since Chicago, and now that we're back together, I would really, *really* like you to do that to me again."

"Now?"

"It doesn't have to be now. But sometime. When you're comfortable. That would really excite me."

"Okay." She rocked forward and draped her arms over his shoulders. "What else? What other things did you discover turn you on?"

He leaned back on the pillows, pulling her down with him. "You're taking this a lot better than I thought you would."

"That's because I'm awesome." She placed a gentle kiss on his mouth.

"Tell me something I don't know."

"Is that a polite way of saying it's my turn to tell you something you don't know about me?"

"If you want." He used his fingers to slowly inch her robe up to expose her bottom.

She propped herself on one elbow, easing her other hand inside the lapel of his robe until the tips of her fingers brushed over his nipple. "I've watched dirty movies."

"What? Like porn?" Her confessions were so normal compared to his, but her timid reaction was so fucking adorable.

Her cheeks filled with color. "Uh-huh."

"And . . . ?"

"I enjoyed them."

"Really now?" He shifted beneath her so he lay flatter, his head on the pillow. "I wouldn't have taken you for the type to watch porn, let alone enjoy it."

"It was exciting."

He caressed the firm globes of her bottom. "How so?"

She tucked her face against his neck. "It turned me on." Her lips brushed his skin. "And . . ."

"And . . . ?"

She squirmed closer, sighing as the apex of her body rubbed against his erection. "And I wondered what it would be like . . . you know . . . to watch a movie like that with you."

Talk about interesting conversational turns.

"Something tells me we wouldn't watch much before we began making our own movie."

"Have you ever done that?" She shoved his robe aside, exposing the left side of his chest and the tattoo of her name over his heart. She traced her fingers over the inked, glyphic pattern.

"Done what?"

"Filmed yourself having sex."

Grabbing the backs of her thighs, he maneuvered her body forward and back, his cock sliding between her lower lips. "Like I said, there's not much I haven't done. I'm just relieved none of my more exploitive endeavors haven't ended up on the Internet."

"Maybe you just haven't searched far enough." She rotated her hips against his cock.

"Maybe so." He reached toward the bedside table. "And maybe you'd better help me get on a condom before this goes much further."

She stretched to the side and tugged on the drawer while he untied her robe. The sash fell away as the silky material opened. A moment later, she handed him a condom and sat up, untying the knot on the belt of his robe as he ripped open the packet.

"Do you want to do that with me?"

"What? Film us having sex?"

She nodded as he rolled on the condom.

"Do you want me to?"

After a brief hesitation, she bit her lip and nodded again. "Don't you agree it would play in nicely with your role-play fantasies?"

He couldn't believe how well this conversation had gone, especially if she was talking about his fantasies as if she were willing—maybe even eager—to participate. There were still things on his list he wanted to tell her, but compared to all he'd already revealed, they were nothing. Well, not nothing, but not nearly as daunting as they had been an hour ago.

"It *would* play in nicely, given the right fantasy. Are you up for that?"

She shed her robe and helped him out of his. "I wouldn't suggest it if I weren't."

Palming her breast with one hand, he brushed back her hair with the other. It had grown out since summer and hung loose around her face, still damp from their shower. "You never stop surprising me."

"What do you mean?"

"Just . . . you. Tonight." He gestured toward the now-dark room. They'd been cast into shadows nearly ten minutes ago. The moonlight and the nightlight in the bathroom were the only things keeping them from being in total darkness. "You've taken all this so well. I was so afraid you'd be upset."

"I guess I'm not your typical girl."

What an understatement.

"I guess not." He pulled her down until her face was only a couple inches from his. "So, were there any positions in this dirty movie you watched that you'd like to try? Anything we haven't done, yet?"

She grinned, playing her fingers through the hair on his chest.

"There was one that looked interesting. The woman was on her side, and the man was behind her. We've nev—"

Before she could continue, he rolled her off him to her side then spooned her, rocking his hips against her bottom. "Like this?"

Jesus! Her ass was sweet. An unbidden groan rumbled from his chest.

She gasped, raising herself on one elbow, glancing over her shoulder at him. "Yes. Like this." She pressed her hips back. "What's this position called? Does it have a name?"

Taking hold of his cock, he guided himself to her entrance. "Sexy spooning, and it's perfect for hitting a woman's G-spot." He drove into her to prove his point.

She threw her head forward and let out an eager, wanton groan.

Gripping her hip, he thrust into her again, reveling in her rising, sultry groans as she collapsed and threw her head back against his shoulder. The difficult conversation he'd needlessly dreaded faded away. He'd been so sure she would reject him, but she had heard the worst about his past and still wanted him. Still loved him. Still found pleasure in his arms. And her unbending acceptance intensified his own, making him take her harder than usual.

Within minutes, he was eagerly speeding toward release, unable to stop the libidinous gratitude from gripping his balls and stroking his shaft as he surged into his woman—*his woman*—claiming her.

He released her hip and shot his hand between her legs to stroke her swollen clit as the head of his cock continued assaulting her G-spot, massaging it, stimulating her closer to her own climax.

Crying out, she fisted the comforter, body arching as she planted the back of her head on his shoulder. "There! Right there! Don't stop."

Not. Stopping. Ever.

Giving her everything he had, he fucked her to within an inch of insanity before blowing apart a split second before she did.

Her body gave out, rolling forward as he surged against her like ocean surf, ending up on her back, pressing her facedown into the mattress. He continued thrusting through his orgasm as she humped the bed and squirmed beneath him.

As lust spent itself and gave way to adoration, he wove his fingers around hers and curled their joined hands into fists in a way that felt like a promise. In that moment, he vowed to protect her, love and honor her, and cherish her forever.

If only wedding vows could be so simple, because he would gladly marry her a thousand times if it were as easy as this. As easy as holding her in intoxicating bliss.

Right now, he was the luckiest man on Earth. He had everything he could possibly want.

For now.

Too bad he couldn't live in this moment forever.

Chapter 5

Never let your fear decide your future.
-Author Unknown

Karma lay on her side, watching Mark sleep. His arm lay slung over his stomach, his head turned toward her as if he'd fallen asleep watching her. His tousled, dark-brown hair hung over his forehead, and she resisted the urge to brush it back.

The moonlight glowing through the window made him look like an angel, so serene. He seemed completely at peace, so unlike how he'd been earlier, when he had looked more like a man standing trial for murder, consumed by guilt and shame over his past. But now he was the picture of tranquility.

What did he dream about? Did he dream? In color? They never talked about their dreams. Did he ever dream about Carol? Or the things he'd brought up tonight?

Suddenly restless, Karma sat up, brushed aside the gauzy curtains, and pulled herself out of bed. She had too much on her mind to sleep. Mark had hit her with a lot tonight, reminding her yet again how little she really knew about him. Her gut told her she'd found the man she was meant to spend the rest of her life with, but her brain kept sending out warning signals, some of which were like slaps to the face while others were more like gentle taps on the shoulder.

She pulled on a pair of underwear and one of his T-shirts, which hung halfway down her thighs, then tiptoed into the living room, slid open the door to the deck, and slipped outside.

The night was cool, but not cold. Refreshing. Maybe even a little invigorating. But then, she was in Saint Freaking Lucia. How could she not feel a little invigorated in a place like this, with its palm trees and tropical breezes?

Pattering barefoot down the stone steps, she descended to the pool, where she eased to the stone deck and dangled her feet and calves in the cool water.

There was still so much she didn't know about Mark. This trip had made her realize that. What if, after they got to know each other better, she didn't fit into his world as well as she thought she would?

He obviously had a lot of money. Karma didn't come from wealth. Her parents had scraped by for a long time before her dad worked his way up the corporate food chain. But even after he earned a comfortable salary, they hadn't rolled in the dough. Karma still owed on student loans, and despite a cozy amount tucked into savings, still lived mostly paycheck to paycheck. She didn't want Mark to simply say, "I'll take care of everything, hon." There was something to be said for making her own way, earning her own money, and paying her own bills. She didn't want to lose her identity by allowing Mark to simply take care of everything.

And then there was Carol. She didn't want to think about that woman when she and Mark were supposed to be on a romantic vacation, but it couldn't be helped. Until Mark made peace with his past, Karma would continue to feel like Carol was a fifth wheel in their relationship.

But now, more than just Carol reared up from his past. What about all that other stuff he'd told her? About Nina, the threesomes, the sex parties? The drugs? Hiring a prostitute? His sex fantasies?

During their conversation, her need for honesty had overruled logic, making everything he'd confessed seem like no big deal. The fact her happy hormones had been flowing like a swollen river, as well, had only reinforced that sentiment. But two hours later, and logic was back in charge. The hot sex was over and reality set in, and the reality was, Mark had been around the block a time or two . . . or ten.

How did she *really* feel about that?

Social norms dictated that she should be furious he had paid for sex. That he was a disgusting, foul man. That what he'd done was wrong. And it was. Very wrong. But the situation wasn't so cut and dry. Mark was repentant. Clearly disgusted at himself for the things he'd done. And he thought enough of her to tell her the truth, and not just tell her, but confess in such a way that made it obvious he needed her approval. That he needed her to understand he was no longer that man but an improved version committed to moving forward on a straighter path.

How could she hold his past against him? Everyone had a past.

But the past didn't have to define the future. Sure, it could affect and mold a person, but that didn't mean the molding process was inherently negative. People did learn from their mistakes, and Mark had already proven he was the type of man who learned from his.

Even so, her own self-confidence had taken a hit after hearing him talk about all the stuff he'd done. What if she couldn't measure up? He wanted her to engage in role-play sex with him. To play out elaborate fantasies requiring extensive planning. But she wasn't Nina or any of those other women he'd done those things with. What if she wasn't any good? What if she tried and failed? Would he be disappointed?

The idea of playing out his fantasies *did* sound exciting, though. And maybe that's partly what this trip was about. Maybe he really wanted to play the part of her kidnapper and for her to play his victim for a few days. Give her a trial run, so to speak. She could definitely see the appeal of playing such a game. Her insides even warmed at the thought of being tied up, pretending to be terrified as he touched her, cut off her clothes, and had his way with her. Wetness even licked her between the legs at the image of him holding her down as she pretended to be scared, aghast that she was responding to her kidnapper with such desire.

But sometimes fantasies played out better in the mind than in reality, so maybe she should just leave that door closed, even if Mark wanted to open it.

She lifted her gaze to the moon. She wouldn't find the answers tonight. For now, she simply needed to put his confession out of her mind so her subconscious could dissect everything he'd told her. She didn't need to ruin their vacation by obsessing over things she had little or no control over. That included Mark's past and all the things she still didn't know about the man she loved.

And she *was* in love with him. That much was certain.

But would that love continue to grow, or would his past eventually prove too much to contend with?

Chapter 6

With everything that has happened to you, you can either feel sorry for yourself or treat what has happened as a gift. Everything is either an opportunity to grow or an obstacle to keep you from growing. You get to choose.
-Wayne Dyer

Mark rolled toward Karma only to land against cold sheets instead of her warm, welcoming body. He brushed his hand over his face, blinking sleepily at the empty bed.

Sitting up, he combed back his hair and glanced around the room through the filmy curtains. She wasn't there. He pushed back the covers and pulled himself out of bed.

"Karma?" He peered into the bathroom then went to the kitchen, finding it deserted.

Slightly alarmed, he returned to the bedroom, put on a pair of shorts and a T-shirt, and stepped out onto the deck.

She wasn't in the hammock. "Karma?"

"Over here."

Relieved, he turned toward the sound of her voice and, after crossing the upper deck, spied her sitting on the side of the pool, her feet in the water.

"What are you doing out here?" He started down the stone steps. "Are you okay?"

"I couldn't sleep."

He faltered. Could she be having second thoughts? "Is something wrong?" He frowned, stepping up beside her. "Are you upset about what I shared with you?"

"No . . . yes . . . no . . ." Her shoulders slumped as she turned puppy eyes up at him. "God, I don't know."

He sat down beside her and dipped his legs into the cool water. As he'd drifted off to sleep, he had worried this could happen. That once the euphoria of the moment passed she would revisit their conversation like she was warming up day-old pizza. Pizza never tasted as good as it did fresh from the oven, and here Karma was, analyzing the soggy crust and congealed cheese, trying to figure out if she really wanted to eat it.

Time for damage control. He'd gotten through the apprehensive discussion unscathed. He wasn't going down now. "Want to talk about it?"

"I just—it was a lot to take in, Mark."

"I know. Maybe I shouldn't have unloaded so much on you all at once." He took her hand. The fact that she let him was a good sign she hadn't turned her back on him. "That's why I wanted to handle the discussion differently."

"You mean, that's why you made a plan?" She grinned as if chastising him. Another good sign.

He lightheartedly bumped her arm with his. "And here you gave me a hard time for planning."

She made a dubious noise. "I still think it's best to just get it out there."

"Yeah, but now you're suffering information overload. See what going against the plan gets you."

Smirking, she leaned into his arm then rocked away again. "I'll get over it."

"Maybe I can help. What's got you stuck?" He felt like they were at least in this together. Like they were finding their way along a new, untraveled path and didn't know where they would end up, but at least they'd end up there together instead of alone.

"I'm just trying to process everything, that's all." She swung her legs under the water, creating small waves on the moonlit surface. "I feel like I should be angry, but I'm not."

"Why should you feel angry?"

"Because that would be the socially appropriate response."

He regarded her for a moment, absorbing the soft warmth of her palm against his. "And since when have you ever been the socially appropriate type?"

Confusion fell over her face.

He pulled her hand into both of his. "Karma, if you were the median woman—the kind of woman who follows the status quo and always does what society expects—you and I wouldn't be here right now." He gripped her hand more firmly and looked her dead in the eyes. "You wouldn't have gone up to my room the night we met . . . then run out a few minutes later." She grinned and briefly glanced away. "You wouldn't have gotten involved with me, because socially acceptable women don't get involved with men they work with, especially when that man is her boss."

She smirked. "You weren't my boss."

He smirked back. "Close enough." He teetered toward her until their shoulders kissed. "And you wouldn't have broken off your engagement and taken me back, either." He paused to admire the way the moonlight reflected off her eyes. "Karma, you are anything but socially appropriate, which is what makes you so extraordinary. It's why you're constantly surprising me. I'm always expecting the socially appropriate response every other woman would give me, but you always give me anything but. You amaze me every day. You take my breath away every morning and leave me in awe every night, and I hope I haven't scared you away, because I can't envision my life without you in it."

"What if I stop surprising you?"

"You won't."

"But I could."

"If that happens, which I doubt, I'll still love you as much as I do now."

Her gaze remained locked to his for a long moment then drifted toward the beach. For a while, they sat in silence, legs dangling in the water, stirring gentle waves.

"What else is on your mind, Karma?" He could tell there was more.

She turned toward him, eyes guarded, lips loosely knotted as if she didn't want to voice whatever was troubling her.

He still held her hand and tightened his fingers around hers. "I can tell something's still bothering you. What's wrong?"

She sighed. "It's not that something's wrong. It's just..." She frowned, hesitated, sucked in her breath. Then she shook her head, closed her eyes, and blurted, "Just how much money do you have, Mark?"

The question came out of nowhere, and before he could stop himself, he burst into laughter. "What?"

She playfully slapped his leg. "Don't laugh. I'm serious." But she was struggling to fight back a smile. Within seconds, she giggled and looked away, kicking her legs more vigorously so water splashed onto their thighs. "Okay, so maybe that was a little funny."

"A little? It came out of nowhere."

But he wasn't surprised she'd asked. He *had* been burning through the cash the past few days.

"I'm just curious, Mark. You've spent a lot of money on this trip. The limousine, the private jet." She glanced toward the villa. "And this place can't be cheap."

"I don't do cheap."

"Obviously. But there's a difference between cheap and frugal. I get the feeling being frugal isn't an issue for you." She dropped her gaze to her hands before meeting his eyes again. When she spoke, there was a tenderness in her voice. "I don't love you for your money, Mark. I've never even thought about it until now. But that's just it. I haven't thought about it. And now I'm getting a glimpse for the first time as to just how affluent you are, and it makes me wonder what else I don't know about you." She turned to face him, one leg still in the water, the other bent on the pool's deck. "I get the impression you're in this for the long haul with me, so if that's the case, I think I need to know more about you. You don't talk much about yourself.

"And maybe that's the reason for my conflicted feelings right now. This was the first time you've really opened up to me about your past, so while I feel closer to you than I've ever felt, it does make me aware we've only really known each other five months . . . and four of those were more about me than you. You've learned so much more about me than I've learned about you, and now you're finally letting me in, and as you do, I start thinking about all the things I don't know. Things I should know if we're going to make this work." She lowered her eyes. "And I want to make this work."

He turned his gaze toward the sea, a little disoriented. He hadn't intentionally kept his wealth a secret. It had just never come up.

He'd prided himself on being able to read her. To know what she was thinking and what she needed before she did. Yet, he hadn't seen this coming. Was he losing his touch?

"Shit, I'm not making any sense," she said as if misreading him. "It's not a big deal. Forget it." She began to turn away but he stopped her.

"No, it *is* a big deal." He scooted closer to her. "To *you*. It's a big deal to you, Karma, so it's a big deal to me."

"But I've upset you."

He shook his head. "You haven't upset me. I promise." He gave her hand a reassuring squeeze. "I just didn't see this coming, that's all."

Letting out a heavy exhale, she bowed her head. "But I don't want to ruin our vacation."

He let go of her hand to cradle her face and lift it so he could look her in the eyes. "Do you really think this could ruin our vacation? That getting to know me better so we can grow closer could possibly be a *bad* thing?"

Her pale eyes glowed in the moonlight, swimming with innocence and doubt. "I don't know. Maybe."

"Karma, I can assure you, you absolutely cannot ruin our vacation by wanting to know me better. And if I were more aware and had been playing closer attention, I would have known I needed to tell you all of this a long time ago."

With a subtle nod of surrender, she offered him a wan smile but didn't say anything.

"I've made no secret that I want us to be together," he said, "so of course you should know everything about me, including the state of my bank account."

"But I don't want to come off like a gold digger."

"Gold digger?" He cocked his head and chuckled. "Karma, you could never be a gold digger."

"But—"

He placed the tip of his index finger against her lips, quieting her. "You are *not* a gold digger. Now, let me answer your question about how much money I have."

With a tiny, chagrined smile tugging at the corners of her mouth, she quieted, giving him the floor. Or, rather, the pool deck.

"Okay, so first, bear with me as I explain the history." He folded his hands in his lap. "I've already told you that my grandfather was a powerful businessman in Chicago. That I chose to follow in his footsteps rather than those of my parents."

"Yes." She shifted so she squarely faced him.

"Well, my grandfather owned a successful shipping company he built from the ground up and hoped to pass down, but that didn't work out."

"Because you're mom wasn't interested, right?"

"Partly. She wanted to pursue dancing, which my grandfather gladly funded. But what I didn't tell you before was that I had an uncle who'd been groomed since high school to inherit the company."

Her eyebrows popped. "I thought he wanted your mom to take over the company."

"Only after my uncle was killed in a tragic car accident."

"Oh." She bit her bottom lip. "That's horrible."

"It was horrible. I still remember the funeral, how everyone cried, completely devastated. Grandpa only had two children, and when Uncle Franco died, that was it. I was too young to step in and help, so when my grandfather got sick a few years later, he decided to sell the business. He'd branched out into other areas than just shipping, so the company was worth a lot when he passed away. The money from the sale, as well as the money he'd invested, in addition to his personal fortune, came to over fifty million dollars. A lot for the time."

Karma gasped, her mouth falling open. "Fifty million? That's a lot for any time."

"Yes." He lowered his voice. "I won't lie, Karma. My family is very wealthy."

Her mouth clapped shut. "I'm sorry. I didn't mean—"

"That's okay. I know it's a lot of money. Sometimes I forget just how much it is, because I've never really known anything else."

"But you don't act like. . ." She trailed off as if she couldn't find the right words to convey her thoughts.

"I don't act like I have money falling out of my ass?" He grinned at the way her cheeks darkened in the moonlight. "I don't drive foreign sports cars, jet set around the world, and throw hundred-thousand-dollar Vegas parties every weekend? Is that what you were about to say?"

She bit back a smile and nodded. "Okay, sure. You could put it that way."

He shifted position on the pool deck. "Yeah, I'm not your stereotypical rich kid. I was brought up with a strong work ethic. My parents never flashed their money around, and they imparted the same values in me. I can afford the finer things, and I enjoy the finer things, but I don't flaunt them."

"Until now." Amusement tickled her expression.

"Okay," he said with a roll of his eyes, "so I've flaunted them in the last few days."

She held up her hand with her index finger and thumb a half-inch apart. "Just a little."

"Maybe a tad." He lifted her hand to his mouth and kissed the back. "But only because I have reason to now." After a brief pause to impart she was his reason, he continued. "So, when my grandfather passed, he left half his fortune to my mother, and the other half to me."

"What about his other grandchildren? Weren't there others?"

"I'm it. Uncle Franco's wife and two children were, unfortunately, killed in the car crash with him, and I'm an only child." He glanced down at their joined hands. "You'd think that since he was Italian he'd have had a massive brood of kids who all had massive broods of their own, but he didn't. I'm the last. At least until . . ." He met her gaze. "Until I have kids of my own."

From the way her lashes lowered and she leaned a little closer to him, he could tell she knew he intended to have kids with her.

"Do you want to have children?" Since they were getting to know one another better, he might as well ask a question or two of his own and determine just how open she was to the idea.

She shyly hid her face. "Yes."

"With me?"

She blinked and met his gaze again, biting her lower lip and slipping her leg back into the water. "Yes."

It was the perfect moment. Moonlit, intimate, romantic.

This was the moment he'd been waiting for. The one he knew would come during this trip. The perfect moment to propose. He should go inside and get the ring and . . .

He sighed, curling his hand around the back of her head and tucking her face against his chest as he kissed her hair. Instead of rushing back to the bedroom for the ring, he remained rooted in place, holding her, eyes closed, the breeze cooling his skin.

He should propose this very moment. Not wait another second. And yet, he just couldn't. Maybe another moment would present itself. A better moment.

They'd just decided they wanted kids together, but he had yet to ask her to marry him. Talk about putting the cart before the horse.

"So . . . you haven't really answered my question." She lifted her head but remained angled toward him. Her feet teased his feet in the cool water.

"You mean, exactly how much money do I have?" Tonight had been revelatory. It felt good to get things out in the open.

"Yes." The single syllable lilted suggestively, as if she didn't want to come off pushy.

He smiled. "Enough."

"Enough for what?"

He chuckled. "Enough that we'll never have to want for anything."

"That's not much of an answer."

He brushed her foot with his and linked their fingers together. "Grandpa left me twenty-five million, which I gained access to when I was twenty-one." He glanced askance at her with a conspiratorial dip of his head. "Grandfather was adamant about making me wait until I was mature enough to understand the responsibility of having that much money. But he needn't have worried." He playfully rubbed his shoulder against hers. "Except for those eighteen months after Carol left, I was very responsible, even from a young age. I wasn't the type to burn through millions of dollars just because I could. When I turned twenty-one, I aggressively invested and turned twenty-five million, plus the interest it had earned waiting for me to come of age, into forty-five by the time I was thirty years old. I think I'm sitting right at forty-nine million now."

Karma's cheeks grew more luminous in the moonlight as if the color had drained from her face. "That's a lot of money."

"Like I said, enough to never want for anything."

She blinked several times and turned toward the ocean.

He remained silent, intuitively understanding she needed a time-out to digest this new bit of information.

Finally, she turned back toward him. "What do you plan to do with all that money?"

"I plan to start my own business someday."

"What kind of business?"

"I haven't decided. At one time, I thought I'd take over the dance studio, but now I realize that's someone else's dream, not mine." And it wasn't his dream anymore because Carol's duplicity had killed that part of his life, as well. "I'm a good consultant, so that's a frontrunner. But consulting is a competitive field, and I'm just not sure my heart's in it. I want to love what I do, not just be good at it."

They sat in silence for a couple minutes, their legs lazily kicking in the water.

It was nice to finally open up. To even the playing field and share more of himself with Karma when he already knew so much about her. The only other person he'd ever come close to doing that with was Carol, but even she didn't know the things about him Karma knew, mostly because she'd been the cause of them. Or at least the catalyst. He never would have met Nina and fallen into a pit of hell had Carol not left him the way she did.

Then again, he wouldn't have discovered all the fetishes he'd come to enjoy, either. Talk about a Catch-22.

But Carol had known about his money. She had all but been a part of the family, even before he'd met her. His parents had known her for two years before bringing her into their studio, so there hadn't been much she didn't know by the time he started dating her.

Even so, like Karma, she'd never come across as a gold digger. Whatever problems they'd had in their relationship hadn't been created by his money. The fact she'd ended up not marrying him confirmed as much. It was her one and only saving grace. A gold digger would have seen the marriage through then divorced him later and taken half his shit. Carol hadn't done that.

She'd never even moved in with him, explaining she wanted to wait until after they were married to move in together and not just "shack up" because he could afford it. Which never really made sense, if he was being honest. In hindsight, that should have been his first sign she was having doubts about marrying him.

Then again, hindsight *was* twenty-twenty.

"Move in with me," he blurted, breaking the silence.

Karma's head whipped around. "What?"

He pulled his legs out of the water and turned toward her. "I've already been hunting for a place of my own. Why don't we make it a place for us? You and me. Our own place, together."

Why shouldn't they move in together? Why shouldn't they find a home they could share? One with enough space to raise a dozen children if she wanted that many.

"That's a big step, Mark. Isn't it too soon?"

"It's not soon enough, if you ask me." He gripped her hands, hugging them within his fists.

Once more, he thought to rush up to the bedroom for the ring, but once more, he remained rooted in place. Why was it so easy to discuss children and moving in together and yet so impossible to broach the subject of getting married?

She searched his face, and then a slow smile crept over her mouth. "Okay. Yes." She took a steadying breath as if she were both nervous and excited and wanted to remain calm. "Let's do it."

Relief and joy rained over him. This was more than he'd ever gotten from Carol, and it felt like validation.

"As soon as we get home, I'll contact my realtor and have her begin feeding me listings again."

Karma's hands trembled within his, but the smile remained on her face.

"Our first house, Karma." Everything was falling into place better than he could have hoped. "We're really going to do this. This is really going to happen for us."

And there he went, putting the cart before the horse again. At some point, he would need to pay attention to the horse and pull out that engagement ring. He refused to return home without making their relationship official.

They'd gotten a lot of important subjects out on the table tonight. Children, money, business, his past, and now the house.

Yet the ring remained hidden out of sight.

Chapter 7

You cannot teach a man anything. You can only help him find it within himself.
-Galileo Galilei

On Sunday, and in need of some mental downtime to let the seriousness of Saturday night's conversations sink in and mellow, Mark took Karma parasailing. Monday, he took her hiking. On Christmas Eve, they took a helicopter tour of the island and circled the twin peaks of Gros Piton and Petit Piton along the southwest coast, as well as the tallest mountain on the island, Mount Gimie, farther inland.

On Christmas, Mark chartered a yacht for a private, twenty-four hour cruise.

Karma had never been on a yacht. The closest she'd ever come was sitting in her dad's fishing boat as he rowed them toward their favorite fishing spot on Peterman Lake.

"What do you think?" Mark handed her a cocktail glass filled with a reddish-orange concoction then eased into the cushioned lounge chair beside her.

Squinting against the sun, she took in the boat's deck, which looked like something from *Lifestyles of the Rich and Famous*, complete with a small pool and amenities that put her apartment to shame.

"Let me put it to you this way. I never want to go home."

Mark laughed. "We have four more days."

She groaned. "Only four?"

He clinked his glass to hers. "We'll make the most of them."

They'd already been making the most of their time in Saint Lucia, participating in a new activity every day. At this point, she just wanted to relax and let the tropical sun and surf sweep her away.

And she was ready for Mark to touch her again. Since their conversation Saturday night, he'd given her a lot of space. It was like he knew she needed time to work through her feelings on everything he'd shared with her. And that was just for the stuff he'd told her before he'd asked her to move in with him.

And how about that? They'd only been back together a month, and they were going to move in together.

Maybe most people—her dad included—would think a month was too soon, but she was learning that she wasn't like most people, which Mark had so eloquently pointed out poolside Saturday night. *Karma, you are anything but socially appropriate, which is what makes you so extraordinary,* he'd said.

She grinned at the memory then sighed as she laid her head back against the cushion and turned her face skyward, eyes closed.

In the days since Saturday night, she'd absorbed everything he'd told her. And, surprisingly, most of the worry she'd felt by the pool Saturday night had dissipated. The man beside her was still the man she'd come to know almost two years ago. He was still the man she'd fallen in love with. He was just more real now. Some of the gaps of his past had been filled in, that's all.

But he'd withheld himself now for three days as if he wanted to give her time to think and digest everything he'd told her. Well, she'd had plenty of time for that. The time for processing was over. She wanted to feel that intimate connection with him again. The one she always felt when they made love. His whole soul seemed to open during sex, and she relished those moments when, for just a brief while, he lay stripped, completely unguarded.

She sipped her fruity cocktail as she peered at Mark from behind her sunglasses. Her drink was surprisingly delicious. She couldn't taste a lick of alcohol, but she knew it was there by the way it warmed her throat on the way down. Or maybe that was just the effect of staring at Mark. His skin was nicely tanned after five days in the sun, which made the ridges in his abdomen pop and the defined *V* leading into his swim trunks practically lickable. But it was his firm pecs and carved arms and shoulders that did Karma in. Mark had the kind of arms that, when he held a woman, made her feel like she was really being held, and not just held but safe.

Her gaze shot to the two attractive waitresses who'd been waiting on them. Were they even called waitresses on a yacht? Whatever their job titles, the way they'd been making flirty eyes at Mark and staring at him since they'd boarded, she would just as soon call them boat bitches.

She thought back to how Lisa had insinuated during dinner Friday night that she was more jealous than she wanted to admit. Okay, so maybe Lisa was right. Maybe she was a little possessive. She'd have to work on that.

She hazarded a glance at the boat bitches eye fucking her man.

Or not.

Taking another sip of her drink, she picked up her sunscreen from the table beside her.

"Could you put this on my back?" She held the bottle toward Mark.

Asking him to put sunscreen on her might have been a barely veiled cliché, but she didn't care. She simply wanted Mark to know she'd had enough time to ponder their discussion and was ready to have his hands on her again.

Beyond ready.

Because his touch was like meth. Totally addicting. And she'd gone far too long without a hit.

She couldn't see his eyes through his blackout sunglasses, but from the way his mouth quirked as he took the sunscreen from her hand, she could tell that he was piecing together her intentions.

As nonchalantly as she could muster, she rolled onto her stomach, lowering the upper portion of the lounge chair.

She heard the click of the cap being popped open, heard the soft gurgle of lotion being squeezed from the bottle, heard the slurping of the lotion as he rubbed it between his hands. Then his warm palms smoothed up and down her back, smearing the sunscreen over her skin.

"You know, I'd intended this bikini for more private viewing." His fingers brushed past the bow she'd tied in the strings midback.

She was wearing the silver bikini. The one that resembled floss rather than swimwear. Changing into the bikini had been another attempt at ending his three-day abstinence.

His fingers teased the bow, and for a moment, she thought he was going to untie it. "I'm not sure I like how the captain keeps ogling you. Perhaps I should ask you to put on something else?" Humor laced his voice.

She turned her head toward him. "And I think the boat bitches need to stop staring at you like you're ice water in the desert."

His hands froze briefly as a wide smile erupted over his face, and then he threw back his head, laughing.

She plopped her cheek on the back of her hand, watching him, pleased with herself.

"Boat bitches?" he said when he continued rubbing sunscreen on the backs of her shoulders.

"The waitresses or whatever they're called. They keep staring at you and giving you flirty looks."

"I can dismiss them if that will make you more comfortable." His left hand skimmed down her spine until he reached her butt. He ran his fingertips back and forth just under the bikini's elastic band.

She had a feeling the women were watching them now, which was why Mark put on such a show.

He bent down and whispered, "Or I could just fuck you right here, right now. That would make it quite clear where my heart is."

She pushed up on her elbows and glanced over her shoulder at him. "Or maybe they'd take it as an invitation to join in, which I will adamantly refuse, of course."

His brow wrinkled, and he pulled his fingers from her suit. "Karma . . ."

She frowned. What had she said wrong? One second, they were playfully teasing each other, and the next he stomped on the brakes.

He straightened. "When I told you I've had sexual encounters with multiple partners, I wasn't saying I wanted to do that with you."

Whoa, wait a minute. How had he inferred that?

"Mark, that's not what I was saying."

But she'd already lost him. He glanced away, the breeze blowing his short hair off his forehead as he laced his fingers contemplatively between his knees.

She sat up and faced him. "Mark, I really didn't mean anything by what I said. I thought we were playing around, teasing each other. You know, playing a sexy game. I didn't mean to upset you."

He bowed his head and uttered a derisive grumble. "I'm sorry. I guess I'm just struggling to put shit back together inside my head."

She wasn't used to seeing Mark so uptight. He was usually so confident and easygoing, but clearly, this self-rediscovery he was going through made him uneasy. Maybe even unsure of himself.

"Is there anything I can do to help?"

"Just . . ." He rubbed his palms up her knees and rested them on her thighs. "Just be patient with me. I promise, I'll get there. I'm just . . ." He sighed and glanced away again.

She scooted to the edge of her lounge chair and draped her forearms over his shoulders. "Give yourself time, Mark, and let me be here for you the way you were there for me two years ago. You know, when you helped me realize I'm no longer the flat-chested tomboy who got teased in school. Remember that?" She bent down, pulling his gaze to hers as she offered him a grin. "Remember how self-conscious I was about my body and how you made me see myself through different eyes . . . *your* eyes?"

That brought a smile to his lips, and his grip on her thighs tightened appreciatively. "Of course I remember."

"I was messed up in the head, too. I saw myself as this insignificant ugly duckling, but you helped me see that I'm a swan."

"I thought you were beautiful. I still do." His hands eased farther up her thighs.

She rolled her head to one side. "But what you saw when you looked at me wasn't what I saw when I looked at myself. Same thing you're going through now. For whatever reason, you're stuck on this idea that your past actions represent who you are now." She slid her arms around his neck, leaning closer. "But they don't. Maybe they influenced who you've become, but that's a good thing. You're a better man now. You've got stronger principles. And that's because of your past. You're the man you are because you didn't want to be that other man anymore."

"But who am I?" He seemed almost to be talking to himself.

"What do you mean?"

He pulled away, dragging his palms down to her knees. "I mean, who am I? I'm changing, Karma. I'm not who I was eight years ago. I'm not even who I was two years ago, a year ago, or even a month ago. So, who am I?" He stood and paced to the rail, where he gripped the top, putting all his weight on his arms.

For several seconds, she stared at his back. At the muscles that bunched and flexed in his shoulders and down the length of his spine. He was a physical marvel. On the outside, he was the physical representation of put-together. One look at him, and you assumed he was a powerful man. A man who knew what he wanted and how to get it. A man in control of every facet of his life.

And that was what Karma had seen the first time they met. And the second. And for the four months they'd spent together two summers ago.

But this man she'd shared a bed with for the past month wasn't the same one she'd met in Chicago. He was troubled, confused, maybe a little lost. In some ways, she loved this Mark more, but in others, she worried he might have changed too much and wasn't the man she'd fallen in love with. But that wasn't necessarily a bad thing, because she had a feeling the man he was becoming was an even better version than the one she already knew.

She joined Mark at the railing, gliding her hand down his back.

He turned his head toward her, his expression bleak. "Have I scared you away, yet?"

"No. Not even close."

"Then you're a tougher person than I am, because, if I were in your shoes, I'm not so sure I wouldn't be running the opposite direction from a guy like me." He forced a smile as if he wanted to demonstrate he was only kidding, but the grim set of his jaw said there was some truth to his words.

She glanced over his shoulder at the boat bitches attentively watching them from inside. Then she leaned provocatively against his arm. "Dismiss the staff, and I'll show you just how much I'm *not* second-guessing my decision to get involved with you." She possessively ran her hand down his back again and over the curve of his ass. Then, with a gentle squeeze, she turned and walked away, into the cabin, and past the boat bitches, who stared after her as if she were crazy for leaving such a fine man all alone.

Let them think they had a chance. She knew better. She could already feel Mark's gaze burning into her backside.

He was hers. Hook. Line. And sinker.

Chapter 8

It takes real planning to organize this kind of chaos.
-Mel Odom

At sunset, Karma sat at the vanity in the impressive master suite, brushing a bit of mascara on her lashes. She'd showered and put on a light green halter dress that matched her eyes and showed off her sun-kissed shoulders, which still smelled like coconuts and bananas from her sunscreen. She twisted her hair into a loose up-do and clipped it in back.

As she'd requested, Mark had dismissed the crew over an hour ago, right after dinner, leaving the yacht theirs for the night.

She'd never been much of a seductress, but tonight, she was going to show Mark just how grateful she was to have him back in her life and that his worries she would leave him were unfounded.

Grabbing a blue and green scarf from the table, she stood and made her way down the carpeted steps from the circular master suite, through the mirrored hallway, pattered barefoot across the enormous cream-colored rug in what she'd deemed the Great Room, because it was large enough to host one of Solar's company meetings, and then up another set of stairs to the upper deck, where she found Mark relaxing on one of the oversized deck couches.

He wore khaki cargo shorts that extended just past his knees and a loose-fitting, navy blue button-up shirt. Two glasses of wine sat on the table in front of him.

"You look nice." He stood and welcomed her into a tender embrace, kissing her cheek. "Mmm, smell good, too."

Old Mark was back, at least for now. She just had to keep him there. She smiled, brushing her cheek against his.

"So do you." The mild but zesty scent of his cologne stirred her senses.

The fact he was acting more like his old self reassured her. The Mark she'd come to know was still there. He was just struggling to find footing with New Mark.

He guided her to the couch and handed her one of the wineglasses as the breeze cooled the back of her exposed neck. She still held the scarf, and the ends lifted on the wind as she wrapped her fingers around the stem of the glass and tilted it to her lips.

Mark watched her drink over the rim of his own glass then settled the base on the arm of the couch.

They were anchored in Piton Bay. Behind them, to the east, the twin peaks rose gloriously skyward. In front of them, the most sensational sunset she'd ever seen filled the sky with burnished warmth, making a long bank of cottony clouds glow rust-orange.

"Thank you for dismissing the staff." She set her glass down and twirled her scarf between her fingers.

"You made it impossible for me to refuse." His mouth twisted curiously as he eyed the scarf.

"That was the plan." She pressed closer, biting her lip as she took his glass, set it on the table, and then unfastened the top button of his shirt.

Except for dropping his gaze to her fingers, he remained still, arms stretched over the tops of the cushions.

"You planned this?" He tsked. "And here I thought you were all about being spontaneous."

She unbuttoned another button and teased the side of his neck with her lips. "Are you really going to lecture me now on the merits of spontaneity?"

Dropping his head back, he chuckled then groaned deep inside his chest as she slowly laved his skin, easing her hand inside his shirt, swirling her fingertips slowly around his nipple, causing it to form a tight peak. "Wouldn't think of it," he whispered distractedly.

"Didn't think so." She pulled herself onto his lap, using both hands to finish releasing the buttons on his shirt. "Besides, I'm beginning to see the benefits of planning."

He dropped his hands to her hips, meeting her gaze with hooded eyes. "I told you so."

Arching her eyebrow, she aggressively pushed his shirt down his shoulders, revealing his tanned chest and torso. Some people didn't burn. They tanned. Mark was one of those. Must be the Italian blood he inherited from his mother.

He grinned at her reaction, making him look even sexier. "Are you seducing me, Miss Mason?"

In answer, she unclipped her hair and gently shook it out before untying her halter. She held the material to her chest for a long moment, then, with a coy smile, let it fall to her waist.

His gaze fell with her top. An instant later, his palms closed over the undersides of her breasts, slowly pushing them up to greet his mouth as he eased forward and closed his lips around one nipple then the other, teasing, sucking, nipping with his teeth.

Yes. This was what she'd wanted for the last three days. His hands on her body. His mouth tasting her skin.

Laying her head back, she gasped to the clouds, holding his face against her chest, arching, reveling in the pleasure she derived just from his mouth. His exquisite tongue, soft, firm, warm . . . alarmingly irresistible.

Addictive.

There was that word again. Mark was her addiction.

Normally, addictions were a bad thing. Not so with him. He was good. So very good.

Dragging his lips from her breast to her throat, he dropped a trail of fire along her skin until he reached her mouth, searing her soul as he gently clamped her bottom lip with his teeth and tugged.

"What are you doing to me, woman?" he said, his voice strained. "You're on fire tonight. I felt your heat the moment you stepped on deck."

She licked her lips and brushed the chiffon scarf over his bare torso, resting her forehead against his. "I need you. I've missed you the past three days."

His hands clutched her bottom as if he had to hold onto something or risk losing control.

Maybe she should help him lose his mental grip.

She lifted the scarf as she sat back. "Would you like to blindfold your kidnappee?"

His fingers curled, and his blunt nails bit into her flesh. A trembling breath escaped his throat as he looked from the scarf to her and back.

Draping the scarf over her wrists, she held out her arms in submission. "Or you could tie me up if you want." A strong breeze blew her hair over her face, and she flicked her head to get it out of her eyes. "It's just that she doesn't feel much like she's been kidnapped when she can freely come and go as she pleases."

His breathing quickened as he stared at the scarf. Then his eyes, dark with lust and something else—something leg-quivering hot—shot to hers. Single-minded intent flashed across his expression, setting his brow in a determined line.

"Do you really want to do this?" he asked.

"Yes."

"Do you trust me?" His words bit from between his lips on a rush of breath.

No question. "Yes." She raised her wrists, the scarf still draped across them, tempting him.

His gaze burned into hers, his body beyond keyed up, his erection hard as a steel rod between her legs.

For several seconds, he didn't speak, but she could see his mind flying in the depths of his eyes.

Finally, he snatched the scarf from her wrists and held it in front of her eyes. She closed them, and he wrapped the scarf around her head, firmly knotting it at the back.

"You've defied me," he said. "You tried to escape. And I warned you not to do that." He lifted her off his lap and set her aside. "I told you there would be repercussions if you tried to get away from me." His voice came from above, so she knew he was standing.

There was the sound of fabric rustling, a zipper unzipping. Then fabric ripping.

"Hold out your hands."

She did, and he looped something soft—his shirt? Had he torn off a piece of his own shirt?—around her wrists several times before knotting it.

Then his voice came from directly beside her ear, soft and tender. "If you want to stop, say 'ginger.' It's called a safe word. This is how I'll know you've had enough and don't want to play anymore."

She nodded.

"Say it now."

"Ginger."

"Good."

Then he was standing over her once more. "You've made me *very* angry." He paced to her left. "How dare you try to run! To *escape*! When I've been so *generous* to you!"

She jumped at the way he yelled, but instead of scaring her, it heightened her awareness. When he'd said he really played the part, he hadn't been joking. But there was something about the raw anger in his voice mixed with the knowledge that this was just a game that spiked her arousal.

He paced back to the right so he was standing in front of her again. She could almost feel the heat pouring from his body and imagined his erection standing high and proud, hard as stone. "What do you have to say for yourself? Are you even going to try to deny that you were trying to escape?"

"I... I don't..." She licked her lips and swallowed. "I wasn't..." What would Mark want her to say? What would take this scene to the next level for him? And for her? Maybe imagining what a real kidnap victim would feel like in such a situation would provide a clue. How would a woman, naked, bared to her attacker, tied and blindfolded react?

Cowering, she lifted her bound arms and tried to cover her breasts. She threw in a shiver to make it seem more real.

"I'm afraid. Don't hurt me."

Mark went quiet, and Karma imagined he was trying to determine whether she was being her or playing the part.

"Please don't stop," she whispered, letting him know she was okay. "I'm not using my safe word." That should reassure him she was simply playing her role. Not that she was really afraid. Because she wasn't. In fact, she was anything but afraid. She was turned on. Unbelievably turned on.

She cringed away, hoping to pull him back into the scene. "You're scaring me."

It only took a moment for Mark to recover. "I'm scaring you?" He surged forward and shoved her knees apart with his legs, making her gasp as electricity zinged up her thighs into her core. "You certainly didn't seem scared of me or what I'd do to you when you tried to run away."

"I'm sorry." She covered her breasts, feeling his eyes on her.

"Oh, no you don't. Don't cover yourself." He tugged on her arms.

She resisted, crying out. "Please don't hurt me."

"Hurt you?" He finally pulled her hands away, possessively planting one of his large hands on her breast, squeezing. "This is mine. Do you understand? *Mine.*" His palm shot to her other breast and squeezed it even harder. "And I'm going to do worse than hurt you."

His voice was so powerful . . . so dominating. He said he didn't get into Domination and submission games, but if he ever wanted to, his voice alone could make her come. She was damn near soaking the cushion she was sitting on, he had her so hot.

This role-play thing was intense, even though she was doing a lousy acting job.

"What do you mean? W-what are you going to do to me?"

There was a quiet thump as if he'd fallen to his knees between her legs, and then his arms brushed her outer thighs as he clutched her dress, which was still bunched around her waist, and pulled it, along with her drenched panties, down her legs. She heard the soft whisper of fabric hitting the cushion beside her.

Then his hands were on hers, and he pulled her arms over her head, behind her. She felt the cold metal railing slide smoothly over her knuckles, felt him tugging and tying, and then her arms were restrained. He'd tied her to the rail.

"You want to know what I'm going to do to you?" he said, yanking her hips to the edge of the cushion.

"Y-yes." Jesus, she was lit up. Her skin had to be glowing red, she was so hot.

"I'm going to make you love me. I'm going to give you so much pleasure that you'll never want to leave me again."

His tongue flicked its way down her stomach, making her pant. His fingers lightly stroked their way up the insides of her thighs, making her legs tremble. Every stimulus elicited an equal response, and she was nearly vibrating out of her skin with the need to come.

Then he shoved her legs open wide, and his mouth landed hard at the apex of her body, his tongue diving deep as the front of his teeth and his upper lip pressed against her clit.

Arching violently, she blew apart, pulling on her restraints, crying out, gasping toward the sky, even though she couldn't see anything but darkness blotched with shifting, glowing orbs from having her eyes closed so long and her body so abruptly pleasured.

His body slid up hers. "See how easily you come for me?" He kissed her between gasps. She could taste herself on his lips, feel the wetness of her release on his chin as he opened and claimed her tongue with his. "See how easily you could love me?"

She nodded, breathless. More, more, more! She wasn't near finished.

He pulled away, leaving the front of her body exposed to the cooling breeze. Her orgasm still cycled through her muscles, liquefying her limbs, quivering inside her belly.

She heard the crinkle of cellophane. Heard the satisfying rip of the packet . . . his moan as he rolled the condom on and stroked her thigh.

"You're so wet. So fucking wet for me." His thumb stroked between her labia. Then he drew his hand away. A moment later, he moaned. "And you taste incredible."

Had he sucked her juices off his thumb? Just the thought brought a broken groan from inside her chest.

"You like hearing me talk about how good you taste, don't you?" He smeared his entire hand between her legs. Then he cupped her and drove his thumb inside her still-trembling core. She practically hung from the railing now, draped off the cushioned seat like lax sinew, moaning with every breath. "You're a naughty girl. You like it dirty, don't you?" He pulled his hand from between her legs.

She jumped when he swiped his fingertips against her lips. The musky scent of her arousal filled her nostrils, and she inhaled deeply.

"That's it. Smell how hot you are for me." He probed between her lips and against her teeth with his thumb. "Taste yourself on my hand."

She did. She sucked his thumb into her mouth, clamping down with her teeth as she swirled her tongue around and around, lapping up every drop of what he'd offered.

"Fuck!" The word snapped from his throat like a reflex. "You've never done that before. So fucking hot. I wish you could feel what that does to me."

He'd fallen completely out of character, and yet, he hadn't. He was Mark, her boyfriend, and Mark, her kidnapper, all in one.

Sucking her mouth off the tip of his thumb, she let her head fall back, surrendering completely. What he was doing to her . . . the way he was making her feel . . . she'd never felt more lascivious.

More wanton. More unabashed and sexual and unbelievably aroused.

"Fuck me. God, please fuck me."

Before she could process what was happening, he grabbed her feet and flipped her to her stomach. The way he'd tied her to the rail didn't restrict her movement, and her head hung between her upper arms as he pressed against her lower back, making her body arch. Thank God for yoga.

The head of his cock slicked her up and down, and then he drove forward, impaling her as she cried out. Her insides clenched, preparing for orgasm number two.

The cushions dipped down on either side of her, so she knew he'd braced himself on his arms.

"You have such a fine ass." He forcefully punched his hips forward, making her cry out as their bodies slapped together. "Maybe I should fuck you there. See if you like it as much as you like me fucking your pussy."

Shit, she was going to come again. Now. Just from his brash language and hearing him threaten her with anal sex.

"I'm coming . . . I'm coming!" She fell against the couch, her insides pulsing around his cock as he pounded into her.

"You like that, don't you?" His deep voice practically growled out the words. "You want me to fuck your ass. Don't deny it."

Right now, she couldn't even think, let along deny him anything. She shook her head then nodded. Damn, she wasn't even sure what he'd asked and whether she should answer yes or no.

"Yes." She could barely speak. Her words sounded more like harsh exhales. "My ass. Fuck my ass."

Right now, it didn't matter what it was. If Mark wanted to do it to her, she wanted him to do it. She was in nirvana, a state of euphoria. The word "no" didn't exist here.

"Jesus!" His body stiffened midthrust and shuddered almost immediately. "Fuck! I'm coming." He fell over her back, pumping hard as he grunted through each spasm.

She hung from the rail like wet laundry on a clothesline. Slack, unable to move, hands relaxed as he spent himself then fell still.

Mark trembled and gasped through one final ripple of pleasure as he pushed himself off her back and pulled out. He untied her wrists, took off the blindfold, then wrapped a large, orange and aqua beach towel around her before pulling her down into the crook of his arm as he laid back on the couch.

She nestled against him, her head on his shoulder, her fingers playing through the sweat-soaked hair on his chest. When she glanced up at his serene, blissed-out face, she saw that his hair lay in damp tendrils against his forehead. His eyes were closed, but he cracked his eyelids and looked at her as if he'd felt her watching him.

The corners of his mouth rose sublimely. "Are you okay?"

Her body sang with warmth and love and everything that made her feel like a woman. "Yes. Are you?"

He nodded. "That was..." He sighed, letting his gaze drift toward the stars.

"Hot." She filled in the blank.

"I was going to say fucking intense, but hot works." His chest rose and fell heavily as he continued to recover.

She rested her cheek on his shoulder again. "I think I understand now why you like role-play sex so much."

He chuckled and brushed back her hair. "And that was nothing."

"Nothing?"

"Mm-hm. Just wait until we do a whole scene."

"That wasn't a whole scene?"

"Huh-uh. I'm talking start to finish. Inception to conclusion. Where it plays out from when we meet to when we fuck."

Why did her heart always skip a beat when he used *fuck* that way?

"So, role-playing isn't just about the sex?"

"It is for some people, but not for me. I like the buildup. I like developing a scene and acting it out. For example, let's say I want to play the part of a racecar driver who needs to learn to slow down in life. And maybe you're a professional women's basketball player taking a break at the end of the season. We meet at a spa."

"That would mean we'd need to make reservations at a spa, right?"

"Exactly. You and I would develop our characters, go off to our romantic weekend, where we'd book separate rooms, and then manipulate the scene as we go."

"Are you saying it would be spontaneous?"

He laughed. The sound was joyous and free. "You're not going to let that go, are you?"

She giggled. "Not any time soon."

He kissed the top of her head. "Well, you're right. It would be more or less spontaneous. We'd meet and make up the rest as we go, improvising as we consummate the role-play relationship on up to the point where we say good-bye and return home."

"So, what we just did was only acting out the consummation."

"Yes." He hugged her more securely against him. "But you were perfect. Absolutely perfect."

She rolled her eyes. "I felt like my acting was horrible."

"Not at all. I really thought you were afraid and had forgotten your safe word. I almost stopped. You were that convincing."

"I sensed that, which is why I said what I said."

"I'm glad you did." He caressed her arm and swallowed a yawn. "So, was there anything about it you didn't like? Do you have any questions?"

"No, but ask me again later. I'm still floating on cloud nine right now." She snuggled closer, draping her leg over his. "I might think of some questions after I come back to Earth."

His body sank more deeply into the cushions. "In BDSM, they call that getting into your subspace. Or some call it headspace."

"Really? Hmm." She closed her eyes, drifting. "Are you into BDSM at all?

"No, but I've been exposed to it." His voice sounded as lazy as hers. "So I know some of the terminology."

"I see." She was more relaxed than she'd been in weeks and curled around him. "You're so smart." It was an odd thing to say, but her brain was rapidly shutting down.

His steady, sleepy breathing was his only response.

So this was what a little psychological fear and resultant arousal could do for you. It knocked you flat on your ass and sent you into the ozone on a ribbon of dreams.

She blinked at the stars one last time before floating into slumber.

Chapter 9

Love is an ice cream sundae, with all the marvelous coverings. Sex is the cherry on top.
-Jimmy Dean

Thursday morning, Karma awoke cocooned within the cream-colored blankets in the giant circular bed in the master suite.

At some point during the night—and she couldn't recall exactly when, she'd been so out of it—Mark had carried her from the deck to the bedroom and tucked her in before sliding in beside her and folding her into his arms.

She rolled to her back, enjoying the way her whole body ached, but in such a good way. A way that said she'd been well fucked. Not made love to, but fucked. By Mark. The master of her body. The king of all things sexual.

And she would gladly let him rule her world if this was how he made her feel.

Speaking of Mark, he wasn't in bed. As usual, he'd awakened before her and, instead of waking her up, let her sleep. He must have known she needed the rest after last night.

God, last night. Butterflies swirled low in her belly as she remembered the naughty things they'd done. Wow. Just . . . wow.

She sat up, rubbed her eyes, then shimmied to the edge of the bed and sank her feet into the thick carpet. She could get used to luxury like this.

A zippy five-minute shower later, and she made her way up to the deck, wearing another of the limitless number of bikinis Mark had bought her under an oversized, off-the-shoulder white T-shirt and khaki shorts.

The staff was back, and the aroma of breakfast wafted from the galley. Mark sat at the table on deck, just under the awning.

"Good morning." He stood and greeted her with a kiss that reached the tips of her toes and made her fingers burn. From the gleam in his eyes, he was remembering last night, too.

Nice.

"Good morning." Her feminine parts quivered just from

glancing toward the couch. Their clothes still lay where they'd abandoned them.

There was something about having a powerful orgasm that made remembering it and everything that had led up to it almost as good as the real thing. Her insides melted. Heat gushed through her lower abdomen. Her legs weakened. If he touched her right now, he'd find her wet and ready, and she might even come on the spot. In an instant, just from seeing him and returning to the scene of the crime, she was ready to drag him back to their room and demand a repeat performance.

Mark grinned and pulled her against him. He was hard. "I can tell we're thinking the same thing this morning." He spoke quietly, provocatively.

She took a deep breath and held onto his biceps for support. "I think you're right."

The waiter—*waiter?*—silently appeared, delivering two plates of crepes drizzled with mashed strawberries. He set them on the table then quickly disappeared.

She arched her eyebrow knowingly. "What happened to the boat bitches?"

"I explained to the captain that they were making you uncomfortable and asked they not return."

It was hard not to smile at that little announcement. "Did you now?"

His palms slid down to her rump and gave her a light pat. "I most certainly did. I couldn't have them distracting you when I want your mind completely on me and what I'm capable of doing to you." He glanced at the freshly made crepes. "The question is, do I fuck you now, or do we eat first?"

Her knees nearly buckled at his possessive, primal tone. "Maybe we should eat first. I think I'm going to need my strength if the look in your eyes is any indication of what's coming."

His eyes narrowed, and he drew closer, their foreheads touching. "You are most definitely going to need your strength. Apparently, your kidnapper feels he needs to punish you some more for trying to escape."

She pressed her lips together then grinned. "I think your prisoner would like that. Very much."

"Then let's eat. We have four more hours until we return to dock. And I intend to make you pay for trying to run away from me." He pressed a chaste yet steaming kiss on her lips. "And pay..." Another kiss. "And pay some more."

If she could still walk by the time they returned to the villa, it would be a miracle.

Chapter 10

People spend too much time finding other people to blame, too much energy finding excuses for not being what they are capable of being, and not enough energy putting themselves on the line, growing out of the past, and getting on with their lives.
-J. Michael Straczynski

Mark peeked into the villa's bedroom. Karma was still sleeping. The sheer white curtains floated lazily around the bed as the breeze blew in through the open doors.

She'd passed out an hour after returning from their day cruise. It was almost time for dinner, and she had yet to stir. Apparently, he'd worn her out this morning. And last night.

Hell, he'd worn himself out and should be in bed with her, catching a few Zs, as well. But he was too keyed up to sleep.

He pulled the sheet of folded notepaper from his wallet and read the remaining items he had yet to share with her from the list he'd made Saturday night. They'd toyed with exhibitionism on the yacht, but what really got his blood pumping was when they'd played last night.

He gulped at the memory, almost unable to think the words. *Yes. My ass. Fuck my ass.*

She'd sounded so desperate, so shameless. Eager to receive him in a way his gut told him she'd never experienced. Had she simply been caught up in the moment and, consequently, would have agreed to anything? Or had she merely been playing her role? It was possible she had only been acting when she'd made her demand. Then again, she could have been serious. Karma never ceased to amaze him with her curiosity and openness. Maybe she really did like the idea of anal sex.

The question was, would she like it his way? Would she be open to all the ways of anal play that appealed to him?

He folded the sheet of paper and tucked it back inside his wallet before glancing toward the dresser. The little blue Tiffany box was still hidden inside, and time was running out. He still hadn't proposed, despite several perfect opportunities. He'd even taken the ring with him on the yacht, planning to ask her to marry him then.

But he hadn't. Like a fool, he'd let another ideal moment pass.

Why was this so hard? He knew she was the only woman he would ever love again. He knew he wanted children with her. They'd already discussed that. They had also agreed less than a week ago to move in together. He already had one foot and half the other inside the door, and yet he couldn't take that last step. He couldn't pop the question.

Bowing his head, he quietly left the room, letting her sleep. Maybe tonight the right opportunity would present itself. Maybe tonight he would be ready to propose.

* * *

Thursday night came and went, and the ring remained out of sight. They spent Friday relaxing then spent the evening in Gros Islet, a fishing village that transformed into a colorful carnival every Friday night. Reggae music filled the streets, and everyone danced. It was a grand celebration and a local tradition. Afterward, he took her back to the villa and made love to her in the hammock.

By Saturday night, their last full day in Saint Lucia, Mark still hadn't found the right time to pop the question, even though he'd had numerous opportunities.

And now he was out of time. They were returning to the States tomorrow.

Standing just inside the open sliding glass door that led from the bedroom to the deck, with the breeze blowing over his face, he crossed his arms and leaned against the frame. It wasn't like he didn't want to marry Karma. He did. More than anything, he wanted to put that ring on her finger and tell the world they belonged to one another. So then, why couldn't he make it happen? Why had he let every perfect moment pass without proposing?

For so long, he'd planned his life to the millisecond. In fact, his best friend Rob had severely blasted him last year for his habit to control every facet of his life, telling Mark to let go and allow himself to live in the moment . . . to free himself from his self-imposed constraints. Mark had been trying to take Rob's advice ever since, and yet, he couldn't get out of his own way long enough to simply be. Just be. To exist and let the spontaneity Karma preached about take over.

And now it was their last night in Saint Lucia. He'd wasted the entire trip worrying about his past misdeeds and searching for the right moment instead of just getting right to it, and now it was do or die time.

Deep down, he knew his reticence was about more than just his control issues and the fact that he was still dwelling on the shit he'd done in the months after Carol left him. As much as he loved Karma, and as badly as he wanted them to be together for the rest of their lives, every time he imagined standing at the front of the aisle, waiting for her to turn the corner in her white dress and stroll toward him, bouquet in hand, her arm hooked around her father's, Mark's heart raced. Dread gripped his chest and suffocated him, even if only on a microscopic level.

Even now, just thinking about it, his breath caught in his throat, and he had to pace away from the door back into the room. Moving helped quell the panic. He stopped in front of the dresser and took a shaky breath. They had already started packing, but the small blue box still sat among his unpacked clothes in the middle drawer.

It was now or never. If he didn't ask her tonight, the trip would end and he would miss his chance. And, other than revealing his shameful past, hadn't this vacation been about setting the perfect stage for him to propose? Of all the reasons he'd brought her here, proposing had been the most important.

He opened the drawer, pushed aside his boxers, and lifted the small box. He hadn't seen the ring since his secret day trip to Chicago last week to pick it up. Karma had thought he'd gone out of town on business, and God love Lisa for helping him keep his plans secret. She'd been extremely helpful in pulling off this entire vacation.

Untying the bow, he sat on the side of the bed as he pulled off the top then removed the case. Lifting the lid, he took a deep breath. The solitary, round diamond set in gleaming, filigreed platinum sparkled up at him. Perfect. The ring was simple and elegant, just like Karma. A timeless classic.

He'd actually been on a business trip when he saw the ring the first time. Work took him up to Chicago about once a month, where several of Solar's customers were based, and where he hoped to land more. He had met his mom and dad for lunch on Michigan Avenue, and on his way back to his car, he'd passed Tiffany's. On a whim, he'd gone inside.

Surrounded by white marble, velvet drapes, and polished metal, he'd asked to see a selection of engagement rings and settings. The salesperson had presented him with tray after tray, and while many caught his eye, none announced themselves as Karma's until the salesperson pulled out the simple solitaire as an afterthought. A shot in the dark, as it were.

As the woman placed the ring on the counter in front of him, a beam of sunlight shone in the window, setting the diamond alight, making the platinum practically glow.

"This one. Absolutely." He'd picked up the ring, admiring it more closely, abandoning all thought as to price. This was his ring.

He'd taken the salesperson's card, and, after an elaborate ploy to determine Karma's ring size, e-mailed the specifics to the store. After that, it was a simple matter of resizing, polishing, perfecting, and picking up the ring so he could reach this moment.

He removed the ring from the slit in the velvet lining and tucked it into his pocket, then made his way to the lower level of the deck, where Karma lounged by the pool, reading a book in the waning sunlight.

"Let's go down to the beach," he said, reaching for her hand.

She glanced up as if she hadn't heard him join her. "Okay." She set the book aside, smiled, and placed her hand in his.

He helped her up, and together they took the stone steps to the beach below.

Mark's heart pounded and raced, but he forced himself not to acknowledge the image of him standing at the front of a church waiting for her to join him.

"Have you had a good time this week?" he said as they walked barefoot in the sand.

The cool, lazy surf washed over their feet.

"I don't think 'good time' can even come close to how much fun I've had this week. It's been exciting and invigorating." Her gaze turned shyly to his. "And eye-opening in a way that makes me look forward to what's still to come."

The wind blew back her hair, and her tanned skin seemed to glow against the burnished sunlight.

"Me, too."

They walked a little farther in silence before Karma said, "So, is there anything else you need to tell me? Anything else you want to get off your chest before we return to the real world?"

He thought about his list then shook his head. "No."

Now wasn't the time to discuss the remaining items he hadn't yet shared with her. That wasn't why he'd brought her to the beach, and he didn't want anything else stealing the spotlight from his purpose. He could tell her about the other things later.

He directed her away from the surf and pulled her down with him as he sat on the sand. She sat between his bent legs, both of them facing the sea.

He pressed his nose into her hair. She smelled of the ocean and strawberry shampoo.

"I can see why this is your favorite place in the world." She leaned back into the cradle of his body. "We definitely have to come here again."

He dug the ring from his pocket and concealed it inside his fist as he wrapped his arms around her. "Maybe we can." He took her left hand in his then slid the ring on her finger. "Perhaps we should come back on our honeymoon."

* * *

Karma was so caught up in the view, the warmth of the sun on her face, the surf ebbing and flowing, and the refreshing breeze, it took her a second to realize what he'd said.

Honeymoon?

What?

Then she realized he was holding her left hand, and he was sliding something onto her ring finger. She looked down and sucked in her breath.

"Oh my God." A stunning round diamond glittered up at her. "Mark?" She turned to face him.

He was smiling, his eyes hopeful. "I searched a long time to find you, Karma. A very long time. Even when I didn't know I was searching. And when I found you, I almost blew it. I almost lost you." He pressed his lips together in a tight smile. Then he glanced down at her hand. "Now that I've found you again, I can't imagine my life without you." He met her gaze as he squeezed her hand. "So . . . Karma Mason, will you marry me? Will you be my wife and guarantee I never lose you again?"

Speechless, she glanced back at the ring that looked like it had cost a small fortune then turned to face him again.

How had he kept this a secret their entire trip? She hadn't even suspected.

The insecurities she'd shared with Lisa last Friday evaporated in an instant. She'd been worried that maybe once they got to know one another they would find they really didn't work as a couple. That the excitement of them would be based on just the sexual chemistry and nothing more. That his fear of commitment would return and be too great for them to overcome. But for him to propose and show he was ready — *really ready* — to commit felt like a reassurance that her worries were unfounded. This was real.

He'd shared the dark secrets of his past, and she'd accepted them. The worst was over, and now she and Mark could move forward together, with nothing else holding them back.

"Yes." She threw her arms around his shoulders and kissed him as he pulled her down on top of him in the sand.

She had known the night he showed up at her apartment three days before Thanksgiving this day would come . . . that he would propose. He'd made it clear that's what he wanted. A life with her.

But she hadn't trusted that feeling and had let fear briefly tease her into thinking their relationship could still fall apart.

Well, no more. They were finally official.

Still, she hadn't expected him to propose so soon. Once more, just as he'd done during their four-month affair two summers ago, Mark had surprised her. Like an ever-changing kaleidoscope, he'd transformed into something else just when she'd gotten used to the image in front of her.

"Is a kidnappee supposed to fall in love with her kidnapper?"

He grinned. "It's been known to happen."

Happiness shone from his gaze, a kind of joy she'd only ever seen in the eyes of children. It was a gleefulness she had never associated with Mark, but seeing it now made her heart beat a little harder. This was real. Maybe he was finally putting his past behind him, ready to try again and embrace his future.

She lifted her hand and stared at the twinkling diamond. "Then consider me fallen."

What had begun as a casual affair a year and eight months ago had finally culminated in the most important relationship of her life. And this time, she was ready. Mark would be her husband. She'd called off her engagement to Brad, but she would never call off this one. Mark was hers. She was his.

End of story.

She was ready for another adventure with her Prince Charming. One that would last the rest of their lives.

Part II

Even though you may want to move forward in your life, you may have one foot on the brakes. In order to be free, we must learn how to let go. Release the hurt. Release the fear. Refuse to entertain your old pain. The energy it takes to hang onto the past is holding you back from a new life.
-Mary Manin Morrissey

Chapter 11

Me? Jealous? Hahahahahahaha! Yes.
-Author Unknown

Karma lightly rapped her knuckles on Lisa's office door.

Lisa looked up from her computer and burst into a smile. "Hey, girl! What are you doing here?"

"Mark and I are viewing a house today. I'm meeting him here, but I'm a little early." She checked her watch, catching a glimpse of her engagement ring as she did.

It had been almost a month since they'd returned from Saint Lucia. Paradise. Where every day had seemed like a dream. Now they were back in the real world, and tropical beaches and day cruises on luxury yachts where she pretended to be a kidnap victim were a million miles away.

Mark had fallen behind from taking a week off for their vacation and had spent most of the last four weeks playing catch-up. Between that and her starting her new job, they hadn't seen much of each other except in passing, so she was beyond ready for them to move in together. At least then she would see him more than a couple nights a week.

To make things even tougher, she was preparing for what she'd been warned was a labor-intensive online editing course that would last a year. But after she completed it, she would possess all the skills and knowledge necessary for her first promotion. Until then, she would work under a senior editor.

Lisa waved her into her office. "Come in. Grab a seat and talk to me. How's the house hunting going?"

She sat in the gray-and-burgundy armchair across from Lisa and set her purse on the floor beside her. "Really good. I think the house we're viewing tonight is the one. We've already seen it once, but there's one other on our short list. But I really like this one. It's my favorite."

"Does your dad know you're moving in together, yet?"

Just the reminder of her dad was enough to make Karma bristle. "He still doesn't even know we're engaged."

"You haven't told him? What about your mom?"

"No. I've been busy. Mark's been busy. Plus, this isn't something either of us wants to say over the phone or in an e-mail, and since my dad doesn't want Mark in his house, and I don't want to share the news without him, we're at a stalemate."

"Sooner or later you need to tell him, even if you have to force the issue or compromise on the how. I mean, Karma, he kind of has to walk you down the aisle and give you away. So, the sooner you tell him, the better."

"Mark and I haven't even set a date, yet."

"What's the holdup?"

"Like I said, we've been busy."

"Too busy to take five minutes and pick a date?" Lisa's e-mail chimed. She briefly glanced at her monitor before dismissing whatever message she'd received and turned back to Karma. "Seriously, Karma. If you want a June wedding, you might have already missed the window." She cocked her head. "I thought you were excited about this."

"I am."

"Then what's stopping you?"

Karma shrugged. "Mark suggested we wait until after things calm down. We're both crazy busy right now, Leese. I start classes next week, I just got my first editing assignment, we're buying a house, we've got to pack, change all our mailing information, move, buy furniture. There's a lot to do."

"Okay, but don't wait too long. There's a lot of planning that goes into a wedding, and you want to get moving."

"You're right. There *is* a lot of planning, which is why we're waiting until things settle down." She relaxed into the chair, smiling to herself. "God, Lisa. Is this really happening?"

"What? That you're buying a house with Mr. Hotness? Or that you're marrying the guy?"

She laughed. "No . . . just . . . well, yeah. All of it." She sat forward and scooted to the edge of the chair, suddenly anxious. "I mean, Lisa, he has money. More money than I ever thought the man I'd marry would have."

Lisa's eyebrows scrunched over her nose as she angled her head curiously. "And this is a problem how?"

Karma rolled her eyes. "You know what I mean. He's rich, Lisa." She'd already revealed to Lisa what Mark had told her about the state of his finances. "And this house is huge. I'm not used to living that way."

"And what way is that? Comfortably?"

She exhaled gruffly. "No, silly. Like I'll need a team of maids just to keep the place clean."

"Well, I think Mark can afford it."

"That's not the point."

"Then what *is* the point? What's wrong with marrying a guy who has money?"

"What if I don't fit into his world?"

Lisa frowned as if she'd never heard anything so ridiculous. "Trust me. You fit."

Karma sighed. "I don't know. This is all so strange and new and . . . I feel like I'm in a whirlwind."

"Which you will come out of once you settle down and get used to things. Just relax, Karma. Count your blessings. You're one of the lucky ones."

"How so?"

"You're in love with a man who loves you. A man who's not just in love with you but *crazy* in love with you. Who just happens to be a multimillionaire and a brilliant businessman. A man who has professional aspirations and doesn't just want to live off his inheritance. Who's got his shit together and sweeps you away on a private jet to a tropical island on a whim. So, let yourself enjoy the moment, girl."

She sighed and pushed herself back in her chair. "Yeah, okay. Maybe you're right. Maybe I—"

A knock on the door interrupted Karma, and she turned to see an attractive blonde she didn't recognize standing in the doorway. The woman appeared to be in her late twenties or early thirties, with large, doe-like eyes. She was dressed impeccably in a stylish, magenta suit. Her skirt hit just above the knee, revealing slender, toned calves. She wore beige peep-toe platform pumps.

"Oh, I'm sorry." The woman glanced toward Karma and smiled apologetically as she took a step back. "I didn't mean to interrupt."

Lisa shook her head. "No, that's okay, Kit. Come on in."

This was *Kit*? Jesus! Karma swallowed her shock but turned incredulous eyes on Lisa. Why hadn't Lisa told her Kit was a walking Victoria's Secret model?

"Kit, this is Karma Mason, Mark's fiancée." Lisa gestured toward her.

"You're Karma?" Kit practically gushed like a fan meeting her rock idol. "I've heard so much about you. Mark goes on and on about how you used to be his assistant." She giggled, and the sound was like tiny silver wind chimes tinkling in the breeze, charming and perfect. "Sometimes I fear I'll never live up to your legacy." She waved her perfectly manicured hand and stepped forward. "It's so good to finally meet you."

Mark goes on and on about how you used to be his assistant.

The statement felt like a knife to the gut. Even now, after two months, Karma still missed working with him. Still felt the loss like it was a personal injury.

She forced a smile and stood. "It's good to finally meet you, too."

She'd almost forgotten that Lisa had told her about Kit during their conversation before Mark whisked her away. She'd said Mark had been struggling to find a new assistant but that maybe Kit would work out. That had been the last Karma heard about the woman, and now, here she was. Looked like she'd worked out all right.

"So, Kit, what's up?" Lisa said.

The impressive blonde handed a file over to Lisa. "That candidate Mark just interviewed?"

Lisa snagged the file and opened it. "Yes?"

"It's a no."

Lisa groaned. "Damn." She wrote the word "No" in red ink along the top margin of the applicant's résumé then closed the manila flap with a smack. "That man is going to be the death of me." Lisa pointed toward Karma. "You'd better warn him that I'm about to do something that could cause him severe bodily harm."

Karma held up her hands. "Hey, I just sleep with the guy."

Okay, where had that stupid remark come from? Marking her territory, perhaps?

Lisa's eyes narrowed knowingly then she turned back toward Kit. "Thank you, Kit. And could you let Mark know Karma's in my office?"

"Absolutely." Kit smiled at her. Her teeth resembled pristine white marble. Bright and perfectly straight. Bleach much? "Nice to meet you, Karma."

"Same here." She gave a little wave and watched Kit exit and disappear down the hall.

She hooked her thumb toward the door. "Do you think those are her real teeth?"

"Really, Karma? Could you be any more obvious?"

"What?"

"You're jealous."

"I am not."

"'I just sleep with the guy'? Really?"

"Well, I do."

Lisa shook her head, eyes flashing upward. "I can't believe you're jealous of her when you're wearing that iceberg on your finger." She gestured toward Karma's engagement ring.

"I'm not jealous."

"You're practically green."

"Fine, whatever. I'm jealous. So what?" She leaned forward and lowered her voice. "But you told me she was average-looking." She pointed out the door. "That is *not* average, Lisa. That is *stunning.*"

"Okay, so I misspoke. But in my defense, she looked average when she came in for her interview. How was I supposed to know she'd turn into . . . *that?*" She flapped her arm toward the empty doorway.

"And you didn't think you should clue me in?"

"What's there to clue in? She's pretty. Who cares? Mark wants *you,* not his assistant."

"*I* was his assistant."

"And now you're not, and he still wants *you,* not Kit, so calm down."

Karma sighed and backed into her chair, feeling a bit silly for her jealous outburst. "Maybe you're right. She's probably really sweet, and here I am freaking out over nothing, right?

"Right."

Rolling her eyes, she briefly dropped her head into her hand then took a deep breath and looked back up. "Ignore me. I'm just being stupid. Mark and I haven't spent much time together since getting back from Saint Lucia, and with my classes starting and everything else going on, it's just going to be that much harder for us to spend time together. I'm just feeling a little fragile right now."

She hadn't felt that way until she saw Kit, though. But just getting a peek at Mark's new assistant had reopened a fresh wave of realization that she and Mark no longer worked together. She'd come to identify their working relationship as part of who they were romantically, and coming face-to-face with Kit for the first time roused new insecurity. Mark *had* moved on. He *had* found a new assistant. He *had* replaced her, despite her irrational hope he wouldn't be able to. She had to accept that phase of their relationship was officially over. She no longer played a professional role in his life. Theirs was purely a personal relationship now, which felt so bizarre given how they'd started.

And damn, Kit was pretty. With lovely legs and attractive feet. Funny how she noticed such things now. She was constantly on the lookout for sexy footwear to satisfy Mark's foot fetish and tease him.

"Did you see her shoes?"

Lisa sat back and crossed her arms. "Her shoes? Really? You're going to talk about her shoes now?"

"I told you about Mark's foot fetish. He's got to be seriously drooling over her shoes, Lisa."

"You're making too much of this."

Karma sighed and slumped her shoulders. "I know, but... I can't help it."

"Try."

"It's not that easy."

Lisa sat forward and folded her hands together on her desk, gaze compassionate. "I know it's not. I know you've dealt with some pretty nasty shit in your past, and no matter how hard you try to forget, it's always going to be there. But you're in a better place now. And Mark isn't going to cheat on you. He's nothing but professional around Kit. Trust me when I tell you you're the only one that makes his eyes sparkle when he sees you."

"Yeah, but what about her? Does she know that, or am I going to have to watch her shamelessly ogle him at the next company picnic? Because, let's face it, Mark is very attractive, and women stare at him everywhere we go. I told you about the boat bitches in Saint Lucia."

Lisa's expression morphed into one a mother might give an objectionable child. "Yes, and then you took great pleasure in informing me that Mark dismissed the boat bitches because he knew they made you uncomfortable. So, you see, Mark is very aware of your feelings and makes every attempt to show you that you're the only one allowed to *ogle* him. And would you much rather Mark be ugly so that no one looked at him at all?"

Karma lowered her gaze. "No."

Lisa leaned forward. "I mean, come on, Karma. He's hot. He's probably one of the top five percent in good-looking men in the country. There's nothing he can do about that except try to reassure you he only has eyes for you. But if you keep getting jealous over Kit and boat bitches and every other semi-attractive woman who comes along, pretty soon he's going to get tired of reassuring you."

Harsh, but Lisa wasn't one to sugarcoat the truth, and Karma appreciated her honesty, even if it stung a little.

Lisa's gaze grew more patient and understanding. "Kit is very professional around Mark. He's her boss, and she handles herself accordingly. No flirtatious looks or anything. She knows he's engaged to you, and she respects that."

"And you know that how?"

"My gut," Lisa said immediately, eyes sharp. "So stop trying to find warning signs where there aren't any."

Karma bowed her head, feeling scorned. Lisa was an exceptional judge of character, so if she said Kit was above-board, she was. "Okay. You're right. I'm being silly, letting my insecurity get the better of me. I know he loves me and that I shouldn't worry."

"That's the spirit." Lisa plucked the lid off her crystal candy dish and nudged the bowl toward her. "Now, have some M&M's. They'll make you feel better."

"Mmm, chocolate. You *do* know how to make a girl feel better." She fished out a small handful of colored candies and tossed them in her mouth.

"Knock-knock."

Karma turned as Mark breezed into the office, his black wool coat slung over his forearm. He swept in and kissed her on the cheek. "How long have you been here?"

Seeing the adoration in his eyes made her feel even sillier for letting envy and doubt get the better of her. "About fifteen minutes."

Lisa stood. "I'm mad at you, Mark."

Mark fished a sampling of M&M's from her dish before Lisa could drop the lid back into place. He grinned as if they were in on a private joke. "Why? What did I do?"

Lisa pointed at the file folder. "You turned down another applicant."

He tossed the candy into his mouth and held up his arms as if innocent. "Then give me someone I can use."

"I have. About ten someones. And you keep rejecting them."

Grinning, Mark took the lid off the candy bowl and helped himself to more chocolates.

"Hey," Lisa warned. "Hands off the bowl, fast fingers."

It was a well-known fact that Lisa guarded her candy dish with an iron fist and only doled out when she saw fit.

Laughing, Mark tossed the M&M's into his mouth and dusted off his hands. "You're too stingy with the treats."

"Whatever. Now, what was wrong with this guy?" She pressed her index finger to the folder on her desk. "I screened him, and he seemed perfect."

"He couldn't look me in the eye."

"He looked me in the eye just fine."

Mark pointed his finger toward the ceiling as if making a point. "Exactly. He could look *you* in the eye, but not me. Why is that a problem for a project manager?" Even though he was giving Lisa a hard time, he kept a smile on his face, so Karma knew he wasn't being as harsh as he made himself sound.

Lisa frowned as if lost.

"Because," Karma said, drawing two sets of eyes her direction, "he's got a confidence problem. He's fine with women, but when faced with an intimidating man, or even with men, in general, he wilts. You need someone who won't wilt when faced with an upset or overbearing customer, which includes about ninety percent of Solar's customer base."

Mark smiled proudly at her then arched his brow at Lisa as he snapped his fingers. "Exactly. That's why I rejected him."

That familiar buzz of accomplishment prickled Karma's skin. Every day working with Mark had felt this way. He'd taught her so much, and she'd been so in tune with him. She'd known what he needed. What he wanted. What he looked for in people. And every proud smile had felt like a reward. Now that they no longer worked together, she had to find another way to reap those rewards and make such a connection with him.

"I knew that." Lisa sank back into her chair and tossed the file aside. "Fine. I'll keep looking."

"Don't worry," he said, "the perfect candidate is out there somewhere."

"Yeah, but he's taking his sweet time getting his ass in here to put me out of my misery."

"Why don't I have Kit screen the applicants with you? She's pretty tuned in to what I'm looking for. An extra hand could take some of the load off your shoulders."

Karma briefly met Lisa's gaze, and despite a pang of loss, she gave a quick, tight nod to let Lisa know she was over her green-eyed meltdown.

"Sounds like a great idea," Lisa said somewhat cautiously, dropping her gaze briefly then meeting Mark's again. "I'll get with her after you leave and work out the logistics."

"Great. Thanks." Mark pulled his coat from over his arm and turned toward Karma. "So, are you ready to buy a house, honey?"

She grabbed her purse and stood, liking the way he called her honey, as if the term of endearment were a public stamp to mark her as his. "I thought we were just viewing it."

"We are, but unless we find something this time around that is an absolute deal killer—which I doubt we will—I think we can make an offer. I know you like this one."

"Do you like it?"

"I like them both. So it's your decision." He took her hand and led her toward the door.

She waved toward Lisa. "I'll call you later."

Once in the car and on the way toward West Clover, where the financially unencumbered lived, Mark said, "So, what was that look Lisa gave you back there about?"

"What look?"

"In her office? After I asked her to work with Kit?"

Of course, Mark hadn't missed that. He was Mr. Observant. Mr. I-Never-Miss-Anything.

"It was nothing."

He glanced at her then returned his gaze to the road as he took her hand.

"You met her, didn't you?"

"Yes. She's . . ." Gorgeous, breathtaking, every man's fantasy. "Lovely."

"Yes, but she's not you."

Obviously.

"She seems capable, though, for you to put your trust in her. That's a good thing, right?"

"Of course, but I would still rather have you as my assistant."

"You would?" She hadn't meant that to come out as surprised as it sounded. Or as pleased.

"I miss us working together, Karma. You always gave me something to look forward to at the office. Work wasn't just about work when you were there. It was exciting. You know, every day since you've left, when I go for my coffee, I wish when I walk out of my office that I would still find you sitting at your desk."

Your desk. He still saw it as hers, even though she'd been gone for almost two months. It was good to know he felt that way.

She dipped her head flirtatiously. "You mean, you don't make Kit get your coffee for you?"

He grinned and gave her hand a squeeze but kept his eyes on the road. "That was only for you."

"Was I special?"

This time he did take a second to look at her. "You still are. *Very* special."

They drove in silence for a while, which allowed Karma's memory to play over their sexy games and all the ways he used to tease her at the office. That first day—when he appeared like a specter only two days after she'd met him in Chicago, all deliciously hot and stealing every woman's attention just standing in the lobby wearing his crisp, tailored suit—she'd gotten his coffee. After that, doing so became a fun diversion. Something to put her in front of him . . . to see him smile as he took that first sip, his grey-green gaze burning into hers like a challenge.

They didn't play games like that, anymore, but then, their relationship was different now. Playtime had taken on a new dimension. Instead of using their professional relationship as a means of foreplay and sexual restraint that turned into an inferno in private, they used heated glances across the kitchen while making dinner, or suggestive caresses while watching TV. He asked for sex by standing in the bedroom doorway, shirtless, arms extended overhead, hands propped against the top of the frame, jeans slung low on his hips, *The Look* firmly in place.

In a way, she wanted some of those playful times back. Not that she didn't like where they were now, but Playful Mark had been so very fun. He'd made her laugh and see things in herself she hadn't known existed. And, to be honest, sometimes she got the feeling Mark was still holding something back. She'd thought they'd gotten everything out in the open in Saint Lucia, but occasionally, the shadows fell over his face in such a way to make her think there was more he still hadn't told her.

"I was wondering," she said. "Maybe tonight we could talk about the wedding. You know, set a date."

Mark's jaw flexed, and a distinct chill rolled off him as his hand tightened around hers. Then he relaxed as if he'd forced himself. "I thought we'd agreed to wait."

Okay, so that wasn't the reaction she'd expected. Both physically and verbally.

"I know, but Lisa mentioned today that we might have already waited too long for a June wedding and made me realize just how much planning a wedding is going to take. I know we're both busy as hell right now, but maybe we should at least set the date so we can get the ball rolling. That way, we're not rushing around at the last minute trying to pull everything off in a month. Good plan, right?"

He let go of her hand and made a left turn. "We've already got so much going on right now. I'd feel better if we waited until after we close on the house to discuss the wedding."

His voice was tight, his words slightly clipped, almost as if he were angry, even though he clearly wasn't. Uptight? Irritated?

Karma couldn't put her finger on the emotion stirring just beneath his words, but it was clear he still wasn't ready to talk specifics about the wedding.

"Okay, we can wait. I just thought I'd suggest it." She glanced out the window at the palatial estates nestled within thick, protective coves of trees.

West Clover was a beautiful area. Magnificent homes on massive plots tended by professional landscaping crews. Everybody who was anybody in central Indiana lived in West Clover. Players from professional sports teams, government officials, coaches, millionaires. It was a Who's Who of the rich and famous.

Mark would fit right in.

Her? Not so much.

But she'd better get used to it, because there was a high probability that within the next hour, they'd be making an offer on a house big enough to hold the enter United States Winter Olympics team and still have room to walk around. Okay, so maybe that was a slight exaggeration, but the place was huge. Bigger than any house Karma had ever imagined living in.

As they pulled into the driveway, Karma cringed inwardly at their realtor's car already parked in front of the four-car garage. Natalie was a shameless flirt. Maybe Karma's jealousy was unfounded where Kit was concerned, but it was more than justified in Natalie's case.

The first time Natalie met Karma, she had seemed taken aback that Mark was already in a relationship. That had been a chilly first meeting, and Natalie still showed her disappointment with every icy, red-lipped smile she gave her.

"Welcome back." Natalie tippy-toed across the ice-patched driveway in her three-inch, peep-toe heels.

Looked like Natalie had gotten the memo about Mark's foot fetish, too.

Karma mentally chastised herself. She really needed to get over this jealousy routine. It wasn't becoming. She hated when other women displayed their ugly, green-eyed monsters. It was a sign of insecurity, and she had no reason to be insecure, other than her silly past that had practically bred that nasty personality trait into her genetic makeup for almost two decades. But she was over that now—or, rather, she should have been, thanks to Mark.

So, yeah, the jealous girlfriend act needed to take a hike.

Mark took her hand, and they met Natalie halfway across the driveway.

"Are you two ready to take another look at your first home?" Natalie's smile seemed more genuine this time around. Maybe she'd moved on to another potential suitor. Or maybe she saw all the places on the left side of the decimal point her commission would include if she closed this sale tonight.

"Lead the way." Mark gestured for Natalie to go ahead then pulled Karma's forearm around his, linking them more intimately.

Just as she'd done the first time they viewed the house, Karma sucked in her breath as they crossed the threshold into the entryway. She loved the relatively open floorplan. Oak hardwood spread toward an angular staircase hugging the left wall. An extra-wide hall opened into an enormous kitchen with high, A-line ceilings and a row of windows overlooking the deck and wooded backyard. The kitchen, living, and dining rooms all shared the same space to create one giant, inviting area.

Mark inspected the kitchen cabinets as she stood aside and let him drool. The kitchen in his temporary apartment was barely an eighth of the size of this one. For a man who loved to cook, such a tiny kitchen had to be frustrating. Just imagine the culinary damage he could do in this eighth wonder of the world.

"I have a feeling this will be your room," she said, running her hand over the polished, dark-grey-and-white granite countertop as she eased up beside him.

He grinned and glanced at her out of the corner of his eye. "Oh, I don't know. I think I might allow you in here once in a while."

"Only once in a while?" She followed him around the counter into the dining area, with its cozy stone fireplace, and then through the side hall leading back to the front of the house, past the side door, the laundry room, and a spare bathroom, before entering what Karma had termed her library. It was a smaller, round room with floor-to-ceiling bookshelves on one side and a small custom window on the other to let in natural light. There was enough room for a modest table so she could use it as a meeting or research room.

An arched doorway led them into what Karma had decided

would become her office.

Natalie had the good sense to hover several feet behind them. She seemed to understand that a good realtor let the client sell the house to themselves.

"And this is your room," Mark said, crossing toward the large picture window overlooking the front yard.

There was enough space for two comfortable club chairs and an end table between them. A wall of bookshelves took up the wall opposite the window, behind where Karma envisioned her desk.

"And you'll be welcome in it any time you like," she said sweetly. Maybe a little extra sweetly because of Natalie poised in the background.

"Why, thank you." He winked and took her hand.

After touring the full basement, with its bar, half kitchen, theater, spare bedroom, and exercise room, they ended their tour upstairs in the master bedroom.

"Natalie, could you give us a moment, please?" Mark said from the French doors that opened onto a private balcony.

"Of course." Natalie backed out of the room and gave Karma an awkward smile. "I'll wait for you in the kitchen."

After she was gone, Mark wrapped his arms around Karma's waist and pulled her against him. "What do you think? Is this home?"

In his arms was home.

She couldn't contain her smile, pressing her palms against his chest. "I love it."

"So do I." He stepped back and took her hand, leading her away from the doors. "I see our bed there." He pointed toward the right then gestured to the left. "And I want to get a Tantra chair that would go nicely right there."

"A Tantra chair? What's that?"

His wicked grin bespoke that whatever a Tantra chair was, it was not a normal piece of furniture. "It's sort of like a chaise lounge but made to help couples find lots of fun and interesting positions for sex. Think of it as an ergonomic sex chair." He led her toward the door. "I'll show you pictures later. But you'll love it. Especially since you're so limber from all that yoga." His eyebrows popped mischievously.

Where did he find these things? "Have you used a Tantra chair before?"

The shadow that occasionally appeared and made her think he still hadn't told her everything about his past crossed his face. "Yes, I've used one."

"When?" Was it with Carol? Nina? One of his other temporary flings?

He kept his eyes on the floor as they headed toward the stairs. "Nina had one."

Nina again. She'd taken up a lot of time in Mark's post-Carol personal development.

"And you liked it?"

"Yes, it's one of the things Nina introduced me to that I *did* end up liking."

They began descending to the main floor.

"What else did she introduce you to that you liked?"

His eyebrows ticked inward. With every step, his body grew more tense. "Maybe now isn't the best time to discuss this."

"So, there's more about *this* we need to discuss?"

A guilty shroud fell over him.

She'd been right. There was more. The fact that Mark hadn't told her when they were on vacation irritated her, because that had been the whole point of the discussion they'd had the night they made their lists.

"Please, let's not talk about this now. Let's wait until we get home." His brow was pinched in the middle, his expression grim.

"Why do I get the feeling there's still something you haven't told me?" she said quietly as they reached the foot of the stairs and stopped. "Something important."

His shoulders wilted as he faced her. A chagrined smile tilted his mouth. "Because, apparently, you're getting to know me well enough to know when I'm hiding something."

"Hiding something?" She frowned and took a step back, crossing her arms. "What are you hiding from me? I thought you told me everything in Saint Lucia."

He scrunched his eyes closed, holding up his hand. "Not exactly *hiding*. That was a poor choice of words."

"Then give me some better ones." If he still felt the need to hide things from her, then they hadn't made as much progress as she thought.

He glanced toward the kitchen, where Natalie was waiting for them. Then he spoke in hushed tones. "It's not that big of a deal. Compared to what I've already told you, this is nothing. I promise."

"Then why are you so upset? If it's not a big deal, then why haven't you told me?"

He closed the short distance between them, his gaze boring hard into hers. "Because, Karma . . . it's personal. It's *deeply* personal. And it's damn hard to find the words to tell you what needs to be said. Do you understand? I want you to know, but I'm afraid of the way you'll look at me after you do."

On one hand, he felt like a complete stranger. How could he say whatever he was hiding was no big thing but express how much he feared revealing it? On the other hand, she wanted to pull him into her arms and tell him not to be afraid. Never to be scared of telling her his secrets, no matter how personal he thought they were or how he feared she would react. They were a team. One. Together in thick and thin, good and bad. The fact that he was still keeping secrets unnerved her.

"You're scaring me," she said quietly.

His frowned deepened as he dropped his gaze to the floor. "I'm sorry."

She forced a tight smile and took one of his hands in both of hers. "What could be so bad that you'd get this upset about it? I don't know what to think, and I'm imagining the worst."

Did he have a terrible disease he hadn't told her about? Did he have a kid with one of the women he'd gotten involved with? More than one kid?

Oh God, what if he did?

He sighed, his posture broken. "It's really nothing bad, Karma. Honest, it isn't. But . . ."

"But what?"

"You might not like it."

She regarded him impatiently. "Will you stop trying to think for me and let me decide for myself?"

"I'm sorry. It's a habit."

"Well, let's see if we can work on breaking it. Because I'm a lot more understanding than you're giving me credit for."

He sighed and closed his eyes for a count of two then opened them again. "I know you are, and I'm trying."

"And that's all I'm asking. For you to try." She searched his face. "So, are you going to tell me what you've been hiding?"

"Yes, but not right now. Later. At home where we can talk openly." He paused then added. "This time, let me do this the way I'm most comfortable."

She narrowed her eyes. "And what way is that?"

He took a deep breath then tugged her hand to follow him as he started for the kitchen. "With a plan."

With a plan. That was so Mark. But she would cut him some slack. This time.

They entered the kitchen hand-in-hand, if not a bit more tense than they had been thirty minutes ago.

Natalie sat at the island, scrolling on her smartphone. She immediately tucked it into her purse and stood. "So, what's your decision?" She looked from Mark to her and back to Mark.

"We want it."

Natalie's smile creased the spackled makeup around her eyes. "I'll start the paperwork tonight."

"Good. And inform the sellers we are highly motivated and want to move in as soon as possible. Whatever it takes." He squeezed her hand as if to impress upon her how he felt about living together. That no matter what came of their discussion later, he wanted *this.* Them. Together. Under one roof. And he wanted it sooner rather than later. No matter the expense.

"Noted." Natalie ushered them toward the front door. "I think you two will be very happy here. It's a fabulous home. Competitively priced. And it's in a great neighborhood. Perfect for kids."

It was like she was putting her own personal stamp of approval on the sale.

They exited, and Natalie locked up then joined them in the driveway.

"I'll be in touch tomorrow to let you know what the sellers said," Natalie said to Mark. "But I have no reason to think this house won't be yours by the end of the week."

"Thank you, Natalie." Mark shook her hand.

Karma did likewise, and then she and Mark departed for Solar so she could get her car and meet him back at her apartment.

Silence engulfed them. But it wasn't an awkward silence. More like the silence associated with someone who was deep in thought.

Mark was apparently working on his plan.

She stared out the passenger window, letting him toil as her own mind wandered.

She had the ring. And now it looked like she had the house. All she needed was the wedding date.

And to know what else Mark hadn't told her.

Chapter 12

Learning to trust is one of life's most difficult tasks.
-Isaac Watts

She should have been happy. Should have been excited. Right now, she and Mark should have been wrapped around each other in bed, turning dreams into plans for their new home. Instead, she was quietly poking the uneaten portion of her salmon. Waiting. Just . . . waiting.

"Are you finished?" Mark reached for her plate.

She set down her fork. "Yes."

He took their dishes to the kitchen, spent a few minutes tidying up and putting away leftovers, then shut off the light and returned to the table, hand outstretched.

"Come on," he said.

"Where?"

"Your bedroom."

If he was going to use sex to sidetrack her, she'd end that idea right now. He needed to start talking. "Mark, I—"

"I'm going to tell you. Trust me."

Why couldn't he just say what he needed to say in the dining room? Or the living room? Why the bedroom?

"Karma . . . trust me."

Then it dawned on her. The bedroom was their sanctuary. It was where he seemed most comfortable with her. Or, rather, more open. Maybe he needed the sense of neutrality and freedom her bedroom provided to reveal his secrets.

She took his hand and followed him down the hall.

Watching him curiously, she sat beside him on the edge of the bed.

The mysterious atmosphere he wove was both agitating and exciting. Maybe even a little erotic. Whatever he wanted to tell her, she believed he'd been telling the truth when he said it wasn't nearly as bad as what he'd already revealed.

But the fact he hadn't told her in Saint Lucia irritated her. She'd thought everything that needed saying had already been brought to light.

As if reading her mind, Mark said, "I wanted to tell you this in Saint Lucia, but it felt like too much. When I found you by the pool that night when you couldn't sleep, obviously conflicted and struggling to process everything I'd already told you, I decided to wait . . . so I didn't burden you with too much too fast."

That made sense. His intentions had been noble. Thoughtful even.

"But if this isn't as bad as all that," she said, "why not just get it over with and tell me? I mean, if all that other stuff was the hard stuff then telling me whatever this is shouldn't have been a big deal."

He sighed and offered a sheepish grin. "I guess this is what they mean when they say it's hard to see the forest for the trees. I'm so deep in the shit that it's hard to figure out what's a big deal, what isn't, and how to think logically. And, Karma, I've been deep in the shit for the past couple months, dredging up old memories, trying to make sense of them, wanting to tell you everything but terrified of how you'll react. I am so thick in the trees that I can't find the forest even if it's wearing a neon sign."

"Okay, okay." She took his hand. "I get it. I'm sorry. I'm trying to adjust, too. This is all happening so fast, and I know you're on your own kind of vision quest right now." He'd made that pretty clear in Saint Lucia, and even though she'd thought he'd gotten past all the mental and emotional rubble, clearly, he hadn't.

"Vision quest. That's a good way of putting it. Because the visions of my memories are definitely sending me on a quest."

"A quest for what?"

His eyes met hers with as much clarity as she'd seen from him in the last few hours. "Me." His mouth set in a grim line. "I'm searching for me."

She held his hand in silence for a few seconds, giving him space to absorb and make sense of whatever his brain was throwing through his mind. Oh, how the tables had turned.

She smiled and inched closer. "Remember how confident you were when we first met?"

He met her gaze almost apologetically. As if he knew he was different now and hoped she wasn't regretting her decision to accept him back into her life.

Turning her body so she was facing him, she said, "I liked that man. He was cocksure, in total control, no cracks whatsoever in his armor." She paused and glanced down at their joined hands. "But you know what?" She met his gaze again. "I like who you are *now* even more."

A small, inquisitive frown bent his brow, but he didn't say anything. Only stared at her, seemingly eager for her to continue. As if he *needed* her to continue.

"You're vulnerable," she said, "and I know you don't do vulnerable. So for you to expose yourself like that means you trust me. Even that you need me. And it feels good to be needed, especially by you. It makes me feel important, like it's a reassurance that my role is no longer that of student, but that of an equal partner." She held up one hand as if she were warding off a counterargument. "Don't get me wrong, I like being your student, because I know you still have so much you can teach me, but I like being your partner, too. Or maybe even *your* teacher, for a change. Like it's my job to be there for you now the way you were there for me then. Like now we're there for *each other* instead of remaining static in the roles we created two years ago. It means we're growing, and I like the balance. The balance of *us*."

Devotion shone from his eyes as if he were looking at a goddess who'd finally revealed herself. "Sometimes I wonder what I ever did to deserve you."

She shrugged. "You made me feel alive. You sat down at that blackjack table and told me not to take that bet. And I did anyway. In more ways than one. And, you know what? I don't regret anything we've done since."

His smile widened. Then he laughed and bowed his head. "You know, we've done this all backward."

"What do you mean?"

"Our relationship." He faced her, holding her hand in both of his. "Usually, two people meet and they get to know each other. And if they like what they learn, they want to spend more time together. Then, if all goes well, they have sex. And then they get to discover all the wonderful things having sex does for their relationship, bringing them closer until they enter into a commitment." He shook his head, expression filled with sad wonder. "We started out with the sex. We got to know each other sexually first, and we were *never* supposed to form a commitment. That wasn't how it was supposed to work. But it did." He stopped as if all the air in the room suddenly vanished. "You found me. You got to a place no other woman was able to get to for six years. By the time I realized that, it was too late. I was already gone. I was already on my way back to Chicago."

His grip intensified as he slid closer. "But I couldn't forget. I couldn't stop thinking about you. I had to find a way to get you back. And when I returned, you didn't want me . . . until finally, you did." His gaze searched hers, filled with confusion, love, and unspoken promises. "And now, here we are, trying to reboot ourselves from square one. Trying to go through the getting-to-know-you phase when we've already reached sex and commitment and are about to move in together."

She shook her head and smiled. "Just so you know, I always wanted you, Mark. I never stopped wanting you."

"I know that now, but for a while, I thought I'd lost you." He caressed the backs of her hands with his thumbs. "But we're all turned around, and I'm fumbling as I try to figure out how to be a normal man again. A normal man who hasn't already fallen in love with you. Who hasn't got this tremendous amount of emotional baggage he's still trying to unpack and sort through. We've taken a very unorthodox path to get where we are, and I feel like I'm fucking everything up." He frowned and looked away. "God, I don't even know what I'm saying. I wanted this to go differently, but now all the words I wanted to say are all tied up inside my head." He searched her eyes. "You do this to me. You make me want to be better when I know I'm not. When I know I've done shitty things. You make me want to settle down when I never thought I'd want to settle down again, which was the only reason I could live with what I'd done. Because if settling down was never going to be in my future, I never had to worry about coming clean and confessing all the shit I'd done.

"I have to worry about that now. Which means I have to worry about the backlash. Like what happened on the yacht when you teased me about the waitresses joining us in a foursome. I was so hypersensitive about what I'd told you about my past I thought you were making a dig at me. That you resented what I'd done. But that wasn't the case at all. You were simply playing, and I took your words out of context, because I've become this man who regrets his past. Who's ashamed of it. And self-doubt made me question you when you'd simply made an innocent comment.

"The man I was four years ago never would have batted an eye at what you said. I would have ridden it for what it was, a playful, sexy game. I would have played along, maybe pushed the envelope and untied your bathing suit, tempting you to do things you've never done before. Exhibitionist things, because I want that. I want to dress you up in a slinky, backless dress and tell you not to wear any panties underneath so I can parade you around a crowded party then slip my hand down the back and slide my finger inside you and make you come in front of all those people. I would get off watching you trying not to reveal what I'm doing to you, not to let on that I'm fucking you with my fingers." His gruff voice deepened as he inched closer on the bed.

Karma was practically panting simply from the mental image his words created.

His gaze cut into hers. "On that yacht, the old me would have stolen you away to bed and fucked you. Hard. Hard enough to make you cry out so that everyone on board could hear you and know what I was doing to you. Old me would have taken you as far to the edge as you would let me without caring about the consequences. Old me wouldn't have cared if you walked away afterward, claiming my proclivities were too much. But this man I am now? I still want all those things and more. I want to strip you, defile you, make you do things you've never done, but I'm terrified of pushing you too hard, because I *do* care. I *do* care if you leave. I don't want to lose you . . . to make you fear me and my fantasies to the point you *do* walk away.

"There's more at stake now, Karma. A lot more. And I can't stand the thought of losing you simply because I want to indulge my fantasies, my desires . . . my fetishes. That's what this is about. I'm afraid. You took my confession in Saint Lucia better than I thought you would, but now it's like I'm waiting for the other shoe to drop. And that's why I withheld revealing everything, because

I'm worried doing so would be just that *little bit* too much. I didn't want to risk tipping the scales."

"You won't."

He let go of her hand and tucked her hair behind her ear before caressing her face. "You say that now, but what if you don't like what I have to say?"

"There's only one way to find out."

He studied her for a moment. "In a lot of ways, you *have* become my teacher. Yes, there are still things I could teach you . . . if you're willing and open to explore them with me. But you're teaching me, too. I may not be the best student, because, like I said, I'm struggling to see the forest for the trees right now, but I'm changing because of you. You're showing me how to trust again. It's just happening in baby steps." He paused. "So, you *are* my equal. We do have a perfect give-and-take between us. I just need to have more faith and trust in that."

"Yes, you do. Because I'm not going to bite. I'm not going to walk away. You keep thinking that, but I'm still here. What's it going to take for me to prove I'm in this for the long haul?"

His hand dropped to her knee. "I don't know. Time. Patience."

"You've got it. You have all the time in the world. And I'm not going anywhere. Ever. Now . . ." She scooted closer so there was hardly any space between them. "What is it you need to tell me? What is it you think I won't understand?"

He squirmed, frowning intently as he inhaled deeply. "Part of it I already told you. Or at least, I hinted at it."

She replayed his soliloquy in her mind but drew a blank.

"I'm an exhibitionist, Karma. I love the idea of being seen having sex. I get hot just thinking about showing you off in public and finding ways to risk us being seen fucking at a party, in a theater, in the car, a stairwell." The grey-green of his eyes darkened under hooded eyelids as his gaze dropped to her mouth and he leaned closer. "I've repressed my exhibitionist side for years, but now . . . with you . . . I want to unleash it. I want to set it free and see how far we can push the edge. I've even fantasized that we've gone to a sex party where people are standing around the bed, watching while I fuck you."

Oh. My.

Karma trembled at the thought. From excited anticipation or abject fear? But really, did it matter? After all, one emotion fed the other, intensifying both.

"There's more," he said quickly, as if fearing she would speak and halt his newfound surrender. "I want anal sex. With you. From you. I want... it's that... I like..." He was stammering uncharacteristically all over himself, suddenly tongue-tied.

Wait. Back up. What? *From* her?

"Wait a minute." She raised her hand, palm out. "What do you mean when you say you want anal sex *from* me?"

His expression tightened as he rubbed his hands over the tops of his thighs. "Uhm..." He glanced down then to the side before meeting her gaze again.

She'd read about stuff like this in her books. "Do you mean... like... you want me to wear a strap-on or something?" She wasn't sure she could do that.

He frowned, his head flinching backward slightly as his brow wrinkled. "Uh... I, uh..." He appeared completely confused. Then his eyes flew open wide as he sucked in a quick breath and shook his head. "No, no. Not that." He uttered a nervous chuckle as he wiped his palm down his face and shifted his weight on the bed. "I'm not talking about anything quite that kinky."

Whew! She wasn't sure she could have done the whole strap-on thing. She was the one with the cave. She had no interest in being the one doing the spelunking.

She let out a breathy giggle. "Okay, that's a relief." The moment she said it, his posture stiffened. Oops. Maybe she needed to show him she was a bit more open-minded. "I mean, not that I wouldn't have given it a try if you wanted me to. I just think I'm more of the ravag*ee*, not the ravag*er*."

He gave her an awkward grin as he cleared his throat. "No, I get it. I know what you're saying, and trust me, I definitely want to remain the giver in our relationship, not the receiver. No need to worry about that."

"Okay then, so what exactly are you saying?"

Based on the way he glanced down and briefly fidgeted his fingers around hers, this was obviously the part he'd feared revealing. After taking another deep breath, he lifted his face and

157

looked her square in the eye. "Karma, just because I'm the . . . ravag*er* . . ." He winked, and even though it was an uncomfortable, pale-faced wink, it made her grin. "Well, that doesn't mean I don't enjoy anal stimulation."

Okay, now she was confused. If he didn't want her to ravage his ass, but he enjoyed a little backdoor stimulation, what exactly was he saying he wanted?

He apparently recognized her confusion and shifted closer and wrapped his hands around hers. "Karma, a man's prostate is like a woman's G-spot. And when it's stimulated, it can be very exciting and set off the most intense orgasms he's ever had. For some men, it doesn't do much for them, kind of the way some women don't get much out of their G-spots being stimulated. But for other men, it does. I'm one of those men. I really, *really* like it."

"Okay." She could definitely understand the whole G-spot comparison, because hers was extremely responsive when he went to work on it. So then, what did anal play have to do with . . . ? Oooohhh, okay. She was beginning to understand where this conversation was going. "And how do you stimulate a man's prostate?" she said suspiciously.

"Well, that's the thing, see . . ." He cleared his throat again and kinked his neck to the side, making one of the vertebrae pop. Deep inhale, harsh exhale. After a curt nod that came off like the punctuation at the end of some you-can-do-it inner dialogue, he blurted, "The best way to stimulate a man's prostate is by inserting something into his anus." He turned his head to the side and rubbed his palm up and down his face as if just saying the words made him itch.

"I see." She pressed her lips together, letting this new knowledge sink in. He wanted anal stimulation. Okay. She got that. Hmmm.

He flexed his shoulders as if trying to get comfortable in his skin again. "It could be a finger, or a butt plug. Or there are dildos specially designed for this kind of thing. Any of those would do the trick."

"You mean . . . to insert . . . inside . . . ?" She got it. She really did. But, for some reason, she needed to hear the words. Or at least an explanation to confirm the thoughts swirling inside her head were on track.

"Yes."

The idea of inserting something inside Mark's ass made for an odd image. Did he bend over on all fours? Lie on his back? Did he want her finger up there? Was this during sex? Before? How would that work? She'd never done anything like this.

Then she suddenly remembered that he'd also said he wanted to have anal sex *with* her.

"You want to have sex with me like that, too?"

Lusty hunger instantly glowed in his eyes as his mind made the mental shift. "God, yes."

How did she feel about that? Would it hurt? She liked when he fondled her ass, especially when he gripped her cheeks like they were handles, and he churned her body hard on him as he took her from underneath. Would allowing him entry to the final orifice his penis had yet to be inside take those sensations to the next level or completely turn her off? If the latter, would that disappoint him? She didn't want to let him down. She wanted to please him. If she ended up not liking anal sex when he seemed to want it so badly, it would be a major downer for them both.

"Oh." It was all she could think of to say.

He gently stroked her hands. "I would take my time. I would prepare you. I wouldn't do this without considering how important preparation is."

This was one time she was glad he was a planner.

"What if I don't like it?"

"Then you don't like it."

"But you want it."

"Yes, I do. I can't lie about that. But if you don't like it, I can live without it. I just want to know you're willing to at least try."

She stared at him for a long time. Expectant hope practically dripped from his face. This was important to him.

"Okay."

His eyebrows rose. "Okay?"

"Yes, I'll try it. I trust you." And if this brought them closer and introduced her to something new she would end up enjoying, pushing out of her comfort zone would be worth it.

Hell, their whole relationship so far had been about pushing her out of her comfort zone, and hadn't she enjoyed every bit of it? Why would this be any different?

Gratitude oozed from every pore as he closed his eyes and bowed his head. "Thank you."

Placing her hand under his chin, she brought his face back up and searched his eyes. "Thank you for trusting me enough to share that with me. I know it was hard."

"I was afraid you wouldn't understand."

"Well, I do." She placed a tender kiss on his lips. "But I have to ask. Why were you so afraid to tell me this?"

He let out a sigh that sounded like relief as he rubbed his palms reassuringly up her thighs. "I didn't want you to think I'm gay."

"What!" She laughed. "Really? You thought I'd think you were gay?"

His eyebrows scrunched together briefly then he let out a staccato chuckle and glanced away, shaking his head. "Well . . . yeah." He shrugged. "A lot of men are afraid to admit they like this sort of thing because others will think they're secretly in the closet or have homoerotic fantasies. So, yeah . . . I was worried your image of me would change, and that you'd think I swing both ways or something."

"Uh, no." She pressed forward and kissed him again. "I would never think that about you. You enjoy having sex with me too much for me to think you're gay."

"Well, I could be bisexual."

She shook her head curtly. "No. Just . . . no. You would never convince me of that even if you tried."

He snapped his fingers. "Well, damn, there goes my April Fool's Day joke."

"Ha. Funny." She placed her hands on his. This conversation had gone better than she anticipated. What a relief to finally have everything out in the open. "So, is there anything else you need to tell me? Anything left that you haven't said?"

She was ready for this whole sordid ordeal to be behind them so they could get back to planning their future.

* * *

Mark's mind shot to his list. There was still one unrevealed item on it. One he'd crossed off but still haunted him even more now than it had then.

I want to dance again.

Rather than push his luck and go for complete disclosure, perhaps he should count himself lucky and call it a day. Karma had handled his latest confession better than he'd expected. She hadn't completely freaked out or looked at him like he was an alien. Didn't that count for something? Could he live with getting ninety percent through his list and leave it at that?

Besides, dancing again wasn't something he could ask of her. That was something he'd shared with Carol. Something intensely personal that would shatter Karma if she knew he wanted it back. He'd already unloaded enough on her and couldn't expect her to take up ballroom dance just for him.

Plus, that item meant so much more than just dancing. So much so he still couldn't put it all into words.

"No. That's it." He lifted her hand and kissed the backs of her fingers. "You've graciously handled everything I've told you, both in Saint Lucia and now, and I couldn't want for anything more."

It was the truth. So what if he had to abandon the fantasy of ever dancing again, both metaphorically and physically. He wasn't even sure he could handle it, anyway. Carol's duplicity might have killed that part of his universe forever. Dance was all about trusting your partner, and she'd killed that for him.

But now, with Karma, he trusted again. And he'd found that trust without dancing with her. There was no need to open old doors, which could lead to a major backfire.

Relationships were about compromise. And this was the compromise he would make for theirs. He would gladly give up this fantasy to have the others. And to have his Karma.

He pulled her onto his lap. "So, I didn't scare you off? You're not freaked out?"

"No. Surprised maybe. A little. But not freaked out." She brushed her fingertips across his forehead, combing aside his hair. "And maybe I'm a little aroused." She grinned in that playful way that hinted at naughty thoughts and secret fantasies.

"Aroused?" He lay back and pulled her down with him. "Why's that?"

"Because . . . what you said about parading me in public . . ." Her lashes fell over her eyes. "That sounds kind of sexy."

Now it was his turn to be surprised. "Really now?"

"Mm-hm." She nodded dramatically.

He slipped his fingers up the back of her shirt, finding her warm, bare skin. "And how sexy does it sound? Sexy enough that you'd like to try it?"

She bit her bottom lip, her eyes twinkling mischievously. "Maybe." Then she froze and narrowed her eyes. "As long as we start slow. I like the idea of secret touching in a crowded room, but that whole sex party thing might be too much."

"Understood." He rolled her over and pushed her farther into the center of the bed before easing back down between her legs. "You know, I've always suspected you had an exhibitionist in you, too." He pushed up her blouse, lowering his head so he could leave a trail of kisses down her stomach. "You've often said and done things that made me think you would get off on being watched. That you enjoy the risk."

Her fingers burrowed into his hair. "And you never thought to bring this up before now?"

He tugged off her shirt then his own. "I was afraid I might have misread you and turn you off if I did."

She half-rolled her eyes, smiling. "When have you ever misread someone?"

He'd misread Carol. Which had led to a level of emotional anguish he never wanted to feel again, crippling him to err on the side of caution every time he thought he knew someone well enough to know what they wanted before they did. At least when it came to the important stuff.

"Trust me, it's happened." He pulled the cup of her bra down and gently closed his mouth over her nipple.

On the inside, he wanted to tear away the rest of her clothes and ravage her to within a hair's breadth of maddening pleasure. To consume her so fully she wouldn't be able to feel where he ended and she began and would lose sight of everything but burning euphoria. But on the outside, he maintained control. As he'd done so many times before, in countless relationships and situations, he quelled his own desires so he didn't upset the newfound balance that revealing his fantasies had created.

There would be time enough to stretch her outside her comfort zone into his later. For now, he just wanted to love her. He wanted to be the safe place she had come to know and trust with her own vulnerabilities.

"I love you," he said, gliding slowly into her after quickly nabbing a condom and slipping it on.

"I certainly hope so, Mr. Strong." She wrapped her legs around his hips and tilted her pelvis welcomingly.

"Why's that?" He rose up on his arms so he could gaze down at her perfectly understated breasts, her pale pink nipples forming tight peaks.

"Because we just bought a very big, very sexy, very over-the-top house together." She swiveled her hips then unlocked her legs and threw them over his shoulders.

Jesus, but she was flexible.

"That we did. Are you ready for this?" He gently rocked into her.

"Now that you've finally shared all your secrets with me, I'm ready for anything."

Not *all* his secrets. But enough of them.

"Then hold on, Miss Mason." He rocked more forcefully into her, making her gasp.

Reaching low, she grasped his hips and dug her blunt nails into his buttocks. An extra shot of arousal flashed up and down his spine.

She grinned as her fingers played over his ass, sending crackles of lightning up and down his back and legs as his cock swelled.

Her gaze bore into his as she pulled him forward. "Shut up and fuck me, Mr. Strong."

Growling, he rose to his knees and grasped one strong, slender leg, holding it to his chest as he kissed her ankle. If she wanted fucked, he would oblige.

That he *could* do.

Chapter 13

Sometimes you don't need a goal in life. You don't need to know the big picture. You just need to know what you're going to do next.
-Sophie Kinsella, The Undomestic Goddess.

Karma loved these tender, peaceful moments after sex, Mark's arms holding her, his face nuzzled in her hair, his warm breath heating her scalp.

Once again, all was well. Another intense discussion that could have ended with shattered hope and broken hearts had, instead, culminated in the two of them making love and tightening one more notch in the cinch binding them together. They'd made it one step further in this journey of them. An "us." A real couple.

She rolled over, facing him. "I think it's time we told my parents."

His palm rested on her naked hip. "That we're engaged?"

"Yes."

Rolling to his back, he let out a heavy exhale as he stared up at the ceiling. Then he rolled his head and looked at her. "This'll be tricky. Your dad hates me." His eyes twinkled in the darkness as he grinned. "I've stolen his daughter to the dark side."

She propped herself on her elbow and rested her other hand on his chest as she kissed his shoulder. "Well, he needs to accept that this is my choice. And we need to force the issue. He's never going to come around if we don't give him a push."

"And you want to push him."

"You'll help, of course." Sirens rang out somewhere in the distance, but she and Mark were tucked into the safety of each other. The rest of the world could be in chaos, but around Mark, she would feel nothing but calm. "And we haven't even told *your* parents."

"We will. But I believe in making that kind of announcement in person." He rolled back to his side so they were facing each other again. "I was thinking we could take a weekend off and go to Chicago after closing on the house. There's this furniture store up there that's been around for decades. I wanted us to go there and pick out a new bed. Something to start our life together. And my parents are having a party for my mom's birthday in a few weeks, so that would be the perfect time." He ran the tips of his fingers around her eye and down her cheek. "We could go shopping . . . buy a bed, maybe a few other pieces of furniture . . . go to my mom's party . . ." He kissed the tip of her nose. "Announce our engagement." His smile faltered briefly before brightening his face once more. "How does that sound?"

"Sounds perfect. For *your* parents. Now, what about mine?" She dropped her head to the pillow, keeping her eyes on his, enjoying the soothing way his fingers slowly skimmed up and down her arm. "My dad's going to be a lot tougher customer than your parents."

"I know." He kissed her, letting his lips cling to hers as if imparting reassurance everything would be okay. "How about we keep it simple and tell them we have news and would like to have dinner with them. We can make reservations at a nice restaurant—"

"Where he can't make a scene, right?"

He laughed. "I hadn't thought of that, but yes, that's a good point. If we're in a restaurant, he's not as likely to make a scene."

She tapped the side of her head. "Gotta think of these things."

"Absolutely." He inched closer, wrapping his arm around her waist and pulling her against him. "So, we invite them to dinner—in a restaurant—and we just tell them we're engaged."

"When? Before dinner? During dessert?" She smirked. "As we're about to get back in our car and come home?"

He chuckled lightly. "I say we get it out right away so you're not worrying about it the whole time. If he gets mad and leaves, then at least our consciences are cleared and we've taken the first step."

He made it sound so simple, but Karma feared revealing their engagement wouldn't go exactly as planned. But, as Mark said, at least the news would be out there. The hard part would be over.

She just wished her dad could be as happy for her now as he had been when Brad proposed. That wasn't going to happen, though. Dad had liked Brad. He despised Mark.

But Dad needed to understand she was marrying Mark. End of story.

They were in this for the long haul.

Even if they still hadn't set a date.

Chapter 14

True friends stab you in the front.
-Oscar Wilde

"Who's bright idea was it to go jogging in this weather?" Karma shot Daniel a scowl, her nose freezing, her legs tingling beneath her thermal leggings and nylon, water resistant training pants that swished like two plastic bags being rubbed together with every stride.

Zach, who trotted on her other side, laughed. "Daniel, I think you just got on Karma's shit list."

"She'll thank me later . . . on her wedding day when she looks absolutely fabulous in her dress."

She expelled a derisive huff. "At this rate, I might *never* get into a wedding dress."

Daniel shot her an inquisitive glance.

"Mark still hasn't set a date," she explained.

The threesome followed a curve along the trail as an icy mist began falling. It wasn't quite warm enough for rain, not quite cold enough for snow. Just right for miserable mist that made the air feel like ice.

"Well, honey, what's that fine man waiting for? A shift in the gravitational forces of the universe." Daniel paused for a few quick breaths. "Get Mark to commit to a date. It's not rocket science."

She laughed. "Did you just use Mark's name in the same sentence as the word commit? Do you not see the irony of that?"

"I thought he was over all that nonsense."

"He is, but—"

"Mm-mm, honey." Daniel waggled his finger. "He needs to shit or get off the pot. That's what I say. If he wants to play, he's gots to pay."

"Amen," Zach said. "He put a ring on it, now he needs to make it real."

Karma slowed to a walk, dragging the boys' pace down with hers. "Okay, you two, cut Mark some slack. He's working on it. We're just waiting until we get moved in to the house and get settled. Then we'll start looking at dates for the wedding."

"If you say so." Daniel jacked his hands up on his hips as he walked, panting. "By the way, how's that going? The new house, I mean."

It had been three weeks ago today that she and Mark had made the offer on the house, which the sellers had accepted four days later, after a quick negotiation on price. Being that Mark had liquidated assets to pay for the purchase with cash, the closing fast-tracked, and they'd signed the paperwork on Valentine's Day. That night they had a quiet carpet picnic in their new dining room to celebrate. They'd chattered the whole time about moving in, what would go where, which rooms would be used for what. But not once did they discuss the wedding.

"Everything's fine. Mark's already moving in, and I notified my landlord on Monday that I'm vacating my apartment at the end of the month. I'm losing my security deposit, but that can't be helped." She waved her hand dismissively. She hated losing the money, but the only way she could get her security deposit back was if she waited to move out until the end of October, and that wasn't happening, so buh-bye security deposit. "And this weekend, Mark and I are going to Chicago for his mom's birthday party. While we're there, we're going to tell his parents about our engagement."

"And what about your parents? When are you telling them?"

"We're having dinner with them Friday night."

Daniel's eyebrows shot upward. "I hope you can still go to Chicago after your dad hears the news. Maybe you should wear body armor to dinner."

She blew air between her pursed lips, making them flutter. "Tell me about it. It was like trying to talk a Colts fan into betting on the Patriots just to get my dad to accept our invitation."

"How did you finally convince him?"

"I didn't. Mom did. And I have no idea what she said. But damn, it took a week for him to agree just to have a meal with us."

Zach bent to one side then the other, stretching. "So, how's everything else going? How's your new job?"

"And your classes? How are they going?" Daniel added.

"Busy and busier." She stopped at a fence and used it for balance as she stretched her quadriceps. "I finished my first assignment for

Winstrom on Monday, so now I'm just waiting to hear back from my boss, and my classes are intense. Sometimes I don't finish my homework until after ten o'clock at night."

Daniel cringed and exchanged glances with Zach. "I bet that's putting a damper on your sex life."

"Not really. Mark keeps things interesting."

Zach made an appreciative noise. "I bet." He'd made no secret that he thought Mark was—how had he put it?—just about the hottest straight man he'd ever met.

Daniel gave Zach's shoulder a light shove. "Hey, you're taken, lover boy."

Laughing, Zach took Daniel's hand, pulled him close, and kissed him on the lips. "Calm down, handsome. I may be taken, but I'm not blind. I can still appreciate a good-looking heterosexual man."

Those two didn't give two shits what the public thought about their shows of affection. They were secure in their feelings, and even if they weren't, they were built like UFC fighters. Zach had even recently gotten a tattoo of Daniel's name across his chest, inspired by Mark's tattoo of her name on his chest, no less. But now he was obsessed with the idea of getting another tattoo on his back. An eagle with outstretched wings on his shoulder blades.

Tattoos or not, Daniel and Zach looked like guys you didn't want to go up against, even though they were as sweet as kittens and didn't have a violent bone in their bodies. That didn't mean they wouldn't shed someone's blood who threatened them, though. If it came to protecting one another or someone they loved, they could definitely lay down the hurt. But they wouldn't be the ones starting the fight.

Daniel possessively bit Zach's lip and held it between his teeth. Then he released it and said, "Just as long as you bring your fantasies home to me, babe."

"You know I do." A sly, heated look passed between them, and then Zach pecked him hard on the mouth once more and pulled away with a wet *smack* as their lips suctioned apart. "You're the only one I want to share my secret fantasies with, babe. You know that better than anyone."

Karma felt a little like a voyeur for witnessing their hotly intimate moment. Then they separated and the three of them headed across the street. Daniel and Zach lived near the jogging trail, which was why Karma usually went to their house for their running dates.

As they walked in silence, Karma's mind mulled over what Zach had said about his fantasies. About how Daniel was the only one he wanted to share them with.

And that made her think about Mark and the conversation they'd had three weeks ago. She still didn't know quite what to think about what he'd told her. About liking anal play. Not just giving, but receiving, too.

She glanced to the side, at her friends' loosely joined hands. Their thick fingers wove together. Easy. Comfortable.

For gay men, was it easier to talk about anal stuff? Was it simply assumed that a gay man liked having dildos and cocks inserted in his butt? That that sort of thing was *situation normal* for them but *situation red alert* for a straight man? And did straight men really enjoy that sort of thing? Because Mark wasn't gay. He was absolutely and completely heterosexual. So then, why did he enjoy stuff like that? He'd explained the biology behind why, but she still didn't fully know how she felt about what he apparently wanted her to do to him, mostly because she didn't know how to do it.

She was so damn green. For all her progress into the world of debauchery, there were still so many things that made her feel like a first grader in a high school trigonometry class.

Daniel chucked her shoulder. "Hey, you okay?"

She jolted from her thoughts. "Yeah, why?"

His eyes scrunched into narrow slits under a furrowed brow. "You sure? You got really quiet on us, and you look like your mind is dwelling on some pretty deep shit. Is everything between you and Mark really as okay as you say it is?"

Zach peered around Daniel's head at her.

"Yes," she said, "everything's fine. I'm just . . . it's just that . . ." She sighed. "He and I were talking a few weeks ago, and he said something that's got me kind of thrown."

"What did he say?" Concern coated Zach's words.

"Yeah. And what were you talking about?" Daniel added.

"It was nothing really, but . . ." She held a greater appreciation for the effort it had taken for Mark to come clean. This was a hard subject to talk about, and she wasn't even talking about herself. Imagine how hard it had been for Mark to reveal to her these were *his* fantasies and turn-ons?

"Okay, you're starting to worry me," Daniel said, letting go of Zach's hand to retrieve his keys from his pocket.

"Really, Daniel, it's not that big a deal. It's just . . . awkward." And really, should she even be discussing this with them? What if Mark found out? Would he be embarrassed? Angry?

They started up their driveway. "Well, you're going to come in, and I'm going to heat us all up a pot of soup to take this chill off." He lifted his gaze to the grey, overcast skies still dropping their misty dampness. Then he glanced at Karma. "And you're going to spill all, awkward or not."

As Daniel unlocked the door, Zach nodded at her as if putting the period on Daniel's statement.

"Fine, just let me get inside your warm house first, but you both have to promise me you'll keep this between us. This is private. No making any smart-ass comments to Mark or anything like that."

"Smart-ass comments?" Daniel shut the door behind them. "Now I *am* intrigued."

In the mudroom, Karma peeled out of her cold, moisture-slicked jogging suit, pulled off her cap, and hung everything on the pegs dotting the wall before joining her friends in the kitchen.

"Okay, girl, start talking," Daniel said before she even had a chance to sit down. He snagged the ceramic teapot from the stove and started filling it with water.

Meanwhile, Zach grabbed a large container of what looked like homemade soup from the refrigerator and set it by the stove.

With a resigned sigh, she parked herself on a barstool and plunked her elbows on the counter. "Mark told me something a few weeks ago, and I'm not sure what to think about it."

Zach and Daniel exchanged glances, each with one eyebrow raised.

"What did he tell you?" Zach spoke evenly. Cautious curiosity dripped from every syllable.

"Okay, so let me say first that when we went to Saint Lucia, he opened up about his past and some of the" — how could she express all the stuff Mark had done in one word? — "*things* he's done. Some of them a bit more on the wrong side of the tracks, if you know what I mean." She held up her hand defensively. "But don't tell him I told you that, okay."

They both cocked their heads and crossed their fingers over their hearts.

"Karma, you've known me long enough to know I would never break your confidence," Daniel said.

"And you've known me almost as long to know I won't either," Zach added. "Whatever you want to tell us stays with us. We're like Vegas, just without the cool costumes."

She knew that, of course. She'd known Daniel since college and met Zach soon after. Other than Lisa, they were her best friends.

Daniel started pouring the soup in a pan. "And it's not like we couldn't see this coming from a hundred miles away. His wrong-side-of-the-tracks activity, I mean."

"Mm-hm." Zach slid a bottle of water across the counter toward her then unscrewed the cap on his own. "Because a man that fine is bound to have some skeletons in *that* closet. What, with all the women he's dated and all that."

Zach had always been the less tactful of the two. Not that he was insensitive. He just had a very thin brain-to-mouth filter. Sometimes it didn't catch everything it should.

"Gee, thanks for reminding me, Z." She swiped the bottle of water and twisted off the cap.

Daniel lightly punched Zach's shoulder. "Nice going."

He held up his hands. "What? I'm not saying anything we don't already know."

Shaking his head in consternation, Daniel turned back toward Karma. "Don't listen to him. He still possesses Neanderthal genes." He stirred the soup. "So, go on. What did Mark tell you that has you so flummoxed?"

Flummoxed. Good choice of word.

"Okay, so he told me all about his past while we were in Saint Lucia, and then a few weeks ago, he said there was more he hadn't yet told me. In fact, it was the night we made the offer on the house."

Was she doing the right thing by revealing to them what Mark had told her in private? But if anyone could relate, it was Daniel and

Zach, right? Maybe they could shed some light on the subject and ease her mind.

She knitted her fingers together. The boys were now parked across the counter from her, all ears.

She was stalling.

"Anyway," she said, "I thought it was going to be this really horrible thing, and then he revealed that he's an exhibitionist. That he has exhibitionist fantasies."

The expression on Daniel's face was the epitome of the phrase, "Is that all?"

"Just wait," she said. "There's more." She felt like one of those advertisements on TV. *But wait! There's more! If you buy now, you'll also receive a second sexual fantasy for free. Aaaannnd, we'll throw in one butt plug and an anal dildo with your order!*

"Go on," Daniel said.

"He wants me to do exhibitionist things with him, too. Like, wear a provocative dress in public where he can fondle me and, maybe, you know, *do it* in the coat closet where someone could walk in on us."

"And this is a problem because . . .?" Zach looked like his mind was working over the possibilities of doing something similar with Daniel at their next social engagement.

"That's not all," she said. "There's more."

"Well then, honey, get to the point. We're gonna grow old and wrinkly at this pace."

"Okay, okay. Give me a second. This is . . .?" What exactly was this? Embarrassing? Abnormal? Perfectly normal and healthy and she was just being silly? "Odd," she finally said. "At least for me."

Daniel pulled his head back and stood up straight, eyebrows pinched. "Odd?" His expression shifted into curious amusement as he leaned forward again and rested his forearms on the counter with a crooked grin splashed across his face. "Oh, I can already tell this is going to be good."

Groaning, Karma dropped her arms and slumped forward until her forehead bonked the counter, which made Daniel and Zach laugh.

"It's not funny," she said, pushing herself back into an upright position.

Zach nudged Daniel's upper arm with his. "Well, if you'd just spit out whatever it is, we might understand what's so odd about it and why it has you in such a twist."

Yes, she definitely felt a greater appreciation for what Mark had gone through to tell her this.

"Fine. Okay. Just . . ." She held her hands in front of her, fingers splayed, palms down, as if she were pressing the air toward the floor. "Mark likes . . . well . . ." She sighed. "He enjoys anal play."

Daniel and Zach frowned and tilted their heads in unison, in perfect sync with one another. They were like twin bobbleheads. Their actions would have been humorous under different circumstances.

Daniel pushed off the counter, eyeing her. "Okay, so he wants to have anal sex with you? Is that what you're saying?"

She felt like she was folding in on herself. "Partly."

"And the other part?"

It was like there was a great big rolling storm cloud hanging over their heads. Just waiting to drop a deluge.

"He says he enjoys . . . you know . . ." Did she really need to say it? Couldn't they infer the rest without her actually having to speak the words?

"What?" Daniel's eyes narrowed as he turned his head slightly to one side as if his mind were racing over what exactly she was trying to tell him.

"You know . . ." Karma nodded tightly, eyes wide, as if that would somehow communicate what she was trying to say better than her voice could.

Zach was the first to get it.

"Oh! Oh my God!" He jumped back and thrust his hands out in front of him as if holding back a rush of Black Friday Christmas shoppers. "Oh, hell, I think I've died and gone to gay heaven!" He started laughing and shoved Daniel. "He likes it up the ass, Danny! Oh my God, that's it, isn't it?" He turned toward Karma and rushed the counter like a winning game-show contestant, eyes bright. "Am I right? I'm right, aren't I? He likes it up the ass."

And there came the deluge.

His reaction almost made Karma laugh. Almost. Except for that on-the-edge-of-crying feeling.

"Yes." She held her hands palms-up, fingers curled into claws as if she were gripping a pair of elephant balls. "But, oh my God, what do I do? I've never . . . this has never . . . just . . . oh my God, guys! What am I supposed to do?"

"What are you supposed to do?" Zach was beyond hysterical, laughing as if he were the happiest guy on the planet, oblivious to her consternation. "Give the man what he wants, honey!" He shook his head as if he still couldn't believe it. "This is so awesome. A straight man who isn't afraid to admit he enjoys taking it up the ass."

And there he went again, being the most tactless man on Earth.

He spun on Daniel, whose face was the picture of amusement. "This is the best thing I've heard all year." He bobbed his head back and forth and shrugged. "I mean, I know the year's barely begun, but I can't imagine I'll hear anything better than this for the next ten months. This is just . . . Oh my God, Karma." He whirled back around. "Thank you. Thank you for making my day."

"Glad I could be of service." She shot them both a helpless look. "Now, help me out. I don't know what to do."

Zach calmed and shimmied up to the counter, all ears and wide smiles. "Girl, he must really love you to tell you something like that. That takes balls."

"Why?"

Daniel finally chimed in. "Because there's this stigma among straight men that if they admit they like *anything* up their ass, people will think they're gay."

Mark *had* told her that.

Zach nodded. "But the truth is, if more straight men realized how good it feels, they wouldn't be such idiots about admitting they like it. Your guy's got a lot of courage to admit something like that. Don't take that for granted, Karma."

"But what do I do?"

"Wear a strap-on and go at him?" Zach suggested.

She rolled her eyes and shook her head. "He already told me that's not what he wants."

Daniel rested his arms on the counter again and bent forward. "How about a prostate plug or something like that to stimulate him?"

Zach's head bobbed up and down vigorously. "Oh yeah. Or maybe one of those prostate stimulator-cock ring combos. Those are incredible."

Daniel smiled at him in a way that said he and Zach possessed firsthand knowledge of this sex toy Zach spoke of. "Oh yeah, I bet he'd really like that. That's uh, yeah, that's a good one." Daniel turned toward her, visibly hot under the collar. "And you would, too. Talk about giving the man staying power and still rocking his socks off."

"And his *rocks*." Zach nodded dramatically. "The anal plug-cock ring thing is hot. Really hot. Daniel and I can definitely vouch for it. We've—"

Karma held up her hand and slammed her eyes shut as if that would turn off her ears. "Okay, okay, okay. I'm learning way more about your guys' sex life than I wanted to."

When she opened her eyes again, Daniel was smiling from ear to ear. "Welcome to our world, my young apprentice. You're one of us now. Pay attention and learn well." He straightened and reached across the counter for his laptop then opened it and began typing. "We're about to educate you. With our help, you're going to blow Mark's mind."

"But I have so many questions. I'm not even sure I can do this."

"Sure you can."

"It's not weird?"

Daniel scoffed. "No, it's not weird. As long as you don't make it weird."

Zach leaned over Daniel's shoulder, watching him type. "This isn't weird at all, Karma. Mark's just a man who's obviously in tune with his body and what he likes. Seriously, if more men would explore their backdoor, they wouldn't be such dicks about guys sticking their wicks up there."

Something about that sentence sounded all wrong, but given the source, should she really expect anything less?

"Why is that?"

"Because, honey, that's where the magic happens. That's where a guy's G-spot is."

"Mark did try to explain that to me."

"Well, listen to the man. He knows what he's talking about. If he likes a little toy up his bum, stick one there and let the fireworks fly, sweetie." Zach placed his hand over hers. "And it's perfectly normal. It doesn't make him *gay* or anything. Which is really a tragedy if you ask me, because that man needs to be gay the way Beyoncé needs to insure her ass."

Daniel looked up, frowning curiously. "She hasn't?"

Zach shrugged. "I don't know, but if she hasn't, she needs to. That's all I'm saying."

She was feeling a little better about this whole issue. Maybe this wasn't the big deal her over-analyzing, hyper-aware mind had turned it into over the last few weeks. And if it could intensify their sex life then it couldn't be a bad thing, right?

"So, I'm just being weird then? This is all perfectly normal."

"That's what we're saying," Daniel said. The compassionate, level tone of his voice further soothed her anxiety. "You don't have to worry about Mark going all homo on you. And like Zach said, he really loves you to share something so deeply personal. I think you've found yourself a winner in that one."

A winner. Mark was a winner. "You're right." She finally allowed herself to smile. "He is pretty terrific, isn't he?"

"Uh, slightly," Zach said.

Daniel spun his laptop around. "That's what you need."

He was on Cārvāka's website. The same place where Mark had ordered her a box full of toys two summers ago. Did everyone know about Cārvāka except for her? First Mark. Now Daniel and Zach.

She stared at the smooth, curved contraption on the screen. It was black and smaller than she imagined, with a flared base that connected to a slender cord attached to a ring. So, this was what Mark wanted? She hadn't even thought to jump online and do a web search.

Daniel angled the laptop back toward him while Zach checked on their soup. "Or you could do something like this." He clicked on a cock ring that was translucent pink with a protrusion that looked a bit like a lobster claw or rabbit ears on one side.

"What's that?"

"That's a cock ring made for him *and* her." He pointed to a tiny silver nub to the side of the rabbit ears. "See that? That's where the batteries go. Three watch batteries." He sounded like he was reading that last part from the product specs.

"Why does it need batteries?" Then she drew in her breath. "Oh, it's a vibrator."

"Yes. And you can't tell me that doesn't excite you even just a little bit."

Her face warmed, so she knew she was flushed.

Daniel began clicking and scrolling. "Or there's these cock rings. This is a set of seven." Daniel began reading off the site. "They stretch to accommodate any size, so that's good. And each of the seven is textured differently to give the woman—or man"—he glanced at Zach as he returned with their soup—"a different sensation. But I think these are made more for a woman's pleasure," he amended.

She lifted a spoonful of soup and blew on it, totally engrossed at this point. When she got home, she would need to spend some time perusing Cārvaka's site. Definitely.

Daniel clicked a few more times. "And then you can pair any of those cock rings with any of these prostate stimulators." He clicked on one made of glass with a broad, rounded handle at the base. "I recommend something like this. It's smooth, not too large, has a nice, gentle curve that will allow it to hit him just right, and with the wide base, you won't risk losing it inside."

"Losing it inside?"

Daniel and Zach both smirked. Then Daniel said, "Inferior anal plugs don't have wide bases and can get accidentally pushed inside. That's not a good thing to have happen."

"Oohhh. Okay. Duly noted." She started eating as Daniel turned the laptop back toward him and continued typing.

She assumed he was bringing up more products for her to look at, or even going to another site, but when he sat back and closed the screen with a shit-eating grin on his face, she got the distinct feeling something was up.

"Happy birthday," he said, his smile widening.

"My birthday was in November." She slowly lowered her spoon into her bowl.

"Then happy belated birthday. Or early birthday. Whatever, it doesn't matter."

"What have you done?"

He pushed the laptop aside and slurped a spoonful of soup and shrugged. "Be expecting a package early next week."

"Daniel!" She reached across the counter to smack him, but he was too fast, pulling away, laughing.

"Hey, I'm just looking out for your best interests, sweetie."

To the side, Zach snickered. He cradled his bowl of soup in front of his chest and had clearly seen what Daniel had ordered for her.

"You didn't stop him?" she said, incredulous.

"Hell no." Zach stepped to the side as if to pull out of range if she decided to slap him.

"I can't believe you two." She settled back onto her barstool. "I'm going to pay you back."

"Don't be silly," Daniel said, taking his place in front of her again. "It's our early wedding present to you. Or a housewarming gift. Something to definitely keep the *house warm*." He winked.

"Fine. Whatever." She slowly stirred her soup. "So, what am I to expect when I open the box?"

"One of everything I showed you," Daniel said as if he were far too pleased with himself. "And maybe a surprise or two."

"What kind of surprise?"

Daniel ate a spoonful of soup then sucked on the spoon for a second as if it were a lollipop. "You'll just have to wait and see."

Zach set his bowl down and dabbed his mouth with a napkin. "Oh, and Karma?"

"Yes?"

"I suggest you do a *loooooot* of research on cock rings and ass dildos over the weekend. A lot of research. You'll want to know how to use them when they arrive." He winked and picked his bowl back up.

Great. Just what she needed for an already busy weekend.

Chapter 15

A relationship with no arguments is a relationship with a lot of secrets.
-Author Unknown

"Good evening. How may I help you?" The modelesque brunette with hair as straight as a ruler and extending at least six inches past her breasts gave her and Mark a practiced smile as they stepped up to the podium.

"We have a reservation," Mark said.

"And the name?" The woman glanced down at her ledger.

"John Mason."

When Mark had made the reservation, he'd chosen to put it under her dad's name because, as he'd said, "I know how your dad feels about me, and I think it would be a nice gesture on my part if he didn't have to say my name if he arrives before we do."

For Mark to consider her dad's feelings showed just how compassionate he was . . . as well as how important it was to make nice with him.

"The other two in your party haven't arrived, yet," the woman said. The small light shining up from under the lip of her podium cast alluring shadows over her features. "Would you like to wait here or be seated and wait at the table?"

Mark glanced at her. "Table?" he said.

"Yes." Something about being seated and ready to order sounded a lot safer for when her dad arrived.

He turned back to the woman. "We'd prefer to be seated, please."

"And would you like to check your coats?"

"Yes, please."

Mark helped her out of hers then handed both to an attendant who stepped forward to take them.

The lady handed them a ticket then sashayed away.

She and Mark followed a third hostess into the elegantly attired dining room. White tablecloths. Sparkling wall sconces. Candlelit centerpieces and glittering stemware. It was the type of restaurant Mark was used to, having come from money. As for Karma, she was still acclimating to this new lifestyle.

"I'm nervous," she said once they were seated.

"I know." He reached for her hand.

Her palms were damp, but Mark didn't complain as he protectively enveloped her hand in his warm, dry one.

"This'll be a lot easier tomorrow with your parents," she said.

Tomorrow was his mom's birthday party. They were heading out around seven o'clock to get in early enough to rest and clean up before going to his parents' in the afternoon.

"I talked to my mom yesterday and told her you were coming with me." He smiled at her. "She's dying to meet you."

"Do you think she'll like me?"

He angled toward her, face affectionately alight. "She's going to love you."

Mark always had a way of making butterflies flutter in her belly. Maybe it was the way he looked at her. Or the tender tone of his voice. Or perhaps the way his skin seemed to melt into hers wherever he touched her. Whatever the reason, ripples teased her tummy.

"How many of your girlfriends has your mother met?"

"Not many." He straightened and glanced toward the white candle in the center of their table. "Carol, of course. Maybe two of the others." His face tightened. "I preferred not to let things go that far. Before, I mean." He bobbed his head abruptly to the side, indicating the past.

She grinned and leaned closer. "When you were honing your mad skills of seduction?"

His mouth screwed into a twisted smile as he met her gaze, eyes twinkling. "My 'mad skills of seduction'?"

"Well, what would you call it? A learning phase?"

He studied her for a moment then leaned in and whispered in her ear, "Would you like me to show you exactly what I learned while honing my mad skills?"

She giggled, tipping the side of her head against his. "I thought you were already doing that."

He chuckled, pressing closer. "No. I mean now. Right now. During dinner with your parents."

Sobering, Karma pulled back, eyes wide, mouth gaping. "You

wouldn't."

He laughed. "Probably not, but that doesn't mean I won't be thinking about it." Even though he was smiling, heat flared from his gaze. He looked like the devil who sat on one shoulder, all wicked smiles and suggestive glances, while an angel preached from the other. She could almost hear his voice inside her head. *You know you want to. You know it will feel good. So naughty but so nice. Come on, live a little.*

"You really want to do that to me, don't you?" She bit her lip, her breath shallow as her gaze remained fixed on his. "Right here. In front of my parents? My *dad*? You must have a death wish."

He closed the distance between them again, gently cupping her face as he lightly kissed her ear then whispered, "What I really want to do is take you back out to the car and fuck you in the parking lot, where anyone could walk by and see us."

She swallowed heavily then let out a little breath. "Oh."

"I told you I like the thrill of getting caught in the act."

"Uh... yes, I know. Um..." Honestly, what he suggested sounded very exciting. She got wet just thinking about it.

"Do you think you're ever going to want to do something like that with me? Not just fantasize about it, but do it? For real?"

She pulled back and searched his dark, hungry gaze. Yes, she wanted to do that. She wanted to know what it felt like to be caught. Or to at least risk being caught. How exciting! The thrill and adrenaline rush would probably be incredible, making for one intense orgasm.

"I..." She smiled. "I think..."

"Are we interrupting?"

Karma jerked away from Mark with such force she nearly tumbled out of her chair.

"Mom! Dad! Hi. Mark and I were just... we, uh..."

Her dad shifted uncomfortably, frowning.

Mark collected himself faster than she did and stood, running his hand down his blue and silver tie. "Mr. and Mrs. Mason, thank you for coming." He didn't dare use first names until invited to do so, especially with her parents. But he did hold out his hand to her father.

Karma held her breath.

After a brief hesitation, her dad stiffly shook Mark's hand. That was a good sign, but it didn't mean her dad had stamped his ticket on Mark's train. This dinner could still go very badly. The tension between Mark and her dad hovered between them like a giant, bloated wedge.

"Hi, Mom." She stood and hugged her mom, keeping her engagement ring hidden so the cat didn't leap out of the bag before she and Mark were ready to make the announcement.

"Hi, sweetie. You look well." Her mom's sentiment was genuine, and Karma got the feeling her mom was the one who'd convinced her dad to be nice and behave himself.

"So do you." She sat back down, her mom on her right, Mark on her left, and her dad across from her.

The four sat in awkward silence while the conversations of the other diners murmured around them.

Her mom was the first to speak. "So, Mark, how are things at Solar?"

"Very good, thank you. Not as enjoyable now that Karma no longer works there, but business is good."

Her mom and dad shot her confused glances.

"You no longer work at Solar?" her mom said.

She met Mark's eye just as he appeared to realize she hadn't yet told her parents about her new job.

"I'm sorry," he said quietly. "I thought you'd told them."

"Not yet." She forced a smile then looked back to her mom. "I left back in December."

"Why?" Her dad's voice held an accusation he didn't express, but he clearly thought she'd been booted because of Mark.

Before he could say something he would regret, she said, "It was my choice, Dad."

"But I thought you liked it there."

"I did, but now that"—her gaze flew to Mark's again—"Mark and I are together, I decided to leave. They offered to transfer me into another department, but those positions didn't appeal to me." She fiddled with her napkin. "So, my old college professor helped me get a job as a junior editor for Winstrom Press in Chicago."

"That's terrific, honey," her mom said. "You always wanted to work in publishing."

"Thanks, I did."

But her dad simply scowled. "And you didn't take five minutes to tell us."

Her mouth fell open. "You haven't exactly been receptive to talking to me lately, Dad."

He squared his shoulders and avoided meeting her mom's accusing, I-told-you-so stare. "Well, you still could have told us sooner than this."

Ah, ever too proud to admit he was wrong.

Irritation rustled beneath her skin. She couldn't believe her dad was making this out to be her fault.

Mark seemed to sense her growing distress and took her hand.

"Karma has been so busy. I'm sure it just slipped her mind." And there was her Mark. Her fiancé. Genial peacekeeper. Tempering her fire by taking some of the oxygen out of the room, but not so much that she disappeared completely. "I surprised her with a trip to the Caribbean over Christmas, and once we got back, she started her new job. And then there are the classes she's taking, which are required for new editors, and, well . . ." From his expression, he was thinking about the house they were moving into in less than a week, as well as the ring on her finger. "It's just been a really busy couple of months."

Her dad harrumphed. "My daughter doesn't need you speaking for her."

Her blood instantly boiled. "He's not speaking for me. I — "

Mark squeezed her hand, cutting her off.

She slouched against the back of her chair. This dinner was falling off course fast. How dare her dad make such accusations against Mark when he'd been dictating how she lived her life since as far back as she could remember. Maybe her dad hadn't spoken for her, and maybe he hadn't told her what to do, but he'd always made his expectations clear. And when she failed to deliver, he'd made his disappointment just as clear, too, which was as bad as, if not worse than, speaking on her behalf, because it affected her more deeply on a psychological level.

Like with Brad. Her dad had wanted her to marry Brad. She hadn't wanted to. By breaking off their engagement, she had suffered her dad's silent treatment as retaliation. It was his way of trying to influence her to go back to Brad, even though he knew she wouldn't.

True, this was the first time he'd gone to such lengths to make his displeasure known, but she'd also never stood so steadfastly against him on such an important issue. Not even when she chose to leave the engineering program at Purdue to pursue journalism instead. Her dad had been furious over that, and he still hadn't quite forgiven her for walking away from what he saw as a lucrative, successful career as an engineer to become a "lowly" writer, but this was her life, not her dad's. And she planned on living it the way she wanted to from now on.

"Forgive me," Mark said. "I realize she can speak for herself, Mr. Mason, but . . ." He pressed his lips into a thin line, nodding tightly as if a path had just presented itself and he'd decided to take it. "Well, sir, I know you don't like me, and I just want to prove to you that I have your daughter's best interests at heart and love her more than anything. And maybe that makes me try too hard to maintain the peace between you two and show you I'm not a bad guy." He paused, eyebrows tight. "I hate that I'm the reason why you and Karma haven't spoken since Thanksgiving. I hate seeing her so upset and knowing I'm responsible for that."

She squeezed his hand, drawing his gaze to hers. Shaking her head, she said, "It's not your fault."

"It's no one person's fault, but if I hadn't fallen in love with you, you and your dad wouldn't be at odds with one another, so I have to take responsibility for my part in this, whether I would change it or not." He turned back to her dad. "And I wouldn't. I will never stop loving your daughter. I can't. She's everything to me, and there's no way I can see a future without her."

Her mom was practically holding her breath, as if she sensed what was coming. As for her dad, a combination of shame, acceptance, and prideful resistance fell over his expression.

Mark lifted her left hand to the table. "Which is why I've asked her to marry me." He removed his hand, revealing the ring.

This was not how they'd planned to tell her parents about their engagement, but, in a way, it was perfect. Even *better* than their plan.

Score one for spontaneity. Maybe there was hope for Mark yet.

Her mom squealed and reached for Karma's hand to get a closer look at the diamond.

Her dad, on the other hand, recoiled and frowned. His upper lip curled in disgust. But at least he didn't make a scene. Instead, he sat quietly, seething.

"Dad?" she prompted. "Aren't you going to congratulate us?"

She deserved that much. He could at least give her that.

He cleared his throat and said, "Congratulations." But the word came out like a tight, dissatisfied grumble instead of a sincere expression of good will. And he didn't offer to shake Mark's hand, either, to welcome him to the family.

Still, his response was a step in the right direction. It showed her dad was making strides, even if they were teeny-tiny baby strides only a microscope could record.

"Thank you," Mark said, maintaining a low key.

"Goodness, Karma." Her mom gushed over the ring. "This is beautiful. Just gorgeous." She hugged her, obviously delighted even if her dad was still cool to the idea. "So, when's the wedding?"

"Well . . ." Karma glanced at Mark. What was she supposed to say? They still hadn't set a date. Surely, now that they were through the hard part with the house and all that remained was moving in, they could choose a date.

Mark's face paled, and he hastily said, "Well, Solar's coming in to spring, which is the busiest time of year, and I'll be doing a lot of traveling and working a lot of late nights, and Karma is swamped with her classes and adjusting to her new job, so we're waiting until things settle down to pick a date. That way, we can focus all our attention on the wedding."

Hold up.

Wait a second.

When had they decided this? The last time the subject of setting a date came up, he had told her they would pick one after they got settled into the house. That was less than two weeks away, so she'd been mentally preparing, looking at her calendar, even doing a little casual legwork to check out the availability of possible venues. And now he was telling her parents they were going to wait until after spring? Until after work calmed down and her classes eased up.

She had news for him on that front. Her classes lasted a year.

They wouldn't ease up until *next* spring. And then Solar would be back into the busy season again. So, what? Was he saying they weren't even going to pick a date until next *year*? Next summer, to be exact?

She was starting to get a little peeved.

"I thought we'd decided we would choose a date after we moved into the house," she said, her voice edged with suspicion.

"House? What house?" her dad said.

Mark cringed and closed his eyes.

Oops. She hadn't meant to reveal they were on the verge of living in sin, at least not like this. They'd been saving that conversation for later in the meal, after letting her dad first get used to the idea they were engaged.

"Oh, um . . ." She felt the color drain from her face. "About that. Mark and I are moving in together."

"You're what?" Her dad's booming voice drew the attention of several nearby diners. "You just got engaged." He shook his head, eyes wide. "You were engaged to Brad less than four months ago, Karma. You and Mark are barely back together, and you're moving in with him?"

"Dad—"

"No, Karma. I've heard enough." He stood. "I was keeping an open mind about your relationship. I even had a feeling the two of you had done something as ill-advised as getting engaged when you haven't even been together four months, but I was willing to let you sort it out. But now you're moving in with him? No, Karma. This is too much. You're not ready. You haven't been back together with him long enough to be ready for this."

She stood and threw her cloth napkin on the table. "Who's trying to talk for me now, Dad? Huh? *'You're not ready'*? How about you let *me* decide when I'm ready? How about you let *me* make my own decisions and you simply support them? Because I would really appreciate that."

They were causing a scene, but Karma didn't care. She'd walked into the restaurant already emotionally keyed up about breaking bread with her dad and Mark at the same table. And then her dad had started in on Mark and ticked her off, and now Mark dropped this huge bomb on her that he still wasn't ready to set a date, and now it felt like her entire evening was crashing like a defunct satellite into the ocean, the wreckage sinking fast.

"I need some air." Her dad started for the door.

"John!" Her mom stared after him then looked back up at Karma.

She slumped into her chair. "Just go, Mom. I'm sorry."

Her mom took her hand and squeezed. "I'm sorry about this, honey. I'll talk to him. He'll come around. Just give him time."

"Well, hell, I seem to have all the time in the world right now, so, sure . . . whatever." Humiliation and anger wrestled inside her chest, making her heart hurt.

Her mom gave her a sympathetic, if not confused, look then stood and addressed Mark. "Thank you for inviting us to dinner. I wish . . ." She shrugged sheepishly. "I'm sorry." With that, she hurried off after her dad.

Silence engulfed them, the air feeling like dead weight.

Mark tried to take her hand, but she snatched it away and spun on him.

"When did you decide to postpone setting a date until after spring?"

"Karma—"

"No, Mark. You told me we would set a date after we moved into the house. We're doing that this week. And now you surprise me during dinner with my parents by announcing you've decided for *both* of us that we're still not ready?"

"I—"

"Just forget it. Take me home." She got up, clutching her pocketbook, and shoved her chair under her table.

Chagrined, Mark slowly stood and followed her back to the entrance, where he retrieved their coats. But she refused to let him help her into hers. She yanked it from his hands and put it on herself then didn't wait for him as she stormed out the door.

At her apartment, they climbed into bed as silently as they'd driven there. It took forever to fall asleep, but she must have, because she awoke in the morning nestled in his arms.

Damn traitorous sleep, always betraying her. She wanted to stay angry with him. Wanted to make him hurt as much as he'd hurt her. But lying there, listening to his peaceful, even breathing, smelling the subtle remains of his cologne from the night before mixed with the scent of his sweat, all she wanted was to cuddle closer.

She had to force herself to pull away.

He wouldn't win her back over that easily. She needed to make a statement. To let him know she wasn't happy about what he'd done, nor about how he'd made her feel.

Not even trying to be quiet, she went to the bathroom and flipped on the water for the shower then shut the door. She didn't slam it, but she also didn't let the latch quietly snick closed. Mark was an early riser, anyway. He could get his ass up and suffer knowing she was still upset.

He instinctively knew to give her space, because when she got out of the shower, he was no longer in the bedroom and the shower in the hallway bathroom was running.

The apartment smelled of eggs, toast, and sausage, though. Then she saw the plate of food he'd left for her on the dresser alongside a small cup of tea and a note.

I'm sorry. Please forgive me. -M

Aw, so okay, that was sweet. No denying it. Still, a sweet gesture wasn't enough to get him out of the dog house just yet.

She set the note down, dressed, and then sat on the edge of the bed while she ate. Still, she wasn't going to give him the satisfaction of forgiving him. Not yet.

By the time she finished breakfast, brushed her teeth, and tossed the last few items in her overnight bag for their trip to Chicago, it was six forty-five. Mark appeared from the bathroom dressed and clean-shaven.

"Good morning." He cautiously eyed her.

"Morning." She raised her chin and carried her bags to the living room after shutting off the bedroom light.

He sighed and joined her, holding a small duffel. "You still haven't forgiven me for last night?" He set down his bag and grabbed their coats from the rack by the door.

"No." She took her coat from him and slid it on then crossed her arms as he made one last check of the apartment to make sure everything was turned off.

When he returned and took her bags before she could pick them up, she relented a little and said, "By the way, thank you for breakfast." But like her dad, she was too stubborn to give more than an inch.

"You're welcome." He smiled and met her eyes knowingly then opened the door.

With a quiet huff, she exited and started down the stairs.

This was going to be a long, uncomfortable ride to Chicago.

Chapter 16

*Sometimes couples have to argue, not to prove who's right or wrong, but to
be reminded that their love is worth fighting for.*
-Nishan Panwar

They were on their way back to where it all began. Chicago.

The Chicago Arts Coalition's annual benefit wasn't for a couple
more months, but she and Mark had already received their
invitation. Well, Mark had. She was his plus one.

And right now, staring out the passenger window of his BMW,
she was a brooding, still-upset-with-him plus one. And conflicted.

Maybe it was last night's fight or the fact he continued putting
off choosing a date, but that tiny part of her that still dwelled in
insecurity's realm poked its head from around the corner of her
mind and took a step into the light.

Did she really fit into his world? Look at how refined he was. She
was simple, unaccustomed to extravagances like gold silverware
and real china on her dining room table, attending elegant parties
with the Who's Who of Chicago's elite, and dropping ten thousand
dollars on chartered flights to the Caribbean.

For the past few weeks, she'd been excited about moving in with
Mark, but now the fact she was shacking up with a rich man
unsettled her. He hadn't changed, but something in her perspective
had. She blamed the voices of self-doubt, though, not him. And not
the woman she'd become. It was her past coming back to haunt her.
The voices telling her she wasn't good enough. That she and Mark
were too different. That they would never work, because she would
always be too humble to handle his wealth.

Of course, reason scoffed at such claims. But right now, fear took
the floor, so whatever words reason offered fell flat.

She was going to meet his parents today, for God's sake. His
worldly parents who owned homes in Italy, London, and Paris.
They were people who walked in small circles open only to card-
carrying members, of which she wasn't one.

The question assaulted her thoughts again. What if she didn't fit
into Mark's world? What if, after she met his parents, it became clear

she was like a glass of milk served with grapefruit salad? The two just didn't go together and damn near curled your toes clean off if you tried to mix them.

Karma didn't want to be milk. She wanted to be sugar. A sweet, perfect complement to tart grapefruit

Despite their argument, she still wanted inside his world. Not as a bystander, but as an active participant who belonged there.

The fact he came from money and possessed enough to bathe in was her problem, not his. This was *her* hang-up. She needed to figure out a way to deal with her concerns, but she also needed to make sure he knew she didn't want to sponge off his inheritance. As she'd told him before, she wasn't a gold digger, and she didn't want to come off like one. That wasn't why she'd fallen in love with him.

Why did money have to be such an issue?

Hopefully, over time, she would get used to this new dynamic. Maybe in a year she would look back and laugh at how neurotic she'd been over the fact he had millions.

Right. She didn't think she would ever get used to that.

Sighing softly, she forced herself to think about happier memories, such as the night they'd met.

She'd been so nervous sitting at that blackjack table while Daniel was off playing poker.

And then there he was. Dark. Mysterious. Handsome. Magnanimous.

Her Mark. Warning her not to take a hit on her cards. But she had anyway. She'd asked for another card only to bust. That had been the start of what she could only describe as an incredible, breathtaking, heartbreaking, and magical journey that led them to right now. In love, engaged, and embarking on both a scary and exciting path into the future.

"What are you thinking about?"

She broke from her reverie and glanced across the seat at him. "Hmm?"

"I just wanted to know what was making you smile like that?"

"Was I smiling?" She hadn't noticed, but now, as her cheeks warmed, she realized she still was.

"Yes, you were."

Their fight and her lingering resistance faltered as she glanced at him and saw the man she'd seen two years ago. Handsome. Powerful. Confident. Master of the universe. At least, of *her* universe. "I was thinking about the night we met."

A grin touched his lips, and a soft, reflective chuckle broke from his throat. "Did I ever tell you about the moment I saw you the very first time? I mean, what I thought the very second I saw you?"

The chill that had plagued them since leaving her apartment instantly dissipated. "I don't think so." If he had, she couldn't remember.

He reached for her hand. She laced her fingers between his.

"I was standing across the room drinking a scotch. At least I think it was scotch. I was feeling pretty miserable and down on my luck." He paused, and a wistful expression fell over his face as if he were remembering. "And then there you were." He shot her a quick, adoring glance. "It was like the sea parted and led my eyes straight to you. God, you were beautiful. You still are." Another glance, a little longer this time, a little more reverent.

Whatever problems stood between them, Mark clearly loved her beyond compare, still as smitten with her now as he had been then. Warmth spilled through her body, and she knew she was blushing from head to toe.

"That red dress"—his eyes darted to her as if he could still see her wearing it—"was almost criminal. You were stunning in that dress. The most alluring woman in the room." His fingers tightened around hers. "And I remember you looked so uncomfortable." He chuckled. "You kept fidgeting and running your hand down the skirt as if you wanted to ensure it wasn't showing off too much of your gorgeous legs."

She giggled quietly as she remembered how awkward she'd felt in that dress. That night was a lifetime ago. She'd come so far. "I'll admit, I've become a lot more comfortable wearing clothes like that."

"Yes, you have." He enforced the sentiment with another squeeze of his hand around hers. "But that night, you looked almost terrified. You had no idea how to handle all the attention, but I could tell you secretly loved it. That's when I knew you just needed a little push and you'd discover how sexual you are."

In the months that followed, he had definitely pushed her. And he'd awakened hidden desires she hadn't known she possessed. He still had the power to do that.

"I remember thinking you looked like a princess meeting the public for the first time," he said. "You liked the attention, but it intimidated you and you didn't yet have the experience to know how to respond." He paused, his expression tender yet possessive. "I knew the moment I saw you that I had to know you. And when I got to know you, I knew I had to have you."

The declaration sent a thrill through her, and warmth pooled between her legs. In this moment, Mark was completely open, and so was she. At times like this was when they became magical. This was when they became one.

His thumb gently stroked the back of her hand. "When the seat opened next to you, I took it. I refused to let anyone else take the opportunity I knew was meant for me. I never imagined it would lead to this. That we would be here now, almost two years later, still together." He lifted her hand and kissed her fingers. "You gave me the greatest gift that night. You blessed me with your presence. When every man in the room wanted you at his side, you were at mine. You chose me." He tore his gaze from the road to glance at her. "You chose me, Karma, and for that I will always be grateful. You found me. You made me a better man."

She scooted to the edge of her seat, leaned over the center console, and pressed her cheek to his shoulder. This was what she loved so much about Mark. He made her feel special. So very special. And loved. If only every woman had a man who made them feel this way, the world would be a better place.

"I love you," she said, wrapping her arm around his torso.

He kissed the top of her head. "I love you, too, princess."

She giggled. "I'm not a princess."

"You're *my* princess."

Once they reached the Palmer House Hilton in Chicago, they couldn't get to their room fast enough. His parents had offered to let them stay at their home, but Mark had insisted on a hotel, and as rabid as they were to be alone, she was thankful he had.

The moment they'd lost last night rose up higher, stronger, more intensely, demanding they commune in the most intimate way known to man and woman.

As soon as the bell hop unloaded their luggage and the door shut behind him on the way out, Mark pressed her against the wall then lifted her so she could wrap her legs around his waist.

His kisses blazed, his caresses burned, and his body surged against hers like a blast of hot air. All Karma could do was hold on, grapple for purchase, and pray she didn't pass out.

As he entered her on the bed a few minutes later, she came. And as he pummeled her body in an unrivaled sensory onslaught, she came again, and again, and still yet again.

He flipped her over, held down her arms, bit the back of her shoulder, and gripped her hips so harshly she knew she'd find bruises there later.

One awful fight and the resulting sexual frustration it had created blasted out of them, culminating in one of the most intense sexual experiences she'd ever had.

When Mark finally collapsed against her back, his cock pulsing inside her, filling the condom he'd managed to roll on somewhere in the midst of transporting her into nirvana, she came again, shuddering in his grasp.

The last bricks of the wall that had gone up between them last night fell, and for a couple of hours, they forgot the world.

Then it was time to get ready to leave.

"Do I look okay?" Karma brushed her hands down the front of her off-the-shoulder grey knit top. The fabric was silky and draped alluringly over her breasts and torso. She wore a black camisole underneath, and a long, silver necklace adorned with round circular links hung around her neck. She'd completed the outfit with dark grey denim trousers and stylish black ankle boots.

"You look perfect." Mark kissed her and helped her into her coat. "Don't be nervous."

He had helped her pick out the outfit and unintentionally matched her in his own denim trousers and dark-grey sweater.

Still, she was second-guessing their decision not to dress more formally. "I feel like we should have dressed up more."

"We're fine. Trust me." He whisked her out the door before she could object further.

His parents' house was magnificent. A behemoth of brown bricks with white trim and a slate-grey roof. Four massive columns rose from five-foot-tall pedestals in front of the paned-glass entrance. It looked exactly like the type of house a millionaire would live in. Easily three times the size of their new home. Maybe even four.

"You grew up here?" she asked as he pulled in front of the wide steps leading to the front door. Which was really an understatement. How did you call *that* a front door? It looked more like the entryway to a palace.

"Yes," he said, shutting off the engine.

"And you *weren't* popular in school?" She remembered him telling her how he'd been bullied, but she couldn't see how someone with this much money couldn't be one of the cool kids. If he'd gone to the school she'd attended, he'd have been the most popular boy there.

"It was a very elitist school."

Shit. She didn't want to see the houses of those other kids if this was considered the low end of the elite spectrum.

"I guess."

The valet—*valet?* The Strongs had their own valet?—opened the door for him as another opened her door and held out his hand to help her out of the car. She took it and stood, gaping at the impressive mansion.

Mark joined her, and she wrapped her arm around his as the valet drove his car around to the back to where Karma was sure she'd find a parking lot fit for thirty cars, maybe more.

"We're a bit later than I wanted to be," Mark said, hurrying her up the stairs. "They're sure to be making final preparations for the party, and guests will start arriving soon if they haven't already."

A butler opened the door and welcomed them inside.

Karma didn't know where to look first. Up or down. An expanse of gleaming, polished marble stretched in all directions beneath her feet, lit by an enormous crystal chandelier that hung like falling shards of ice from the ceiling. The crown molding gracing the tops of the white walls was more like art than architecture, and twin, winding staircases curved up either side of the substantial foyer. In the center, directly below the rounded balcony that looked over the foyer, sat a table black as onyx, upon which stood a colossal flower arrangement inside a massive hand-painted vase. Bright-pink roses, yellow daffodils, tall sprigs of lavender, and white Star lilies gave the foyer its only splash of color. But what a splash it was. More like an explosion in the otherwise colorless but opulent entryway.

Then she glanced at the butler. He wore a black and white tuxedo — with tails. She suddenly felt severely underdressed. She was so not in Kansas, anymore. If the hired help could make her feel this inadequate, how would the other guests make her feel?

"Welcome home, sir," the butler said.

"Thank you, Henry. You look splendid."

"Thank you, sir. May I take your coats?"

"Yes, please." Mark helped her out of hers. "Karma, meet Henry. Henry, this is Karma Mason." He offered no explanation as to their relationship status. Then again, he was proper enough to know he should tell his parents they were engaged before he told Henry.

Henry's expression perked as he regarded her, taking her coat from Mark. "My pleasure, miss." He gave a little sideways bow of his head, obviously understanding exactly how special she was in Mark's life for him to bring her home to meet the parents.

She nervously nibbled her bottom lip. "Nice to meet you, too."

Henry took Mark's coat, smiling. "Nice to see you're finally settling down, sir."

Mark chuckled. "Okay, Henry, stop calling me sir." He turned toward her. "Henry only behaves this way when my parents have a party. Don't let him fool you. He's a scoundrel. And excellent at cards. He's the one who taught me how to play blackjack and poker."

"I've never seen you play poker," she said.

"I never really liked the game."

Henry glanced side-to-side as if making sure he wasn't being watched, then he took a step forward, grinning mischievously as he spoke to Karma. "He only doesn't like the game because he played against someone once who apparently had a better poker face than he does and ended up losing ten thousand dollars of his inheritance."

She shot him a questioning glance. "Ten thousand dollars?"

That shadow Karma thought was gone made a reappearance and flashed across Mark's face. "It was the last time I ever played." He shifted his gaze to Henry. "And quit telling her stories like that,

Henry, or you'll scare her away." He meant it as a joke, but Karma could hear the hint of fear in his voice.

Henry winked and took a step back, becoming the picture of propriety again. "Of course, sir."

"Good man." Mark took her hand and led her in the direction of conversation and laughter as Henry opened the coat closet to put away their coats.

She stole a peek into the extra-large, lighted, walk-in closet as they passed. Fur. A lot of fur jackets hung inside. And purses that looked like they could put Coach to shame. She was fairly certain she saw a gold Chanel emblem on one made of baby's-butt-soft leather the color of honey. At least it *looked* baby's-butt-soft. And there went her black, quilted North Face coat to mingle with the designer labels. Her poor coat was going to get an inferiority complex in there.

And didn't she knew how it felt? She was way out of her league here. If this party were a representation of the food chain, her league was somewhere down around small farm animals. A lamb or potbelly pig. The people she was about to meet were lions. If she wasn't careful, they'd eat her alive.

"You're so tense," Mark whispered, squeezing her hand. "Relax."

"I'm trying." She took a few deep breaths. "It's just . . . this place is really big. Bigger than I imagined. It's kind of intimidating."

"Try not to think about that."

"Okay, okay." She needed to get her mind off the grandeur oozing the smell of money all around her. "Remind me again what your parents' names are. Adler and Giada, right?

"That's right. Adler is a family name, and Giada is Italian."

"Giada. Like the chef, right?"

He frowned as if confused.

"You know," she said, "the petite, wafer-thin Italian chef with the big teeth who's always smiling? The one on the Food Network who always calls it *mozzarella*?" She did her best at pronouncing the word with an authentic Italian accent.

"You mean, *mozzarella*?" He corrected her, making what was such a familiar word sound intensely foreign . . . and a bit sexy. Like a new word altogether.

"Yeah, that." She smirked at his teasing grin. "But that Giada. You know who I'm talking about, right?"

"*Sì. Credo di sapere di chi stai parlando, adesso.*"

She both loved and hated when he threw his Italian at her. Loved it because it sounded provocative. Hated it because she couldn't understand a lick of what he said.

"What did you just say?"

He ushered her through a hall with toffee-colored walls toward a set of open double doors. "I said that I think I know who you're talking about now."

"Show off."

He chuckled as he guided her into a grand ballroom as opulent as the one at the Palmer House Hilton, only on a much smaller scale. Still, that wasn't to say the place wasn't huge. It was. Bigger than eight of her apartments combined. Maybe more. It was hard to compare the square footage.

About a dozen people dressed in everything from suits and flirty cocktail dresses to tuxedos and evening gowns sat in a sitting area along the far wall, drinks in hand, caught up in discussion.

She exchanged glances with Mark, wordlessly conveying her anxiety over dressing so casually. But he merely grinned, winked, and pulled her into the room as if everything were normal.

"Marcus!"

All heads turned their way as a slender, elegant woman who had to be Mark's mom rose from her seat at the head of the group, threw out her arms, and glided toward them, holding herself like a queen coming to welcome home her son, the prince. A man bearing a striking resemblance to Mark followed.

"Happy birthday, *Mamma*." Mark hugged her. Then he shook his dad's hand.

"It's so good to see you." Giada's Italian accent graced every syllable. She stood back and looked Mark up and down. "You look good. Lean. Like a tiger." She winked at him then turned her gaze on Karma, her smile beaming. "And you must be Karma." Without warning, Giada enveloped her in a strong, consuming embrace. "The one to steal my son's heart." She spoke softly but proudly, as if she had never thought this day would come. Then she released her and pulled back, her dark eyes—eyes so much like Mark's in the same shade of dark green—dancing over Karma's face. "And so lovely." She turned toward Mark. "You've done well, Marcus."

He took Karma's hand and gave her a look that came across as part relief, part pride. "She honors me, *Mamma*."

"That she does." Giada pinched Mark's cheek.

"Pleasure to meet you, Karma. I'm Adler, Mark's father." Adler shifted his glass of wine to his left hand and extended his right. He had a firm handshake, just like Mark's.

"Nice to meet you," she said.

Adler and Giada held themselves almost regally, but not haughtily. Shoulders relaxed, backs straight, heads held high, with warm, generous smiles on their faces. They definitely possessed the posture of champion ballroom dancers.

Mark glanced toward the group in the sitting area. "I was hoping Karma and I could have a few minutes of privacy with both of you before the party."

Giada beamed. "Of course." She gestured toward the door. "Let's go somewhere we can talk." She stopped a waiter on their way out. "Could you bring four glasses of champagne to the sitting room, please?"

"Certainly."

And then Karma was following Mark's parents into a smaller, elegantly appointed room with burgundy walls, furnished with a green and gold settee, a solid dark-green upholstered sofa, which looked more grey than green once she got closer, and two burnished-gold club chairs. A small fire crackled in the brick fireplace, which was framed by a mahogany mantle adorned with a collection of ceramic cats, some small, others almost life-sized.

Karma peered closer, admiring one that was solid matte-black, smooth and sitting tall and proud the way she'd seen cats in Egyptian paintings.

"My mom collects cats," Mark said from beside her, his hand resting on the small of her back. "When I was in your apartment the first time and saw your collection of ceramic elephants, it reminded me of them." He turned an affectionate smile toward her, their eyes meeting.

"And of your mom," she added.

"Yes."

The memory was a delicate connection to their past. To how they met, as well as the first time she invited him into her home. Now his interest in her collectibles made more sense. Why hadn't he just said then that his mom collected ceramic cats, which was why her elephants had caught his eye?

Karma glanced back to the matte-black cat as the answer came to her in a flash of clarity. That night, Mark had had no intention of letting their relationship come this far. At the time, he'd still believed he could simply walk away and not fall in love with her. So of course he wouldn't have revealed anything personal about him or his family. That hadn't been part of his plan.

Ever the planner, he'd never seen her coming, had he?

Contained. That was how Mark had lived until they met. Self-contained within an impenetrable skin. And yet... she had penetrated him all the way to the center of his heart.

Love and hope and something that felt like a bubble full of giggles expanded inside her chest, and she slid her arm around his waist, pressing closer. His arm eased securely around her waist in response. They were cause and effect. Echoes of one another. When she moved, he moved. Theirs was such a personal, almost supernatural weaving of motion.

Almost like a dance.

It was just one more piece of evidence proving she had succeeded where all others had failed. Isn't that what he'd told her? That she had enabled him to love again? Not because she'd held a gun to his head and told him to love her or die. No. She'd gotten through and awakened his heart by letting him go. By freeing him to fly back out into the world without her. Only then had he seen how important she was to him.

He'd told her all this over the last four months, but it hadn't fully sunk in until this very moment. He'd said all the words, but now she felt their impact.

He loved her. Really, truly, deeply loved her. And it was because she'd let him walk away that he'd realized that.

Mark had come back. For her. And even though he wasn't the perfect man she'd built him up as in her mind, he was so much more. Still larger than life. Charitable. Thoughtful. Almost to a fault.

Humble.

Strange how she now saw Mark as humble when two summers ago, she never would have used that word to describe him. Back then, he'd been almost cocky. But that was before she knew he had millions. A person wasn't able to hide wealth like that if they didn't possess humility.

Giada appeared at her side and lifted down one of the figurines. Her long, elegant fingers caressed the shiny surface as if she were holding a baby. "You collect, too?"

Karma nodded. "Yes. Elephants."

"Why elephants?"

"I got one as a gift when I was younger, and then I got another, and before long, I had a whole set. How did you start collecting cats?"

Giada's eyes sparkled. "I've always loved cats, but Adler's allergic. So, since I can't have real cats, anymore, I surround myself with these." She drew her hand through the air in front of the mantle.

"She has an entire curio of them in the family room and two more in the upstairs hall," Adler added. "And plenty more displayed around the house.

Giada set down the cat then reached for Karma's left hand, her thumb stroking down her ring finger as she lifted it.

Karma bit her lip and exchanged a worried glance with Mark. His face was relaxed, but his expression filled with awareness and expectation. His gaze dropped to her hand in his mom's.

"I assume this is what you wanted to discuss with us, yes, Marcus?" Giada tilted her head maternally, in a way that said, "I'm your mother. How did you think I wouldn't notice such an engagement ring on Karma's finger?"

She had probably spotted the ring the moment she laid eyes on her from across the room a few minutes ago.

"Yes." Mark's subdued voice did nothing to hide the way he lifted his chin and chest, the rooster strutting, wearing a purely masculine grin, possessive and proud. "Karma and I are engaged."

Giada closed her eyes and drew in a long, deep breath as a smile spread over her face.

"Congratulations, son," Adler said, shaking Mark's hand.

Unshed tears glistened Giada's eyes when she opened them

again, and she slowly shook her head as she took both Karma's hands. "I never thought . . ." She sighed as if forcing herself not to cry. "Welcome to the family, Karma. What a lovely birthday present this is."

Giada swept her into her arms and hugged her close, whispering, "Thank you for making my son happy. I never thought he would find such happiness again. Thank you. Just . . . thank you." She almost sounded like she was praying.

When Giada finally released her, she quickly brushed her fingertips under her eyes and blinked rapidly, glancing away from Mark as if she didn't want him to see her crying.

The waiter returned with flutes of champagne, which Adler passed around.

"A toast," he said, raising his glass. "To my son and his future bride."

Everyone clinked glasses and drank. It was a far different reception to the news than they'd received from her parents the night before. Or rather, from her dad. Her mom had been happy enough.

"So," Giada said, "when is the big day? When's the wedding?" She looked expectantly from her to Mark.

Whoosh!

There went all the air in the room. Sucked out as if by a factory-sized vacuum. And most of the warm and fuzzy gushiness she'd felt toward Mark barely five minutes ago rushed out with it. She'd only just forgiven him for springing the news that he wanted to wait until summer to set a date, and now, right on the heels of their ugly fight's demise, came an unwelcome reminder of it.

When neither she nor Mark answered, Giada's smile wavered. "You *have* set a date, haven't you? You can't get engaged and not set a date."

Apparently, in Mark's world, you could. Too bad they didn't live in Giada's.

"We're waiting until after things slow down at work," Karma said, darting an accusing glance toward Mark. "And I just started a new job and have classes, sooo . . ." She sounded like she was making excuses for why her homework wasn't done. *You see, there was a pile of dishes in the sink, and I needed to take the car in for an oil*

*change, and then my dog ate all the pencils in the apartment and I was too
busy trying to come up with believable excuses about why my homework
wasn't done to actually do it, so that's why it's not finished. My bad.*

Damn Mark for sucking her into his delay game. Now *she* was
spouting his excuses, even though she didn't buy them for a second.
He'd put her in an awkward position. One that felt more like a trap.

"And we just bought a house," Mark added, "so we're trying to
get settled there, too."

Nice diversion, Mark.

"A house!" Giada pressed her hands together in supplication.
"How lovely. You must invite us down once you get settled."

Mark took out his phone and pulled up a series of pictures he'd
taken during their first walk-thru, seeming all too content to let the
subject of their pending nuptials fall into the background.

She was getting the feeling Mark would never be ready to set a
date, even though she didn't have much to base that on. Her gut just
told her this was an issue. That his reticence wasn't just a passing
irritation but a huge problem. The question was why?

Somehow, she knew Carol was part of the answer. Mark had
confessed everything else that had been holding him back. But he
still never talked about Carol. She needed to find a way to get that
woman out of their lives if she and Mark were going to have their
happily ever after.

"Well," Giada said, studying Karma with a compassionate eye,
"you don't want to wait too long to set a date, Marcus, especially if
you're trying for June."

Karma looked at Mark as he stuffed his phone back in his pocket,
but he avoided meeting her gaze.

She wanted to say, "See, I told you so." Lisa had said the same
thing about trying for June, and now his mom said the same thing.

Of course, they didn't *have* to have a June wedding, but, in all
honesty, Karma wouldn't mind one. June was her favorite month.
Not too hot, not too cold. On the precipice of summer. Colorful with
everything newly come back to life after winter. It was the perfect
month to get married . . . for new beginnings.

Oh well, there was always *next* June.

As long as Mark didn't put a kibosh in that, too.

Chapter 17

A true friend never gets in your way unless you happen to be going down.
-Arnold H. Glasow

Karma nibbled on a tasty *amuse-bouche,* as Mark called it. Single, bite-sized *hors d'oeuvres.* This one was a tiny cheese and bacon stuffed pastry decorated with chopped baby lettuce and herbs.

Waiters carried tray after tray of *amuse-bouches* among the guests. Cherry tomatoes cut in half with tiny chunks of mozzarella between the two halves and speared on a toothpick with a small strip of fresh basil; bacon-wrapped shrimp; bite-sized gourmet pizzas; finger sandwiches; sushi; even miniature bowls of different kinds of soup, and so much more. Karma had yet to see two trays alike.

Then, of course, there were the drink trays. The party was a smorgasbord of fine food and potables.

"Tell me about this poker game that ended your poker-playing days," she said, dusting her hands on a cocktail napkin as Mark grabbed them two more flutes of champagne from a passing tray.

Mark handed one to her, his eyes shifting restlessly. "What's there to say?"

Had they not gotten past all this secrecy by now? "Obviously, quite a lot, from the way you're dodging the question." She crossed one arm over her chest, holding her glass in the other.

Wilting, his head dropped to one side as he met her gaze. "Okay, I'll tell you, but you're probably going to think I'm a flake."

"You? A flake?" He might be flaking on setting a wedding date, but in all else, flaky was not in Mark's bio.

He held up one hand. "Just . . . okay . . . here's what happened. I was out with a bunch of friends. Rob, a few of the guys I worked with, a couple of buddies from school . . . and Antonio."

"Antonio?" Why was that name familiar? It was something important.

"Carol's dance partner," he reminded her.

Her eyes opened wide. "Ooohhhh." Antonio. The guy who stole Carol out from under him.

Mark took a sip of champagne and moved them away from the

bar. "I was winning big. Really raking in the chips."

"You played with real money? Not just for fun?"

"We usually just played for chips, but that night, it was for real. Real money. Real stakes."

And why not? He was filthy stinking rich.

"I was up ten thousand dollars and was dealt an amazing hand. Full house. Aces high. Only two hands could beat that. Four of a kind and a straight flush. The odds were in my favor, so as the bets came around, and players dropped out while others—Rob included—continued to bet, I went all in. When Antonio turned his cards, he had four queens. Four of a kind. The bastard had never even flinched. Talk about your poker faces. I thought he might have had a straight or a flush, or maybe even a lower full house than mine to keep betting, but the prick had four of a kind." The shadow that wouldn't completely die played over his face.

"When was this?"

He snorted and shook his head as he glanced down into his glass. "My bachelor party. Can you believe that? Not only was Antonio fucking my fiancée behind my back, stealing her away from me, but he beat me at my own game. He took my ten thousand dollars *and* my fiancée." His gaze drifted away as if he were watching a memory. Then he snapped out of it and glanced back at her as he sipped his drink. "I never played again."

"She really hurt you, didn't she?"

"They both did."

She frowned into her glass, her teeth worrying the inside of her bottom lip as her mind churned with a sudden revelation. "Do you think that might be why you're so hesitant to set a date for our wedding?"

"No, no." He shook his head, frowning, responding a little too hastily. "I just . . . you know . . . things are so busy. And I want to be able to focus on our wedding. I don't want to feel rushed, okay?" He took her free hand in his and squeezed. "I promise I'm not intentionally putting it off, Karma." But the fearful shadows darkening his eyes said otherwise. "I want us to be together for the rest of our lives. I swear to you."

But being together was not necessarily the same as getting married. What if Mark was content with simply living together and raising kids without actually tying the knot. What if he was fine with a commitment like that. One where he had no intention of leaving but didn't want to make it legal, either. There were men like that. Good men who were loyal to their women. Who stayed with them through good times and bad, in sickness and in health, until death do they part, even when they weren't legally required to do so. Maybe she and Mark could have such a relationship. Would that be enough for her?

She sighed and glanced up at him. "Okay," she said, relenting. "I just thought talking about her and what happened might help. Or even talking *to* her. I'm not sure if you ever have, but—"

"I'm with you now, Karma. You have me." He shook his head. "Let's enjoy the party and not talk about it, anymore, because, really, there's nothing else to discuss."

Wasn't there? Why did she get the feeling he was diverting again? And just because he didn't want to talk about Carol didn't mean she didn't want to. She had questions. And the more he avoided discussing Carol, the more questions she had.

Before she could push the issue further, Mark's best friend Rob broke through the crowd with a perky blonde at his side.

"Mark, hey, good to see you here," Rob said.

Mark let go of her hand and man-hugged him. "Rob. Man, you look good." He stepped back to Karma's side. "You remember Karma?"

"How could I forget?" Rob shook her hand. "Mark damn near drove me nuts last year when he was back in Chicago obsessing over you."

"Really?" She looked from Rob to Mark. His face flushed crimson.

The blonde giggled. "Yes. Mark definitely had it bad for you. I got to witness some of his mania firsthand. I'm Holly, by the way." She held her hand out, and Karma shook it.

"Nice to meet you." She turned back to Mark. "Is that true? You were *obsessing* over me?" She grinned. "And suffering *mania*? Really?"

Mark tossed a playful glare at Rob. "You just had to open your big mouth, didn't you?"

For the next thirty minutes, Rob and Holly shared stories about

Mark's behavior during the year they'd spent apart. About how he'd blown up at Rob for setting him up on a blind date with an overly talkative Chicago Bulls cheerleader. About the way Mark had snapped at Rob the night he told him he was marrying Holly. About how Mark turned his manic energy toward a crushing cross-training routine, which had allowed Rob to dole out some retribution for all the shit he'd taken, since he'd been Mark's personal trainer.

But even though Mark laughed along with them and even added his own amusing anecdotes, Karma could still see that damn shadow hovering around him, especially when Holly asked, "So, when's the wedding?"

It was like the punchline to a bad joke, and it simply wouldn't go away. Everyone wanted to know when the wedding was, but she didn't have an answer.

Before she could reply with the pre-decided excuses Mark had made, someone brushed her arm.

"Excuse me."

Karma turned to find Giada beside her, taking her hand.

"I'm stealing Karma for a while." Giada pulled her away from Mark's side then wrapped her arm conspiratorially around Karma's, leaning in like they were old friends. "I hope you don't mind, dear, but I want to show you off a bit."

It seemed the news of her and Mark's engagement had made Giada's day, if not her entire year.

Giada pulled her into the other half of the room. Over here, the guests seemed of a different class. Richer. More refined. It was like the party had segregated itself, and she and Mark had remained on the side of the lesser man. Over here was quite another story.

Her head spun as Giada swept her from one person to the next, all of whom were dressed to the nines, wearing more money than she made in a month. And the women! They didn't look real. Like perfectly coifed mannequins, not an ounce of fat on them. One wore a body-hugging sheer black turtleneck with what appeared to be leather leggings on slender legs extending for miles. Except when Karma got closer, she could tell the material was some kind of shiny, stretchy fabric, not leather. And her strappy shoes looked more like art deco than footwear.

This half of the room was definitely a study in the best clothes, shoes, faces, and boobs money could buy. Even some of the men looked botoxed.

She got the once-over more times than not, especially from the women. Through narrowed, suspicious eyes, they efficiently swept over her casual, non-designer attire before they forced a polite, tolerant smile and blinked several times as if waking themselves from a dream. The message conveyed was clear. "You don't belong here."

But she was with Giada, and Giada was the goddess of the evening, so they put on their fake smiles, perfectly feigned all the right congratulatory words when Giada proclaimed she was her future daughter-in-law, and oooed and aaahed over her ring the way they were expected to. Then they huddled in their tiny conclaves, whispering and staring, as Giada led her off. Karma had looked back a couple of times to catch them in the act.

Without saying a word, they let her know she *wasn't* a member of the coveted circle. She *didn't* belong.

Giada glanced across the room and smiled, "They're about to serve cake. Come along, dear."

Karma stopped her. "Um, where's the restroom?"

Giada gestured toward the rear exit from the ballroom. "There's one back there, but if it's occupied, take the stairs to the second floor. There's another down the hall to the left." She leaned in and winked. "That one's only for family."

Family. She was officially family now. If only her dad could be so benevolent.

She slipped out and didn't even waste a stop at the larger community bathroom. She wanted privacy. Somewhere quiet to calm the insecure, paranoid voices in her head, which were telling her she didn't fit in with these people and that they were all talking about her.

Upstairs, she found the restroom, freshened up a bit, and then stepped back into the hall. It was so peaceful up here. She could barely hear the party.

For the first time in over a half hour, she took a full breath. How nice not to have people staring at her, whispering about her, probably making fun of her outfit.

She adjusted the off-the-shoulder collar. As she did, she glanced up and down the hall. It was a lot wider than an average hall in an average house, with carpeting so thick it felt like firm pillows as she took a few steps to the left, away from the stairs leading back down to the party.

Feeling a bit like she was doing something wrong, she placed her hand on a heavy, brass doorknob and twisted. The door opened into a large bedroom not quite as big as the master suite in her and Mark's new house, but bigger than the one in her apartment.

A queen bed rested along the far wall, and walnut bookshelves and a matching built-in desk big enough for a Fortune 500 CEO shared a wall with the door. There was even a leather couch and small end table that held a lamp, as well as another set of bookcases along the far wall.

The room appeared preserved. Like Julia Child's kitchen at the Smithsonian Institute.

Was this Mark's childhood bedroom?

She took a step inside and spied a picture of a much younger Mark wearing a red graduation cap and gown.

It *was* his room. She smiled and walked farther inside, feeling like she'd just found a long-lost piece of Mark's history.

*   *   *

Mark pulled Rob aside. "I need to talk to you." He couldn't let this go on any further.

Rob's face filled with concern. "Is everything all right?"

Mark shook his head. "Yes and no. Let's just . . . I need to talk to you." He nodded toward the exit.

"Okay, give me a second." Rob turned to Holly and said something to her. She nodded then smiled sympathetically at Mark as Rob turned back around. "All right. Where to?"

"Let's go to the pool room."

"Lead the way."

A couple minutes later, Mark opened the door and led Rob inside the room that held his parents' indoor pool. It wasn't a big pool. More of a place for his mom to swim laps. She was an avid swimmer and swam at least fifty laps a day.

Mark flipped on the lights and led Rob to the small bar in back beside the staircase leading to a loft sitting area. He grabbed two bottles of water and a large bag of peanuts in the shell and tossed them on the bar before taking a seat.

"Okay, so what's up?" Rob said. "What's got you so upset? Are you pissed I told all those stories about you from last year? I didn't mean to—"

"Hell, no, I'm not mad about that, Rob."

"Then what's wrong, because I can tell something's wrong."

He blew out a frustrated breath. "I'm fucking everything up. I'm blowing it, Rob." He broke open a peanut with enough force that the nuts flew across the bar. He discarded the shell and grabbed another, opening it more carefully. "I'm totally blowing everything."

"Whoa. Back up. How about you start from the beginning."

Mark let out a sarcastic laugh, meeting Rob's gaze. "I don't even know where the beginning is. All I know is that I'm destroying everything I returned to Indiana for. If I can't get my head together, I'm going to lose her."

This had been eating at him for weeks, ever since he'd told her about his anal fantasies. She hadn't mentioned the conversation again. It was like she was avoiding it.

Last night, he'd started to broach the topic while they'd waited for her parents to join them for dinner, but his timing had been about as good as gunning the gas after the stoplight had already turned red.

"Karma? Are you talking about losing Karma?"

"Yes."

"Okay, so lose her how?"

His laugh sounded as self-deprecating as he felt. "Oh, let me count the ways, Rob." He split open another peanut shell with his thumbs then plucked out the nuts and popped them into his mouth.

"Talk to me, Mark." Rob turned on his barstool to face him. "Let's hear it. Maybe then I'll know how to help."

Mark ran through the conversations he'd had with Karma, trying to figure out where to start. "Okay, the beginning." He broke open another peanut. "Saint Lucia." He glanced at Rob.

"Where you took her for Christmas."

"There was more to that trip than just asking her to marry me."

Rob had been in on the planning of the Saint Lucia trip, so he knew all about his intention of proposing. "I wanted to tell her about my past."

"I thought you'd already done that."

Mark shook his head. "No. You don't understand." He raked his fingers through his hair. "Man, Rob, you don't know the half of it. I told her things I never even told you. Stuff I never told *anybody*."

Rob's forehead crinkled. "I thought I knew everything about that time in your life."

"Well, there was some shit that I was too ashamed to admit, even to you." He sighed. "I'm sorry, man. I never meant to keep you in the dark. I just didn't want to talk about it, let alone remember it."

Rob shifted on his barstool and spun a peanut with his fingers. It made a papery scraping sound like gears grinding, only really quiet. "You don't need to explain, Mark. I get it. What you did tell me about—I mean, what I witnessed with my own eyes—was pretty bad. And I've known you for-fucking-ever. Long enough to know that if you're carrying around shame about the other shit you did, it had to be *really* bad. Shit that you'd *want* to forget."

"Yeah, well, I told Karma. I had to."

"Why?"

"Because I didn't want to move forward until she knew the worst there was to know about me. I wanted to know I'd told her everything. That way I could have a clean slate, no secrets, nothing to hide. A totally fresh start."

"Yeah, but it could have backfired. And for you to be sitting here pissing into your pile of peanuts about how you're destroying everything tells me you're thinking it has. So, what's going on? Tell me what you told her. Come clean with *me* so I can help."

"God, Rob." He hung his head then glanced at him sideways. "Do you really want to know?"

"Yes."

After a couple of false starts, Mark finally got going and slowly spilled his guts about his deviant past. Nina, the sex clubs, the threesomes, the prostitute, the drugs. He unloaded everything he'd told Karma all over again, this time to his best friend.

Afterward, Rob sat in silence for a long while then said, "Shit, Mark. I never knew."

"No one did. No one but me knew how bad it got." He drained his water bottle. "I'm sorry. I should have told you a long time ago."

Rob perked up, shaking his head. "Hey, you don't owe me an apology. Like I said before, I get it. I totally get it. Your head was fucked up back then."

"Yeah, but you got me back on my feet. Without you, I'm not sure I would have made it back. I owed you."

"You didn't owe me anything. You're my best friend. We've shed blood together. Since we were kids, you've had my back as much as I've had yours. You would have done the same thing for me under similar circumstances."

Mark grabbed another peanut. "Yeah, maybe. But there's more." He rested his forearms on the bar as he pinched the shell and split it open. "And this is where I might have crossed the line with Karma."

"What do you mean?"

"I mean that I got off on some of that shit, Rob." He slung the broken peanut shell toward the trash can behind the bar with more force than was necessary. "I liked some of it. As fucked up as most of it was, some of that shit was hot."

Rob didn't say anything for a few seconds, then, "And you told Karma that?"

He crunched into a peanut like he was biting off the head of a tiny demon. "Yes. I told her. And I told her I wanted to do those things with her."

"And . . . how did she respond?"

"That's just it. At first, everything was great. She seemed open to the idea. I thought I'd hit the jackpot."

"And now?"

"She hasn't brought it up again."

"Have you?"

"Once. Last night. Before dinner with her parents."

"And . . .?"

"She seemed . . . I don't know . . . I thought things were going well, but then we got into a huge argument, and she didn't bring it back up, even though we made up today."

"And I take it you didn't bring it back up, either."

"No."

Rob cleared his throat and rested his arms on the bar. "Okay, I don't know exactly what type of sex acts we're talking about here, and I don't want to know. That's between you, your god, and Karma. But maybe she's still getting used to the idea. You ever think of that?"

"Yeah, maybe." He didn't really think that was the case, but what did he know? He was too caught up in the thick of the situation to see clearly.

They sat in silence for a couple of minutes, eating peanuts, Rob sipping his water. Then Rob set his bottle down in a way Mark had come to know meant he was about to get smacked with a Rob-ism. One that would hit him right between the eyes. Hard.

"Go ahead," he said, glancing at Rob. "I know you've got something on your mind."

Rob sighed and bowed his head. A couple of seconds later, he looked up and said, "Okay, I'm just going to put this out there. Don't get mad. Just hear me out."

"Fine. Whatever. Just say it."

"Did you ever stop to think you're subconsciously pushing her away?"

"What? Why would I do that?"

"Because you're you, Mark. You spent six years pushing away every woman you got involved with. You even pushed Karma away. Which led to some fabulous stories we all laughed over tonight, I might add, but that's beside the point. The point is, you pushed her away."

"But that was before."

"Do you really think it's that easy to change?"

"What are you saying? That I'm intentionally pushing Karma away again without realizing it?"

"I don't know, but it's possible." Rob sat forward. "Think about it. Keeping women at arm's length became a way of life for you after Carol. Then you met Karma, and she changed everything. Except you can't just walk away from your past like it never happened. You can't just snap your fingers and make all your bad habits evaporate. It's not that easy."

"You don't think I know that, Rob?" He thumped the side of his fist on the bar.

"I don't know, man. You tell me."

Mark sat back and waved his hand down the front of him. "You call this easy? What I'm going through? Does this look easy to you?"

"Mark, come on, give yourself a break."

"Getting to this point hasn't been *easy*. Opening up to her about my past wasn't easy. Sitting back waiting for her to acknowledge what I told her?" He shook his head. "Not easy, Rob. So, don't preach to me about shit being hard, because I'm living it. I'm there. Right in the middle of fucked up. Because it's not just all this shit I'm dealing with. It's the wedding, too." And here he went through part two of his troubles. "I've proposed. I've given her the ring. I can't see my life without her. But every time I think about the actual ceremony, I freeze. I panic. I get a pain deep down in the center of my chest." He poked the tip of his index finger against his sternum. "I get nauseous, start perspiring. I freak out."

"Have you told Karma this?"

"No."

"Why not?"

"I've already upset her enough by sharing my past with her. She won't even talk about the other shit. I can't throw this on the fire. It'd be like a can of kerosene." He made a noise like an explosion, popping his splayed hands out in front of him. Then he sighed and grabbed another peanut. "I can't disappoint her again. I can't tell her that I'm scared shitless of our wedding. That I'm terrified of standing at the front of the aisle wondering, worrying, fucking *freaking out* that she won't appear at the end of it and walk down that aisle toward me! That would devastate her. She deserves better than that."

"She *deserves* to know the *truth*."

"And what if the truth is too much for her to take, and she leaves?"

Rob leaned away, his eyes narrowing. "That's what you're really scared of, isn't it? That she'll leave."

Mark stared at him for several seconds, hardly breathing. The thought of Karma leaving him was enough to send ice through his blood.

"Yes," he finally said. "I'm terrified she's going to walk away."

"Why?" Rob searched his eyes. "I saw how she looked at you back there. I heard the tone in her voice when she talked about you.

She loves you, man. Maybe your relationship isn't perfect, but whose is? I don't see a woman preparing to run when I look at Karma. I see a woman in love. A woman who just wants to marry you."

He lowered his gaze to the pile of peanuts and broken shells on the bar. "Yeah, and I can't even suck up enough courage to set a damn date." He frowned at himself as he met Rob's gaze again. "I can't even give her the one thing she wants."

"You will. Have faith."

"I don't know, Rob. I just don't know. Maybe I'm not redeemable. Maybe I'm too fucked up to be good for any woman, anymore." He shook his head shamefully. "Two years ago, I had my shit together. I—"

"Hold up." Rob raised his hand. "Your shit was *not* together. If you think that, you're delusional."

Mark huffed. "Yeah, well at least I knew what I wanted and how to go after it. Now . . ."

"Are you saying you regret this? That you regret meeting Karma?"

He scowled. "No. Hell, no. But I'm stuck. Something in my head is stuck. I want to marry Karma, but every time she wants to talk about the wedding I go into a total lockdown. Shouldn't I be excited about this? I thought all that shit with Carol was behind me by now. Like now that I know I've found the woman I'll be spending the rest of my life with I should be more than ready to walk down the aisle—unable to wait even one more day."

"And you're not?"

"No." The shame exhausted him. For weeks, he'd forced himself not to show how heavily his thoughts weighed on him, but now he let himself give in. His shoulders caved, he closed his eyes, and he let the morose take him.

"Why not?" Suspicion dripped from Rob's words. Obviously, Rob knew there was more. And he knew it was bad.

And he was right.

"There's still something I haven't told Karma. One last thing I haven't shared with her." He thought about the last item on his list. The one he'd crossed off but weighed so heavily on his soul he could barely stand sometimes.

Was that why he'd been thinking more about Carol as the weeks passed? He couldn't understand why she kept infiltrating his thoughts. It wasn't that he wanted her back or that he regretted things hadn't worked out. He was completely devoted to Karma and wanted no one but her. But his thoughts kept taking him back to Carol. Not constantly, but at some of the most inopportune times. Like when he was lying in bed at night. When he was just about to fall asleep. Then his subconscious threw an image of Carol — of some past memory — into his head. A memory of happier times. And then of his wedding day. He'd even dreamed of that day, waking with a start, covered in sweat, heart racing, breath coming in hard bursts. It was like there was some vital component he was missing. Some key that would unlock everything and finally let him go. But he couldn't find it. Couldn't figure out what it was.

"I keep thinking about Carol," he said quietly.

"Excuse me?" Rob sounded fit to bust something. "What do you mean, you've been thinking about Carol? Like, you want to get back with her or feel like you're settling for second best by choosing Karma?"

Mark rose back to his full height, scowling. "Hell no. That's not what I meant. Not even close. That's why I'm so confused. I *don't* want her. But I can't stop thinking about what happened. I have fucking nightmares about it, for Christ's sake. Isn't that going to be just fabulous when Karma and I are living together and sharing a bed *every* night instead of just a few nights a week? So far, I've only had the nightmares when I'm alone."

"Well, maybe your subconscious is trying to tell you something."

He scoffed, feeling tapped out. "Like what?" He'd been trying to solve this riddle for over a month.

"Like maybe it's time you and Carol talk. Bury the hatchet. Discuss what happened, so you can both move on once and for all."

He crumbled another peanut shell. "We already *talked*, and I *know* what happened."

"Uh-huh. Sure you did."

"What's that supposed to mean?"

Rob leveled him with a cut-through-the-bullshit stare. "Do you *really* know what happened, Mark, or are you relying on that emotionally heated confrontation the two of you had at her place after you found her in bed with Antonio on your wedding day? Because that's the last time you two actually *talked* to one another. And I use that term loosely, because from how you've described it, there was more *yelling* than *talking* going on that day. And yelling usually doesn't go hand-in-hand with rational, air-clearing conversations. So, I'll ask again. Do you really know what went wrong with Carol? Or are you still running from the truth?"

Mark frowned, words failing him.

"I thought so." Rob finished his bottle of water and tossed it in the recycle bin.

"Okay, so maybe you're right. Maybe Carol and I haven't talked. What do I do about it now?"

Rob tilted his head and raised his eyebrows. "Well, let's see. How about you . . . gee, oh, I don't know . . . talk to her."

Could the solution to his problems really be that simple? It sounded too good to be true. Besides, the last person he wanted to see was Carol. The last time he'd seen her, he'd barfed his guts out. He wasn't sure he'd be able to contain his upchuck response if he had to face her again.

"I don't know, Rob."

"Well, think about it." He stood. "It could go a long way toward making things right. Not only for you and Karma, but for Carol, too."

"You say that is if I should feel sorry for her." He scowled. "I don't care how she feels."

"Well, maybe you should. Maybe that's what's eating at you. Because I'm sure she still carries a lot of guilt over what happened. Then again, I could be wrong about that, but for all Carol's faults, she seemed like a pretty conscientious woman. I wouldn't be surprised if she's been burdened with her actions for the past eight years. Giving her the opportunity to apologize and clear her conscience could go a long way toward helping you both let go of the past."

Mark cleaned up the bar and tossed the remaining peanuts back into the cupboard.

"I'll think about it. No promises. We'll see."

They started for the exit. "Are you and Karma sticking around tomorrow?"

"Yeah."

"Do you want to come over for lunch with Holly and me?"

"Can't. We're going furniture shopping."

Rob nodded. "That's right. You're moving into your new place Friday."

"Yep. Less than a week." And his head was in every shithole known to man instead of focusing on the happiness that he and the love of his life were finally going to be under the same roof.

Rob opened the door out of the pool room then stopped. "You're on the verge of having it all, Mark. Don't blow it."

"I'm trying not to."

"Try harder. And while you're at it, open up to Karma about what it is you want. If she hasn't brought up whatever the two of you talked about a few weeks ago, and it's that important to you, then you do it. You bring it up." Rob nodded in the direction of the party. "Now, go find your woman and tell her how much you love her. Better yet, show her."

That much he could do. Telling and showing Karma how much he loved her wasn't the problem. The problem was in getting out of his own way long enough to do what needed to be done to cement their future.

Chapter 18

Never give up on something you really want. It's difficult to wait, but more difficult to regret.
-Xuan Ta

"Knock-knock."

Karma jumped and nearly dropped the picture of a young Mark holding a basketball she'd been looking at. She turned to find Giada standing in the doorway.

His mom smiled warmly and glanced down at the two small plates she held in her hands. "I brought you a piece of cake."

Caught. She'd been caught prowling through the house like a sneaky thief.

"I'm sorry, I just—"

"I see you found Marcus's room." She entered and extended one of the plates and a gold fork toward her as if she found nothing whatsoever amiss of Karma's secret snooping.

Karma set down Mark's picture and took the plate. "I didn't mean to snoop. I was just looking for a quiet place to think."

"You mean a quiet place to get away from those stuck-up high-society girls, don't you, dear?" Giada slipped a small piece of her own cake into her mouth as if she were eating a bite of caviar.

Karma's face heated as she stammered for a proper response. Had she insulted Mark's mom without realizing it? "No, I . . . it's just that—"

Giada bumped arms with her, smiling. "I needed to get away from them, too." She dabbed a cocktail napkin on her lips. "These parties can be so tedious."

"But it's your birthday party."

Giada scoffed and rolled her eyes. "Yes, but if I don't invite *everyone*—including those I'd rather not—I would never hear the end of it." She gestured for Karma to join her as she sat on the edge of Mark's childhood bed. "It's one of the compromises I've had to make to live the life I do."

It sounded like there was a lesson in there somewhere.

"I put up with those people because I have to." Giada waved her fingers dismissively toward the door. "But they're such bores. Not like you." She wrapped her free arm around Karma's and squeezed like they were best friends who'd run off to tell each other secrets. Then she pulled away and picked up her fork again. "Have some cake, dear. Let's eat my birthday cake and talk about you and Marcus and how wonderful it is you two are together."

She stabbed off a piece of cake. "You're really happy he's engaged, aren't you?"

Giada's eyes danced as her entire face lit up. "Ecstatic."

The orange flavor of the confection exploded over her taste buds. "Mmm, this is incredible."

"I know." Giada winked and took another bite. "I love orange cake, so I hired this fabulous pastry chef who makes the tastiest treats to make my birthday cake. He trained in France and is the best baker in Chicago. If only you lived here, we could hire him to bake your wedding cake." She took another bite then waved her fork back and forth. "But don't worry. I'll ask him to recommend someone in Indianapolis."

"But we don't even know when the wedding will be, yet."

"Yes, but you will." She patted Karma's leg reassuringly.

Karma took a few more bites of her cake, glancing around the room at all the pictures, trophies, and trinkets lining the shelves. There was one of Mark with a woman who had blond hair. He looked a bit older than he'd been in the basketball picture. Still young, though. Eyes not as wise . . . or jaded. Happy.

"When was that picture taken?"

Giada followed her gaze then pursed her lips as she glanced away. "About nine years ago."

Karma stood and set down her plate, inspecting the picture more closely. "Is this Carol?"

Giada stood and placed her plate next to Karma's on the desk. "Yes," she said so softly she was barely audible. "You know about Caroline?" Was that disappointment in her voice?

Karma nodded. "What can you tell me about her?"

Maybe if she learned something about Carol, she could figure out how to break her spell on Mark. Unlikely, but right now, anything was worth a shot.

"Well . . . Caroline was the daughter I never had," Giada said wistfully. But a note of distress fell over her words. "She still is, despite what happened."

Karma wasn't sure what to make of that statement. How do you think of the woman who jilted your son as a daughter?

Her confusion must have shown, because Giada offered her a patient smile and patted her hand. "She was an orphan, dear."

Ooohhh.

Giada glanced away as if staring into the past. "Her mother died when she was four. Then her father passed away five years later. Only nine years old, and she'd lost both her parents."

"Oh my God." Karma looked back toward the picture of Carol and Mark on the shelf. She was finally beginning to understand Carol a little bit better, even if this wasn't what she'd expected.

Giada guided her toward the couch. "She ended up moving to Milwaukee to live with an aunt," Giada said as they settled on the leather cushions. "But she'd been very close to her father, especially after her mom died. She missed him terribly and fell into an awful depression after his death, from what her aunt told us. So, understandably, she started seeing a therapist twice a week to help her sort out her feelings and adjust to her new circumstances."

Giada dipped her head to one side. "I guess she mentioned a few times in her sessions that she enjoyed dancing, which gave her therapist the idea to try classes as a means to give Caroline focus again. So her aunt signed her up for lessons." Giada smiled. "And to hear her aunt tell it, she was a natural, taking to the Latin ballroom dances instantly."

Giada sighed, and fond recollection filled her eyes. "Her aunt told me dance gave Caroline purpose again, and she worked hard to earn money to take more lessons. She cut the neighbors' lawns in the summer, shoveled snow in the winter, sold lemonade, washed cars, worked in horrible fast-food restaurants." Giada let out a soft laugh. "Every cent went toward dance lessons.

"And she was good. What Adler and I call a natural talent. We discovered her at a junior competition when she was sixteen. Just a sophomore in high school, and already a star. She ended up winning that competition, and Adler and I introduced ourselves. We wanted her to come and dance for us after high school. We already knew she would make a valuable addition to our company, and we knew we could make her even better."

Karma remained quiet, listening intently. She wasn't sure she liked humanizing Carol. It was so much easier to remain detached and pissed off at her when she was two-dimensional. But she'd wanted to learn more about the woman. She was getting what she'd asked for.

"For two years, Adler and I kept in touch with her. We went to her competitions, took her and her aunt to dinner, got to know them, and... well... her story touched us, especially me. I'd always wanted a daughter, but it just wasn't in the cards for Adler and me." She sighed wistfully. "After she graduated high school, her aunt agreed she should come to Chicago to study with us. I promised her I would take care of Caroline as if she were my own. And I meant it."

She turned her gaze back to the photograph. "And then she met my Marcus." She pressed her lips together. "He fell so hard so fast. He was still in business college, but he worked at the studio, too, teaching, helping out. He was the first dance partner we paired Caroline with, and they began dating immediately.

"I won't lie," Giada continued, "part of me wanted to see if matching him to such a talented partner would push his own dancing to a new level and convince him to give professional competition a shot, but it became apparent that Carol's talent was even greater than his, and while Marcus was clearly interested in dancing with her because of their relationship, his heart just wasn't in competing. It wasn't fair to either of them for us to keep forcing them to be partners.

"That's when we found Antonio. He was extremely talented, and we paired him with Carol. It was magic." She lifted her shoulders and flicked her eyes upward. "The two of them together made the perfect partnership." She angled her head toward Karma and lifted her elegant eyebrows. "I just never knew *how* perfect until it was too late."

Giada blinked and lowered her gaze, pausing introspectively. "You know, I think her father's death was one of the reasons for what happened between her and Marcus. She'd been lost when they met. She hadn't had a strong male figure in her life for nine years and latched onto him. He's always been steady. Solid. With a strong personality. He was her first serious boyfriend, and in hindsight, I think she saw him as a replacement for her father. Someone she could admire, look up to, even idolize." She shook her head. "But that's not what creates everlasting love. There has to be more to it than that. Yes, admiration and all the rest play a part, but it can't be all one-sided and starry-eyed. There has to be a genuine connection . . . an honest give and take. Between Marcus and Caroline, he did all the giving, and she did all the taking. Not because she was selfish, but because she didn't know how to give back to him. That wasn't the type of relationship they had. He was more a savior than anything. A man who briefly grounded her again. That was his purpose in her life. To show her that people come and go . . . that it's normal to experience love and loss . . . that it's nothing to fear."

Giada let out a heavy exhale, stood, and crossed to the picture of Mark and Carol. She picked it up, and her expression tightened as she stared at it. "Marcus and Caroline were only meant to be stops along the way for each other. They were never one another's destination. I realized that after their relationship ended."

Karma remained seated, not knowing what to say. So she remained silent.

Giada lifted her gaze and grinned affectionately at her. "You're the destination, dear. The same way Antonio was the destination for Carol." Her eyes twinkled. "Marcus is different with you. Better. Happier. Complete. The moment I saw him today, I sensed it. He's the happiest I've ever seen him, and I know you're the reason."

Karma's face heated as she smiled. "He's done the same for me. I've never been this happy."

"I can tell, dear. It warms my heart to see the way you look at my son." Giada winked at her then glanced at the picture of Mark and Carol again. "You know, some have asked me why I never kicked Caroline out of our studio for what she did." Giada turned to face her again. "But how do you kick out someone you love as a daughter—someone who's already been kicked around enough in life, and who you promised to take care of—and still show devotion to your son?" She set the picture down and brushed her fingers down the glass as if she were caressing both Mark's and Carol's faces. "She hurt Marcus, but I still love her. I still want what's best for her. And I still want what's best for Marcus."

She returned to the couch and settled beside her again. "Marcus loved Caroline, and she *did* love him, at least for a while. In her own way. But they were too young. Neither really knew what they wanted. But the way she ended things left Marcus badly wounded." Sadness filled her eyes. "For a while, I thought I'd lost my son. He was no longer the Marcus I raised but this angry, withdrawn stranger, leaving and coming home at all hours. But after a while, my Marcus began to come back to us. But he never fully returned to who he'd been before. There was always a darkness hovering over him, even when he was smiling."

Karma thought about the shadows that occasionally crossed Mark's face. "I've seen it. That darkness, I mean."

"So you know how concerning it can be."

"Yes."

Giada took her hand. "Back then, I never knew what would set him off. The most unexpected subjects affected him badly. I can't say he got angry or upset. He just became . . . well . . . ambivalent. As if he'd shut off that part of his heart."

Karma imagined what Giada had witnessed were Mark's first steps into the disconnected lifestyle that eventually brought them together.

"Carol's name was the worst, of course," Giada said. "I used to be so nervous trying to talk to Marcus about her. He would grow so moody and agitated then turn off completely. I learned to avoid talking about her. I never knew what to say, so I said nothing to keep from upsetting him."

"I know the feeling." Karma looked down at her hands. "I don't like to say her name around him even now." She glanced back up and shrugged sheepishly.

Giada's shoulders slumped. Not much, but enough for Karma to notice. "She's still causing trouble, isn't she? Still interfering with his happiness after all this time." Her eyes sliced into Karma's. "Tell me I'm wrong. I *want* to be wrong."

Karma couldn't tell her what she wanted to hear. Carol *was* still interfering. She *was* still in Mark's mind, even if he didn't admit it.

"I can't." Quiet agony laced her voice. "Because I think she is."

Giada murmured something in Italian that sounded like verbal disappointment then took Karma's hand in both of hers. "He loves you. You know that, right? I can see his heart in his eyes when he looks at you. I can feel the love he feels for you. A mother knows such things."

Karma nodded. "I know he loves me, but . . ." So many of her old insecurities had been stirred to life tonight.

"But what? Tell me, dear." She gave her hand an encouraging pat. "I can tell something worries you." Her eyes were kind, her words gentle, not prodding.

At the moment, everything worried Karma. The money, Carol, the wedding that might never happen because Mark wouldn't set a date.

Tears stung her eyes. For weeks, she'd held her fears inside. She'd kept them hidden, trying to appear strong while inside she suffered. Now, with just a few kind words and the discerning eye of a wise matriarch who wasn't blind where her son was concerned, her protective shield fell.

"He won't set a date," she quietly blurted with a sniffle. "He keeps pushing it off."

"And you fear Carol is the reason."

"Yes. It's like he can't let go of her. Carol is always there. Always in the shadows. Always between us."

Giada let out a heavy breath. "Marcus has always been one to feel things deeply. His emotions run deeper than those of anyone I've ever met. Not only does he love deeply, which is why I know you two will find your way through this, but he hurts deeply, too. He internalized the pain of what Carol did to him at such a profound level it nearly destroyed him. He became a Marcus I no longer recognized after Carol left him at the altar. I feared for him. I really did. Then he met you." Her face filled with happiness. "And you brought back the son I knew and remembered. For the first time since Carol, I recognized him again. He was my Marcus. My boy. All because of you. You're good for him, and he knows it. So don't give up."

Karma glanced around the room. "I don't want to, but I'm so confused right now."

Giada's forehead creased as she frowned quizzically. "What do you mean?"

"It's not just Carol, or the fact that Mark's dragging his feet to set a date, but . . ." How could she say this tactfully? "I've never dated a man like Mark. A man who has so much . . . um . . ."

"Money?" Giada offered with a suggestive tilt of her head.

Karma winced and dropped her gaze. "It's such a culture shock. I don't want him paying for everything. He's already given me a set of credit cards. He's hinted that he wants to pay off my student loans. He chartered a private jet to fly us to Saint Lucia for Christmas. I don't want to leech off his money. I don't want to be seen as a gold digger, because I'm not. I want—"

Giada grabbed her hands and clutched them to her chest. "Dear, you are not a gold digger. The mere fact that you cringe at the idea is proof enough you're not. And Marcus would never have fallen in love with you if you were."

"But—"

She held up her hand. "Hear me out, dear." She scooted closer. "You're not making Marcus pay for anything. He wants to take care of you. It's how we raised him. To be the provider. To be responsible for his *famiglia*. Providing for you is his purpose. Do you understand?"

The look on Karma's face must have conveyed she didn't, because Giada pursed her lips and turned her gaze upward as if searching for a better way to explain.

"Okay," she said a moment later, standing. "Think of it this way." Her accent stroked her words in a way that made her sound wise. "You're two dancers. Man and woman. Together." She lifted her arms and swayed smoothly side to side. "The man is the foundation. He's the rock. Without the man, the woman has no support." She halted and met Karma's gaze. "Now, you may be asking yourself, if Mark is your foundation—your rock—then what are you to him?" Giada paused only a beat before continuing, speaking slowly, dragging out the words to give them weight. "You are what gives him purpose." She lowered her chin pointedly. "Without you, Marcus is just an empty frame. No purpose. Nothing to hold. Without him, you are a piece of silk on the wind, nothing to keep you grounded. But together, you are art. You are beauty. You are strength." She placed her soft palms on either side of Karma's face, a wistful expression in her eyes. "As one, you are breathtaking." She took her hands away and lifted them as if she were catching rain. "With support, a woman can leap higher." She spun once. "She can spin faster." She bent to the side. "She can bend more deeply." She straightened and clasped her hands loosely in front of her. "She can do all these things because he's there giving support. She can do more because of him." Giada sat down beside her once more. "The two of you are synergistic. Better together than apart."

Leave it to a dancer to create such fabulous imagery.

"Some people . . ." Giada bobbed her head toward the bedroom door to indicate the people they'd left in the ballroom. "They let their money go to their heads. They become entitled, thinking happiness and materialism is owed them. That they're somehow better than those with less and should be treated differently. As if they're special." She scoffed. "Mark isn't like that. That's not how we raised him, and he knows better than to think that way."

Karma understood completely now why she'd never noticed how much money Mark had until he'd started spending so much of it on her. He wasn't one to show off his financial status. He never held himself the way the others downstairs did. And he never looked down his nose at *poor people*. And he didn't do any of those things because his mom and dad had raised him better than that.

"I just don't want to lose my identity," Karma said.

"You won't. You're simply building a new one with Marcus. You're still you, and he's still him, but together, you're becoming someone new. A pair instead of two individual people."

Giada took her hand again. "One more thing, dear. If Marcus is buying you extravagant gifts, it's because he feels you're worthy of his money. He's never been one to squander his fortune. Marcus is *very* responsible. For him to spend so much on you means he sees a future with you. A long, fulfilling future he wants to invest in. Trust me on this."

"Then why won't he set a date for our wedding?" This conversation had been such an eye-opener, but in some ways she was more conflicted now than she'd been an hour ago.

Giada's gaze drifted back to the picture on the shelf. "If I had to guess, I'd say he's still battling old ghosts."

"But how long will he be battling them?"

She shrugged. "That I can't tell you. But just be there when he's ready. He'll come to you. I know he will. He sees his salvation in you."

The question was, salvation from what?

*   *   *

Mark heard voices coming from his bedroom and made his way down the hall.

"Karma? *Mamma?*"

It took a moment for an answer to come, and then his mom said, "In here, Marcus."

His steps quickened until he reached his old bedroom and pushed open the door. Karma and his mom were sitting on the couch he'd fallen asleep on many times in his youth while studying. Two half-eaten pieces of cake sat on his old desk.

"What are you two up to in here?"

His mom stood and gave Karma a wink. "Just getting to know my future daughter-in-law better. You've kept her hidden from me far too long, honey. Shame on you for that." She gave his arm a gentle swat. "But we had a fabulous visit, didn't we, dear."

With a nod, Karma smoothed her palms down her pant legs. "Yes. It was very . . . educational."

He frowned and cast a suspicious glance between them. "Okay, what were you two really talking about up here?"

"You know better than to ask your *madre* such a question," his mom said, playfully chastising him. Then she turned toward Karma, patting her hand. "Just a little girl talk, right?"

Karma stood and joined him, wrapping her arm around his, and shared a secret glance with his mom. "That's right. Girl talk. Top secret stuff."

Something about the way her eyes sparkled made him smile. She looked utterly adorable. Coquettish yet innocent, a combination that always lit his fire.

His mom gathered the plates and carried them to the door. She stopped, stacked one plate on top of the other, and put her hand on the doorknob. "I'll leave you two alone." She pulled the door closed.

As soon as the latch clicked, he pulled her against his body. His conversation with Rob dissipated in a blink, leaving only his love and the intense chemistry he and Karma shared. She was his home base in a game of hide-and-seek. The place he could come back to time and again and find safety from the shit running after him from his past.

Her compassionate gaze, so full of love, met his. Whatever she and his mom had talked about had hushed whatever discontent was left over from his surprising announcement last night and his continued avoidance of the subject of their wedding date today.

"I told you my mom would like you." His arms settled around her waist, holding her close.

Her palms skimmed up his chest, coming to rest just below his shoulders. "I think I'm her new best friend." She let out a soft laugh. "She seems *very* happy we're engaged."

His mom had witnessed in one way or another the residual effects of Carol's betrayal, including the long string of women he'd dated but never let himself get involved with beyond a certain point. For her, seeing him finally settling down was probably an answer to a prayer.

"I think she was beginning to think I would never fall in love again." He sighed. "And, honestly, so did I."

She snuggled closer, pressing her pert breasts against his chest. "Only because you wouldn't allow yourself to love and be loved."

Trailing the tip of his finger down her exposed shoulder, he pushed the loose fabric of her blouse even lower, revealing more skin. "I didn't allow it with you, either, but you got through anyway. I still fell in love with you." He tucked his chin, bringing his face within an inch of hers. "*Hard*."

Her fingers linked at the back of his neck and pulled him even closer as she turned her face up to his. The moment her lips brushed over his, a waterfall of heat poured over his body. His eyes drifted shut, and his arms coiled tighter around her lithe form.

He deepened the kiss and sought her tongue with his, inhaling her breath. And again, deeper still, he invaded her mouth, his arousal rapidly rising. When she moaned a moment later, hot shivers danced down his spine straight into his scrotum.

He pulled away, already breathless, his right hand under the back of her shirt, pressed firmly against her skin.

"You ready to leave?"

She nodded, bottom lip caught between her teeth.

"Me, too." Searching her face, he forced himself to take a step back and wrapped his hand around hers. "Let's go back to the hotel so I can show you just how hard I've fallen."

"I'd like that." She hesitated, blinking up at him, eyes doe like and beguiling. "Maybe we can . . . you know . . . rent a movie?" Her eyebrows rose suggestively.

"What? You mean, like a dirty one?"

She nodded, her cheeks flushing red as she lowered her eyelids a split second before she ducked her head and tucked it against his chest.

He chuckled, stroking her hair. "It's too late to go all shy on me now," he said. "You've already planted the seed. This is a done deal."

He'd thought she wasn't interested in pursuing the fantasies they'd discussed, but maybe Rob was right. Given her bashful reaction just now, perhaps she'd just needed time to adjust to the idea. After all, watching a dirty movie was her fantasy, and if acting on her own fantasy made her behave this shyly, he could only imagine how she felt about acting on his.

"I know." Her voice was muffled against his shirt, and she giggled nervously.

Pulling away, he placed his thumb and forefinger under her chin and tilted her head so he could look into her eyes.

"Why are you so nervous? This was *your* fantasy."

"I know it was, but . . ." She fought back another giggle, pressing her lips together. "I've just never watched a dirty movie with someone else in the room. It's . . . just . . . this is going to be—"

He placed his fingertips over her mouth. "Sexy as hell. That's what it's going to be."

She blushed and lowered her eyelids. Then she lifted her gaze to his again, her long, delicate lashes framing her pale-green eyes. "You make it sexy."

"So do you." He gave her hand a light tug. "Now, come on, let's get out of here, and I'll teach you how sexy you can be when there's a dirty movie on in the background."

"Another lesson?" she said as he opened the door.

"If you want to think of it that way." He led her down the hall. "But I choose to think we're beyond lessons. Now . . ." He stopped abruptly and pushed her back against the wall, driving his hands up the front of her shirt until he grasped the scalloped lace cups of her bra and peeled them away from her breasts. Her nipples budded instantly against his palms as he squeezed them, making her gasp.

"Mark!"

"Now, we're exploring," he said, finishing his thought.

She moaned against his mouth as he claimed her lips, tonguing her until she gave way and allowed him in.

The sounds of laughter rang up the stairs from the party. Music and chatter echoed up and down the walls. At any moment, someone could come along and see them. Maybe another couple searching for a private corner would steal away upstairs and find them there, locked in their own passionate moment.

The thought alone was enough to supercharge his arousal to the point he dragged her open collar down to expose one of her breasts.

She writhed against the wall, gripping a handful of his hair as he ducked and closed his mouth around her nipple.

"Mark, oh my God, Mark . . . what if someone sees us?"

A rush of heat flooded his blood at the idea. "Let them."

"But . . ."

He sucked her nipple, releasing it with a pop, then stood and straightened her clothing, covering her again. "Don't worry. Tonight's about your fantasy, not mine." He cleared his throat and gently pulled her away from the wall. She seemed a bit unsteady on her feet, so he gave her a moment to gather herself. "But I would like to talk about mine again someday soon, if you're still open to them."

She bit her lip. "Yes."

"You are?"

She nodded. "Yeah, why?"

"I just . . . we haven't talked about them since I brought them up, so I wasn't sure."

Her cheeks colored as she smiled. "I'm interested. I just needed some time to, you know, do a little research."

He grinned. "Research?" Wow, he'd been so off-base with his assumptions. He'd gotten bent out of shape over nothing.

"Well, yeah." She ran her hands down his chest and rested them on the sides of his waist. "You hit me with some stuff I've never heard of or done before." Then she gave him a flirty look and said, "And my teacher likes me to study up on new things before I try them, so that's what I've been doing."

He narrowed his eyes. "Ah, yes, your teacher. Something tells me he'd be pleased to hear this."

She rose on her tiptoes and gave him a sweet kiss. "I hope so," she said against his lips.

He kissed her back then eased his arm around her, his hand at the small of her back. "Come on, let's get back to the hotel before I take you back to my old bedroom." He bobbed his head down the hall then ushered her toward the stairs.

They briefly returned to the party, wished his parents a good night, and then Henry retrieved their coats as the valet brought around his car.

Sexual tension hung over them the entire drive back to the hotel, but thirty minutes later, after a steamy kiss in the parking garage, one elevator ride filled with suggestive glances and coy touches, and a firm caress of her firm ass as he unlocked their door with his other hand, they were once again alone.

The moment the door shut behind them, he spun her toward the wall and slammed her against it, bending to grab her just under the curve of her bottom, hoisting her off the floor. Her legs wrapped around his hips, her arms clamping around his shoulders.

"Do we even need the movie?" she said, rolling her hips forward on a moan.

Holding her with one arm, he pressed the other against the wall, dry humping her. "No, but we're going to watch one, anyway." He wasn't going to shortchange her fantasy. Not when so many possibilities could unfold in the aftermath.

Hopefully, this would open the way toward living out more of both their fantasies. That's what he wanted, for them to enter a new level of trust and openness with one another.

"You're going to drive me crazy," she said, dropping her head back so he could lave her neck.

"But it's a good crazy."

Her forearm wrapped around his head. "God, yes."

After expending the initial rush of sexual energy, Mark gave her one final kiss and stepped away from the wall. She unwound her legs and found her footing a moment later.

God, he was torqued. If he wasn't so committed to acting out her fantasy, he would have abandoned the dirty movie and taken her that instant, but he was nothing if not a connoisseur of pleasure, and he refused to rush anything he could savor instead.

"Why don't you take a relaxing bath while I check out our options," he suggested, nodding toward the large flat screen hanging on the wall.

Her eyebrows lifted curiously. "A bath? You want me to take a bath?"

He reached around and patted her on the bottom. "Just setting the mood."

The corners of her mouth curled upward. "Even now, you're such a planner."

He caressed her kiss-swollen lips with his thumb, enjoying the way they bunched then parted on a breathy exhale as she leaned toward him, taking his thumb into her mouth. Her tongue swirled around it, the suction awakening a lusty ache in the pit of his stomach.

"You're trying to distract me," he said softly, bending his neck until their foreheads tapped together. His gaze remained glued to the way her rosy lips tightened around the base of his thumb, the same way it would around his cock.

He moaned, swallowed, forced himself to breathe.

Then she pulled away, releasing his thumb with a naughty grin. "I think I'll take that bath now and leave you to ponder your obsession with planning." She winked then spun and disappeared into the bathroom, leaving him with a straining erection and the lively awareness they were about to venture into yet another arena of their evolving relationship.

Chapter 19

Your body is the church where Nature asks to be reverenced.
-Marquis de Sade

When Karma reentered the room, wearing nothing but her robe and smelling like vanilla soap, all the lights were off and Mark was sitting on the white love seat by the window overlooking the city of Chicago. He was wearing nothing but a pair of black briefs, his gaze turned toward the view outside.

"You sitting all alone out here in the dark?" She pattered barefoot across the carpet.

His gaze slid to hers, one corner of his mouth lifting in a cool grin. It was *The Look* times a hundred, and it sent a hot ripple down her back to land squarely between her legs.

Patting the cushion beside him with one hand, he raised the TV remote in the other, aiming it at the flat screen. A moment later, the screen came to life. She joined him, her nerves fluttering as she sat beside him while he pushed a couple of buttons until the movie he'd selected started.

"What are we watching?" she asked as he set the remote on the table and wrapped his arm around her shoulders.

His dark eyes twinkled when he turned to look at her. "Does it matter?"

Heat flooded her cheeks. "No."

It wasn't that she'd never watched a porno. She wasn't *that* innocent. But what little porn she had watched had been in private. Something about watching an X-rated movie with someone else felt weird. Almost too personal. Like she should be doing this alone.

"So, we're just supposed to sit here and —"

"Ssshhh." He held his index finger in front of his lips then pointed to the screen. "The movie's on. No talking." The playful yet carnal shadows in his eyes made it clear he didn't care whether she talked or not.

She smirked and swallowed a giggle, turning her attention to the screen.

The movie started simply enough, as most pornos do. And from what she could tell, the loose plot to dress up all the sex was about a trio of friends on vacation whose car breaks down at night in a small Texas town. Oh, but wait. There just so happens to be an auto shop within walking distance where three hot, tattooed mechanics are on duty.

Once the hot guys towed the car into their garage, it didn't take long for the action to start as couples paired off.

When the sex grew intense, Karma refused to look at Mark. She could feel him watching her. Feel his gaze focused intently on her instead of the movie.

"Why are you watching me like that?" she eventually asked, fidgeting.

When he spoke, his voice purred quietly over every syllable. "Because I like watching how turned on you're getting."

She swallowed as the man on the screen flipped the woman to her stomach and penetrated her with enough force to shove her forward at least two feet, sending her sprawling on the bed—yes, this autoshop had an upstairs loft, complete with a king size bed. Go figure.

But what made warmth bloom between her legs was the aggressive way the man fucked the woman. This was hardcore sex. Abandoned sex. The kind of fucking that left a woman internally bruised but in such a delicious way. A way that left no doubt she'd been fucked by a man driven by his own pleasure. Something about such impulsive, uninhibited wantonness sent Karma's arousal into the atmosphere.

Mark's breathing had grown heavy, and his erection tented his briefs. He was no longer watching the movie, but that didn't mean he wasn't still experiencing its effects.

Or maybe watching her was what got him so hot.

"So . . . how do I look when I'm turned on? Does it excite you?" she whispered, still unable to look at him but growing more aroused by the second.

He leaned closer, gently pushing the lapel of her robe to the side, exposing her breast. "Very." He let out a heavy, tremulous breath that washed over her shoulder.

She glanced at the flat screen, staring at the way the muscles in the man's arms bulged as he held himself above the woman, his hips rolling and thrusting at a bruising, rapid cadence. The woman cried out, her hands curled into tight fists around wads of bedsheets, straining the fabric as she held tight, back arched, ass in the air, her cheeks rippling with every powerful thrust.

She wanted Mark to take her like that. Hard, almost reckless. Just once, she wanted to feel what such licentious fucking felt like. Mark always catered to her pleasure. Always made sex more about her gratification than his own. Not that he didn't enjoy himself. He did. And the sex was incredible. But just once, she wanted to be fucked like the woman on the screen. To know what Mark felt like when he selfishly took her for his own enjoyment. If she got off, great. If not, he'd get her off next time.

Mark bent and kissed the top of her breast. "Do you like what he's doing to her?" Mark murmured, brushing his fingers over her nipple.

"Y-yes." She licked her lips, her eyelids falling halfway closed.

"What's so exciting about it?" He trailed his tongue down to her nipple and swirled it in a circle, coaxing her flesh into a tight peak.

She placed her hand on the back of his head, her chest heavily rising and falling. "How rough he is."

His teeth nipped her budded nipple. "You like it rough?"

"Yes," she whispered, trying to focus on the action taking place on the TV, but increasingly falling prey to Mark's ministrations.

The truth was she didn't know if she liked it rough or not. The only way she'd been taken that way was in Saint Lucia, on the yacht, when she and Mark had engaged in role-play sex. But she'd loved the hell out of that, so it was a safe bet she did, in fact, like it rough.

"How rough?"

She moaned as he pushed her hair aside and brushed his lips over the side of her neck then raked his teeth over the same area.

"This rough?" He scraped her neck with his teeth again, harder this time, as he tightened his grip on her breast. Then he bit her. Not hard enough to draw blood, but hard enough to make her sharply suck in her breath.

Her head fell back and heat exploded between her legs. Somehow she managed to make a noise that resembled "Uh-huh."

Rough was nice. Very nice.

"Or," he said, drawing the word out, "this rough?" In one fluid motion, he whipped his arm around her waist, yanked her onto his lap, and forced her robe open. Grabbing the waist tie, he pulled it free of the belt loops, swung it around her, and tied her wrists behind her back, confining her.

The next moment his mouth closed over her nipple, teeth bared, and she cried out, throwing her head back again.

"Is this how rough you like it?" He sucked her nipple, tugging it between his teeth.

She nodded urgently. "Yes . . ." She gasped as he gripped her hips and yanked her forward as he thrust against her. "God, yes!"

He nodded over her shoulder to the TV. "Does my prisoner want to be taken like that?" She didn't need to see what was happening in the movie. The sounds of hard fucking made it clear.

But they were also back to acting out his kidnapper fantasy. Nice. Now they could enjoy both their fantasies at the same time.

"Y-yes."

Using her tied arms as a lever, he yanked her haphazardly off his lap, stood, spun her around, and tossed her facedown on the bed. She bounced, and the hem of her robe flipped up to reveal her naked bottom. With her hands bound, there was nothing she could do to cover herself. Nothing she could do but lie there, exposed, and lift her head to watch him peel out of his briefs and snag a condom from the drawer of the bedside table.

He was still rolling it on as he crawled onto the bed behind her, straddling her thighs as he maneuvered her around to face the TV.

"Then watch," he growled in her ear, grabbing the fabric secured around her wrists and pulling. Her upper body lifted off the bed, her arms stretched down her back. "Watch him fuck her the way I'm going to fuck you."

OhGodOhGodOhGod! She was so going to come the moment he entered her. Her core clenched, and he wasn't even inside her, yet.

The head of his cock nudged in close, probing as he used his free hand to brusquely slick her up and down.

Panting, she kept her eyes glued to the TV. The man slowly pulled out then speared the woman hard. Again. Then again. Then the man slammed into her and pumped viciously, sweat glistening his arms and shoulders.

Donya Lynne

A moment later, Mark thrust into her, using her binding as a handle to tug her back to meet his body.

She cried out then gasped at the depth and force behind his violation, her body vibrating all the way to her marrow as her muscles swiftly surged toward orgasm.

"Yes, yes, yes . . ." Each affirmation burst from her on a breath, in perfect sync with his harsh, maddening rhythm, her release spiraling like a tornado, wrapping around her, consuming her, coiling tighter . . . tighter. How much more could she take? The pleasure was unlike anything she'd ever felt, intensifying beyond her normal boundaries, sending her higher than she'd ever flown.

And Mark knew it. He knew she was on the verge of having the most intense orgasm of her life.

"That's it," he growled, cranking her arms lower with one hand as he gripped her hair with the other.

His hips slapped loudly against her bottom, his delirious pace stealing her ability to think rationally. Her existence resided solely between her legs, at his control.

Pulling her up to her knees, he clamped his arms all the way around her waist, fucking her like a caveman, harsh and animalistic, grunting in her ear, his sweat slicking her skin.

But the new angle made his cock slam head-on with her G-spot, and that was all it took to make the storm cloud of mounting sexual tension explode.

"Oh my Gooooooooooood!" She'd never been a screamer, but as her muscles split apart and sent wave after wave of explosive tremors through every cell, she couldn't rein in the vocal release matching her physical release ounce for ounce.

A second orgasm rushed to claim her before the first was even finished. And then a third, smaller climax that felt more like an aftershock rippled through her thighs and lower abdomen.

If not for Mark's arms holding her up, she would have fallen in a useless heap, unable to do much else than close her eyes, shudder, and let the outbreak of pleasure totally consume her.

His groans turned into growls, which turned into staccato grunts, and then his body halted midthrust as every striated muscle contracted. In that split-second, he didn't utter a sound, not a breath or even a whisper. Then he twitched an instant before bucking hard against her, letting out a primal growl from deep within his chest.

Great, shuddering gasps poured from his throat, his hips jackhammering as if they had a mind of their own, completely out of control.

Tumbling forward, she slammed into the mattress as he fell over her back, his hands fisting on either side of her head, gripping the comforter as he continued pumping into her.

For several seconds, his body rocked forward and back, milking his release, and then he slowed, breathing heavily, until finally collapsing, completely spent.

So maybe they hadn't gotten fully entrenched in the kidnap fantasy they'd played out in Saint Lucia, but that hadn't mattered. Just pretending to fall back into those personas had done the job.

"Fuck," Mark bit out a moment later, still lying on her back, her arms between them, which couldn't have been comfortable for him.

She still couldn't talk, too consumed by the enormity of what had just happened to form coherent sentences.

He groaned as he pulled out of her then rolled to the side, landing on his back beside her. Then he took a deep breath and sat up to untie her.

"Come here." He swept her into his arms and lay back on the bed, head on the pillows, his fingers combing her hair away from her face. "Are you okay?"

She nodded, still breathing hard.

"I didn't hurt you?"

She shook her head, snuggling closer. He cocooned her in his embrace, tucking her cheek against his chest.

His heart thump-thump-thumped, pounding hard against her ear.

"I've never felt you come like that," he said. "So hard. How many orgasms did you have?"

"Three, I think." The euphoria still snarled her in its grip, making it hard to think.

"Three times so fast." He sounded impressed, exhaling a proud breath.

"I've never done that before." Her arm hung lazily over his waist.

"I've never been able to make a woman do that, either."

She pulled back. "You? Mr. Sex God?"

He grinned, his eyelids heavy. "Surprised?"

She tucked herself against him once more. "A little."

"Why?"

"Because when we met, you seemed like you knew everything about sex. I just assumed this was status quo for you."

He shook his head, his fingers trailing up and down her arm. "No. You're the first."

The first. No woman before her had experienced what he'd just given her. Three back-to-back orgasms. Not Carol. Not Nina. Only her.

She wrapped her arm more securely around him, pressing closer.

"I've never experienced this kind of chemistry with anyone else, Karma. Not even close. You're the only one." He rolled her to her back and sank down on top of her, kissing her long, slow, and hard. When he broke away, he added, "But then, I've never loved anyone the way I love you."

She wanted to ask him, "Not even Carol?" but didn't. Mark wasn't one to make such a proclamation if it wasn't true, so she should take him at face value. If he'd loved Carol as much as he loved her, he would have phrased his statement differently.

"Nobody," he said, as if reading her mind.

He lifted off her and rolled her to her side, pressing up behind her, holding her tight. "You make me feel safe, Karma." He sounded fully relaxed . . . completely content.

"You make me feel safe, too." She sighed and sank into his embrace, closing her eyes as the front of his body melded against the back of hers.

Home. He was her home.

She vaguely heard the couple on TV still having sex as she drifted off to the sleep a few minutes later.

*   *   *

She wasn't sure how long she'd slept, but when she woke, the TV was off and the room was dark. There was nothing to hear but silence and Mark's quiet breathing.

He was still behind her, but she didn't think he was asleep. He breathed more evenly and more deeply when he slept.

She blinked her eyes open. She was facing the window. Facing the glow of Chicago's city lights at night. There was something both relaxing and invigorating about the city and the —

Her thoughts cut off.

Mark was hard.

Not completely hard, but enough for her to know he was definitely awake. Awake and turned on.

But it was where she felt his growing erection that caused her thoughts to seize up.

It was nestled between the cheeks of her bottom.

Hello.

Not that she thought he'd put his penis there on purpose. More like he'd awakened, found his penis had somehow slipped in there while he was sleeping, and then, rather than pull it out, he'd let himself play a little. And when Mark played, an erection wasn't far behind.

He shifted his hips ever-so-slightly, which caused his cock to press more snugly against her backside, positioning the head at the threshold of that which was yet to be discovered.

Oh wow. That was . . . *hot.* Surprisingly hot.

Butterflies awakened low in her belly and quickly morphed into slowly rolling lava. And when he ever-so-gently applied subtle pressure, heat seeped into her core.

He wasn't trying to push inside, but he wasn't pulling away, either. It was as if he wanted his presence known but didn't want to scare her. Was he testing the waters?

The whole situation was so taboo. So naughty. So . . . *exciting.*

He remained firmly in place, growing harder as the minutes ticked by. And as he swelled and the head inflated, he naturally stretched her. But the process was so slow she felt nothing but pleasure. Pleasurable pressure invading her as tenderly as a man could invade an anal virgin like her.

She didn't say a word. Just closed her teeth around her bottom lip and tried not to make a sound. The restraint of not talking, not moaning, not even breathing too loudly, created an even greater sexual energy around them. It was as if by stripping away the sense of sound, all the other senses were intensified, making her focus on his sweat-slicked stomach pressed against her back, the tension in his arm around her waist, the feel of his cock as it eased a fraction of a half-inch inside her.

She knew he was awake. And she knew *he* knew *she* was awake. But half the fun was in pretending she was still asleep. Or *trying* to pretend, because she was failing miserably at faking sleep. She was too aroused. Too desperate for more.

As he eased another quarter of an inch inside, a quiet rumble whispered from his throat then abruptly cut off as if he'd briefly lost his focus then strangled it again.

He was inside her. Not far. Maybe half an inch. Maybe a little more. The point was, he was inside her. He was making one of his fantasies come true on the heels of giving her one of hers. And he'd taken such tremendous care doing so she felt no pain. As in . . . *none*. There was tightness, pressure, a feeling of fullness even though only the tip of his head was in there, but not a lick of pain.

She'd been worried about the pain. It was one of the reasons why she hadn't brought the subject of anal sex up since they'd talked about it a few weeks ago. She'd been reading about it . . . learning what to expect. And the one thing that had come up repeatedly was that there would be a lot of pain.

And if he'd just gone at her and impaled her, she could see how pain could be a problem. But they'd been at this for at least ten minutes, and the head of his cock wasn't even all the way inside her, yet. So, yeah, the guy was a study in care and patience, steadily preparing her rather than mercilessly violating her.

But the longer he teased her sphincter, the more he roused her desire.

Which surprised her, because good girls didn't do this kind of thing. Did they? They didn't let men stick their penises in their asses. Butt sex was forbidden for good girls. Too eccentric. Verboten. And if good girls *did* do this sort of thing, they certainly didn't enjoy it.

But God, she did enjoy it. She was enjoying it immensely.

She'd always thought she was moral and virtuous. But maybe she wasn't. Just as Mark had put on a mask of confidence to hide the emotional insecurity of his past, maybe she'd simply been hiding the bad girl she really was, and the good girl was the façade.

Mark gently brushed her hair off her neck as if wanted to pretend she was still asleep and didn't want to wake her. But when he pressed his lips against her nape and licked a fevered trail to her shoulder as he ran his hand down her abdomen to between her legs, she gave up all pretenses, dropping the deception.

Letting out a sigh, she dropped her head back and lifted her leg, draping it over both of his as he shifted behind her, pressing closer.

His cocked inched a little bit farther inside.

Okay, so there was a pinch of pain, but not enough to make her want to stop.

"Is this okay?" he whispered, massaging her clit with his fingertips. His voice sounded patiently strained.

"Yes," she whispered back. She let out a breathy moan as he relaxed his hips, drew his cock back, and then nudged forward again, driving in a little farther.

She'd never felt anything like this. Such naughty pleasure mixed with such intimate trust.

He continued pumping in those same shallow thrusts, creeping a tiny bit deeper with each advance. Such an incredible feeling.

His fingers on her clit. His cock in her ass. Only a couple inches, but enough to make her want more. Or at least to try for more.

She was panting, her chest heaving, her senses totally overwhelmed. The slow build and heady anticipation were damn near shredding her nerve endings.

"Fuck," he quietly bit out.

He was covered in sweat. It slicked her back, her ass, the backs of her thighs. She peeked over her shoulder and saw perspiration beaded over his brow. His hair was damp. His jaw was tight, as if he were subjecting himself to superhuman restraint.

His eyes flitted to hers, and an abrupt gasp burst from his throat. He looked almost desperate . . . crazed . . . visually begging her.

"I'm not gonna last," he said. The desperation leaked into his voice, tightening his words. "Oh, Jesus . . ." His brow pulled toward the bridge of his nose as his eyes rolled back and closed. "Fuck . . . oh fuck . . ."

His chest and shoulders quivered, then his hips jerked, briefly driving him deeper. Then he quickly pulled out of her, snatching his hand away from her clit to grip his cock as he heaved against her.

Warm fluid spurted over the upper swell of her ass as he rolled her to her stomach, bent over her, one hand pressed against the mattress beside her head.

The bed twitched with the force of his silent orgasm as he emptied onto her back. Then he grunted as he shuddered again.

She closed her hand over his and pushed her upper body off the bed, tilting her head back. In yoga, this was called a cobra pose. But in bed with Mark, it was just another way to coax him into kissing her.

He grinned as she looked at him upside-down. Then he crawled forward, lifted onto his knees, and gripped the side of her head with his free hand as he gave her a backward kiss. As he did, a bead of perspiration dropped from his hair and landed on her neck.

"Wow," he said a moment later as he pulled away, releasing her.

She collapsed back onto the bed with a loud sigh. "I was just going to say that."

He eased off her back and let out a breathy, confounded chuckle that made it sound like he hadn't expected what they'd just done. "Let me get a towel."

He disappeared into the bathroom. A couple seconds later, the tap turned on. Then it shut off and he returned, holding a white washcloth in one hand and a hand towel in the other.

"Are you okay?" He bent beside her and wiped the washcloth over her back then gingerly slid it over her bottom.

"I'm fine." She turned her head to watch him as he used the hand towel to dry her. He was grinning ear-to-ear, but in an almost sheepish way. "How about you?"

He licked his lips then pressed them together as his gaze met hers. "Actually, I'm a little lost for words right now." His dimple cut into his right cheek as he smiled and stood.

He went back to the bathroom. There was more running water, and then a couple minutes later he shut off the light, returned to the room, and climbed into bed beside her.

After pulling the sheet over them but leaving the comforter folded at their feet, he rolled onto his side toward her. She was still on her stomach, but her head rested on her arms, facing him.

He let out a contented sigh as if he were about to make a confession. "I didn't plan that."

Her eyebrows shot up. Really now? This was new.

"Are you saying that was" — *gasp* — "spontaneous?" She sucked in her breath and made an *O* with her mouth, coyly covering it with her fingertips.

He rolled to his back with a defeated grumble. Then he looked back at her, the grin still plastered on his face. "Go ahead and tease me, Miss Mason. I can take it."

"I'm sure you can, Mr. Strong." She lifted on her elbows. "But now I think you see the merits of spontaneity, don't you?"

"I do." He shifted back to his side and ran his fingers down her spine. The sensation felt nice. Relaxing. His hand came to rest on her rump. "The question is, did you like it?"

His expression was hopeful, expectant.

She relaxed, laying her cheek on the back of her hand as she settled against the mattress again. "I did."

"Enough to want to do it again?"

She nodded. "It was . . . um . . ." How could she put how she felt into words? "Wow, Mark. Just . . . wow. I really, *really* liked that. So, yes, I want to do it again."

He practically beamed as he let out a relieved exhale. "Good." He nodded, his grin growing wider. "I'm glad."

She giggled lazily as she watched his gears begin to turn. "And you're already planning for next time, aren't you?"

"Maybe." He squeezed her rump.

She shook her head. "He sees how good spontaneity can be then goes right back to planning," she teased.

"Hey, you can take the man out of the planner, baby, but you can't take the planner out of the man."

She laughed. "That doesn't even make sense."

He laughed with her then stretched. A moment later, he wrapped her up in his arms.

"Baby, if I'm not making sense right now, it's because you've blown my mind. Just totally . . . blown. My. Mind. And I love it."

And she loved it, too. She loved him.

And for now, wedding date or not, that was enough.

Chapter 20

The hardest part about growing is letting go of what you were used to and moving on with something you're not.
-Author Unknown

After waking up deliciously sore all over, especially between the legs, Karma shared a shower with Mark, and then they spent the day picking out furniture at a store called Smithe Furniture & Design. Talk about high end. Smithe was the best of the best, and the prices reflected it.

An in-store designer helped them build an entire bedroom suite around a magnificent four-post bed, and then they selected a new dining room set and living room furniture, as well as a desk, chairs, and small conference table for her office and side room. Before they left, they scheduled an appointment for a local designer to visit their home.

So, this was how the rich shopped for furniture, going to great extent to make everything just right. The most extent Karma had ever gone to for a piece of furniture was to measure the space where she wanted it to go. Boom! Done. Just buy it and have the delivery dudes do the rest.

Clearly, life with Mark would see a lot of changes to her standard operating procedure, something she'd better get used to.

Back in Indianapolis, the week wound down faster than she could track, and suddenly it was moving day. The movers arrived, and within an hour, her apartment was empty. Of course, she'd taken special precautions to keep the unopened box of toys Daniel and Zach had bought for her tucked away in secrecy, stowing it in the trunk of her car. The last thing she needed was for Mark or the movers to open that box as they helped unpack at the house.

The first week of March was spent dividing time between work, studying, and unpacking what they'd had the movers leave for them. She fit in meals when she could. And Mark couldn't take off from work, because things were just too busy. Which meant she did a lot of unpacking on her own.

Funny how he could buy and move into a house during the busy season but not set a wedding date.

She pushed the thought from her mind. No good came from dwelling on what she couldn't change, and he'd assured her that after things settled down, they would pick a date. She trusted him.

The second full week they were in the house, Mark had to fly out of town on business, so she was on her own when the furniture truck and the designer they'd hired pulled up mid-morning on Thursday. She put away her studies, which she was falling behind on, and trailed alongside the designer—who'd introduced herself simply as Andrea with the flash of a business card—as she dictated where the furniture was to be placed and made notes about additional options she and Mark should consider. She pulled out fabric swatches and giant binders of fold-outs, with pictures of various items in a multitude of shades and textures. She led Karma from room-to-room, pointing out where a table could go, or perhaps a decorative clay vase. She made suggestions, hinted at painting certain rooms different colors, and left Karma with a stack of information " . . . you need to discuss with your husband."

She hadn't corrected her. Andrea didn't need to know she and Mark weren't married, yet.

By the time Andrea cleared out four hours later—a full two hours after the delivery truck left—Karma was thoroughly exhausted and mentally drained. No way was she going to get any more homework done tonight, putting her even more behind. She would have to burn the midnight oil for the next three days if she was going to get her assignments finished.

But at least the house finally felt like someone lived in it. Like *they* lived there. As she slowly toured from the living room, through the dining room and kitchen, and back to her office in the front of the house, for the first time since moving in, she felt like she was home. Her things mingled with his in the same space. Her books, his books. Her blender alongside his coffee maker.

In the parlor, the couch they'd made love on in his Chicago apartment sat next to the end table from her apartment. This was their space now. And as the weeks passed into months, and then into years, the nooks and crannies would become infused with their essence to the point where they wouldn't be able to remember which piece of furniture belonged to whom.

She could actually see her and Mark here now. Feel his arms around her as they watched a movie in the living room. Feel his body on her as they made love in their new bed. Feel his hands on her swollen belly as his baby kicked and moved inside her. See his smile as he held their son or daughter for the first time. Hear the future giggles of their children. Hear their tiny bare feet thump against the hardwood floors as they raced into the kitchen for a treat. See them getting off the school bus and racing up the driveway as orange autumn leaves fell from the two large maple trees in the front yard. And always, Mark was right there. Beside her. Holding her. Loving her.

Her whole life flashed before her eyes, but instead of the life she'd already known, it was her future. One she never thought she'd have two years ago but now seemed more real than the smooth, cool wood beneath her fingers as she skimmed her palm across the surface of her new desk.

Everything was coming together. Finally, blessedly together.

She spent the rest of the afternoon setting up her office.

Then she went upstairs to finish unpacking the bedroom.

After emptying the final box and placing the contents in their new bureau, she turned toward the medium-sized box sitting in the corner on one of the sheets she'd put down to protect the carpet.

It was time.

Time to finally unpack the goodies Daniel and Zach had ordered for her.

She hefted the box onto the bed and grabbed the utility knife from the dresser, zipping it down the taped seam. Setting the knife down, she bent the two flaps back and peered inside, face flaming.

Holy butt plugs, Batman.

She hastily glanced toward the hallway as if Mark would pop in that very moment. Thank God he wasn't due back until tomorrow. She wasn't ready to unveil her bounty. She needed to read up on how to use these things, what precautions to take, what to expect, and anything else she could discover. And anal plugs and prostate vibrators were definitely things she wanted to learn more about before poking them around Mark's backside. With knowledge comes confidence. So, yeah, until she had both, these little gems were going into the bottom of her panty drawer. All the way in the bottom, where she buried them under a mound of cotton and satin delicates.

Dusting off her hands, she gave the room a satisfied glance then gathered the broken-down boxes and took them downstairs to the garage, where she piled them alongside the rest of the recycling.

Then she went to the dinosaur-sized kitchen, heated up some chili for dinner, took it to the living room, and kicked her feet up while she watched the news on their new, extremely comfortable couch.

As she ate, she felt like she sank deeper and deeper into the cushions. Her eyes grew heavy. Finishing her chili, she set the bowl on the coffee table then leaned back again, letting her head rest against the cushion. Maybe she would close her eyes for a few minutes. Just a few to rest them.

Before she knew what hit her, she was asleep.

Chapter 21

Best friends. They know how crazy you are and still choose to be seen with you in public.
-Author Unknown

"I can't believe it's already April," Lisa said, coming in and taking off her jacket.

Karma hung it in the coat closet then did the same with Daniel's and Zach's.

"It's about time you invited us to your *mansion*." Daniel's gaze swept left to right as he nodded approvingly. "Very nice, Karma. You've moved up in the world."

She rolled her eyes. "Well, I'm still little ol' me."

"Honey," Zach said, "there is nothing little or old about you *or* this fabulous house." He shot Daniel a smirk. "Why don't we live in a house like this. It's not like we can't afford it."

"If you remember correctly, babe, you're the one who wanted to buy the house we're living in now."

"Yes, but that was, like, five years ago. It's time for an upgrade."

"We'll discuss it."

As the two continued bantering as they wandered toward the hall, Lisa slid up beside Karma and hugged her.

"How have you been? I haven't heard much from you in a while."

"I've been so busy." Karma's shoulders wilted just from thinking about the whirlwind of the last month. "There's so much to do, and no time for any of it."

Lisa's eyes brightened and she sidled closer, her expression one of sly curiosity. "*Wedding* planning?"

Daniel and Zach spun around at the word and rejoined them. "Did he finally agree to a date?" Daniel said.

Karma exhaled impatiently. "No." She gave Lisa a playful glare. "Thanks for getting everyone's hopes up, Leese."

"Hey, honest mistake. I just thought that was why you've been so busy."

"I wish." She gestured for them to follow her. "Come on. I'll give you the tour." She figured they'd start upstairs and work their way to the basement before ending in the kitchen, where they were going to make homemade, single-serving pizzas then have a movie night.

"So, what's been keeping you so busy?" Daniel said.

"Work. School. Moving." She paused halfway up the stairs to look over her shoulder. "And Andrea the tyrannical interior designer."

"Who?" Zach laughed, falling back in step beside her.

"Andrea is the interior designer Mark hired. She stops in every few days to check on things and suggest more furniture." She waved to the walls. "See this lovely shade of taupe? This was Andrea's idea." She came to the top of the stairs and pointed to a narrow glass table along the wall. "That table? Andrea." She stopped and did a Vanna White between two landscape paintings hanging on the wall. "And these?"

"Let me guess," Daniel said. "Andrea."

Karma gave him the wink and a gun. "Bingo." She started down the hall to the bedroom.

"You don't like her suggestions?" Lisa said.

She pushed open the bedroom door and flipped on the light. "Oh no, I love them." Andrea had done a superb job incorporating her style with Mark's to give them both what they wanted.

"Then what's the problem?"

Karma welcomed them into the master suite. "The woman just doesn't know *when to stop.*" Everyone laughed at the way she opened her eyes and pretended to choke herself. "At this rate, she's going to burn through Mark's entire inheritance before summer."

"Wow, Karma. This is . . ." Lisa gaped when she finally turned her attention to the room.

Karma had to admit, their bedroom was impressive. It was one of her favorite rooms in the whole house. Lots of natural light came through the large windows and French doors leading to the private balcony. And the cream-colored carpet reminded Karma of vanilla ice cream.

Which reminded her.

"Shoes off." She waved at their feet. "No shoes in the bedroom." She'd never had to worry about such things before, but with this luxurious layer of clouds on her floor, she wasn't letting anything that could stain, maim, discolor, or otherwise dirty it into its midst. She needed a sign on the door that said, "No shoes, wine, or tomato sauce beyond this point."

Everyone dutifully took off their shoes then wandered the bedroom like they were viewing a museum exhibit.

"Jesus, Karma!" Zach called from the bathroom, followed immediately by, "Daniel! Get in here. You've gotta see this."

Lisa disappeared inside the walk-in closet. A few seconds later, as Daniel entered the bathroom, Lisa poked her head out, her face the picture of impressed.

"My whole apartment can fit in here, Karma," she said at the same time Zach said, "This is the kind of master bathroom I want in our next house. Check out that showerhead. And the tub. And . . . what? A refrigerator? Karma!" He came to the door and looked from her to Lisa and back again. "You have a refrigerator and coffee bar in your bathroom? Seriously?"

"What?" Lisa abandoned the closet and hustled into the master bath. "Holy shit, Karma!"

Karma propped herself against the doorframe. "And the towel racks are heated, too."

"No way." Zach ran his fingers over one of the racks.

It was comical watching her friends marvel the way she had the first time she viewed the place with Mark. Now it felt like she was finally getting used to it. Something she never thought would happen.

After a couple more minutes of ooing and ahing, Karma said, "Okay, so are you guys ready to see the rest of the house?"

"I don't know," Lisa said. "I might never want to go home. This is kind of depressing." She walked out into the hall and picked up her shoes. "Do you and Mark need a roomie?"

Everyone laughed as she led them through the hall in the opposite direction to a wing of bedrooms and another hall that extended like a mini-catwalk to an empty room she and Mark hadn't decided what to do with, yet. It was over the garage and large enough to be a bedroom, but not laid out as one. It could be a home office . . . or a playroom for the kids someday . . . or maybe even an *adult* playroom. Mark had hinted at converting it into something they could use just for them. A place where he could put the Tantra chair he still planned on ordering

"See," Lisa said as they peered inside the first bedroom on their way back through. "It's already got a bed and everything. You'd never even know I was here. I promise."

"Yeah, but then you'd have to listen to Mark and me having sex," she teased. "We can be pretty loud."

Daniel chuckled. "Sounds like you've been using your new toys." He exchanged glances with Zach.

"Toys?" Lisa said, perking up. "What kind of toys?" She arched one eyebrow.

"We bought Karma a few toys as an early bridal shower gift," Zach said. "Special toys she can use with Mark. Man toys."

"Really now." Lisa eyed her.

She shook her head. "Sorry to disappoint you guys, but we haven't used them yet."

"What?" Daniel's mouth fell open. "Doesn't he like them?"

She turned for the stairs. "Come on. You still have to see the main floor and the basement."

"Oh, no you don't." Daniel caught up to her and grabbed her hand. "Haven't you even shown them to him? Does he even know you have them?"

"We've just been so busy," she said, trying to break away.

"Excuses, excuses. Now you're starting to sound like him putting off the wedding date."

Lisa crossed her arms. "Would someone please tell me what kinds of toys we're talking about so I can catch up."

At the same time, Zach and Daniel said, "Butt plugs and cock rings."

"Excuse me?" Lisa's forehead wrinkled as a dumbfounded expression overtook her face. "Butt *whats* and cock rings?"

"Plugs," Daniel grinned and let go of Karma's hand. "Mark has a thing for having his prostate stimulated."

"You weren't supposed to say anything," Karma said, huffing at them.

Daniel held up his hands as if warding off further scorn. "Sorry, but I figured she knew already. You usually tell her everything."

Lisa cocked her head to the side. "I'm lost."

"Oh, God. Not you, too." Zach glanced from Lisa to Karma. "Do women simply not understand the power of the prostate?"

Karma started down the stairs, thinking of Nina, who had likely been the one to introduce Mark to the power of *his* prostate. "I'm sure some do."

"Well, men need to do a better job cluing you ladies in. Everyone says the way to a man's heart is through his stomach, but they're wrong. The prostate is the gateway to keeping a man satisfied, honey. Tickle him right, and he'll never leave you."

Lisa brought up the rear, no pun intended. "What do butt plugs, or whatever you called them, have to do with a man's prostate?"

At the bottom of the stairs, Daniel and Zach stopped and looked at her. "We'll show you later."

The way Daniel spoke with a hint of mischief prickled Karma's awareness. "What do you mean, you'll show her later?" she asked suspiciously. "What have you two done now?"

Zach laughed and reached out his hand. "Give me the keys, babe. I'll go get it."

Daniel smirked and nodded then handed over his keys. "Might as well."

"Get what?" Karma watched Zach dart out the front door.

"You'll see." Daniel motioned for her to continue the tour.

Reluctantly, she took them to the basement. Zach showed back up as they peeked into the workout room, where Karma's stationary bike and treadmill were already set up, along with a combination of his-and-her-free weights.

He handed her a gift-wrapped box.

"What's this?"

"Just another early bridal shower gift."

She and Mark didn't even have a wedding date, and already she was receiving bridal shower gifts.

"Go ahead. Open it," Daniel took Zach's hand, and the two watched like proud, gay Jedi Masters as their apprentice finished building her first light saber.

She sliced the paper with her fingernail then ripped it back to reveal a black and red box. Actually, it was *two* black and red boxes. As the paper tore away, the boxes tumbled out and nearly fell to the floor before she secured them in her hands with a little help from Lisa.

"What is it?" Lisa said, peering closer.

On one box, in bold red letter, was the word ADAM. On the other was the same red font, only it read EVE. On both packages, in small, clean script, were the words, *From Eve's temptation came Adam's desire.*

"It's a his-and-her gift," Zach said, stepping forward and taking the boxes. "See, this is for the man." He lifted the Adam box, displaying the image of the black probe-looking thing with two slender, curly-Q handles at the base. "And this is for you." He handed her the Eve box and pointed. "See, it's for Kegels. And this . . ." He lifted the Adam box again. "Well, this will blow Mark's world. I'm telling you. Guaranteed."

Daniel nodded so aggressively she knew they were speaking from experience.

Lisa took the box from Zach. "So, are you telling me this . . ." She pointed at the black thing that looked a bit like a large, swollen thumb, bigger on the end than at the base. "This goes inside his . . . his . . ."

"His ass," Zach said, ever the blunt one.

Lisa covered her mouth, eyes wide. "Oh my God. Seriously? Mark likes that. He actually wants you to do this to him?"

Daniel nudged Lisa's shoulder. "Trust me, she *wants* to do this to him." He turned his attention to Karma. "Karma, even if he had never told you he liked this sort of thing, he would be forever grateful to you for giving him this. Trust me, he will never come harder or longer or as many times in a row as this little baby will allow him to do. Just . . ." He exchanged eager glances with Zach. "Yeah, this one is a keeper. Absolutely. It takes a bit to get used to if he's never used one, but once he hits the spot . . ." He rolled his eyes and raised his hands in front of him as if praising Jesus. "Wow, Karma. All I can say is wow."

"And thank you," Zach added. "Because if you hadn't shared with us what Mark told you, Danny and I never would have done a little shopping for ourselves, and we never would have discovered this precious little darling. So, *yeeesssss*, Karma." He grabbed her hands and practically bowed fealty. "Thank you, thank you, dear God, *thank you.*"

Okay then. Apparently, the Adam was a must-try. "You're

welcome, I think." She giggled at the way Daniel and Zach gushed over themselves to convince her of the Adam's potential.

Lisa handed the box back to Karma. "Well, I'm sold. Next time I've got a man in my life, I'm making him try one of those."

"You won't regret it," Zach said. "Danny and I did a lot of reading on the website about it, and while men who've used it raved about how they could walk around with it in, they rarely made it past an hour, because the thing just sets them off. Just, like, in a blink." Zach snapped his fingers. "It would move a certain way, and then it was orgasm city, just out of nowhere. One testimonial said the guy sprayed his cabinets and didn't even get an erection. He said that his wife tried to get him to the bedroom, but that every few steps, it would start over. He just kept coming. And then I guess the sex was off the charts, even for her. When he finally full-on ejaculated, it lasted for five minutes, and his wife just kept coming with him. And Danny and I can vouch for the accuracy, because—"

Karma and Lisa held up their hands at the same time, cringing. "We get the idea."

"Yeah," Lisa added. "TMI. *Way* TMI."

"Sorry." Zach grinned as if he was anything but sorry. "Just got carried away."

"Obviously." Karma glanced down at mankind's greatest sexual secret.

And was it hot in the basement or what? She couldn't listen to Zach carry on any more about how the Adam could send Mark's ejaculatory reflex into outer space without wanting to excuse herself to relieve a little of her own frustration. Mark had been gone a week, and he'd only been home ten days out of the last thirty. After what they'd done to each other in Chicago, that wasn't enough. She was seriously Jonesing for a repeat performance.

As if reading her mind, Lisa said, "When does Mark get home?"

"Tomorrow." He'd flown to Florida Monday, then to Minnesota Wednesday morning, and then into Chicago Thursday night. He'd spent Friday with a client, and then had dinner with his parents. Today, he was visiting with Rob and Holly, who had recently announced she was pregnant.

When Mark got home tomorrow, she was determined to corner him for a little private time.

She glanced at the boxes in her hands.
Okay, make that a *lot* of private time.

Chapter 22

Life begins at the end of your comfort zone.
-Neale Donald Walsch

Mark shook Rob's hand then gave him the tissue-wrapped gift he'd bought last night at Tiffany's. Nothing big, just a silver picture frame. Something to put their first baby picture in.

"Congratulations," he said, hugging Holly.

"Thank you." She placed her palm on her stomach, already doting on the unborn child who, from what Rob had texted last night, was already giving Holly terrible bouts of morning sickness. But there was no sign of sickness right now. Holly's cheeks were flushed, eyes bright, lips plump.

"You look good," he said to her.

"It's a good day." She grabbed Mark's hand and led him into the living room. "A perfect day for what Rob and I have planned for you."

"I told her not to do this," Rob said, laughing, "but she's shown me the light."

He cast Rob a questioning glance, feeling a bit like a dog being led on a leash. "And what light would that be?"

"To never disagree with a pregnant woman. It doesn't end well."

Holly laughed. "Don't listen to him. I'm not that bad. I'm really quite agreeable, given the circumstances."

Now Rob laughed. "Really? Is that what they're calling it now? Agreeable? You practically grew horns and a forked tail."

"I did not."

Rob took her hand. "Okay, maybe they were little tiny horns. And they were kinda cute on you."

"Just wait till I hit six months," she said. "You'll want to move out."

Rob shook his head. "Never."

The love between Rob and Holly warmed Mark's heart. For so long, he and Rob had sworn they would never fall in love. Never get married. Never have kids. They'd been avowed bachelors.

Now Rob was married and expecting, and Mark was on his way.

If only he could simply get past the one tiny roadblock impeding his progress.

"So, what's this about a plan you two have for me?" he asked.

Holly's face brightened. "Well, Rob explained to me that you're having trouble talking to Karma about the wedding and that you have these panic attacks every time you try."

Mark angled his head at Rob. "He did, did he?"

Rob cleared his throat, chagrined, as he fought back a sheepish smile.

"Rob tells me everything," Holly said dismissively. "But that's not the point. The point is, it gave me an idea."

"Well, it gave *us* an idea," Rob added.

Holly nodded. "Right. Us. This was kind of a joint effort."

Rob took over. "See, Holly's heard of this thing called immersion therapy where people are gradually exposed to the very thing they have a phobia to."

"Patients look at pictures of what they fear," Holly said, "or they talk about it, or sit in the same room with it . . . or even watch movies which contain the object of their fear." A gleeful smile broke over her face, and she dashed to the entertainment center. When she returned, she was holding a stack of DVDs. "So, Rob and I are immersing you." She started reading off movie titles. "*Father of the Bride*, *The Wedding Singer*, *My Best Friend's Wedding*, *Bridesmaids*, and *My Big Fat Greek Wedding*, which is my personal favorite."

Mark glanced at Rob. "You're serious?"

"I told you I wasn't sure this was a good idea, honey," Rob said to Holly.

"Nonsense. This'll work. I know it. Now, sit." Holly pointed to the couch. "I'm making Cuban ham sandwiches for lunch. Then we're ordering out for dinner. We're doing this."

Mark glanced warily from Holly to Rob, "Is she possessed?" He pretended that he was scared to touch her as she passed him on her way to the TV.

Rob chuckled, "I told you, man. It's the hormones."

"You two, hush." Holly threw them both warning glances. "Mark needs this."

This. An intervention. Only not for drugs.

He hesitantly rounded the couch and plopped down, waiting as

Holly loaded the DVD.

"Do you think this will really work?" He had his doubts, but anything was worth a try. And it wasn't like he had anything better to do today. He'd been running all over the eastern third of the country for a month. He could use a day on the couch. But it would be nice if he could return home tomorrow and be able to surprise Karma with a wedding date. This immersion therapy might not work *that* fast, but even if it only helped a little, that was better than nothing.

"I don't know," Rob said. "It could work. Then again, we might just spend the day watching a bunch of wedding movies and have nothing to show for it other than losing our man cards."

He relaxed into the couch. "Why couldn't I have been afraid of clowns?"

"Clowns? Man, no way. That would suck."

"Oh, because being afraid of weddings doesn't suck?" He speared Rob with a frustrated glance.

"Yeah, I guess you've got a point." Rob reached for the newspaper, which Holly immediately snatched from his hand.

"No. You." She snapped her fingers. "Watch." She pointed to the TV as the opening credits began running on a backdrop of champagne bubbles.

"Hey, why do I have to watch? Mark's the one with the phobia."

Holly dropped the newspaper on the kitchen counter as she headed for the fridge to start lunch. "As the pre-designated best man and Mark's best friend, it is your duty to sit with him through this," she said. "You have to help him."

Rob turned around and looked over the back of the couch. "Help him how?"

"By occasionally reminding him that he needs to imagine himself in the place of the actors playing the grooms in these movies and by pointing out things that could be triggers as they come up." She spoke as if this all should have been apparent to him already.

"Are you kidding me?"

"No. Now, be quiet and turn around. The movie's starting."

"This had better work," Rob grumbled to Mark as he faced the TV again.

Mark leaned toward him. "You're telling me. But, man, I'm glad

I'm not in your shoes for the next nine months."

Rob uttered a soft huff. "When Karma's pregnant and you're up to your nads in raging female hormones and morning sickness, I'll remind you that you said that."

Holly clapped twice from the kitchen. "Quiet! You two need to take this seriously. This is Mark's future we're talking about."

Mark exchanged a secret smile with Rob as he shifted back to his side of the couch.

"Yes, ma'am," Rob said. "Taking things seriously in here."

Holly sighed but didn't reply.

Mark turned his attention to the movie as the camera panned to Steve Martin, wearing a tuxedo, sitting in a chair among the aftermath of what was obviously his character's daughter's wedding.

In less than twenty seconds, as Steve began comparing getting married to a wedding, something clicked inside Mark's mind.

A wedding wasn't the same as getting married. One was an event, the other a deliberate action. Getting married was what happened between two people who were in love. To get married was to dedicate yourself—heart, soul, and spirit—to another person and to receive that same promise in return.

A wedding was just where that vow took place.

In other words, he was through the hard part. In his heart, he was already married to Karma. So why the hang-up over the easy part? When he really thought about it, a wedding was like putting a period at the end of a sentence. The sentence, which took all the work, was already finished. A period just made it official and easy to read.

But phobias didn't care how easy something was *supposed* to be. They hit where it hurt. Where they could do the most damage. Phobias held no compassion for the victim. And didn't he know it.

Steve Martin continued his soliloquy about his character's daughter and her new last name. Banks-MacKenzie.

He'd never asked Karma whether she wanted to take his last name or hyphenate hers. He'd just assumed she would be Karma Strong after they got married. But maybe she wanted to be Karma Mason-Strong.

As the movie's opening narration continued, more lights went on inside Mark's head. Steve Martin was playing the father of the bride, a role Karma's dad played in real life. No wonder John was so against him. Mark was stealing his daughter. Maybe John had known even before Mark did that Karma's heart was lost to him forever. Maybe it was like a fatherly sixth sense kind of thing.

And just like George Banks in *Father of the Bride*, John would do anything to keep his daughter as . . . well . . . his daughter. He wouldn't want Karma running off to get married. Because that would mean she was all grown up. Her own person. No longer in need of her dad.

Mark knew how close Karma and her dad were. She was the very definition of a daddy's girl, and not just because she thought so, but because John thought so, too. He'd been her rock until Mark came along. Now Mark was her rock. Mark had replaced her dad in a lot of ways. He had become the most important man in Karma's life, a role John had filled until last November, when Mark came back and gave Karma's then-fiancé, Brad, the boot.

It all made sense now. John had liked Brad, because on a subconscious level, he'd known Brad wasn't anyone he needed to worry about. Brad never would have been her rock. But Mark was, which made him the enemy.

As the movie got underway, his mind churned over the revelations firing inside his head. It was like a dozen tiny but monumental connections were being made. All from less than five minutes of a movie.

Maybe there was something to this immersion therapy idea. He still wasn't sure he could discuss a wedding date without losing his lunch, but the clarity he was obtaining about everything else was certainly worth the effort and couldn't hurt.

For the next seven hours, he lost himself inside the movies the same way he'd done with all the books, magazines, and online forums he'd read years ago when learning about women, what they wanted, and how to give them pleasure. Watching the movies was just another type of research.

Holly, emotional from her fluctuating hormones, dabbed at her eyes with a tissue at the end of The Wedding Singer and laughed herself to a different type of tears while watching Bridesmaids.

But it was *My Big Fat Greek Wedding* that gave Mark his most powerful reaction of the night. Toula reminded him so much of Karma his heart actually hurt. Toula started off as an invisible wallflower, a beauty hidden behind large glasses, a bad haircut, and frumpy clothes. A plain caterpillar. And then she metamorphosed into a butterfly. Beautiful, strong, and vivacious.

Just like his Karma.

And then he was suddenly missing her so bad it hurt. He'd been gone a week, and, right now, he needed to see her more than anything. He wasn't supposed to head out until tomorrow morning, but that wasn't soon enough. He really needed to be with Karma tonight. If nothing else, these movies had reminded him of how much he loved her . . . how much his soul needed hers to feel complete.

He was about to excuse himself to go home when Rob threw out his arms toward the TV.

"Okay, I can't take any more of this!" His hands curled into fists.

"What?" Holly appeared affronted.

"This! These movies! One chick flick after another after another." Rob grabbed a car magazine on the coffee table and aggressively waved it in the air. "I need speed. Action! Car chases and guns!" He stood and paced. "This . . ." He flung his arm toward the TV. "This is about to drive me insane. At least give me a nude-booby shot!"

"Hey, this was *your* idea," Mark said, reminding him how this all got started.

"It was more Holly's idea than mine!" Rob yelled. Then he realized what he'd said and how he'd said it and darted a worried glance toward Holly.

She looked like she was on the verge of crying.

"Oh, honey, I'm sorry. I didn't mean that." Rob rushed to her chair and knelt in front of her, taking her face in his hands. "I'm sorry. Don't cry."

Wow, those hormones were powerful little fuckers. Mark needed to remember that.

He scooted to the edge of the couch. "Hey, you guys did this for me. Holly . . ." He raised his chin toward her as she warily met his gaze. "You did good."

Rob glanced over his shoulder. "What's that supposed to mean?"

Mark stood. "It means that I miss my fiancée. I need to go home.

"You mean . . ." Holly smiled. "Did our immersion therapy work?"

He smiled. "I'm not sure I'm ready to talk about the wedding without having a panic attack just yet, but I'm a lot closer to being ready than I was eight hours ago. This was a big help. Thank you."

Rob helped Holly up, and the two followed him to the door, where they said warm good-byes. At least it appeared Rob was out of hot water.

For now.

In his rental car, Mark checked the time. Not quite seven thirty.

He pulled out his phone and sent Karma a text.

I'm on my way home.

A few seconds later, she replied. *Thought you weren't coming home till tomorrow.*

Tomorrow's not soon enough. I miss you.

Awe. ☺ But what about your airfare?

Due to the nature of this week's trip, he was supposed to fly home in the morning. He didn't normally fly between Chicago and Indianapolis, because when everything was taken into consideration, including driving to and from the airports, checking in, grabbing any checked luggage (and this time, he'd checked a suitcase), and especially O'Hare's propensity for flight delays, it was faster to drive three hours than take a short, forty-five minute flight.

I'll gladly eat the airfare to get back to you tonight. See you soon. I love you.

I love you, too. Drive safely.

Maybe he wasn't quite ready to discuss their wedding, but he was more than ready to hold Karma in his arms again. After all, he already saw her as his wife. In his heart, they were married. Which meant the hard part was over, right? All he needed was the period at the end of the sentence to make it official.

But as he hit I-94 out of Chicago, something told him there was still one roadblock in the way of his happiness. One piece of the puzzle he still hadn't dealt with, and that until he did, he wouldn't be able to move forward.

And he had a sinking feeling in his gut he knew exactly what that final piece was.

Chapter 23

Love is the ability and willingness to allow those that you care for to be what they choose for themselves, without any insistence that they satisfy you.
-Wayne Dyer

Freshly showered, Karma pulled on a pair of flannel shorts and a T-shirt then climbed into bed. She fluffed her pillow and piled it on top of another, then set both against the headboard and relaxed. It was almost 10:00, and Mark would be home any minute.

After he texted that he was on the way home, Lisa, Daniel, and Zach had helped her clean up before taking off. But not before Daniel gave her one last, short pep talk about introducing Mark to her new arsenal of toys.

In preparation, she'd moved them from her panty drawer to the top drawer of her nightstand. It would be a lot easier to get to them there, especially if things escalated the way she thought they might when Mark got home.

There had been a bit of urgency behind his texts, and, with Mark, urgency usually meant sex.

She trembled in anticipation. How would he react when he saw her new toys? She could almost see the look on his face now. One of surprise, but also one of power. An expression that said he was both pleased that she wanted to indulge his fantasies but also that he planned on showing her just how much pleasure he could give her for doing so.

She clicked on the TV, needing something to distract her mind. Otherwise, the waiting would drive her crazy.

Twenty minutes later, she heard his footsteps on the stairs.

She sat up, hugging her knees to her chest, ready.

And then he was there. Her sexy, larger-than-life man. He entered the bedroom and met her gaze as he set his bags beside the door.

"Hey." He smiled, but the gesture was more a hungry display of salacious seduction than a show of happiness and affection.

"Hey." She let go of her legs and let them fall Indian-style to the mattress.

He pulled his shirt over his head and tossed it to the floor as he crossed the room toward her.

His lips met hers, and she practically pulled him down on top of her.

"I missed you," he said, between kisses, pushing his hand under her tank top.

"I missed you, too."

In the fiery rush that followed, as their clothes fell away and he rolled on top of her, held down her arms, and claimed her body, she forgot all about the toys. This moment was about welcoming her man home. About untamed love and unbridled passion. Devotion conveyed through swift and furious affection.

She gripped him with her legs, drove her nails into his back when he finally released her arms, and held on tight as he drove into her hard and fast, making her cry out with every thrust.

Afterward, neither could move for a long time. He lay on top her, his skin slick with sweat, both of them panting.

Finally, he kissed her neck then pushed himself up on his arms. This time his smile *was* one of happiness and affection. "I'm going to grab a shower." He bent and gave her a quick kiss.

She sat up as he rolled to the edge of the bed, stood, and then disappeared into the bathroom. A moment later, the shower turned on and she heard the glass panel click closed.

She glanced at the drawer on her nightstand. She wanted to show him what she'd done. That she was ready to explore his fantasies with him. Now.

With a quick glance at the sliver of light shining between the partially closed bathroom door and the frame, she took a deep breath and hopped out of bed. Yanking open the drawer, she pulled out her stash and tossed everything on the bed. Then she grabbed the Adam and took it with her as she eased open the bathroom door.

Mark had his back to her, and the bathroom smelled of sandalwood. Mark's soap. Shampoo suds trailed from his hair, down his neck, over his cut shoulders. The muscles of his back rolled under his skin as he brushed his hands forward and back over his scalp.

She quietly opened the glass door, set the Adam on the built-in stone shelf, and glided up behind him, lightly brushing her palms over the back of his shoulders.

He stilled then glanced over his shoulder, blinking as suds slid past his eyes. The dimple cut into his right cheek as he smiled.

"Hungry for more?"

"I'm nowhere near satisfied." She slicked suds down his back, letting her fingers linger on the tight swells of his ass. He really did have a fine ass.

And it was time she gave it the attention it deserved.

* * *

He could barely breathe as she massaged his butt, pressing the front of her body to his back as she did, rolling her taut nipples against his skin. He couldn't see her, but the way she was moving reminded him of the way a belly dancer moves, only much slower, and only with her breasts, not her hips. Sexy as hell.

She was different tonight. More seductive. More in control. The power was in her court, and she wasn't afraid to wield it.

He liked that.

Her fingers slid between his cheeks, and he had to press his hands against the wall in front of him as a wave of arousal rocked him forward.

Jesus!

He moaned, dropping his head between his outstretched biceps. Trails of sudsy water rained down from his hair.

She released him then slithered her hands around to his cock and balls as she pressed her groin against his ass.

He'd come less than fifteen minutes ago, but damn. He was ready to go again. Growing hard and swollen.

He watched her delicate hands fist and stroke him. Tiny soap bubbles coated both his cock and her fingers, making the friction slick.

"Hold out your hand," he said, picking up his bottle of shower soap. He poured some in her palm then groaned when she gripped him and went back to stroking, harder this time, working the slippery lather between her hands.

Then her left hand disappeared, reappearing a second later from between his legs. She'd reached under him from behind to cup his balls, but as she did, she rubbed the heel of her hand against his perineum.

Fuck!

He saw stars, flexing his arms and legs to keep him upright as his knees quaked.

The fingers of her left hand slid back. Farther still. Until her middle finger found his anus and began rubbing in small circles.

Oh God. Holy fuck. He'd dreamed of this, but he'd begun to think it was something she'd never want to do. He didn't know why she'd waited until tonight to go down this path, but he was grateful she'd finally gone there.

"Is this what you want?" Her voice was soft yet commanding, and every hair on his body stood on end at the power she had over him in that moment.

Both legs shuddered as her finger pressed inward.

He gasped, nodded, licked his lips. "Yes."

"What's it feel like?" She took her time, just as he had with her in Chicago, gently letting just the tip of her finger enter him.

His hands became claws, his nails scratching the stone tiles. "Good. It feels good." He could barely talk as he gasped for air, his toes curling and flexing.

No one had done this to him in a long time. A long damn time. And doing it to himself was like giving himself a massage. It didn't feel nearly as good as when someone else did it.

Her right hand continued to stroke as her left pressed between his cheeks.

"Stop me if I hurt you," she whispered, letting her finger delve deeper.

"You're not . . . you're not hurting me. Jesus, Karma. I didn't think . . ." He grunted as a wave of euphoria whipped through him, causing him to weave forward and back. "I didn't think you wanted this."

She pressed her cheek against the back of his shoulder. "I just needed time to figure out what I was doing."

Hallelujah for her doing her research!

"Trust me, you're doing fine. This is . . ." Another shock of arousal rocketed through him, stealing his voice as her finger stroked home base. "Jesus!" His whole body shuddered, his muscles contracting violently. "Right there. There . . ."

God bless her daring desire to please him! The tip of her finger hit the spot again. And then again.

And then he was a goner.

Everything went dark as his entire body convulsed and he shot his load against the tiled wall.

Karma cried out behind him, and when he opened his eyes again, he was on all fours, his cock still emptying.

"Mark! Oh my God, are you okay?" Karma was on her knees beside him, one hand on his back, the other holding his shoulder.

All he could do was moan and hold his eyes closed as his cock pulsed several more times, his abdomen jerking through each contraction.

"Mark?"

He finally sucked in a long, heavy breath, opened his eyes once more, and smiled. "Where did you learn that?"

"What?" She shook her head as if dispelling brain fog. "Mark, you fell." She stared at him with wide eyes. "Are you okay?"

He'd come so hard he'd fallen to the floor. Maybe that was why everything had gone dark for a second. He'd almost passed out.

"I'm fine." He took several deep breaths then unsteadily pulled himself to the bench in front of him and leaned his back against the cold, wet wall as he reached for her hand. She took it, and he helped her onto his lap. He needed his arms around her, her body against his. "Where did you learn how to do that?" he said again.

She bit her lip and smiled, relaxing. "I've been reading."

He drank in her face. Her beautiful, adorable face. "That must have been some reading."

Warm water still rained down over them from the oversized, square showerhead, but he was in no hurry for their shower to end.

Her cheeks flushed red, and she looked over her shoulder and bobbed her head toward one of the shelves. He could just see the profile of something black and red poised on the edge.

"I'd intended to use that, but then . . ." She giggled as if at herself. "Then I got a little carried away. That was, uh . . . just wow. I thought I'd be squeamish, but then I saw how you reacted, and it turned me on, and then I couldn't stop."

He kissed her, letting his lips linger on hers. "You have my permission to get carried away like that any time you want, baby."

Her shy but proud smile warmed his heart.

"But . . ." He pushed her to her feet and stood. "Now I'm curious what this is." He crossed the small space and picked up the black and red object. He'd seen something like this before but had never used one.

"It's called the Adam." Karma took it from him and held it up. "It goes in like this, and this little curly thing . . ." She pointed at one of the slender plastic curls that extended from the base. "This presses against your scrotum. And this presses against your prostate." She pointed to the other end. "I guess men who've used this say it gives them really powerful orgasms. The strongest and longest they've ever had. You can even walk around with it in. I guess it can be pretty intense."

The longer she talked, the bigger his smile grew, until finally she cocked her head at him and said, "What?"

"Nothing, Miss Mason. I'm just amused that you seem to have found something *you* can teach *me*."

"The student becomes the teacher?"

He pulled her into his arms. "I think I'm going to like being your student."

"Will you bring your teacher a shiny red apple?"

"If that's what she wants." He reached around her and shut off the water. "But right now, your student is famished." He pulled two warm towels off the rack and handed her one. "And for what he has planned for his teacher tonight, he's going to need a lot of energy."

"Is he now?"

It felt like the remnants of one more crumbling barrier had come crashing down, and even though one still remained firmly in place, he'd take what he could get. And right now, what he wanted to take over and over was Karma.

"Yes," he said, slinging his towel around her like a rope and tugging her to him. His gaze tore into her. "Fucking burns a lot of calories. And I plan on fucking you all night, especially if you help me use this." He pointed to the contraption she referred to as the Adam. "Are you up for that?"

She grinned and skimmed her palms over his chest. "I'll just say this. I've missed you *a lot* in the last month."

"Then I have a lot to make up for, don't I?"

"Mm-hm. And I've got more where that came from." She pointed to the Adam.

"More?"

She nodded. "A *lot* more. You and I have quite a night of experimentation ahead of us, baby."

"Then, by all means, let's hurry up and eat so we can get started."

He took her hand and led her from the shower. He was so close to having it all. His future was right in front of him, just outside his reach.

Just past the lone specter still haunting him.

Carol.

Chapter 24

A journey of a thousand miles begins with a single step.
-Lao-Tzy

Mark paused Bride Wars on his office computer, grabbed his phone, and hit Rob's speed dial.

He'd run Rob's advice from the night of his mom's birthday party over and over in his mind all week. What if Rob was right? Maybe he needed to talk to Carol. In hindsight, they'd never really talked about what happened eight years ago. Like Rob had said, they'd yelled at each other, their emotions too high to think reasonably and truly listen, and then . . . nothing. They'd had virtually no contact beyond the occasional run-in at the annual arts benefit, where they avoided each other like men avoided Medusa.

But Carol wasn't attending this year's benefit, according to the current attendee list he'd coaxed out of his dad. Thank God for small blessings, since he was going with Karma.

"Hey, man. What's up?" Rob said.

"I think you were right," Mark blurted without offering a greeting.

"Okay, this sounds serious. What was I right about?"

"Carol. I think I need to talk to her."

"Ooo-kaaay. What brought this on? Don't tell me it was the immersion therapy."

"No. I mean, I don't think so. It could have been. I mean, I've been staying late at the office every night this week watching wedding movies, so you tell me if it's working."

"You're not serious."

"Dead serious. Bride Wars is paused on my computer right now. Karma thinks I've been staying to get caught up on work since we're leaving tomorrow to head up to Chicago for Saturday's benefit."

"You've been lying to her?"

"Not totally. I've been working." He gestured toward the frozen image on his computer as if Rob could see him. "I've just been watching movies, too. And it's working. Somewhat. At least, it feels like it is." In a lot of ways, he felt more open. "Watching these movies has, at least in some cases, helped me gain perspective. But . . ."

"But you still can't talk about setting a date."

He rocked forward and planted his feet squarely on the floor beneath his desk. "No. And I think I finally figured out why."

"Because I was right and you've realized you need to talk to Carol?"

He snapped his fingers. "Exactly."

"I told you so."

"Yeah, yeah. Spare me the lecture. I need your help."

"Anything. Name it."

"I need you to ask Holly to invite Karma to lunch Sunday."

"And what are you going to do?"

"I'm going to see Carol. I'm going to resolve this once and for all."

"Whoa, man. You sure about this?"

Mark stood and paced to the window. "Hey, this was your idea. Just like the immersion therapy. So don't you puss out on me now and tell me you weren't serious.

"I was dead serious. I think you need to talk to her, but you sound a little intense."

"Maybe because I am. This needs to happen. I need to end this now, so I can move forward with Karma. If I don't get my head out of my ass, I'll eventually lose her. She won't want to stick around forever. I've already made her wait long enough."

"Okay, okay. Calm down. I'll talk to Holly. But man, I should warn you that I don't think it's a good idea to lie to Karma. Holly and I can work something out to keep her busy so you can handle this, but I think it would be better if you told her the truth."

"No. I don't want to worry her, and I need to do this without worrying what she's thinking. If she knows I'm going to see Carol, she'll be upset, and that won't sit well with me. I'll be preoccupied, and I don't want that to happen."

"Okay, fine. I've got your back. I'll take care of it."

Mark took a relieved breath. "Thanks, Rob. I owe you one."

"Like I said before, you don't owe me anything. Just . . . deal with this shit once and for all and put it behind you." He paused. "I'll see you Saturday then, okay?"

"I'll be there. Thanks, man."

He disconnected, returned to his chair, and pushed play on his computer. Less than five minutes later, his phone chimed with a text from Karma.

Mom and Dad invited us over for dinner, if you can believe that. Maybe my dad is finally coming around. I told them you were working late but I could go. So, I'm heading to their house. You want me to bring you something?

He hated missing dinner with her parents, especially if her dad really was starting to come around, but he did have official work to do. Maybe he should shut off the movie and finish up so he could at least get home at a decent hour. But, surprisingly, he was getting a lot out of these damn wedding movies. Maybe not what Rob and Holly had intended, but still. Something was better than nothing.

No need to bring me anything. Enjoy yourself and tell your parents I send my regards. I'll be home in a few hours. I love you.

And he did. He loved her so much. She deserved to have all of him. And by the end of the weekend, that was exactly what she would have. One way or another, Carol's occupation of his mind, no matter how minimal, would come to an end.

* * *

Karma read Mark's text and smiled.

I love you, too. See you when you get home. Xoxoxox

The incredible weekend they'd had four days ago still caused butterflies and flames to flicker in her belly every time she recalled the things she'd done to him, and all the ways he'd thanked her for doing them. For twenty-four hours, there had been no work, no parents, no pending wedding date, no Carol. Just them. Their bedroom had been an oasis they left only to eat and recuperate before starting over again.

But he'd seemed distracted ever since. Not in the bedroom. That was the one place he remained laser-focused. It was in the mornings when he was getting ready for work, or in the evenings as they watched the news or grabbed a late snack before bed, when his mind seemed to be elsewhere.

Maybe he was distracted by work, or maybe it was nothing at all.

They were still getting acquainted with the idea of living together. Perhaps this was just how Mark was, and as they settled into a routine, things would feel more normal.

She turned onto the street that led to her parents' house and nearly came to a stop when she saw Johnny's car in the driveway. She and Johnny didn't get along, but Johnny and Dad got along even worse. The last time they'd seen one another was last summer when Brad proposed.

This could be an interesting dinner depending on whether Johnny could keep his egotistic, pompous attitude in check.

"Hi, honey," her mom said, opening the door. "Where's Mark?"

"He has to work."

"Well, that's too bad. I was looking forward to visiting with him." She closed the door behind her.

"Yeah, well, I'm sure Dad will be pleased."

Her mom blew out an abrupt laugh. "Oh, I don't know. I think Mark's starting to grow on your father."

"Really?" Hell must have frozen over.

Her mom stepped closer and said in hushed tones, "It was *his* idea to invite you two for dinner, so if Mark *isn't* growing on him, at least he's trying."

"I guess that's a start." She glanced past her mom toward the sound of voices in the living room. "What's Johnny doing here?"

Mom smiled in that way that indicated some forces in nature just couldn't be explained. "I think Johnny's trying, too."

"What do you mean?"

"He's been coming around more since you've been gone. Spending time with your dad. I can tell he's trying not to be so argumentative."

What the hell had happened since Thanksgiving. Had the rest of her family entered an alternate dimension?

She followed her mom into the kitchen, where chicken pieces coated with a double layer of buttermilk and seasoned flour sat on a sheet of wax paper next to a large iron skillet.

Mmm, fried chicken and mashed potatoes. The good stuff.

"Why don't you go watch the game with your dad and brother while I finish up in here," her mom said.

"You sure you don't need any help." Part of her dreaded leaving the calm safety of her mom, but she knew she couldn't avoid her dad and brother all night.

"I'm fine. Go on." Her mom waved her toward the family room.

Practically tip-toeing, she went to the doorway to the living room and peered inside. Johnny and her dad were watching the game together, engrossed in the action.

Before the Mark Strong Apocalypse, she was the one Dad watched sports with. The two of them had spent at least one day a week catching a football game, basketball game, or whatever sport happened to be on. It had been their thing. *Theirs*. Not theirs and Johnny's. Johnny had never figured into what had been special father-daughter time. Now, Dad was sharing that special time with her pain-in-the-ass brother. When had her dad and Johnny gotten so close?

Johnny threw his arms out in front of him. "Charging! Where's the call, ref?"

"The officials obviously have their favorite, and it isn't us." Her dad groused over the call, crossing his arms the way he always did when he was getting worried a game was already over.

"Don't give up on them just yet," she said, entering the room.

Dad smiled at first as he uncrossed his arms and motioned as if he was about to stand and hug her, but then he cleared his throat and settled back in his chair once more, glancing behind her at the TV. It was odd behavior. Kind of like her dad didn't know how to act around her, anymore. As if he wasn't sure what his place was now that she had Mark.

"Where's Mark?" he said, right on cue.

"Working."

"This late?" he said disapprovingly.

"We're driving up to Chicago tomorrow for a charity benefit on Saturday his parents help plan every year, so he's trying to get caught up before we leave." She turned to Johnny. "Where's Estelle?"

"At home with the baby."

Karma took a seat on the other side of the couch. She hadn't seen her niece in months. "You should have brought her. I haven't seen her in a while."

"Well, you haven't been around."

She shot Johnny a scowl, and he held up his hands as if warding off an argument.

"I'm just saying, Karma, if you want to see her, just come around more often."

"I would if Dad would accept the man in my life."

"Look, I'm trying," her dad said. "That's why I invited you both to dinner. But, of course, your guy couldn't make it."

"That's because he's trying to be a good provider. Would you rather I get involved with a deadbeat."

"No, but—"

"John," Mom called from the kitchen. "Could you come here and help me, please."

In other words, Mom was nipping this conversation in the bud and would have a few private words with her dad before dinner to ensure everyone got along tonight.

Sighing, her dad pushed out of his chair. "On my way, dear."

Johnny went back to watching the game, seemingly intent on not antagonizing her further, which was surprising, given their history. Johnny had been the ringleader who had riled the masses to tease, taunt, and humiliate her in school. And he'd continued hating on her into adulthood.

Maybe he was finally growing up and turning over a new leaf.

Karma listened to the quiet admonishment her mom gave her dad, as well as to the chagrined way his dad kept saying, "I know, dear, I'm sorry."

The way her mom kept her dad on the straight and narrow was actually kind of cute. They'd been married forever, and it was because they both knew how to bring the best out in each other, which was something she was beginning to understand in her relationship with Mark.

Theirs was a dance of compromise and will, each highly motivated to make the other happy.

Except Karma still felt like there was one area of Mark's heart that remained closed off to her. One part of Mark's soul that Carol still possessed.

It was time Karma forced the issue. Not this weekend. Not with the benefit. She wouldn't risk ruining that. But one night next week, she and Mark needed to have a long, difficult conversation. Difficult because this was sure to disrupt the comfortable intimacy they'd created in the last week.

But she didn't want comfortable. She wanted forever. She wanted *all* of Mark, not just part of him, and she didn't want to compete with Carol's memory, anymore.

A few minutes later, her mom called them to dinner, and she stood and followed Johnny to the kitchen table, but even as conversation flowed more easily than it ever had, if not a bit tense at times, her mind still dwelled on Mark.

He needed to address the situation and evict Carol once and for all.

If he didn't, she had a terrible feeling it would eventually destroy their relationship.

Chapter 25

The body is meant to be seen, not all covered up.
-Marilyn Monroe

"You want me to wear *this*?" Karma lifted the sparkling, midnight-blue mermaid dress. He had to be joking.

Mark pulled his starched shirt on and began buttoning it as his gaze met hers in the mirror. "Yes."

"But . . . it's backless."

"I know."

She turned her gaze to the dress again. "What I mean is, it's *extremely* backless. As in, it will barely cover my butt."

When she glanced back at his reflection, he was grinning. "I know."

She let the garment fall over her forearm and eyed him suspiciously. "What do you have up your sleeve?"

His grin twisted into a smirk as he tore his gaze from hers and looked at his reflection, turning up the collar of his shirt so he could drape his tie around the back of his neck.

Resigning herself that this was her outfit for the evening, she crossed behind him on her way to the bathroom. He took her hand, stopping her.

"Don't wear any panties," he said, catching her eye.

Her mouth fell open. "But . . ."

One of his thick eyebrows arched in warning. "No panties, Karma."

His command had *exhibitionist fantasy* written all over it. And the charity benefit was to be his playground. *Their* playground.

She suddenly understood his reason for buying her this dress. As usual, there was a purpose—a *plan*—to everything he did. And as he went back to knotting his tie, the teacher persona fell more into place with every twist and swish of silver silk around his neck.

"Yes, Mr. Strong." She grinned and disappeared into the bathroom.

*   *   *

Mark grinned over his shoulder as she shut the bathroom door. *Yes, Mr. Strong.* She knew what he had in mind for tonight. Or, at least, she had some idea what he was planning, or she wouldn't have given him that look and used that tone of voice right before closing the door.

After checking his reflection one last time, he draped his tuxedo jacket across the foot of the bed, rotated one of the club chairs near the window so it faced the bathroom, and settled into it, crossing his ankle over the opposite knee.

When she reappeared a few minutes later, his heart nosedived into his stomach. God, she was beautiful, her skin glowing in contrast to the midnight-blue fabric. He angled his head, admiring how the dress hung alluringly over her slight curves and caressed her narrow hips.

"Turn around for me," he said. "Let me see."

She sighed but smiled coquettishly. "I can't believe I'm going to wear this dress in public." Biting her bottom lip, she did as he asked and slowly spun around, allowing him to take in the whole package. The sweetheart neckline revealed more of her breasts than she was normally comfortable with, but that was nothing compared to the way the back of the dress plunged all the way to the upper swell of her perfect ass, baring her entire back.

She faced him once more, shoulders drawn in shyly.

"Come here," he side.

As she traversed the room, the fabric flared and swished around her feet. In her heels, the hem would barely whisper against the floor, which was exactly what he'd intended.

When she stopped in front of him, it was with a subtle air of defiance, as if she were challenging him to resist her.

If only she knew. Resisting her wasn't even on the table. He'd chosen this dress expressly so he would be forced to covet her the entire evening and make it impossible for him to resist.

He stood and slid his arm around her waist. His fingers eased just under the fabric barely covering her ass. Then his whole hand disappeared inside the dress to cup her right cheek. There was just enough give to the fabric that he could fondle her everywhere.

"This is what I can do to you in this dress," he whispered in her ear, squeezing. She shivered against him.

Then he slid his hand lower until his fingers found her swollen, slick lips. He kissed her earlobe.

"And I can do this, too..." He flicked one strap from her shoulder with his free hand. The dress fell away to reveal her breast, her nipple budding immediately upon exposure.

He could feel her fighting not to squirm as he slowly slid his finger inside her.

"And you plan on doing this to me at tonight's benefit?" she said, her voice trembling ever-so-slightly.

"If I'm lucky." He removed his finger and stepped behind her, nudging her toward the window as he eased the second strap off her other shoulder. The dress fell into a puddle at her feet, revealing her naked body. "As you can see, it's very easy to take off."

Her body tensed as he pressed her farther forward, until she was only a few inches from the glass.

There was another hotel across the street. Several of the windows had their drapes open, and in one room, a man was sitting at his desk, working on his laptop.

"See that man?" he asked.

She nodded. Her shoulders were tight, and it seemed as though she were forcing herself not to cover herself.

"All he has to do is look up, and he'll see you." He reached around and cupped one breast, swiping his thumb back and forth over her nipple. "Anyone could open their curtains at any moment and see you standing here, naked, my hands caressing you, getting you hot."

Her chest rose and fell heavily.

"Does that excite you?" he said.

She nodded. "Yes," she whispered.

"And you want this?" He wrapped his arms around her and pressed his erection against her bare bottom.

She sighed. "Yes."

"You want everyone to watch me fucking you, too, don't you? It turns you on. Gets you hot. Hotter than you thought it would." He bent forward and nipped the back of her shoulder.

She nodded, practically panting, her fingers curling against the glass.

He caressed her naked abdomen and whispered, "I always knew

you were an exhibitionist. Like me. So like me." He kissed her shoulder, nuzzling, caressing. "We complement each other so perfectly, Karma."

If he searched a hundred years, he wouldn't find anyone he was more attuned to. Karma fit him in every way, arousing not just his body but his mind, opening herself to every fantasy, every possibility. He'd never met anyone else as open to pushing outside her comfort zone, but Karma was a living sponge, absorbing all his lessons and wanting more.

"Touch me . . . please," she whispered.

"I *am* touching you." A dark chuckle rumbled from his chest as he pressed more firmly against her back and lightly pinched her nipples. "See . . . feel that?"

She moaned and dropped her head back against his shoulder. "I know, but . . ."

"Ssshhh." He released her and took a step back. "You'll get what you want." He knelt and began slowly dragging the dress up her legs.

She made a disappointed noise, halfway between a groan and a wordless curse.

"You know," he said, his fingers caressing her hips as he pulled the fabric higher, "I'm going to be hard all night with you in this dress." He tapped her hands, and she held them out so he could maneuver the straps over her arms.

He could feel her disappointment, as well as the waves of arousal pouring from her body. She didn't want to put her clothes back on. She wanted to keep them off. To be pressed against the window and fucked until she screamed his name and left an imprint of her body on the glass.

"Please touch me." The plaintive, make-me-come plea nearly made him cave. His cock even twitched.

Tapping into his reserved determination, he finished redressing her and adjusted the shoulder straps before checking the bodice.

"Not yet," he said, turning for the dresser and the black, velvet-lined jewelry box he'd set there earlier. "But soon."

He plucked the gold necklace from the velvet pillow and shifted back toward her before dangling the delicate golden links in front of her.

She sucked in her breath. "What's this?"

"A gift." He draped the necklace around her neck and fastened the clasp at her nape before kissing the sensitive stretch of skin.

Then he pulled her back against him and secured her in his arms. His lips brushed the tender expanse of skin just below the hairline of her upswept hair. "When I touch you later — really touch you in the way you want me to — you'll be so ready to come you won't be able to stop yourself." He turned her to face him. "It could be at the bar . . ." his hands glided over her hips, and he inched closer. "In a shadowed corner . . ." He dipped his head to kiss the side of her neck then brought his lips to her ear. "Or maybe on the crowded dance floor."

She trembled and gripped his biceps through his shirt as he slipped his hand under the dress again and squeezed her left cheek.

"And I'll touch you there . . ." The tips of his fingers came precariously close to stroking home base. "And you'll come. Right where anyone can see you."

"I'm close to coming now."

He grinned. "I know you are. I can tell."

"Please . . ."

He shook his head and pulled his hand from inside her dress then took a step back. "Patience." He sat on the edge of the bed and picked up one of her shoes then nodded toward the chair behind her. "Please . . . sit."

She did, adjusting the chair so she was directly in front of him. He lifted her foot and let his fingertips whisper over her toes, along the arch, and then he gently grasped around the heel. "You have such beautiful feet."

"Said like a man with a true foot fetish."

"If only we had more time . . ."

"We have all the time in the world." Her tone hinted she was referring to more than just this evening.

He met her gaze as he smoothed his palm down the top of her foot to her toes again. "Yes, we do."

*   *   *

Mark slipped on her strappy high heel as if he were the prince placing the glass slipper on Cinderella's dainty foot. After securing the leather strap around her ankle, he lifted her other foot and repeated. Then he stood, slipped into his tuxedo jacket, helped her out of the chair, and smiled warmly as he held out his arm. "Shall we, Miss Mason?"

The arousal he'd awakened by putting her on display like a living mannequin still thrummed through her blood. He'd known just what to do and just how to goad her to send her salacious hunger through the ceiling. But this was Mark, the master of her body, heart, and soul. He simply seemed to know what she wanted and needed before she did.

And this was why she knew . . . somehow . . . some way . . . no matter if he could kick Carol completely from his life or not . . . they would make it. Somehow, they would survive for the long haul. Because he knew her soul. And she knew his. She couldn't imagine ever finding another man who could do to her the things Mark could. Who could set her on fire with just a glance, a word, a touch. A breath of whispered adoration.

She looped her arm around his as he handed her the sparkling dark-blue pocketbook he'd bought to match the dress. Then he guided her out of their suite, his head held high. He was her proud suitor, eager to show her off to the world. And she was eager to be shown, the queen to his king.

Carol be damned. Karma was in this to win. Mark was hers, and she would fight for him. She would find a way to pry Carol's claw-like hold from his heart.

She would never give Mark up. Not now. Not after all they'd gone through.

He belonged to her.

Chapter 26

Keep calm and let go.
-Author Unknown

Keeping his hand at the small of her bare back, where it was never far from striking distance, Mark paraded Karma around the ballroom full of distinguished guests. They stopped briefly to visit with his parents then moved on to view this year's exhibits in the exhibition hall before returning to the ballroom.

Every so often, he teased her by poking just the tips of his fingers inside her dress, giving a little squeeze, ever reminding her of his power, never letting her forget how quickly he could turn her from pleasant socialite to wanton sex fiend with just a stroke.

He introduced her to everyone, paying particular attention to the men whose eyes fell to her neckline and then to her back as they passed. He enjoyed their envious gazes, which fell right in line with the fantasy he wanted to weave.

"You're enjoying showing me off a little too much," she said coquettishly, leaning close.

He pulled her even closer, ducking his head so he could whisper in her ear. "What can I say? It gives me perverse joy to see these men stare so appreciatively at what's mine."

She arched her eyebrow. "Oh? So you own me now?" But the way one side of her mouth twisted in an amused smirk made it clear she knew he was only teasing.

"Of course not." His fingertips dipped inside her dress. "Just feeding the fantasy."

And the fantasy was to deem her his. To do with her as he pleased and parade her through the room like she was his personal sex slave. To create envy in those who couldn't have her. But it was all just semantics meant to heighten the game.

"Well, like I said, you're enjoying this far too much," she said, teasing him as he guided them to a cocktail table in the casino room with its dim lighting and red-dominated décor.

"You've no idea." He winked as he took a sip of his scotch. "I love that all these men . . ." He gestured with his glass, sweeping it right to left, "are looking at you." He sidled closer and traced her bodice with the tip of his finger, letting it linger between her breasts. "But only I get to see what lies beneath this dress."

Her chest lifted as if pulled by a magnet, and she leaned into him. From the glint in her eye, she was hyper aware of how little she was actually wearing and where his fingertip was.

"Only my eyes get to see you in the way these men can only fantasize about." He outlined her collar bones with his fingertip, swirled it in the hollow between, and slowly burned a trail down her sternum as her breathing deepened, making her chest expand heavily with every inhale.

The air between them quickly heated, coming alive, lust's blazing tendrils wrapping around them.

His eyelids fell as his gaze dropped to where his finger played between her breasts. When he spoke again, his voice was a deep, predatory growl. "I want you so bad it hurts."

And he didn't just mean this very instant. He meant for the rest of their lives.

"Then take me."

Did she understand his double entendre?

Her gaze locked onto his mouth then jumped to his eyes a split-second later. In that instant, he had never been more certain about his feelings. From the moment he first set eyes on Karma, his life ceased being his alone and became one with hers.

He bowed his head, stroking his palm across the bare stretch of skin exposed by the dress's deep neckline as if he wanted to reassure himself she was real and not just a mirage. "Sometimes I wonder what I ever did to deserve you."

It was an odd thing to say at a time like this, but he didn't care. It was how he felt, and the words spilled before he could stop them.

She closed the remaining distance between them and pressed her hand between his legs, making him suck in a breath. She'd never made such a bold move, and it damn near set his body on fire for how incredibly sexy it was. Her eyes lit with mischief and daring as if she didn't care who saw her stroke him through his pants.

He certainly didn't care. Let them watch. Let them see how strong their bond was. So strong that the world around them disappeared and left only them. To love and touch without concerning themselves with what the rest of the world thought.

"You saw what no one else did," she whispered. "That's what you did to deserve me."

What she didn't know was that she did the same for him. She saw the man no other woman had ever taken the time to see. The vulnerable man hidden beneath a confident exterior. The man who'd been hurt, was scarred, and who had desperately wanted to fall in love again, despite his fears.

That's why she'd been able to break through his defenses when no other woman could. Because she was different. Because she had never viewed him as a trophy or a stepping stone on her way up the gold digger ladder. His money and social status had never factored in to her feelings for him. Not once. She'd fallen in love with him for *him*.

Her hand stroked him up and down, and any resolve he'd maintained for the past two hours evaporated as a plaintive moan broke from his throat.

He dropped his hand to hers and linked their fingers together.

"Come with me." He snatched their cocktail napkins from the table then turned and led her away, his pace brisk and strong.

She had to quicken her steps, but she kept up as he pushed through the back exit of the ballroom into a service area. He hurried them away, around a corner, around another corner, looking, his eyes constantly searching.

"Where are we going?" she said, giggling and breathless as she took two hasty steps for each one of his.

He loosened his tie, already broaching on out-of-control. "Somewhere I can fuck you into next week," he said, voice gruff but restrained, eyes constantly searching . . . searching.

Jesus, didn't this hotel have a back hall or a service elevator or —

His gaze lit on a heavy metal door. The sign on the wall indicated it was a stairwell.

It would do. Quite nicely, in fact.

He shoved the door open, pulled her through, and then slammed it behind them. The lighting was dim, the stairwell monochromatically grey. Dark, but not too dark.

Before she could even turn around, he was on her, shoving her against the wall, unbuttoning his jacket, releasing his tie, his mouth seeking hers as she quickly recovered and began unfastening his pants.

Their passion fed their urgency, and their urgency fueled their passion in a vicious cycle of desire. Reason and logic evaporated as carnal hunger took over.

It was that sexy as hell conference room sex he'd never forgotten from two summers ago all over again, only more out of control. More abandoned. Wanton and lusty and shamelessly liberating. And hot as fuck. The only thing that would have made it hotter would have been if someone came up the stairs and stopped to watch. Just the idea that someone stood on the landing below, peeking over the metal banister, was enough to send his excitement into the stratosphere.

He tugged the shoulder straps down her arms, and the dress fell in a heap, leaving her in only her necklace and her shoes. Her lovely shoes with her dainty toes poking out from under the strap.

He dropped his pants, shoved his shirt tails aside, and rolled on the condom he'd pulled from his pocket.

"I'm not going to last long," he said, lifting her off the floor.

She threw her arms around his shoulders, her legs already around his waist. "I won't, either."

Then he was inside her, her back slapping the cold concrete wall as he thrust into her hard and fast.

Within seconds, she came, crying out so that anyone passing in the hall could have heard her. Jesus! But the thought sent a shard of lust straight into his balls.

"You want someone to find us, don't you?" he said, voice strained, breath coming as hard as his thrusts.

She trembled and shook her head. "No . . . I . . . oh God, I'm going to come again."

"Fuck yes . . . make it loud." If someone actually walked in on them while she was coming, he'd shoot his load. Hard. The fantasy realized.

As her insides tightened for orgasm number two, he hooked his arms one-by-one under her knees and opened her legs, splitting her, driving deeper, and deeper still as he pushed forward and planted his hands on the wall on either side of her shoulders, hiking her legs upward. She was completely vulnerable, her legs open and supported on his arms.

And she came again, crying out louder this time, giving him what he wanted, pushing her boundaries beyond her comfort zone. For him. No woman had ever sacrificed herself so completely for his pleasure before. And from the way her eyes sparkled and the corners of her mouth briefly curled upward, she liked the new version of herself she was becoming.

"Someone's watching us," she whispered, licking her lips and glancing over his shoulder.

Holy fuck! Holy shit! Yes!

He groaned then grunted, his body taking over for his brain, jack-hammering his hips like a piston in a high-powered engine as his thrusts quickened and deepened as if driven by an outside force.

He was about to come.

"Fuck, fuck...oh *fuck*." He slammed into her, pumping hard, coming as he gasped and shuddered.

*   *   *

Karma's insides spasmed a third time as his cock jerked and filled the condom. Then he glanced over his shoulder toward the empty stairwell.

When he looked back at her, he wore a confused expression. "I thought you said . . ."

She grinned, still trying to catch her breath. "I lied."

His eyebrows lifted in disbelief. "Why?"

"Why do you think?" Her grin widened as she searched his eyes, which lit with awareness a couple of seconds later.

"You wanted to heighten the fantasy for me."

She nodded. "Did it work?"

A single trail of perspiration broke from his hairline and trickled down his temple. "Hell, yeah, it worked. Couldn't you tell?"

She held up her hand with her thumb and forefinger a centimeter apart. "Maybe just a bit."

With her legs still spread eagle and pinned to the wall, they took another quick moment to catch their breath, and then Mark helped her down before hastily ripping off the condom, using one of the cocktail napkins he'd swiped to wipe himself off and then wrap around the condom, which he then tossed into the large trash can in the corner.

He pulled up his pants as she secured her dress back into place, and then she helped him button, tuck, and tie himself back together.

"How do I look?" he said, brushing his fingers through his hair, still out of breath.

"Dashingly handsome." She brushed her thumb over the layer of perspiration just below his hairline.

"Am I sweating?" He dabbed at his forehead with the other napkin.

"A little." She pulled a tissue from her pocketbook and giggled as she helped wipe away his sweat.

He grinned. "What's so funny?"

"Did we just do that?" Her legs were still trembling, and she nearly teetered over.

Mark caught her and laughed as he steadied her. "We sure did." Then he tucked his face against the side of her neck as he always did after sex. By now, it was a trademark move. "I love you."

"I certainly hope so after what we just did," she said, setting off another round of laughter.

He sighed, kissed her shoulder then pulled away.

"Do I look okay?" She pressed her palms down the front of the dress.

Smiling, he nodded. "You're glowing."

Heat rushed into her cheeks as she smiled back at him. "So are you."

He held out his hand as he ran his other down his tie. "We should probably get back to the party."

She gave him a sly look. "Do you think they've missed us?"

"Probably not." He ushered her through the door and took her hand, leading her at a more leisurely pace in the direction they'd come from.

Taking a detour, they came out in the main hall leading to the grand ballroom. As they entered, he bent and whispered in her ear, "I'm not finished with you tonight, Miss Mason."

She casually plucked a flute of champagne from a passing tray then met his gaze head-on. "I'd be terribly disappointed if you were."

She was more than up for the challenge. Tonight, she was his equal in every way. She had never felt so bold, so decadent...so *magnificent*. And as she sashayed with newfound confidence alongside him as he greeted old friends and nodded at others, introducing her at every turn, she didn't think she could be any happier.

Nothing could spoil her mood tonight. Absolutely nothing.

Chapter 27

Holding on to anger is like grasping a hot coal with the intent of throwing it at someone else. You are the one who gets burned.
-Buddha

"You're more beautiful tonight than the night I met you," Mark said, brushing a stray strand of hair behind her ear. It must have fallen out during their wicked stairway tryst. "And I was pretty enchanted by you that night, so that's saying something."

They were seated at one of the round banquet tables, their chairs so close to each other it was like they were sharing one seat. The wait staff was still clearing the dishes from dinner, which they'd barely made it back in time for.

A full jazz ensemble played an easy, romantic tune made for slow dancing.

She tugged on his tie and kissed him. "Well, you're not so bad yourself." In his tailored black tuxedo, he looked wicked sexy. Something about Mark in a suit always undid her. "Wanna dance, handsome?"

"It would be my honor." He helped her up and led her to the dance floor, where he turned and pulled her into his arms and swayed her to the gentle beat.

Two years ago tonight, she'd met Mark here. At the same charity benefit, in the same hotel. Maybe the dress had been different—and the shoes—but once again she was Cinderella, and he was her prince.

Talk about coming full circle. Here they were, back where it had all started.

Only this time, she wouldn't flee his room after he took her upstairs to their suite. She would let him touch her. Let him push her against the wall, just as he had in the stairwell. Let him drive his fingers into her hair, crush her mouth with his, and undress her. She would let him toss her onto the bed, hold her down, bury himself inside her until she cried his name and felt him twitch as he slammed his hips into her and came.

She swayed closer, her body melting at what they would do to each other after the benefit was over.

"I feel so close to you tonight," he whispered, bending his head toward hers so his chin kissed her temple.

"Me, too." She closed her eyes and drifted on the music, her palms soaking up the warmth of his chest.

After the song ended, they made the rounds again then visited with his parents before returning to the dance floor for another round of slow dancing. Then they stopped by the bar and ordered a single scotch for him and a glass of champagne for her.

As they waited for their drinks, he leaned his elbow against the polished edge of wood and angled toward her, his hand on the curve of her hip, his thighs bookending her legs, the front of his body gently pressed against the side of hers.

"One more drink," he said, "and then I'm taking you back to the room."

"You're going to bail early?" She placed her fingertips at the base of her neck, feigning shock.

"I'm highly motivated. Besides, I've been to enough of these gigs they no longer hold my interest."

She laughed. "Is that so?"

"Only one thing interests me right now, baby." His eyelids lowered as his gaze fell to her neckline.

She slid her fingers from her neck to between her breasts, tantalizing him.

The bartender set their drinks in front of them, and Mark tore his eyes away to pick up her flute of champagne and hand it to her. "Drink up, Karma. The sooner we finish, the sooner we—"

"Mark. Karma. Hey."

She looked over Mark's shoulder as he turned. Rob and Holly were walking toward them.

Mark gave her an apologetic smile. "Okay, so that'll be a raincheck."

She giggled and gave his arm a playful push. "Don't worry," she said quietly, "I'll keep warm for you."

He narrowed his eyes and smirked, letting out a quiet growl, then turned just as Rob and Holly joined them.

He and Rob shook hands, and she hugged Holly. "Good to see you again," she said.

"Same here." Holly stepped back and looked her up and down. "And this dress is incredible."

"Thanks. Mark made me wear it." She winked and gave Mark a sideways glance.

Holly laughed. "It's sad when a man knows what looks good on a woman better than the woman does, isn't it?"

Karma liked Holly. She was funny and smart and always seemed to have a smile on her face.

"Where have you two been?" Mark said, chucking Rob's arm. "You're late."

Rob pointed toward Holly. "Holly's morning sickness was pretty bad today. She finally fell asleep this afternoon, and I didn't want to wake her, so . . . we're running a little behind."

"But I'm fine now," Holly added then turned to Karma. "And I'd love to have you over for lunch tomorrow, if you're available." Holly hugged her hands beseechingly. "Rob's being fabulous about everything, but I could really use a woman's opinion on the nursery, and I don't really have any close female friends to giggle with over baby clothes and things."

"I'm not sure when we're leaving." She looked inquisitively at Mark.

"There's plenty of time," he said. "Go ahead. You two should make an afternoon of it." He paused then glanced toward Rob. "That way Rob and I can catch a few games of hoops at the gym. Right, Rob?"

Karma frowned. Something in Mark's tone was off.

Shaking off the feeling there was something they weren't telling her, she returned her attention to Holly. "Sounds like we've got a date."

Holly's smile brightened the room.

"So, how far along are you now?" she asked.

"Just under two months." Holly took Rob's hand. "And the morning sickness has been dreadful. But don't worry. I usually get a few good days after days like the one I had today. I should be fine tomorrow."

"So, it's settled," Rob said. "The girls will talk baby clothes, and you and I . . ." He glanced at Mark, and an unspoken message passed between them. "We can go for some much needed one-on-

one at the gym so I can show you how it's done, son." He grinned. "But enough about tomorrow. I'm ready to gamble away some serious play money." He nodded in the direction of the casino room.

Mark gave her another apologetic glance as he took her hand and fell in step behind his friends as they made their way from the ballroom. "I'm sorry."

"It's okay. The delay will just make it better when we get back to the room."

But she couldn't shake the feeling that the three of them were hiding something from her. That whole exchange back there had been too weird, full of unspoken messages.

The crowd in the casino room was thicker than earlier. Practically shoulder-to-shoulder in places.

"Damn! What's with the crowd?" Rob said.

"I don't know. It wasn't like this earlier. But it seems to be concentrated around the poker tables."

"Yeah. Wonder what's going on."

Mark and Rob navigated them through the jostling crowd, and then Mark came to a dead stop, his hand tightening around hers, as Rob and Holly continued cutting through the throng. Mark's mood shifted so drastically a cold draft swept from his body like a phantom.

"Mark? What's wrong?" She glanced up at him and frowned.

The color drained from his face, which was hard as stone.

"He wasn't supposed to be here." The words were almost a murmur, void of emotion. He didn't sound angry . . . or upset . . . or anything really. Just . . . dead.

"What?" She followed his stare to a black-haired man as he revealed his cards. Those around him gasped then began clapping. Apparently, he'd won. And based on the mountain of chips in front of him, he'd been winning a lot.

So, this was what everyone was here to see. A big bad poker game.

What was the fascination with this card game?

"He's not supposed to be here," Mark said again, a little louder this time. "They weren't on the list. I'm not ready for this." He spoke distractedly, and his gaze was darting around the crowd as if he were looking for someone, his agitation palpable.

"Mark, are you okay?" Rob said as he and Holly returned. The concern on Rob's face was enough to make Karma realize something was terribly wrong.

"Am I missing something?" Karma asked as Rob grabbed Mark's shoulders and gave him a gruff about-face and started directing him back through the crowd. "Who was that? Will someone please tell me what's going on?"

"That's Antonio," Rob said under his breath.

Antonio . . . Antonio? So familiar. Where had she heard—? Oooohhh! Carol's Antonio. The man who'd helped send Mark into the pit of Hell eight years ago. The man who'd taken Carol from him.

But what had Mark meant when he'd said he wasn't supposed to be there?

What was going on? Why did she suddenly feel like an outsider?

*   *   *

"I'm fine, Rob. Ease up." Mark pushed Rob away and straightened his tux as best as he could in the thick sea of humanity. He hadn't been expecting to see Antonio here tonight. Nor Carol. And if Antonio was here, Carol was sure to be nearby. "He just caught me off guard is all. I'm fine." He took Karma's hand again and tugged her toward the door. "Let's go. We need to leave."

He continued scanning the crowd. He didn't want to see Carol, and yet, he couldn't not look for her. She was like a fatal car accident you couldn't *not* look at, and he was rubbernecking like he couldn't get enough of the bloody gore, even though he couldn't see her yet.

But his panic was about more than that. This week, he'd come to the realization he needed to see her again. To talk about what had happened between them once and for all. And the way his heart was racing this very second felt like a sign he was finally on the right track. This wasn't so much panic in his chest as it was anticipation. Anticipation that he was on the verge of letting go so he and Karma could move forward.

And yet there was still too much mental shit getting in the way. Like a rush of sewage from a busted pipe, he wanted to spill all. Right now. This second. That's what seeing Antonio had unwittingly done to him.

But that's not how he'd planned this trip. Tonight was for Karma. Tomorrow was for Carol. And all the days after would be freedom. Except if he saw Carol right now, he might not be able to wait. Such was his eagerness to finally purge her from his system.

He had to get out before he saw her.

Without looking, he turned for the door, plowing into a woman carrying two glasses of champagne, her head turned toward a second woman gliding along beside her as if they were in deep conversation.

Mark let go of Karma's hand and captured the woman's arms to keep her from falling, righting her so forcefully that he pulled her against his body.

Champagne spilled down the front of her dress and his tuxedo, but that wasn't what caused every hair on his body to stand on end.

"Mark!"

He stared down into Carol's unmistakable blue eyes, unable to breathe, unable to think, completely stripped of the ability to speak.

She'd cut her hair since the last time he'd seen her. She'd always had long hair. It barely hit her shoulders now. Why did he even notice that? Strange how the mind notices the oddest things when under tremendous duress.

Finally, he found his voice. "Carol."

Karma gasped behind him. "Carol? This is Carol?"

He was still holding her arms, their bodies closer than they'd been in eight years, touching. Her breasts crushed against his chest.

He felt nothing. Not a hint of attraction. Not a glimmer of the affection he'd once felt for her. She was still beautiful, but he no longer loved her. His heart belonged to another now.

Antonio burst through the crowd and shoved him away. "What are you doing, Mark? Leave her alone! Jesus!" He tore Mark's hands from her arms.

He stumbled back, confused, unable to decipher the battle of emotions raging inside him. How could someone he no longer loved still hold such power over him? He could fall in love with another woman and even ask her to marry him, but he couldn't even talk about the wedding or set a goddamn date for the fear Carol had planted inside his heart. He wanted to hate her, but he couldn't.

And he wanted to hate Antonio, too, and yet, that emotion simply wasn't there. What was there was a horrible, sinking dread that crawled through his veins, making his skin itch, making him want to scream for the fucking torment it caused.

"Back off, Antonio," Rob said, holding his arm out to keep Antonio away. "It was an accident. He ran into her and simply kept her from falling, that's all."

"Mark?" Karma's timid voice came from beside him, and he felt her hands wrap around his.

He was scaring her. He didn't mean to scare her. But what kind of man could he be for her when he was so fucked up in the head like this?

"I'm sorry." He glanced toward Antonio then at Carol. "I didn't . . . I didn't, uh . . . " He frowned, not sure what he intended to say. No words came. "I'm sorry," he said again as he took Karma's hand and headed for the door without another word.

Chapter 28

Nothing ever goes away until it teaches us what we need to know.
-Pema Chodron

Karma had a death grip on Mark's back.

He surged over her like a man on a mission. His right arm extended past her face, his hand gripping the headboard for leverage as he pounded into her like he had something to prove.

This wasn't making love. And it wasn't sex. It wasn't even fucking.

This was an exorcism.

What he was doing to her wasn't about pleasure. It wasn't about sharing or indulging a fantasy. She was a vessel and nothing more. Right now, she sensed that Mark simply needed the physical exertion. The physical contact with someone he trusted. The emotional release that communing with her would bring.

He whispered no tender words. He wouldn't look her in the eye. In fact, he kept his eyes closed. Was he seeing his demons? Was he commanding them to leave his body with every robust thrust? Channeling them so that when he finally spent himself, and his muscles released, they would be cast out?

Slamming his other hand into the pillow, a mangled groan broke from his throat as his pace quickened, becoming more brutal.

All she could was hold him and let him use her. Some women might think that diminished their power. But not her. Whatever had happened tonight, Mark was hurting, but he had turned to her. Before he'd shut her out by closing his eyes, she'd seen his anguish and his plea. It was as if he hoped she could help him. But she hadn't known how except to give him her body.

And she was happy to do so. If this was what he needed, she would gladly give it.

He growled, his body falling into orgasmic tremors even as he continued driving into her, grunting hard, his arms taut as he held himself away from her rather than collapse into her grasp.

She was ready to welcome him against her, to feel him come back into himself and tuck his face against the side of her neck as he always did and wrap his arms around her and hold her like he would never let go. That was the Mark she knew. The one she expected to come back to her now that he was finished.

But this Mark? She didn't know him.

As soon as his orgasm was over, he pulled out of her and left the bed. Before she could gather her wits, the bathroom door closed with an abrupt click. A moment later, the shower turned on.

She sat up and stared numbly into the dark emptiness. What had just happened here?

* * *

Mark huddled on the floor of the shower, his hands over his face, silent sobs wracking his body.

How could he have used Karma like that? He had never had sex with her without giving her an orgasm. Her pleasure was always first and foremost, but tonight, after returning to the room, he'd ripped that dress off her as if it had been a poisonous sheath.

Then he'd pushed her onto the bed and fucked her like an animal. No passion. No tenderness. Just feral instinct.

And he'd seen the way she'd looked at him. As if she didn't recognize him. Like he was a stranger. And yet even that hadn't stopped him. He'd closed his eyes and turned away. He couldn't take her looking at him like that. Like she was on the verge of fear.

He dropped his hands and tilted his head back against the cold tile, eyes closed.

He was supposed to protect Karma.

To love and protect, wasn't that how the vows went? See, he couldn't even honor her the way a man should honor his woman. Even though they weren't yet married, he should be able to at least cherish her in the way a wife deserved to be cherished, shouldn't he? If he couldn't, what was the point?

This was the problem with marriage. Too many men couldn't honor their vows. Maybe Carol had somehow known he wouldn't be able to honor his, which was why she left. Why she ran off and found a man who would treat her better than he could. A man like Antonio.

Antonio had come to Carol's rescue tonight in a matter of

seconds. He'd seen Mark too close to her, and he'd come to protect her the way Mark should have protected Karma.

Antonio was a better man. He was the kind of man Carol deserved. The kind of man *Karma* deserved.

His stomach churned with self-loathing the way it did every time he bumped into Carol. Seeing her always opened old wounds. Always made him see his failings. Reminded him of the life he'd once had but lost. And now it felt like he would never get it back.

But the worst was what he'd done to Karma.

Karma.

She was out there, probably wondering what she'd done wrong. She hadn't done anything wrong. It was all him. All his fault.

His stomach roiled.

Damn it.

He didn't want . . . not this time . . . please . . .

He lurched from the shower and fell in front of the toilet, clutching his stomach as he threw up what was left of his dinner.

"Mark?" Karma knocked on the door. "Are you okay?"

He swallowed a gag and cleared his throat. "I'm fine. I'll be fine." He scrunched his eyes closed and covered his mouth so she wouldn't hear him sob.

"Are you sure?"

He nodded and took a deep, shaky breath. "Yes, just . . . dinner didn't agree with me."

Silence.

Of course, she wouldn't believe him. She was a smart woman. She could see through his lie and knew why he was sick.

He needed to pull himself together. Or at least as together as he could.

After flushing the toilet, he finished his shower, brushed his teeth, then returned to the bedroom with a towel wrapped around his hips.

The TV was on, turned to the local news. The newscaster was blathering about a double homicide on the Southside. Nothing new for Chicago.

He felt Karma's eyes on him as he pulled a pair of flannel pants and a T-shirt from his bag. He couldn't even look at her. He couldn't meet her eyes after what he'd done.

"Are you okay?" She spoke cautiously, as if she feared his reaction.

"Fine." He tossed the towel aside, pulled on his pants, then sat on the bed as he put on the shirt.

"I got you a Sprite from the vending machine. For your stomach."

He saw the bottle of soda on the table on his side of the bed, and guilt flooded him again. No way did she believe his stomach was upset from dinner, and yet she played along, allowing him to think she believed him. "Thanks."

Awkward silence stretched between them as he kept his back to her, unmoving, his mind racing down a dozen terrible paths.

"Want to watch a movie?" Her voice betrayed her eagerness to right their ship so they could sail blissfully onward once more.

He closed his eyes and bowed his head. "No." This was one time the ship would remain capsized.

"Okay," she said quietly, obviously disappointed.

He should apologize. He should turn around and look at her. Hold her. Tell her everything was okay.

But he couldn't. Right now, he couldn't bear to see the scared, wary look in her eyes. The same look Carol had given him when he'd found her fucking Antonio when she was supposed to be marrying him. The same look she'd given him tonight when he'd grabbed her arms to keep her from falling. He didn't want to see that look in Karma's eyes, because that would make everything far too real.

Instead, he lifted the covers and climbed underneath, on his side, facing away from her.

"I'm going to cancel my visit with Holly tomorrow," she said quietly. "So we can head home early."

"That's fine."

He couldn't see Carol, anyway. Not after what had just happened. He wasn't ready. His reaction tonight proved that.

The TV clicked off, and Karma lay down behind him. A moment later, her hand pressed against his back. Warm and compassionate. Loving.

And all wrong, because he didn't deserve her love.

"Karma, don't . . ."

"Mark . . . ?"

He stiffened as her palm caressed up to his shoulder. "I don't want to be touched right now, Karma. Please." The sad part was, he did want to be touched, but he couldn't stand the thought that the poison flowing through his veins might be contagious. Karma didn't need to absorb any of that. He'd already done enough damage.

Her hand abruptly stopped, and a moment later she removed it as she sighed. "I'm sorry. I just . . ."

"I don't want to talk about this."

"I know, I—"

"Karma, please." He squeezed his eyes shut.

"Okay." Her voice sounded choked. As choked as his heart felt.

But what she did next nearly undid him. Nearly made him break all the way down to his marrow.

She leaned toward him and pressed her lips to the back of his shoulder. Warm and pure and sweet. Such a simple kiss, but overflowing with love. Love he hadn't earned.

"I love you," she whispered. Then she rolled away from him and settled herself under the covers on her side of the bed.

Mark's silent tears fell to his pillow.

He was blowing it. He was losing everything he ever wanted all over again.

Chapter 29

Some steps need to be taken alone. It's the only way to really figure out where you need to be.
-Mandy Hale

Karma pulled her damp hair into a ponytail and gathered her things from the bathroom. In the bedroom, Mark still sat in the chair by the window where she'd left him to take her shower. His head was back, eyes closed.

She had barely slept last night, but she might have gotten at least an hour or two. Mark was lucky if he'd slept at all. Every time she woke up, he was either sitting on the edge of the bed, standing by the window, staring out at the lights of Chicago, shoulders shaking as he silently cried, or in the bathroom throwing up. He'd vomited at least three times.

Whatever memories Carol and Antonio had stirred to life, they were eating him alive.

The only other time she'd seen Mark like this was when his assignment at Solar ended and their affair was over. But whatever was happening now was ten times worse, and she didn't want to think about why.

She also didn't know what to say to make it better. She knew that seeing Carol and Antonio was the reason for his breakdown, but from everything he'd told her about how seeing her used to affect him, it had never been this bad. The night they'd met, for example. Hadn't Mark told her he'd seen Carol that night? That he'd gone to his room, thrown up, and then returned to the party relatively unscathed? Then he'd made his move on her at the blackjack table, and the rest was history.

So, why this severe breakdown? What was it about this time that made seeing Carol so intensely distressing?

"I got you some peanut butter crackers and another Sprite." She set them on the table beside him.

His head jerked away from the back cushion, his bloodshot eyes opening a sliver. "What? Oh . . . thanks." He sat forward and twisted off the cap, and the spitting hiss of carbonation broke the air.

He sipped his soda and nibbled a cracker while she finished packing. Then she sat down across from him, ignoring the much-too-cheerful newscasters.

"Are you feeling better?"

"Yeah, sure." He averted his gaze, glancing out the window instead of at her.

The wall was going up around him again. The wall she'd broken through two summers ago. That damn thing was back, all because of one ill-timed run-in with Carol.

"I was worried last night."

He plunked the soda bottle on the table. "Don't do that."

"Don't do what?"

"Worry about me."

"But . . ."

"Karma, I'm not worth it." He got up and marched to his bags on the bed.

Anger straightened her back. "Excuse me?" She stood and faced him. "You're not *worth* it? What the hell, Mark?"

He fisted the fabric of his bag. "What I did . . . last night . . ." For the first time since they left the benefit, he looked her in the eye. The pain radiating from his gaze stole her breath. "To you, Karma. What I did to you last night never should have happened. How can you stand to be near me right now?"

So that's what this was about? Last night.

The *exorcism.*

What did he think? That he'd hurt her? That she hadn't wanted to give herself to him when he needed her? That was what people who loved each other did. It didn't always have to be perfect. Sometimes love was ugly, and that was okay, as long as love was still at the heart of everything they did.

She found her voice as he looked away again. "That was my choice, Mark."

"What? To be used and tossed aside like you meant nothing?" He slammed his bag against the mattress. "You didn't *choose* that. I took it from you."

"You didn't *take* anything from me! I willingly gave it!"

His head whipped around. "Why? Why would you do something like that for someone like me?"

He was talking to her as if they were more like strangers than an engaged couple, which was really starting to piss her off. The fact she hadn't gotten much sleep didn't help.

"*For someone like you?*" she said with irritation, planting her hands on her hips. "First of all, *someone like you* is the man I'm in love with, and I think he deserves everything I can give him, especially when he's been through hell. So quit insulting him, because it's kind of like insulting me." She crossed her arms. "Second of all, I gave myself to you willingly *because* I love you. Because last night you needed something different. And sometimes I simply want to be here for you to give you what *you* need for a change instead of you always giving me what I need." She dropped her hands to her sides, the sleepless night messing with her brain, mixing everything up. "Ever since Christmas, you keep telling me you're not good enough, and I keep telling you that you are. It's like you don't want to believe me."

He kept his head down, fists closed around the strap on his bag.

"Do you believe me, Mark?"

His jaw flexed as he closed his eyes. "I don't know." He picked up his bag and turned for the door. "Are you ready to go?"

Obviously, he was still too deep in his pit of despair to listen and see the good standing right in front of him. She understood that. She'd been in similar self-pitying funks more than once. It didn't mean he actually believed what he was saying. Sometimes, when the will had suffered a devastating blow, it was just easier to wallow in the shit for a while than to actually climb out of it.

And he hadn't slept. And he'd been sick. He had to feel like death. Give him a good night's sleep and a healthy dinner, and then he'd be ready to talk more sensibly about what had happened last night.

"Yeah. I'm ready." She gave a cursory glance around the room, turned off the TV, and grabbed her bag.

They just needed to get back home. Back to the familiar and away from whatever reminder Carol and Antonio had awakened in him last night. Then they could put this incident behind them and get back to moving forward.

Chapter 30

One day you will wake up and there won't be any more time to do the
thing you've always wanted. Do it now.
-Paulo Coelho

Mark didn't talk much on the drive home, and she was too
exhausted to care.

Once home, he disappeared upstairs and collapsed on the bed
while she napped on the couch. She didn't see him again until
dinner, which was a silent meal of soup and sandwiches. Then he
returned to bed and slept straight through to Monday morning.

He was up, showered, and out the door by 5:00, before Karma
had even fully awakened.

That night, he worked late, arriving home after she was already
in bed.

Same thing Tuesday.

And Wednesday.

By Thursday, they'd barely said two sentences to each other
since Sunday morning, and she might have gotten a total of ten
hours of sleep. He seemed to be getting worse, not better, and
Karma had no idea how to break through the thick-as-Hoover-Dam-
and-just-as-tall wall he'd erected between them.

For the first time, she worried their relationship might not
survive.

She didn't know what to do, what to say. She didn't even fully
understand what was wrong. Carol was at the heart of it, but his
behavior seemed extreme for Carol to be the only problem.

This was something more, but he wouldn't talk to her about
what that was.

And it didn't make sense. After all the confessions about the
things he'd been holding back from her . . . after reassuring her there
was nothing else . . . what could possibly be so bad that Mark would
completely shut her out? It was as if he were preparing her for the
worst. That any second he would tell her he was leaving.

Just the thought frayed her already fragile emotions. She hadn't
slept well all week, grabbing only a few hours each night, and now

Donya Lynne

she was freaking out, paranoid he might already have one foot out the door. What if he left? Where would she go? What would she do?

All day Thursday, she paced her office, restless, unable to focus on her assignments, chewing her fingernails, which was something she hadn't done since high school.

Thursday night, she couldn't sleep and went downstairs to watch dismal late-night TV until she nodded off on the couch around four in the morning.

By Friday afternoon, she'd had enough. She'd given him five days. Tonight, she would sit him down and force the issue. Because she couldn't take this, anymore. They were living under the same roof but felt more like roommates who merely tolerated one another than two people who were supposed to be in love and building a life together.

She wanted her fiancé back. She wanted to bring to light whatever was bothering him so they could deal with it and move on. And if they couldn't? Well, then they needed to talk about what that meant. Because if he was still hung up on Carol—and it seemed as though he was—then she couldn't stay. If he was never going to get over that woman, her ego couldn't take a blow that big.

Dropping her head into her hands, she began to cry. Her happily ever after was crumbling to pieces, the glass slipper shattering while she was still wearing it.

A week ago, they'd been so happy. Now, she was as miserable as when he'd left two summers ago. It felt like they were coming to an end all over again.

How had it come to this?

* * *

"She's going to leave me."

"What?" Rob said.

Mark leaned back in his chair, raking his hand through his hair, holding his phone to his ear with the other. "She's going to leave me," he said again. "I just know it."

"Karma? You're crazy."

"No." He sighed, shaking his head. "I'm fucking it all up, and she's going to walk." Of course Karma would leave. They all left.

One way or another, every woman he had ever cared about left him.

"Is this about last weekend? Are you still hung up on what happened with Carol?"

Mark stood and paced to the window. "You don't get it. You don't know the horrible shit I did to Karma when we got back to the room."

"What do you mean?" Concern laced Rob's voice.

"I fucked her."

Silence.

"And I didn't just fuck her, Rob. I used her. I used her like she was nothing more than a whore I'd picked up off the street. And then I just shut down. I couldn't even look her in the eye after that." He rubbed his palm over his face. "What kind of asshole does something like that to the woman he's supposed to love."

"Was she upset?"

"That's the sick part. She seemed okay with what I did. She said she wanted to be there for me when I needed her."

"Then what's the problem?"

He flung his hand to his side. "What do you mean, what's the problem? She obviously doesn't know what she's saying. She obviously doesn't understand what I did was wrong. That I'm not the kind of man she needs. I mean, why would she need someone who's going to treat her that way? She deserves better."

"Are you listening to yourself," Rob said. "Listen to what you're saying." Rob paused before continuing, as if he were carefully choosing his words. When he spoke again, his words came out firm and slow. "You're pushing her away. This isn't about her wanting to leave you. This is about you being terrified of the *possibility* that she *might* leave without having any proof that she will."

"Wait a minute, I—"

"No, you wait a minute, Mark. You're transferring your fears onto her as if they're hers and not yours. She told you she was okay with what happened, and yet you're sitting there thinking she lied. Has Karma ever been known to lie?"

"No, of course not."

"Then why would you think she's lying now?"

"But she doesn't understand what I did . . . that what I did was wrong."

"Bullshit. She understands what you did better than you do."

Mark bobbed his head back, frowning. "What?"

"You heard me. Karma is more in tune with what you need than you give her credit for. You were fucked up after you ran into Carol and Antonio. Anyone could have seen that. They caught you off guard, because they weren't supposed to be there. But shit happens, and they were. And it jacked you up the way seeing them always does. Only this time, you had Karma to help you through it. She saw how fucked up you were. She knew you needed to let off steam. And she *willingly* let you vent that steam on her. She knew exactly what she was doing and why, and now you're discrediting her choice, diminishing it by saying she didn't know what she was doing. Mark, you need to take a really hard look at your fiancée. She loves you and is undeniably devoted to you. And it sounds like she's willing to do whatever it takes to get you through this. Maybe it's time you level with her one hundred percent."

Mark slumped into his chair. As usual, he was too deep in his own shit to know which way led out. It took Rob to give him some perspective.

"You're right." He hung his head and dragged his hand over his face. "Fuck, I've been such an ass."

Rob sighed. "Remember at your mom's birthday party when I told you I thought you were subconsciously pushing Karma away? You swept my concerns under the rug. Well, do you believe me now? Do you think there might be some truth to that, after all?"

"Yeah, okay." Mark dropped his hand to his desk and let the chair catch him as he rocked back. "Maybe you were right."

"You're too deep in the forest to see the damn trees, buddy. I'm not. I'm above looking down, and I can see exactly where you are and where you need to go to get out of the weeds."

"In other words, I'm still fucking things up and might have already pushed Karma too far to save our relationship." He couldn't lose her. He'd die if he did.

"That's not what I'm saying. If you'd pushed her too far, she'd already be gone. But you've got to fix this."

Mark swiveled his chair around and checked his calendar. He had to get on a conference call in ten minutes. "Tell me something I don't know."

"You need to talk to Carol, man. The sooner the better. And maybe Antonio, too." Rob spoke definitively, as if he'd reached inside Mark's mind and pulled the words straight from his thoughts.

"You got her number?" Mark straightened and grabbed his pen.

"Yep."

"Give it to me."

It took Rob a few seconds to pull it up, and then he recited the information as Mark jotted it on his notepad.

"Call her now," Rob said. "Tell her the two of you need to meet this weekend. Don't take no for an answer. Then go home, tell Karma you're sorry for being a total boner for the past week, tell her you're going to talk to Carol and resolve this once and for all, and then make love to her until she can't see straight. *That's* what Karma deserves, Mark. She deserves the truth. And she deserves to know you love her enough to fix this."

Mark glanced out the window at the refreshingly blue skies. It was a perfect day to finally set things right and get his head out of his ass once and for all. "Man, when did you turn into such a romantic."

"It's Holly's fault."

"Of course it is."

Rob chuckled. "Okay, now go. Do this. I'll talk to you later."

"Definitely. And Rob?"

"Yeah?"

"Thank you."

"What are best friends for?"

They said their good-byes, and then Mark took a deep breath and dialed Carol's number. Shit, his hands were shaking. But, damn it, he could do this. He *had* to. His future with Karma depended on it.

Her voicemail picked up.

"Carol, hey, it's Mark." He cleared his throat, shifting uncomfortably in his chair. "I know I'm probably the last person you expected to hear from, but . . ." He took a deep breath. "I think we really need to talk. It's been long enough, and I can't . . . I don't want . . . I mean, I'm trying to move on with my life, but . . ." He was tripping over his tongue like an idiot. "Just . . . please give me a call back. I promise, I just want to talk. I just want to put closure on what happened between us, and I can't do that until we've cleared the air." He rattled off both his office number and his cell number. "I hope to hear from you soon. And, about Saturday night, I'm sorry for how I reacted when I saw you. I, uh . . . I just hadn't expected to see you there." He cleared his throat. "Please apologize to Antonio for me, too."

He disconnected and took a shaky breath. Okay, that hadn't been so bad. He'd blathered like an imbecile and set the world record for how many times someone could say the word *just* in thirty seconds, but he'd gotten out what he needed to say and hadn't spun into a gastrointestinal meltdown.

But now he needed to shift gears. It was time for his conference call. He poked his head out the door. "Kit?"

She glanced up from her computer. "Yes."

"Can you answer my line while I'm on my conference call?"

"Sure."

"And if someone named Carol calls, please interrupt me. It's very important I speak to her right away."

"Absolutely. I'll interrupt if Carol calls." She nodded once. Her sign that she'd programmed his directive into her brain.

"Thanks." He closed his door and returned to his desk.

One way or another, this shit with Carol was getting resolved by Monday, even if he had to drive up to Chicago and force the issue.

Chapter 31

Don't worry when I fight with you. Worry when I stop, because it means there's nothing left for us to fight for.
-Author Unknown

Karma wandered blindly into the cavernous walk-in closet, her fingers skimming the sleeves of Mark's suits.

She'd showered, and water still dripped off the ends of her hair. The robe Mark had bought her two summers ago hung loosely from her shoulders.

She'd gone running with Daniel to help clear her head. He'd known something was wrong, and even though his curiosity and concern had been written all over his face, he hadn't pushed for details.

But something had happened during their run that now played on repeat in her thoughts.

They had decided to run the winding, looping trail they normally took in reverse. Why they would change things up today of all days was a mystery. But Daniel had led her left instead of right, and she'd simply taken his direction in stride.

As they crested a shallow rise she'd jogged over a hundred times from the other direction, she came to an abrupt stop and gasped. The rolling meadow, dotted by trees, spread out in front of her like an enchanted, undiscovered land, bright green with uncut springtime grass and young leaves. It had been unseasonably warm the past couple of weeks, so the first bright yellow dandelions were blooming, adding a touch of charm.

"Wow."

Daniel stopped and gave her a quizzical glance. "What?"

"Nothing. It's just . . ." She waved her hand toward the view, lit magically by the sun with not a cloud in the sky. "It just looks a lot different coming from this direction. Prettier." Breathtaking was more apropos.

Laughing, Daniel jogged in place to keep his legs loose. "Isn't it funny how that works? You see something over and over and never really see it. Then, one day, you change your perspective, and suddenly everything looks different."

. . . you change your perspective, and suddenly everything looks different.

Was that what she needed to do with Mark? Maybe she'd been seeing him through rose-colored glasses all this time. Seeing what she wanted to see instead of what was really there.

She had spent the rest of her run in silence, her mind sorting through all her memories of Mark while her body went through the motions of keeping up with Daniel.

For months, Mark had continually insinuated he wasn't good enough for her, and she'd kept telling him that wasn't true. Well, maybe it was. Maybe she needed to get real and take off her blinders and see Mark for the man he kept trying to convince her he was.

Her bare feet sank into the plush eggshell-colored carpet. Her mind resisted the idea that Mark was an unredeemable, broken man with nothing more to offer.

She plucked the navy pinstriped suit she loved so much off the rack. Even the hanger was top-of-the-line, made of polished wood and soft curves so it didn't stretch the fabric.

Peeling back the collar, she read the label. Hugo Boss. Nice. Not cheap.

She put the suit back and picked up another. A shimmery charcoal grey with a delicate, weaved pattern in the wool. Armani.

She continued reading the labels. Ralph Lauren. Gucci. Stefano Pilati. Carlo Brandelli. Tom Ford. And so many more.

But there were just as many regular joe labels as designer ones. Hanes, for example. He owned several Hanes T-shirts like the ones he wore to bed or to play basketball in.

Basketball.

Her gaze fell to the duffel bag tucked in the corner as another memory struck her. The bag was the same one he'd taken to the basketball court when she'd driven up to Chicago to surprise him after kids broke into his apartment two summers ago. That had been a bizarre weekend. He'd gotten angry at her for finding . . .

She turned toward his dresser. On top sat the small, ornate box she'd seen on this same dresser in Chicago.

Her lips parted as she exhaled, her heart skipping a beat. She remembered the night they'd argued at his apartment all too well.

She'd found a pair of wedding rings and a diamond necklace in his gym bag, and, hypnotized as any woman would be by all the sparkles, she'd slipped the woman's ring on her finger.

Mark had caught her, and he'd erupted. He'd accused her of snooping, lecturing her and snatching the jewelry from her. Then he'd thrown both the ring and the necklace in that box, slamming the lid closed.

He'd been so angry that night. The ring had been Carol's. The necklace had been meant as a wedding gift to her. One he'd planned on giving her on their honeymoon.

But then Carol had jilted him, leaving him standing alone in front of hundreds of guests so she could run off with Antonio.

She didn't want to think the jewelry was still here, but dread siphoned through her veins as she crept toward the dresser, eyes on the box.

Gingerly, she placed her fingertips on the sides of the lid, took a deep breath, and lifted.

Inside, she found his platinum and onyx cufflinks and matching ring, his Tag Heuer watch, a Rolex, a pair of Montblanc pens, a few trinkets, and there . . . buried beneath it all . . . were the necklace and his and her wedding bands.

Her heart fell.

It was as she feared. Carol was still there. Still getting in the way. Still standing between them. How could she not be when Mark couldn't even let go of jewelry that had been meant for her. Hadn't he said in Chicago it was time he got rid of it. He had assured her he would. And yet, here it was, still among his most personal possessions.

She blinked back tears. He was still holding on to his past. Still unable to break free.

But there was something else in the box. Something that looked completely out of place amid thousands of dollars' worth of jewelry.

A folded sheet of notepaper.

Wiping her eyes, she took out the piece of paper and unfolded it, frowning when she saw it was the list he'd made in Saint Lucia. What was this doing here?

Her eyes scanned down the bullet points of things he'd feared telling her. The drugs. The crap he'd done with Nina. The sexual role-play, exhibitionism, anal play . . .

Wait.

The last item.

I want to dance again.

The line of print was crossed out, but still, he'd written it down. Why?

"What?" she murmured aloud, crinkling her brow and shaking her head.

What the hell did he mean by wanting to dance again? They had danced. In fact, they had danced at the benefit last weekend.

Then, like a bucket of ice water being tossed in her face, it dawned on her. He wanted to *dance*-dance. Professional-style dancing. The way he had with Carol. In a way Karma wasn't capable of. She couldn't waltz or foxtrot or cha-cha. That wasn't in her wheelhouse.

No wonder he had crossed that item off his list. Because he knew she could never fill Carol's shoes and dance the way he wanted to dance.

But hell, just because she would never be an international dance champion like Carol didn't mean she couldn't take lessons and become proficient enough to indulge Mark's wishes. Hell, Mark could teach her himself. She knew from what he'd told her about his dancing past that he could.

Or maybe he didn't want to. Maybe he wanted a level of dancing that was too atmospheric for her to achieve. Or maybe he just didn't think she could learn.

All right, sure, she would never measure up to Carol when it came to dancing, but that didn't mean she couldn't dance at all. Look at the celebrities on those reality TV dance shows. Those celebrities weren't dancers, and yet they learned how to turn two left feet into some fancy moves after a few lessons. So could she if Mark would just give her a little credit.

Icy chills erected goosebumps down both arms as she glared at the crossed-off item on his list, then at the wedding bands and necklace.

Was this why he had yet to set a wedding date? Because he wanted their first dance as husband and wife to be a performance and not just a regular ol' dance? Or was it because, as she'd feared, he was still hung up on Carol? Maybe it was both.

Such thoughts were irrational, but screw rational. She was exhausted, emotionally drained, and had just found Mark's ex-fiancée's engagement ring and bridal gift among his things, along with a curt reminder of just how fabulous Carol had been.

And she was beautiful, too. Gorgeous blond hair, legs from here to there, svelte body. She recalled the way Mark had looked at Carol after running into her — literally — last weekend.

Maybe that was why Mark felt so ashamed of the way he'd fucked her afterward. Like he'd had something to prove. Maybe that's why his eyes had been closed. Because he'd been seeing Carol. In his mind, he'd been fucking Carol, and Karma had just been the vessel to get him there.

With angry, sad tears burning her eyes, and humiliation tying her stomach in tight knots, she got dressed then grabbed her phone from the nightstand.

After two rings, Mark's cell sent her to voicemail, which meant he'd seen she was calling and had forwarded her. He didn't want to talk to her.

Well, she wanted to talk to him, and it was high time they talked, so she dialed his office number.

"Mark's office, this is Kit."

Huh? Why was Kit answering his phone? "Is Mark available?"

"Is this Carol?"

Double huh? Even Kit knew about Carol? Just how far removed from Mark's life had she become in the last week? "No, this is Karma."

"Oh, hi, Karma. Sorry about that. Mark's on a conference call and told me that someone important named Carol was supposed to call and to interrupt him when she did. I thought you were her. You sound different than you normally do. Do you have a cold?"

"Uh, no." But she suddenly felt sick.

"Oh, okay. Do you want me to have Mark call you back when his conference call ends?"

Her phone beeped with a text message.

"Just tell him . . . on second thought, no thanks." She hung up and read her text. It was from Mark.

I'm on a conference call. Will call you back when I'm done.

So, he wanted to be interrupted when Carol called, but her call could wait? Nice to see how *she* rated.

She wasn't going to take that. *She* was his fiancée, and her patience had run out. They needed to talk, and they needed to talk *now*.

She grabbed the jewelry and the list from Mark's dresser, shoved them into her purse, stuffed her feet in a pair of tennis shoes, locked up the house, and drove to Solar.

Lisa was at the reception desk talking to Nancy.

"Hi, Karma," she said. "What are you doing here?"

"Seeing if I can get a little face time with my fiancé." She marched past. "*If* he can work me into his schedule."

"Whoa, okay." Lisa caught up to her at the stairs. "What's this about?"

"It's about how I'm done sitting quietly by while Mark continues to hold a flame for Carol."

"What? Wait a minute. Who says he's holding a flame for Carol."

They were at the top of the stairs, rounding the corner where her old desk — now Kit's — came into view at the end of the hall.

"He'll take *her* call and not mine," Karma said. "What does *that* tell you?"

"Karma, wait a minute. I think you're jumping to conclusions. Maybe we should go down to my office and talk. Get you calmed down."

"Oh, I'm calm, Lisa. I'm perfectly calm." Liar, liar, pants on fire.

"Karma, you are *not* calm."

She stopped and spun on Lisa. "You know what, you're right. I'm not. But I'm not going to sit around waiting, anymore. He needs to make a decision, and he needs to make it now."

She was done. She had reached her boiling point. There was only so much she could take before she exploded, and she'd been holding all her worry, frustration, and heartache in for months. Like an overfilled balloon, there was only so much tensile strength she could impose on herself until she popped and blasted around the room like a manic torpedo without missile lock.

"A decision about what?"

"Everything. Everything, Lisa." She started for Mark's office again.

Kit popped out of her chair. "Karma? Hi. Is everything . . . ? Wait! He's still on his call . . ."

She grabbed the door handle, giving the perfectly coiffed Kit an over-the-shoulder glance. "I don't care. I'm his fiancée. And I'm pulling rank." With that, she played the entitlement card afforded to significant others — which she had never played before — and pushed open Mark's door, leaving Kit and Lisa staring after her like she had just barged in on the President of the United States.

Mark looked up from his desk. "Karma?" He sat upright and glanced at his phone. "Excuse me, guys, but I need to hop off. Something important just came up."

Well, how about that? She was something important. She rated, after all.

He disconnected, stood, and came around the desk, worry etched on his face. "Why are you here? Are you okay? Is anything wrong?"

What a loaded question.

If not for the hell she'd been through since last Saturday night — and especially for the last hour — his concern would have warmed her heart. Unfortunately, she was in no mood for placation.

She crossed her arms and raised her chin. "I want to set a date."

"What?" His eyebrows scrunched together. "You came all the way down here and pulled me off a business call to set a date?"

Undeterred, she straightened her back and said, "If you really want to marry me then let's set a date, Mark."

"I thought we decided —"

"No, *you* decided!" She jabbed her finger toward him. "You decided for both of us, and, like an idiot, I went along with you!"

He quickly shut his door so the entire office didn't hear her outburst. "Karma, what's wrong? Obviously, this is about something other than our wedding." He reached for her arm as if to guide her to a chair, but she flung off his hand.

"Do *not* touch me right now." Hadn't he said the same words to her last weekend? Well, now it was his turn to keep *his* distance.

He held up his hands and took a step back. "Okay. Just tell me what's wrong."

"Why can't you set a date, Mark?" She crossed her arms. "Why can't you sit down with me and help me decide when we'll get married?"

He sighed, but not from impatience. More from frustration. Maybe even guilt. "I thought we had agreed to wait. We've both been busy . . . with the house, with—"

"Bullshit." She stepped back and held up her hand. "It doesn't take that long to pick a date, Mark. So quit making excuses."

"I'm not making excuses."

Right. Sure.

"Really?" She shook her head and paced to the window. "Why don't you just be honest with me. You don't want to marry me, do you? You want Carol. You *still* want Carol."

"What? Why would you say that?"

She gestured to his phone. "I called you, and you sent me to voicemail. So I called your office line. Imagine my surprise when Kit asked me if I was Carol. Then I find out that you told her that if Carol calls to interrupt you. So . . . Carol's important enough to take her call. But when *I* need you . . ." She couldn't keep her voice from rising. "When *I* fucking need you"—she glared at him, her whole body trembling as she planted her palm on her chest—"because I'm *losing* my *fucking mind* over why you won't *talk* to me, I get tossed into voicemail." Tears erupted in her eyes, and she blinked several times, fighting the burn as her chin and bottom lip quivered.

He was looking at her like she was Dr. David Banner about to mutate into the Incredible Hulk. "Karma . . ."

She cleared her throat and brushed her hands over her face, pulling herself together as best she could. "No, no. I'm fine. We're here now. Let's do this." She pulled out her phone and brought up the calendar. "Let's set a date, Mark. You want to marry me *soooo* badly, right? So let's go. What works for you? Or maybe I should get with Kit, since she's got a better handle on your life right now than I do. I mean, she knows about Carol. I'm just the ignorant fool left wandering around like an idiot."

"Karma, please . . ."

"It's okay. We're going to set that date now, right? So, everything should be fine, right?" She flipped through the months. "How about September? That gives us four solid months to prepare."

He remained rooted across the room, motionless, expression flat.

"September doesn't work?" She flipped through a few more months. "How about November or December? No, no . . . too many holidays. Too many *excuses.*" She shot him a nasty glare. "But January could work. It's winter, so work will be slow. Oh wait." She snapped her fingers. "There *might* be a blizzard. We'd better keep looking, because we simply can't set a date on the off chance a blizzard will interfere, can we?"

"Karma . . ."

She ignored him as her tears began to fall again. "No . . . no. I can fix this, Mark. I can find the perfect date, because I know your schedule is so extremely tight and you can't possibly work me in without a little help."

"Karma . . ." He spoke more loudly, but she kept on, flipping to February.

"Can't do February. There's still the threat of a blizzard. And Valentine's Day would just make our wedding pale in comparison." She choked back a sob. The volcano was about to explode. "March. Hmmm. No, things start to ramp up at work in March. Same with April. You can't possibly marry me in spring, because work comes first, right? July is out. Still too busy at work. And then we're back to autumn." Her shoulders momentarily slumped before she raised her head and screamed, "A whole fucking year and a half from now!" before breaking down in uncontrollable sobs.

The days of silence, the sleepless nights, the inability to eat, and all her old insecurities had culminated into what could only be described as a Texas-sized nervous and emotional breakdown.

In a flash of movement, Mark rushed toward her, took her phone, tossed it on his desk, and tried to pull her into his arms.

"NO!" She pushed him away. "Give me a date, Mark! Give me a goddamn date when you want to marry me!"

"Karma, let's discuss this when you're not so upset."

She stopped crying long enough to give him a sarcastic laugh. "So now we can't set a date because I'm upset, like it's my fault?" He tried to reply, but she didn't let him. "I'm upset because we haven't set a goddamn date, Mark! Do you get that?" It was just one of the reasons why she was upset, but it was close to the top of the list.

He tried to take her hands, but she pulled away, flinging herself toward the window.

"Karma, you're angry. And I understand why. Really, I do. I

wanted to talk to you about this tonight, okay? Can't we just wait and talk about this tonight? At home? This isn't the right time—"

She whirled on him. "I'm beginning to think it's never going to be the right time!" She shook her head and swiped the tears off her face as he stared at her in stunned silence. "I've been waiting for months for you to get off your ass, Mark. I've been patient. I've given you space. I've been supportive and put my trust in you that you had my best interests at heart."

"I do."

She held up her hand, cutting him off. "No, Mark. You don't get to do that to me."

"Do what?"

"Lie to me."

"I'm not lying!"

She shook her head. "Yes, you are. You're still hung up on Carol."

Mark tensed and took a step back, his face scrunched as if he were in pain.

"See." She gestured toward him. "That. The way you just reacted when I said her name. She's still in there." She tapped her forehead. "She's right there in the front of your mind all the time. It's like there's three of us in this relationship. You, me, and Carol. And I'm getting the short end of the stick."

"You're not getting the short end of the stick." He shook his head and motioned as if he wanted to pull her into his arms then thought better of it and stayed where he was.

"The hell I'm not. For months, I've felt her just sitting there. Between us. Competing with me for your attention!" She reached into her purse and pulled out the jewelry and the sheet of crumpled notepaper. "And then I found this today." She tossed the rings and necklace on his desk then smoothed the sheet of paper as best she could as she read. "I want to dance again."

She wadded up the paper and threw it at him. "I'll admit that it took me a minute to understand what you meant. I was like, we dance. We've danced plenty of times. And then the light went on. You want to dance all those dances you danced with Carol." She was blowing up like a temperamental teenager, but she was beyond giving a fuck. Her patience had run out. She was completely tapped.

"Carol, with her long legs and her perfect body and her ability to captivate a room with one high kick. She's who you want. She's the one you want to dance with. She's the one you were fucking last Saturday night. Not me."

He shook his head, mouth gaping as if he wanted to say something, but she didn't give him time to speak before continuing.

"That's why you felt so awful about it, isn't it? Because you wanted it to be Carol you were in bed with, not me. I was just a conduit. My body was just a vessel for you so you could fuck Carol one more time."

"Karma, no. That's not—"

"No, Mark. Just stop." She was sobbing now. Tears soaked her cheeks and dripped from her nose. She sniffled and wiped her face. "You've had your chance. Now it's my turn." Some of her steam was gone, having already been expended. "I can't compete with Carol, so if she's who you really want, I'm out."

"I don't want Carol."

She sighed and stared down at her engagement ring. "I want to believe you, Mark, but . . ." She twisted the ring off her finger. "Ever since Christmas, you've been telling me you're not good enough for me. Every time something from your past popped up, you tried to tell me that I deserved better. And I kept telling you that you *are* good enough. That you need to let *me* decide what I want." She paused. "It's like you've always expected I would walk away, so you were testing me. Seeking validation but all the while pushing me away." She held out the ring. "I love you, Mark, but I can't keep validating you if won't believe me. And I can't keep living like this when Carol is always in the way. I can't be your conduit to the past, anymore. I want to be your future, not a reminder of what you once had."

"Karma, please . . ." His voice broke, and he refused to take the ring.

She breathed a shaky sigh and set her engagement ring on his desk, next to his keyboard, and retrieved her phone. "You need to keep this ring until you're really ready, Mark. Until you've dealt with whatever hold Carol has over you and you're ready to move forward with me." She started for the door.

His arm shot out and he grabbed her around the waist, pulling her to him.

She gasped, and he swallowed the sound as his mouth crashed down over hers.

And damn her traitorous body for reacting, flaming to life and reaching for his. Her lips meshed perfectly with his, as hungry for him as he seemed to be for her. She drank him in, clutching his shirt, holding on not just with her body but with her heart and soul, as well.

When he pulled away, his agonized eyes searched hers. "You felt that, didn't you?

She couldn't answer, but she'd felt it everywhere. She could still feel it.

"You did. I know you did." He cupped her face in one hand. Plaintive tears glistened his eyes. "Believe in that, Karma. Believe in that feeling, because it's real." He tipped his forehead to hers. "I love you. You love me. Isn't that enough?"

"It *was* enough." She sniffled as she began to tear herself away. "But not anymore." It took every ounce of her resolve, but she pushed out of his embrace. "Getting married was your idea, Mark. *You* proposed to *me*. You're the one who said you wanted to spend the rest of your life with me. Now you're asking me why our love for one another can't be enough?" She brushed more tears from her cheeks. "So you don't want to get married, anymore?" She shook her head, trying to make sense of what was happening. "Did you even want to give me that ring?"

"Of course I did."

She thought back to that day on the beach. The sun had been setting. It had been their last night in Saint Lucia.

Their *last day*. Oh God, how had she not seen this before?

Because, as with the running trail today, she'd only been looking at Mark from one perspective. Now she was looking at him from every angle, finally allowing herself to see the truth.

"Then why did you wait until the last day of our vacation to propose?"

His shoulders tensed. "Karma, don't."

"Why?" She saw the truth in his eyes. "You were afraid, weren't you? You meant to ask me sooner so we could make Saint Lucia an engagement vacation. But you were too scared."

"Karma, please—"

"How many times did you want to propose to me before that night? How many?" She was catching a second wind, her anger rising once more. She felt so foolish. So . . . cheap.

And yet she still loved him. Damn her heart's betrayal. She loved him, and she always would. But that didn't mean she wanted to be around him right now. She took a step toward the door.

"Karma, you don't understand."

"No, I think I do." Another step. "I bet Carol didn't have to wait for a proposal. I bet you just couldn't *wait* to put that ring on *her* finger. But me? I just get what's left over, right? I always get the leftovers." She turned toward the door, gripping the handle.

"Karma, please don't go."

"I'm going to spend a few days at my parents' house." She fought not to cry as she opened the door and glanced back at him, standing beside his desk, shocked anguish marring his features. "I need a few days to think. I suggest you do the same."

With that, she hurried from his office, nearly barreling over Lisa, who had remained outside Mark's office waiting for her. No doubt she'd heard everything.

"Karma?" Lisa raced after her as she ran to the stairs.

She needed to get out of there. "Not now, Lisa," she croaked through another round of sobs.

"Will you just wait a minute!" Lisa caught up to her on the sidewalk outside and grabbed her arm. "Give me thirty seconds to grab my purse, and I'll go with you. Okay? Just wait for me. I don't want you driving in this condition."

She nodded, unable to speak for the tightness in her throat as her gaze flitted around the parking lot.

Lisa disappeared inside, and a few seconds later, Mark burst through the door.

She turned away.

"Please don't do this, Karma. Don't leave me. You can't. Oh God, Karma . . . please . . ." He sounded like he was on the verge of a global meltdown worse than anything she'd ever seen, but then again, so was she. And he needed to know how it felt.

She kept her back to him, because if she turned around, she would fling herself into his arms and hang on like he was her very breath. "Don't follow me, Mark. Just leave me alone. I need some time."

And so do you.

If she had any hope of everything being okay ever again, she needed to see this through.

Lisa returned and pushed her toward her car. "Let me handle this, Mark. I'll make sure she's okay."

Lisa directed her into the passenger seat, where she kept her head down, willing herself not to look back at Mark.

"I'm taking you to my place," Lisa said, backing out of her space. "I've got lots of ice cream in the freezer."

Karma burst into uncontrollable sobs as they pulled out of the parking lot, and she finally relented, turning to see Mark still standing at the entrance, watching her drive away.

Was he crying the way she had two summers ago when she watched him drive away?

More importantly, would the two of them ever get their relationship right?

She bowed her head, eyes squeezed shut, her shoulders shaking. Only Mark could answer that question. Because it was his past that stood in the way of their future. Until he dealt with Carol, they didn't have a chance.

*　*　*

Mark watched Lisa's car disappear around the corner, carrying away the best thing that had ever happened to him.

Oh God, what had just gone down here? Had Karma left him? Had she just ended their engagement?

A painful throbbing sensation took up residence in his chest. Like a heart attack only worse. How could such emptiness hurt so much?

He couldn't breathe, couldn't think, could barely move.

Panic tightened his chest, and his stomach rolled.

Shit!

He hurried inside to the men's room and threw up his lunch, retching over and over until every muscle protested and all that came up was air as he dry-heaved into oblivion.

When he was finally able to walk again, he practically dragged himself up the stairs to his office. His legs were so weak, his body like lead.

Kit jumped up from her desk when she saw him. "Mark . . . are you okay? Can I get you anything?"

He shook his head. "Please clear my schedule for the rest of the day, Kit. Thank you." He shut his office door without waiting for her single nod of understanding then collapsed in his chair.

He'd fucked up. He'd waited too long to come to his senses and he'd let her get away. His Karma. All because he was too self-involved with the shit he'd been carrying around to give her what she needed. As he rubbed his palms up and down his face, his cell phone rang.

He didn't want to talk to anyone. Didn't want to see anyone. He just wanted—

It was Carol's number.

With renewed hope, he answered. "Carol?"

"Um . . . hi, Mark. We were teaching a class when you called, so . . . umm . . ."

"I need your help, Carol." Every cell in his body sprang to life, set to code red, working toward one goal: Get Karma back.

And he knew Carol was the answer to making that happen the way a meteorologist knows a hurricane is a fucking big-ass storm.

"My help? Mark, are you okay?"

"No." He shut down his computer and began gathering his things, the sheet of crumpled paper, and the jewelry. He paused and took a deep breath as he picked up Karma's engagement ring. His heart shuddered at the prospect he might not ever see it on her finger again.

He couldn't let that happen. He *would* put this ring back on her finger. Failure was not an option. And Carol was the key.

"Carol, I need you to help me save my marriage."

Chapter 32

Sometimes you have to walk away and let karma take over.
-Author Unknown

An empty Ben & Jerry's container sat on the coffee table beside a much lighter Kleenex box than it had been an hour ago.

Karma had cried so much while relaying what had happened with Mark that Lisa had retrieved a small metal waste can from the bathroom so she could throw away her tear-soaked tissues rather than pile them on the table.

But now she was both talked out and cried out. Her eyes felt like they'd been rubbed with vinegar-soaked Brillo pads, her face was puffy and hot, and her voice sounded like she was Kim Carnes singing "Bette Davis Eyes," one of her dad's favorite songs from back in the day.

Lisa took her hand. "Mark loves you, Karma."

"I know he does, but I just can't do it, anymore, Leese."

"Maybe you misunderstood what he meant by wanting to dance again. Maybe he wants to dance with *you*."

"Then why didn't he tell me? Why did he put that on his list of things he was too scared to tell me then not bring it up? He confessed everything else on that list, so why not that? And why did he cross it off?"

Lisa shrugged. "I don't know. Maybe because he was worried about how you would react, because he knew you'd make the connection to his past. Or maybe he just changed his mind."

She tossed another spent tissue into the trash can. "Well, what about last weekend. What about that?"

"Do you have any proof that he was really thinking about Carol while he was having sex with you?"

"No, but—"

"Then maybe he wasn't."

"But it makes sense, given everything else."

"Just because it makes sense doesn't mean it's the only answer, or even the right one. You know how Mark is. He's the quintessential mystery man. Who knows what's really going on inside that complicated brain of his?"

Karma grabbed the Ben & Jerry's pint then plunked it back down when she remembered it was empty. "Why are you defending him?"

Lisa huffed. "Karma, I just can't believe that the Mark we've come to know . . . the Mark who is madly in love with you and has expressed his devotion to you in so many ways, including tattooing your name over his heart . . . who tread through fire and brimstone to come back to you . . . would still be holding a flame for the woman who jilted him. Think about it. He's revealed all these deep dark secrets to you. Things he's never told anyone else, not even his best friend. Isn't that what you said?"

Karma didn't like this shock logic Lisa was tossing at her. "Yes."

"Okay, so do you think he would confess all that to you if he didn't love you? And not just love you, but love you more than he's ever loved anyone? So much so that you're the only person he trusted to reveal that stuff to?"

Chagrined, Karma sank into the couch, crossing her arms. "I guess."

"So let's look at what might really be going on here. What do we know about Mark? We know that he's a damn stubborn control freak." Lisa began ticking items off on her fingers. "He's an internalizer. He internalizes *everything*, right? He also keeps everything close to the vest, revealing very little about himself. He takes responsibility for things out of his control. For example, he blamed himself for Carol leaving him, when that was all on Carol. Mark takes things personally at a deep level. To him, dancing again could be symbolic for something far different than what you and I consider dancing. Why? Because that's just how Mark is. He's profound, mysterious, and more sensitive than he lets on. I know this, because *you* know this . . . because you tell me these things all the time."

Karma uncrossed her arms and sighed. "What are you saying? That I overreacted?"

"Not necessarily. This could be just the swift kick in the ass he needs." Lisa handed her another tissue as tears bubbled at the corners of her eyes again. "Mark holds onto a lot of fear. He's afraid of losing you. Maybe even overly afraid, which is why it was so hard for him to reveal all his secrets in the first place, and why he kept trying to push you away. He probably didn't even realize he was doing that."

Now that the drama of the day was winding down and she'd expelled her pent-up frustration, Karma felt a little silly for some of the assumptions she'd made, even if they held a hint of validation. But still, she couldn't just take him back if he was unwilling to change. He needed to show her something to convince her he was willing to work for their future. Whether that was getting rid of the old jewelry, actually setting a wedding date, or explaining what the last item on his list really meant, or all of the above, she needed *something*.

As if reading her mind, Lisa said, "You need some good food and a good night's sleep. Maybe even an intense yoga session. You haven't been sleeping, which is messing with your mind, and you haven't been to yoga class in weeks. You're probably just out of balance. You know yoga helps you see things more clearly."

"I've been too busy."

"Well, tomorrow morning, I'm taking you to the gym."

She groaned and flopped her head on the back of the couch. "Lisa, I don't have my clothes."

"I'll loan you some of mine."

"Lisa —"

"Nope. Not gonna hear your excuses, sweetie. You're going, and that's final. You'll feel better and be able to think more clearly so you can sort all this out."

There was no sense arguing. Lisa was in mom mode.

"Fine. I'll go."

Lisa's phone pinged with a text. She picked it up as Karma dabbed her eyes and blew her nose.

A second later, Lisa grabbed the empty ice cream container and started for the kitchen with her phone.

"Is it him?" Karma asked. She'd turned her own phone off so he couldn't reach her and talk his way out of the dog house.

Lisa stopped and gave her a sheepish smile. "He wants to know if you're okay."

She missed him. She wanted to be in his arms right now, but the image in her mind was a fantasy that included him putting her engagement ring back on her finger as he poured out his soul, promising never to let Carol come between them again. The reality was that it would take more than a simple assertion of his intent to make it happen. She wanted actions, not words. She needed him to actually make a change, not just say he was going to.

"What are you going to tell him?"

Lisa shrugged. "The truth." She hesitated. "Do you want to talk to him?"

"No." If she did, she would cave. And she couldn't do that. Mark needed to get his head out of his ass, and the only way that was going to happen was if she stuck to her guns.

But as Lisa disappeared into the kitchen, all Karma wanted was to hear his voice.

No matter how angry she was right now, she still loved him. She still wanted him.

And she still wanted to marry him.

*   *   *

Mark sat behind the wheel of his car, waiting for Lisa to reply. He couldn't leave until he knew Karma was okay.

His phone pinged and he quickly checked the message.

She's better but still upset. But don't worry. She's staying with me tonight. I won't let anything happen to her.

What a relief. Thank God for Lisa.

He replied, *Thank you. I'm heading up to Chicago tonight. And I'm not coming back until I've fixed this.*

Her response came within thirty seconds. *I know you're working through some serious shit right now. But maybe this will help. She still loves you. She's crazy about you. So, go get your shit together so you can come back here and put a smile on her face again.*

Lisa's text made his heart flutter. Karma still loved him. There was still hope.

See you in a few days. He wouldn't ask Lisa to tell Karma he loved her. He needed to show Karma that when he returned home.

He set his phone down and backed out of the driveway, headed for Chicago. Back to where it all began.

Within the next twenty-four hours, the last eight years would finally come full circle and he could re-chart the path he'd always been meant to take.

And this time, he would get it right.

He *would* dance again. And he would dance with Karma.

Part III

The couples that are "meant to be" are the ones who go through everything that is meant to tear them apart and come out even stronger than they were before.
-Author Unknown

Chapter 33

Forgive the person and their actions, never give in to hate, let it go, set it free, and karma will take care of what is meant to be.
-Author Unknown

Karma gathered a few things from her bedroom while Lisa waited downstairs. With Mark gone, she could stay here instead of going to her parents', but doing that felt all wrong. If she was going to stay in her own home, she wanted Mark to be with her. Even though she didn't want to be around him right now, staying in their home without him there felt all kinds of wrong.

She would stay with her parents a few days and wait to see what happened once Mark returned from Chicago. Lisa had told her that was where Mark said he was going. That he intended to fix things while he was there. Maybe a miracle would happen and he'd come home a changed man.

Either way, Lisa had been right. Yoga class had made her feel better. More calm. Mentally balanced. And after finally getting a decent night's sleep, a lot of what had happened yesterday came into clearer focus, making her realize she'd gone a bit too far over the deep end.

Amazing what a lack of sleep could do to shred already-frayed emotions.

"You got everything?" Lisa said as she came down the stairs. "I'm going to be late for my hair appointment."

Karma adjusted the strap of the duffel bag over her shoulder. It was Mark's, but Lisa didn't have to know that. She just wanted to keep a small piece of him with her.

"I think so." She locked up.

Less than fifteen minutes later, Lisa pulled into her parents' driveway. "I'll be back after I get my hair done to take you to pick up your car."

Her Civic was still at Solar.

"I'm not going anywhere, so I'll be here."

"Maybe we can go see a movie or something. Grab a bite to eat."

Karma smiled. "It's a date." She climbed out of Lisa's car then turned around. "Thanks for listening to me last night, Lisa."

"No problem, girl. Someday maybe you'll get the chance to do the same for me. If I'm ever so lucky to have boyfriend troubles, that is." She winked then shifted the car into reverse. "I'll see you in a few hours."

"See you later." She started up the sidewalk as Lisa backed out.

Before she could even ring the doorbell, her mom opened the door.

"Oh, honey. What's happened? Are you okay?"

She had called her mom this morning, giving her a heads up that she was coming over for a few days, but she hadn't gone into the details. Admitting she and Mark were briefly separated wasn't something she relished explaining, especially to her father.

"I'm fine, Mom." She lugged her bag inside.

Her dad stood at the far side of the front room, arms crossed, jaw set, eyebrows furrowed. "He hurt you, didn't he?"

She set her duffel on the floor. "Dad, I don't want to get into it right now."

He uncrossed his arms, his frown deepening. "I knew this would happen. I knew he wasn't the right man for you and you were moving too fast." But his voice was tinged with regret and disappointment, as if he'd actually started to accept Mark but didn't want to admit it.

She sighed, bringing her hand toward her face, and tipped her forehead against her fingers. She felt a headache coming on. "Dad, it's not like that."

"What did he do to you, Karma? I swear I'll—"

"No, Dad!" She held up her hand and shook her head. "Mark didn't do this. I did. Okay? *I* did this."

The last thing she needed right now was her dad rubbing salt in her self-inflicted wounds. Yes, Mark had hurt her. Yes, Mark's behavior had pushed her to this point. But she was the one who had walked away, not the other way around. No doubt, Mark would have stayed with her. Mark never would have walked away or threatened to leave. After all, he had walked through fire to come back to her. He had tattooed her name over his heart, for God's sake, branding himself as hers. Thinking he would actually leave her had been utter nonsense.

But for all the progress he'd made, there was still one last vestige from his past that haunted him. A residue that needed to be washed off his soul.

If her walking away instigated the cleansing process—and she prayed it did—then the pain knifing her heart would be worth it.

"What do you mean, *you* did this?" her dad said.

"I walked away, Dad. I left him." After the last twenty-four hours of suffering, her aggravation began to mount. All she wanted was to park on the couch in the family room, turn on a game, hold a plateful of her mom's homemade cookies in her lap with a glass of cold milk for dunking nearby, and not think for a few hours.

But her dad had other ideas. "Good. Mark wasn't good enough for you, any—"

"DAD, STOP! Just stop it!" Her hands curled into fists, and she squeezed her eyes shut. "I still love him! I still want to be with him! Don't you understand?"

Confusion shrouded her dad's face, and for a few seconds he stared at her as if he weren't sure who she was. "Frankly, Karma, I *don't* understand. If you love him, why did you leave?"

"Because he's got to work through this on his own, Dad. Maybe if I leave him he'll wake up and finally let go of the past so he and I can have a future." She'd never told her dad about what had happened to Mark. About how he'd been left at the altar. Her dad had never given her a chance. In her dad's eyes, Mark had become the bad guy the moment he saw him in her apartment that first time nearly two years ago. After that, there had been no convincing her dad that Mark was a decent, kindhearted man.

Maybe it was time to tell her parents about the man she'd fallen in love with. Maybe now her dad would listen. She needed him to listen. But more than anything, she needed his support.

"Dad, I need you," she said, feeling her scratchy eyes well with tears again. She was like a rainstorm that simply wouldn't go away. Just when she thought the tears were over, they started again. "I hate that we've become so estranged since Thanksgiving. I miss spending time with you, watching games with you, talking on the phone."

He cleared his throat and shuffled his feet as he glanced at the floor. "Me, too." His voice broke, and he pulled in a hard inhale through his nose.

"Can't we just..." She sighed as the weight of her emotions pulled down her shoulders. "Dad, I just need to be here right now. Around you and Mom. Someplace familiar and comfortable where I'm not alone." She implored him with her eyes. "And I want to tell you about him without you thinking the worst. I want you to understand why I love him so much."

"Karma..."

"Please, Dad. Give him a chance."

"I've been trying to, honey, but you just left him. How am I supposed to respond when all I want is to see you happy. And you're not happy right now."

She nodded stiffly. "I know, but it's only because..." She took a deep breath. "He's struggling with something that happened to him a long time ago, Dad. And he's been struggling with it for a while. I needed a break, and he needed the kick in the ass. *That's* why I left him. *That's* why I'm here. Because he needs to handle this once and for all, and my being around wasn't allowing him to do that."

She, her mom, and her dad stood in a silent triangle for several long moments, and then her dad sighed and gestured toward the living room.

"Okay, honey. Let's go have a seat and talk."

Her mom started for the kitchen. "I'll make us some hot cocoa."

Cocoa made everything better, and if she was going to spill her guts about Mark to her dad, Mom had better keep a mainline of cocoa in production. This could be a long afternoon.

As soon as she had a mug in her hand, she started talking, and she didn't stop until she'd explained everything. Carol. What she'd done to him. Its effect on Mark, and by extension, its effect on her. The rings, the necklace, the commitment phobia. All of it.

By the time Karma finished relaying the highly edited version of her and Mark's story, two hours had passed, and she'd gone through three cups of hot chocolate and a short stack of Oreos.

"So sad about his past," her mom said, squeezing Karma's hand. "Just awful." She retrieved the empty mugs from the coffee table then disappeared into the kitchen.

Karma turned toward her dad. "So, you see, everything goes back to Carol. She really did a number on him, Dad. It created this intense fear of weddings. He wants to get married, but it's like he's terrified I'll do what Carol did and not show up."

"I won't let that happen," her dad said, surprising her.

"Huh?"

His cheeks filled with color, and he briefly averted his gaze as he shifted in his chair. "I'm the father of the bride, right? Doesn't that mean it's my job to make sure you get to the church on time?"

"What are you saying?" She didn't dare hope that she'd pulled her dad from the dark side to the Mark side.

Her dad leaned forward and rested his elbows on his knees. "Karma, have I ever told you about how your mom and I almost didn't get married?"

She thought about it a second, surprised to realize he hadn't. "No." She thought Mom and Dad had been solid from the get-go.

He grinned, his forehead crinkling as if he'd even forgotten this story until now. "Well, it's true." He leaned back. "As you know, I met your mom while we were both in college. She was a freshman. I was a senior." His expression smoothed out as if he were reliving fond memories. Then mirth twisted his mouth into a lopsided smile. "Her dad didn't like me, either. He said I was too old for her."

"Grandpa didn't like you?" This came as a shock. Her grandpa got along great with her dad now.

"Surprising, isn't it, given how close we've become? But yes, in the beginning, your grandpa and I didn't get along. He forbade your mom from seeing me. Said I was too old for her. And when she transferred to Butler from Notre Dame so she could come with me to Indianapolis after I graduated, her dad was furious." He grew quiet for a few seconds. "The pressure almost got to your mom. During her first semester at Butler, I thought I might lose her, especially when I was working long hours trying to make a name for myself."

"What did you do?"

"I wooed her. I refused to lose her. She was my angel." He smiled and gave her a meaningful glance. "A man can't lose his angel, Karma. He'll never recover from that."

He held her gaze for a long time then reached for her hand. She slipped hers into his.

"Karma, I've not been Mark's biggest fan. I'll admit that. But now that you've shared a bit of his story, I'm sorry I haven't given him more of a chance. I didn't realize what he's been through." He sighed, shaking his head. "And I can see how much you love him and how he looks at you when you're together. Like at dinner that night at the restaurant. It was the way I used to look at your mom." He squeezed her hand. "You're Mark's angel, honey. He won't let you go. I guarantee it."

"And you're okay with that?"

He made a pained face then smiled again. "He deserves a chance."

This was more than she could have hoped for. Her dad finally getting on board with her relationship and, in effect, giving his blessing. She hopped off the couch and hugged him. "Thanks, Dad."

"You're my baby, Karma, and I just want what's best for you. Sometimes I forget that you know what that is better than I do."

Karma breathed a sigh of relief. She'd won her dad over. Now she just needed Mark to take care of his end. Hopefully, he was doing that this very minute.

Chapter 34

Forgiveness is the most powerful thing you can do for yourself on the spiritual path. If you can't learn to forgive, you can forget about getting to higher levels of awareness.
-Wayne Dyer

Mark pulled up to Carol's brownstone.

He was the epitome of self-control. The physical embodiment of disciplined restraint. At one time, he'd thought those characteristics were a good thing. Traits that served him well in anything he chose to pursue.

He'd been wrong. Because the only thing he wanted to pursue right now was Karma, and self-control and disciplined restraint were anything but beneficial. They were a curse. Tragic, destructive tools that destroyed the intimacy and magic they shared. All because he couldn't let go, couldn't release the past.

At one time, he thought he could force Carol's memory to remain buried in his mind. But guarding those memories took energy. A lot of it, especially over the last few months as his fears resurfaced. The expense of mental power detracted from the affection he should have been showing his fiancée . . . his future wife.

He gazed past the brick sidewalk and concrete flower beds, still dormant from the previous winter, which was finally abating in the Windy City, to the red brick building. The bricks were more a peachy-pink than red, with a variety of intricate detailing around the windows. A series of pale concrete steps led to the inset, light-brown double doors, framed by a concrete arch that mimicked columns on either side. Three red clay flower pots sat on the top steps, near the handrails. Freshly potted begonias soaked up the late afternoon sun.

The home was a substantial upgrade from the brownstone she'd lived in while they were dating. She and Antonio were obviously doing well for themselves.

Taking a deep breath, he forced down his anxiety. He had to do this. It was time. Hell, it was way past time. He and Carol should have had this conversation years ago.

He'd allowed Carol to contaminate his and Karma's home, their bedroom — *their bed* — long enough.

No more hiding.

No more dragging his feet.

No more letting the past dictate his future.

There was only one way to make that happen. And it stood behind those brown doors at the top of the steps.

Patting his pocket to check that the rings and necklace were still there, he opened his door and made his way up the sidewalk. He hadn't willingly put himself in Carol's path since the day of their wedding. Every time he bumped into her, he lost control of his emotions and his upchuck reflex, so this meeting could go very badly if he wasn't able to hold himself together.

Before he started up the steps, he scanned up and down the quiet Chicago street and rubbed his palms together then wiped them down the front of his jacket.

No more fear. He couldn't live in fear, anymore.

Taking a deep breath, he strode up the concrete stairs and pressed the doorbell.

Within seconds, he heard footsteps. Through the thick glass panes, he saw Carol approach, and his heart did a quick nosedive before he could stop it. He quickly picked it up and slammed it back into his chest.

Calm the fuck down. She's just another human. No one special. Not anymore.

He heard her unlock three separate locks, and then she pulled the door open.

Her wary eyes couldn't meet his at first, and then she smiled nervously and met his gaze before looking over his shoulder to the street below. "Hi. You found the house okay?"

"Yes, thank you."

An awkward silence stretched between them. Then she stepped aside and gestured for him to come in.

The mouthwatering scent of garlic and herbs greeted him, and a moment later Antonio appeared at the far end of the hall, wiping his hands on a towel as if he'd been cooking. A round white table and dark grey chairs sat behind him. That must be the kitchen.

Looked like Antonio was the chef in the family. Interesting.

Seemed they had something in common. A love of cooking.

Antonio approached, tossing the towel over his shoulder, and held out his right hand.

Mark took it, and for the first time in eight years, he and Antonio shook hands.

"Mark," Antonio said in greeting.

"Antonio."

They studied each other for a moment.

"Smells good." Mark nodded toward the kitchen.

"Thanks."

"What are you making in there?" He nodded toward the kitchen. With his penchant for cooking, which he hadn't had near enough time to indulge with the busy schedule he'd been keeping, he couldn't resist engaging in a little culinary chitchat.

"Homemade tortellini."

Impressive.

"Nice." Mark nodded but didn't say anything further. As much as the topic interested him, he hadn't come here to talk about food.

Antonio seemed to pick up the vibe and cleared his throat as he glanced toward Carol. "You gonna be okay?"

She nodded. "I'll be fine. Mark and I just need to talk."

Antonio took a slow backward step toward the kitchen. "Okay, well, I'll be in the kitchen finishing dinner if you need me." Casting Mark a wary glance, he inched away then turned and disappeared.

Carol gestured into a narrow sitting room where two tall, skinny windows overlooked the street. Mark took a seat on the edge of a white couch with one black throw pillow and another that was light-grey. He propped his elbows on his knees and sat forward, too tense to relax.

She sat across from him in a matching easy chair.

"Are these real hardwood floors?" He glanced past the throw rug under his feet to the shiny, dark wood.

"Yes. We had them refinished before we moved in two years ago."

"You've done really well for yourself." He scanned the cream-colored walls, the intricate crown molding, and detailed plaster work on the ceiling. Fancy.

"I hear you've done well for yourself, too." She smiled.

"You have?"

She tilted her head to one side as if she couldn't believe he'd asked. "I work with your parents, Mark. I hear about you all the time."

How hadn't he considered that before? Of course she would know more about his life than he knew about hers. She was his parents' prize pupil, as well as their top choreographer.

After what had happened between them, his parents hadn't gotten involved in the fallout. There was a lot of behind-the-scenes relationship drama in professional dancing, and his parents had learned to work around it. His relationship with Carol hadn't been the first dance casualty they'd witnessed, nor the last. Besides, given Carol's past, his mother had always held a soft spot for her. He hadn't expected his mother to kick Carol to the curb after what had happened.

"Yeah. Sorry." He rubbed his hands together between his knees.

Another awkward silence drew out between them.

He dipped his head in the direction of the kitchen. "He sounds like he's a good cook. What kind of tortellini is he making?"

"Spinach with five cheeses. And he's making bruschetta, too. It's kind of his specialty. He cooks it at least twice a month."

Mark bobbed his head in a passing effort to nod. "You always did like Italian food."

And Italian men. First him, and then Antonio.

"Yes." She folded her hands over her lap. Her legs were pressed tightly together, her shoulders pulled in.

She looked almost afraid. Guilty. Like she was preparing herself to hear the worst and shoulder the blame for everything that had happened between them.

Oddly enough, his heart went out to her. He wasn't here to castigate her.

"Thank you for agreeing to see me."

She relaxed a little. "Well, after that phone call, how could I say no?" She paused. "You're right, Mark. We need to talk about what happened. We both need to let go, because, I'll be honest, there's a part of me that's never been able to let go of what I did to you. I feel so guilty. I hurt you and ripped out your heart, and then had to listen to your parents talk about how you fell into this horrible depression, that you were drinking, and that you were behaving so recklessly." She paused. "I guess that was my punishment for doing what I did. Maybe that's why they kept me on at the studio, so they could remind me of what I'd done to you by letting me hear all the awful things you were going through." She shook her head and waved her delicate hand in front of her face as if warding off tears. "About how you couldn't settle down with anyone, because you'd lost your ability to trust." She rolled her eyes to try and stop her tears and dabbed at the inside corners with her fingertips. "I mean, they never said these things directly to me, but I heard them talking enough times to fill in what was going on. They were so worried about you, and I knew it was all my fault."

Mark had never known. And from her body language and the way her words cracked with emotion, she'd been suffering almost as badly as he had all these years, only differently.

Guilt could be a miserable mistress.

"Carol . . ." He wanted to reach for her hand but didn't. "They kept you on at the studio because they love you, not because they wanted to torture you. My mom still thinks of you as the daughter she never had. You have to know that."

She sniffled. "I know." She dabbed at the corners of her eyes again. "But for years, I've listened to them worry over you, knowing I was to blame. And I couldn't do anything about it. I couldn't take back what I'd done or make it better."

"Why didn't you talk to me?"

She let out a sarcastic laugh. "Do you want to know how many times I wanted to? How many times I tried and almost picked up the phone to call you?"

He shook his head, numb. They'd both suffered so long, neither of them able to get out of their own way long enough to fix their situation.

She snorted out a self-abasing huff. "But really, Mark? Would you have listened? Look at the way you reacted every time you saw me. You looked at me like I was diseased."

"Carol, I'm sorry. I'm so sorry. I never meant to make you feel that way."

Her delicate eyebrows scrunched together. "And then you moved to Indiana last year to be with . . . Karma, is it? I think that's her name, right?"

"Yes." Just the mention of Karma's name brought a smile to his face.

"I thought it was all over. That I could finally let go of all the guilt and shame I'd been carrying around. But then we bumped into each other last weekend, and I knew it wasn't over, yet. I knew you still hated me, and I still felt all the guilt, and—"

"I don't hate you, Carol." He leaned forward and placed his hand over hers on her lap. "And you don't have to feel guilty, anymore." Seeing her so torn up felt all wrong, maybe because he'd shouldered so much of the blame and couldn't wrap his mind around her taking it away from him.

She took a shuddering breath, blew it out, and bowed her head as tears fell from her eyes. "I'm sorry for what I did to you, Mark. So unbelievably sorry."

A weight lifted off Mark's heart as he wrapped his fingers around hers. "I'm sorry, too, for my part in all this. I never listened to you. I stormed into a future without taking you into consideration. I planned our whole life without asking for your input. No wonder you left. I didn't let you have an equal say."

She shook her head. "No, Mark. What I did was wrong. I never should have let things go as far as they did."

"I pushed you away. You didn't know how to tell me it was over, because, like you said, would I have really listened?" He'd been so one-track-minded back then—in a lot of ways, he still was—he wasn't sure he would have listened had Carol tried to tell him she didn't love him. He was the kind of man who listened more to actions than words, and Carol knew that. Sure, she probably could have communicated her actions sooner than on their wedding day, but she probably hadn't known how. "You were young, Carol. We both were. We both made mistakes."

"But I ruined your life." She dabbed at the corners of her eyes again. She'd always been an elegant crier. "I'm not so out of touch that I don't see what I did to you . . . that I don't know how my actions affected you." She sniffled and placed her hand back in her lap. "I was beginning to think you would never allow yourself to fall in love again, Mark."

He hung his head. Guilty.

"Yeah, me, too." Where was his sweet Karma now? He met Carol's gaze again as he released her hand. "But that's why I'm here." He dug inside his pocket and pulled out the rings and the necklace then placed them on the small, round coffee table.

"What's this?" Her blond, daintily arched eyebrows crinkled.

"Our wedding rings and the gift I was going to give you on our honeymoon."

"Mark . . ." She held up her hand and gave a tight shake of her head.

"I need you to take them."

"Why?"

"Because it's time for me to let go of the past so I can have a future with Karma. I can't do that when I'm still holding on to what happened and letting it control me."

The rings and the necklace were symbolic. They represented who he'd let himself become. They also represented his fierce desire to maintain control. It was time to be reckless again. *Spontaneous.* Time to let go and let someone—or some*thing*—else control his destiny. Time to loosen his grip on every aspect of his life and put it in Karma's hands.

"I don't want them, Mark."

He pushed them closer. "Then sell them and donate the money . . . or put it in a trust for your baby." She'd had a baby last year, right? She could use the money for her child's future.

She studied his face for a long time. Then she turned her gaze to the jewelry. "Are you sure?"

"Carol, these items have been sitting in a chest on my dresser for eight years. They weren't made to be boxed up. Let someone else give them new life."

After a brief hesitation, she finally said, "Okay. If it will make you happy, I'll sell them and put the money away for Krissy's future. I can do that."

"Krissy?"

She smiled. "My daughter."

He'd never heard whether Carol's baby was a boy or a girl. "You had a daughter?"

She nodded. "You want to meet her?"

They were over. He and Carol were finally done. He finally had the closure he should have sought eight years ago, and the lightness in his soul confirmed it. All it took was the two of them sitting down like adults and talking things out. For him to see her as human again. To see that she'd been hurting as much as he had all these years. For them both to say they were sorry.

"I'd love to meet her," he said.

She stood and held out her hand. He took it and stood. A moment later, she stepped into him and hugged him. "I'm so happy for you, Mark. Thank you for giving me this opportunity to unburden myself."

He couldn't believe he was hugging his ex and not having a panic attack. That he wasn't on the verge of throwing up his breakfast. He hadn't even been able to eat all his lunch at Rob and Holly's earlier, for fear he'd only revisit it once he got here.

"And thank you for hearing me out," he said. "And thank you for taking the rings." He released her, shaking his head with a bewildered huff. "Why didn't we do this years ago?"

"Because you weren't ready." She stepped back and ran the fingers of her free hand up and down his arm. "And maybe I wasn't, either. But we're both ready now, especially you. You've finally found the woman you're supposed to spend the rest of your life with, Mark, and that can be a highly motivating thing."

He couldn't argue with her there.

If he'd known that talking to Carol would result in such a freeing sensation, as if he'd eradicated all the dark matter in the universe to allow in only the light, he would have done it a long time ago. But that's the problem with fear. It suffocates you. It shackles your ability to function, reason, and see the path that's sitting right in front of you. It's the snake that coils around your throat, choking you, squeezing until there's no life left.

But all that was gone now. He could breathe again. Really breathe. And for the first time in nine years, his future was crystal clear. No shadows darkened the edges of his mind. No fog obscured the view. All he saw was Karma standing beside him, in a white dress, holding his hands, taking vows to be his to love and cherish above all others for the rest of her life. And for once, the vision filled him with happiness, hope, and elation. Not panic. Not fear. Just enthusiastic anticipation.

Antonio quietly entered the room, holding two glasses of red wine, one of which he held toward Mark. He took it with a nod of thanks. "How's everything going in here?" Clearly, he'd been keeping tabs on the conversation from his hidden vantage point.

Carol slid her arm around his waist and took the wine he offered her. "Great. Everything's just . . . perfect." She blinked back happy tears as she nodded at Mark. "I think we're going to be okay, aren't we?"

Mark looked from her to Antonio and back again. "Yeah, I think we will."

Carol nudged Antonio toward the doorway. "Come on. Mark wants to meet Krissy."

"She's in the kitchen, in her high chair, slobbering on a piece of bread." Antonio took Carol's hand and led her out.

As they made their way down the hall, Antonio exchanged a questioning, intimate glance with Carol. Her smile widened, and she nodded once. Then he said over his shoulder, "Mark, would you like to stay for dinner? We've got plenty."

Why did he get the feeling that he and Carol had planned all along to invite him to stay if things went well?

"I shouldn't impose—"

Carol touched his arm. "Please. Stay. It would make me feel better, and we can talk a little more. The three of us."

Mark glanced from Carol to Antonio, who nodded. "Yes, please stay," he said. "I feel like I owe you—"

Mark held up his hand. "You don't owe me anything, Antonio. It's *me* who owes *you* an apology."

Antonio appeared to have shouldered a heavy burden, as well, for his contribution to what had happened eight years ago.

"And yet I feel like *I'm* the one who needs to apologize."

"Let's call it even. The past is the past. Carol ended up with the right man." Mark grinned. "And I ended up with the right woman."

Understanding crossed Antonio's face as they entered the kitchen. "We're even then. I can do that."

"On second thought," Mark said, his grin widening. "You do owe me one thing."

"What's that?"

"A chance to win my ten thousand dollars back."

Chapter 35

A woman can't be alone. She needs a man. A man and a woman support
and strengthen each other. She just can't do it by herself.
-Marilyn Monroe

Karma sat across from Lisa on the couch in her parents' living room.
She still hadn't heard from Mark. She wasn't sure if that was a good
sign or bad. On one hand, if he wasn't calling her, he could be busy
unknotting his past and tossing it out. On the other, he could just be
giving her the space she said she wanted.

"How are you holding up?" Lisa said.

"About as well as I can be."

"At least your dad has finally come around." Lisa and her glass-
half-full optimism always knew how to make the best of every
situation.

"True."

Her dad had finally accepted Mark, more or less. She couldn't
expect him to be all lovey-dovey right out of the gate, but at least
her dad no longer cursed Mark's name and was ready to welcome
him into the family. The only problem was, what if Mark could
never move forward? What if he couldn't get past Carol's duplicity
and would always hold back a piece of himself? Could Karma live
with that? Could she accept him if he never fully got over his fear of
commitment? Other than that, he was perfect in every way.
Charming, sexy, affectionate. It was only when he had to face his
past that he locked down and became a stranger.

But she wanted *all* of him, not just the best parts. She didn't want
to always be thinking that at any moment he could have a
meltdown or withdraw from her. That something would spark a
painful memory and drag him into a pit of despair where she
couldn't reach him.

Then again, she loved him. As such, shouldn't she accept the bad
with the good? To support him when he suffered, and to be waiting
for him once he reemerged from his dark moments and once more
became the man she had fallen in love with?

She could drive herself crazy thinking about this, because her thoughts kept swirling in one long, vicious circle.

"You know, things could be a lot worse, Karma." Lisa curled her socked feet under her and leaned her head on her hand, which was propped on her elbow against the back of the couch.

"I know." She hugged the throw pillow she was holding more snugly against her tummy.

She and Lisa had gone around and around, trying to follow her wicked line of thinking about just how much shit she should accept.

Lisa tilted her head to one side. "The vows *do* say for better or for worse, in good times and in bad."

"That's if we can even make it to the wedding. Mark is so terrified that I'm going to leave him at the altar the way Carol did that he can't even set a date."

"Then *you* set one. Take control."

"But I want him to be a part of it. I want him to want this as much as I do and to have a say."

Lisa leaned toward her and touched her knee. "I know you do. Every woman wants her future husband to participate. But maybe Mark just can't. Maybe you'll just need to do this for him. It doesn't mean he doesn't want you, that he doesn't love you, or that he doesn't want to spend his life with you. I mean, like I told you last night, everyone can see how much he loves you, Karma."

Karma sighed and laid her head back on the arm of the couch. She didn't want to plan their wedding without him, but maybe that was the compromise she would have to make if she really wanted this to work. After all, weren't relationships all about compromise?

"Maybe he'll get his head out of his ass while I'm gone," she said. "Maybe I'll go home, and he'll have miraculously moved on and be ready to get married next week."

"I wouldn't hold my breath."

"Gee, thanks. And here I thought you were the optimistic one."

"I am, but I'm also a realist." Lisa sat forward. "Hon, maybe you're expecting too much from him. Maybe you should be happy with what you've got. Most women would kill to have a man who adores them the way Mark does you. You do *not* have to worry about his eye wandering. Mark isn't even the slightest bit interested in anyone else. He only has eyes for you, even if he has been a lug-head lately."

"I don't know, I—"

Her mom's scream cut her off. In an instant, both she and Lisa were off the couch, rushing toward the kitchen. When Karma flew around the corner, she found her dad writhing on the floor, his hand gripping his chest. Mom was holding him up.

"Oh my God! What happened?"

"I don't know! He was complaining of indigestion, and a few minutes later, he collapsed!" Her mom shot pleading, terrified eyes toward her as her dad grunted through what sounded like an enormous amount of pain.

"Heart attack," Lisa said beside her.

Without thinking, Karma snatched the phone off the counter and dialed nine-one-one.

"Nine-one-one, what's your emergency?"

"My dad is having a heart attack. We need an ambulance." She rattled off their address.

She stayed on the line with the nine-one-one operator, relaying information as her dad's condition deteriorated.

On the outside, she forced herself to keep it together as the operator told her help was on the way, but on the inside, she was falling apart. Was she going to lose her dad today? Was he going to die and never walk her down the aisle? Now that he'd finally accepted Mark, was he never going to be able to give his official blessing? Never be there to meet his grandchildren? Never go fishing with her again or do all the millions of little things that made her Daddy's little girl?

The train of chaos in her subconscious could have sent her into an emotional and nervous breakdown if not for the need to remain calm and get help. Her mom was disintegrating into an emotional mess. Dad couldn't help himself. Lisa was—

Lisa!

She spun around. "Call Johnny. He needs to know. His number is in my contacts on my phone."

Lisa shot out of the kitchen and returned a minute later, her phone to her ear.

Sirens rang out in the distance, and Karma hurried to the front door, throwing it open and running into the front yard to flag them down.

Once the ambulance arrived, time flashed, everything happening faster than she could track. The EMTs rushed inside, strapped her dad onto a gurney, busily attended to him in a flurry of activity, and then hurried him into the ambulance. The sirens turned back on, and with the neighbors gawking from their yards, the EMTs whisked him away.

Mom was delirious with worry, crying, pacing, frantic to get to the hospital.

"I'll drive," Lisa said as Karma locked up the house.

"Good, because I'm not sure I can drive right now." Now that her dad was in the hands of the doctors, she was unraveling fast.

That was her dad. Her hero. The first love of her life. She couldn't lose him. Not like this. Not today. Not ever.

Tears streaked her cheeks as she bustled her mom into Lisa's car and hopped into the passenger seat.

She needed her fiancé. Her future husband. Her rock. Because right now she wasn't sure she could stand on her own without falling right back over.

Giada's words from the night the two talked in Mark's childhood bedroom came back to her. *Mark is your strength. You are his purpose. Together, you build something strong that can weather any storm.*

She finally understood. She got it now. Mark was her foundation, and she was his reason for being. They needed each other. Everything else was inconsequential. What was marriage but a symbolic ritual to show the public that two people who loved each other had chosen to spend their lives together? The choice had already been made. She and Mark had already chosen one another. Was a wedding more important than that? Was a wedding necessary to make their love for one another stronger than it already was?

All marriage did was make an already committed relationship legal in the eyes of the government. She and Mark could just as easily take that step without holding a grand event where a few hundred people gathered to witness their vows. They could just go to a Justice of the Peace and not dither around with making plans for a gargantuan, intimidating affair that would upset Mark.

Compromise. A relationship was all about compromise.

But right now, she just needed him. She needed his arms around her. She needed his power, his strength, his stability.

In one brutal moment of clarity, she understood the truth. She didn't need anything else but him. Just him. Without Mark, she was barely half.

Fishing her phone out of her purse, she dialed his number.

* * *

"Dinner was terrific," Mark said to Antonio. "You're one talented cook."

"You two should compare notes," Carol added.

He wasn't sure he was ready to become best friends with Antonio, but he could start by getting to know the guy. He'd never given him a chance before, but anyone who could make homemade tortellini that incredible couldn't be all bad.

"Sure," Mark said. "I'm always looking for recipes I can steal."

Antonio snorted at his light-hearted ribbing. "Only if I can steal your meatball recipe. I really hated you during Carol's pregnancy. All she wanted were your damn meatballs, and I could never seem to get the recipe quite right."

"Is that so?" He smiled at Carol as they stacked their dirty dishes.

Krissy cooed up at them and slapped her hands on the tray of her high chair. She had Carol's blue eyes and her dad's black hair. She was going to be a stunner when she grew up. He could only hope to have a couple of such beautiful girls of his own someday, but only if Karma took him back.

She *had* to take him back. He had to make her see he was no longer afraid. That he was finally all-in. Really and truly all-in this time.

Carol ruffled Krissy's hair and kissed her forehead as she sat down beside her. "Poor Tony. All he heard about for nine months was about Mark's incredible spaghetti and meatballs." She leaned over and kissed her husband.

"So, yeah, Mark," Antonio said, "The next time Carol's pregnant, I'm getting that meatball recipe from you. I don't care what it takes."

"Only if you hand over your tortellini recipe. That was incredible."

"Consider it done."

The three of them had chatted more about the past during dinner, talking openly for the first time about what had happened. About how he and Carol had been so young. *Too* young. Neither knowing what they or the other really wanted. More apologies went around the table, and then, as is often the case over good food and good wine, the apologies and tension gradually gave way to laughter and pleasant conversation.

Carol asked about Mark's job, his plans for the future, and Karma. He asked about life with a baby, their dancing, and their recent win in Europe. The conversation was an equal give-and-take, no one dominating, discussion smoothly flowing.

"So, when are you going to have more kids?" he asked. That was one thing they hadn't discussed, yet.

They looked at each other, and Carol smiled. "We're trying now."

"Really?" He glanced at Krissy as she gave a random squeal of laughter. "What about dancing?"

"We'll still dance for now, but Antonio wants to open a restaurant someday, and I'd like to have more time to raise a family. So we're looking at making some changes in the next few years."

Mark recalled the burst of flavors that had blown his mind from the first bite of Antonio's tortellini. "Let me guess," he said to Antonio, "you want to open an Italian restaurant."

"Yes. Authentic Italian from the Motherland."

"I think you're on to something there." He nodded at their empty plates.

"Thank you." Antonio glanced at Carol, who smiled back.

Mark knew what she was thinking, because he was thinking it, too. When she opened the door tonight and let him in, they'd been strangers. Three people who had tiptoed around one another for eight years. Now, after a couple hours of good conversation and good food, they sort of felt like friends. Friends with a long way to go before they were completely comfortable with one another, but friends with potential, for sure.

But then, that's how forgiveness worked. Truly forgiving someone lifted away not just the fear, but the resentment and animosity, too. It swept away all the inconsequential goo, leaving behind a clean beginning.

Mark wasn't blameless in what had happened with Carol. He was as much responsible as she was. He couldn't fault her without faulting himself, especially when he realized that this was the path their lives had been meant to take.

Maybe some good would come out of this now.

Carol and Antonio had just begun to clear the table while he kept Krissy entertained when Karma's ringtone began serenading the room. Maybe it was cheesy, but he'd selected the 80s song Lady in Red as her ringtone. It seemed so fitting given how they'd met.

He pulled his phone from his pocket.

"Karma?

"Mark?"

Immediately, he knew something was wrong. She was crying.

Every cell in his body locked up as he shot to attention. "What's wrong? Karma, are you okay?"

"I need you." She sobbed. "My dad had a heart attack."

Carol and Antonio stopped and watched him, concern etching their faces.

"I'm coming. I'll be there as soon as I can. Where did they take him?"

She rattled off the name of the hospital.

"Mark, I'm sorry I got mad at you. I—"

"Ssshhh. Don't worry about that right now. That's the last thing you should be thinking about. Just hold tight until I get there, okay? I'm leaving Chicago now. I'll be there as soon as I can."

She whimpered, making a sound that sounded like "Okay."

He paused then said, "I love you."

"I love you, too."

"Everything's going to be okay."

She sobbed. "I don't know, Mark. It's pretty bad."

"Ssshhh. I'm on my way."

He disconnected then turned to his hosts. "I need to go. There's an emergency."

Carol nodded. "Of course. Go. You need to be there."

She and Antonio followed him to the front door, where she gave him a quick hug.

"Thank you for coming, Mark." She didn't need to say any more to express how important their conversation had been to her. She looked relieved, as if she'd finally forgiven herself.

Mark knew exactly how she felt. Finally facing the past had completely freed him. The air was clear again. "Thank you for dinner."

Antonio held out his hand, and Mark shook it.

"Don't be a stranger," Antonio said. "And about those meatballs . . ."

Mark grinned. "I'll e-mail the recipe as soon as I get the chance. But you're sworn to secrecy. I've never given that recipe to anyone."

"I'll guard it with my life," he said.

With a curt nod, he gave them each one final glance then turned and hurried down the steps.

With a wave out the passenger window, he hit the gas and sped away.

Karma needed him.

And he needed her.

And this time would be forever.

Chapter 36

*We are made wise not by the recollection of our past, but by the
responsibility for our future.*
-George Bernard Shaw

Karma paced in a small waiting area in the hospital. It had been
over two hours since she talked to Mark.

She bit her thumbnail as she crossed the room again. She had to
have walked five miles over a ten-foot stretch of carpet since
arriving here.

Mom sat with her eyes closed in the corner, finally silent. She'd
cried herself out and had locked herself into prayer mode for the last
hour. Johnny and Estelle sat on the other side of the room, huddled
together, Johnny's face hidden against Estelle's shoulder, the baby
sleeping in her stroller beside them. Johnny had broken into quiet
sobs several times in the past two hours. Karma wasn't used to
seeing him like that, especially where Dad was concerned. Johnny
had always nitpicked Dad. He had been like sandpaper rubbing
smooth metal, dulling the shine, streaking the surface with
scratches. Yet now he crumpled under the possibility that they
could lose their father.

When he stood, head bowed, shoulders slumped, shirt ruffled,
and made his way from the room with a quiet word of reassurance
to Estelle that he needed to get some air, Karma waited a moment
then followed him.

She caught up to him at the elevator, skirting in just as the doors
began to close.

Johnny was wiping his palms down his face but stopped as she
rushed in. They exchanged glances.

His eyes were bloodshot. She imagined hers probably were, too.

After holding her gaze for several seconds, he glanced toward
the floor and shuffled his feet.

Karma had been thinking a lot about Johnny since seeing him at
their parents' house, hanging out with Dad like they were best
buddies.

"You and Dad have gotten closer in the last few months," she said quietly.

He dragged in a deep breath and looked up at the blinking numbers above the doors. "Yeah."

"Ever since he and I had a falling out."

The doors opened, and Johnny wasted no time vacating the elevator.

She followed.

"What made you wait so long to make nice with Dad, Johnny?"

"Not now, Karma. I don't want to talk about this now."

"I'm not mad, just curious. Talk to me."

She and Johnny had never had the best sibling relationship that ever was. As kids, he'd been horrid to her, teasing, making fun, instigating his friends to bully her at school. He'd been an awful little brother.

But something about Johnny was different. He wasn't as cocky. He was nicer. Almost humble.

"Why are you so interested all of a sudden?" He passed through the doors that led outside the emergency room entrance.

"I just want to know. Dad and I haven't been talking much, and now I see how close you two have become when the two of you have been at each other's throats since we were kids. Is it so wrong I want to know what's changed?"

Johnny paced to the side, away from the lights of the entrance. The sun had set an hour ago, casting the area in shadows.

Finally, he stopped and hung his head. When his shoulders shuddered, she knew he was crying again.

"Johnny, hey, it's going to be okay. He's not going to die." She slid her arm around his shoulders.

The meager contact must have jolted him, because in a blink, he turned and crushed her to him as he sobbed against her shoulder. So sudden was his outburst that for a moment, Karma couldn't breathe. Her whole body froze. Then her own emotions overflowed, and she hugged him hard, crying with him.

She and Johnny had never shown each other affection. They had never bonded over anything. They'd been at odds for as long as she could remember. Yet now they held each other the way a brother and sister *should* when faced with the knowledge that they were blood relations who had to rely on each other to get through the hard times.

"I always resented you, Karma," he said between sobs. "You were always Dad's favorite. He loved you better than he loved me. You always got his attention first, and I got what was left." He coughed through another sob. "You and Dad went fishing together. You did things together. He never did anything with me."

He was confessing. Purging what sounded like years of hidden pain. And Karma's heart broke. She'd never known he'd felt this way. That he'd harbored such sorrowful, resentful emotions all these years.

Suddenly, his behavior made sense. The teasing, the bullying. He'd been lashing out at her out of jealousy.

She hugged him harder, rocking him. "Oh, Johnny, I'm so sorry. I never knew. Dad and I never meant to exclude you."

There were few things as tragic as a grown man coming undone. Trying to maintain control in the face of such raw anguish was nearly impossible.

"And now that he and I have finally starting having a relationship, he's in there"—he jerked his arm toward the entrance—"maybe dying, maybe dead already, and I'll never get to know him. To really know him, Karma. Not the way you did."

She directed him to a concrete bench and sat down beside him. "Johnny, you can't think that way. He's going to be fine. He's going to make it. And when he does, he's going to need both of us. You and me. We're still a family." She pulled him against her. "But no matter what happens, you're still my brother, okay? I love you, and we'll get through this together."

His green eyes met hers, and he wiped his fingers over his face. "I've been such an awful brother. I'm sorry. I was just jealous. You and Dad were so close, and I felt like I was left out of everything."

"I know. But the past is the past. We're going to be better now. We're going to make a better future. You, me, *and* Dad. We will." She squeezed him. "You'll see. Dad's going to make it, and we're going to be fine. Next fall, all three of us will get together every Sunday and watch football. And we'll go fishing together and do all the things we never got to do as kids."

He gave her a weak smile. "I can't believe you actually fish. You're a girl. Girls don't fish. Do they?"

The comment came out of nowhere, kind of like a poorly timed punchline but in a poetically perfect way.

"Come with us next time, and I'll show you how it's done, baby brother."

His face pinched, and a second later, he barked an abrupt laugh. "I don't know why I said that. It just . . . I don't know . . . it just came out." He laughed again.

Unable to stop herself, she laughed with him. The maniacal laughter of two people who had reached their monthly limit of emotional insanity. This was the worst possible time to laugh, given their dad was inside undergoing life-saving surgery that may or may not be successful, and yet, in that precious moment between brother and sister, laughing felt as normal as breathing.

"Come on," she said a few minutes later, "Let's go back inside. See if there's any news about Dad."

He agreed and, with a bit more hope in his eyes, returned to the waiting room with her.

Unfortunately, there still wasn't an update.

So, she settled into the seat next to Lisa, who took her hand and said, "He's going to be okay."

"I know." She had to believe it, or she would lose her mind.

The minutes dragged. Every time she checked the clock on the wall, it felt like twenty minutes had passed when only five had. Little by little, the hour crept toward eleven.

It had been over three hours since she'd talked to Mark. Where was he?

Around ten after the hour, she closed her eyes. She was physically drained. Totally exhausted. Emotionally spent. Her only consolation was that if the doctors hadn't come to give them news, yet, that was a good sign. If Dad hadn't made it, the surgeon would have come in by now to tell them.

A few minutes later, still resting her eyes, she felt the air stir. A familiar electrical charge pulsed around her. A scent. Something recognizable.

She opened her eyes and sat up, glancing around, trying to understand where the feeling was coming from. A moment later, Mark appeared in the entrance to the waiting room.

"Mark . . ." Practically leaping out of her chair, she rushed toward him, crashing into his body as his arms engulfed her.

Her rock. Her foundation. Her strength. He was here.

He kissed her hair. "I'm sorry it took so long. There was an accident outside Chicago."

He was here now. That was all that mattered.

"How is he?" he asked. "Is there any news?"

She reluctantly pulled away, shaking her head. "We're still waiting."

He directed her into a seat, never taking his arms from around her. As soon as she was seated, she buried herself against him again, unable to get close enough. He was so warm, so strong.

She latched onto him as if she would never let him go, and he tucked her face against his chest, holding her securely, making her feel safe. Protected.

He was her strength. She was his purpose.

She so totally got what that meant now.

Lisa finally took her leave, telling Karma to make sure she called as soon as she heard something, and for the next hour, she, Johnny, Estelle, Mark, and her mom sat in silence, simply waiting for word.

Another hour passed.

She could tell Mark wanted to talk to her. She could *feel* it. There was a subdued tension about him. Almost as if a hum of energy coursed in invisible waves around his body, encapsulating her, invading her, seeping into her soul. Maybe that was why she'd felt him before she saw him.

Whatever had happened in Chicago had changed him. He was different. He *felt* different. Not just physically, but emotionally. It was like he'd undergone a shift. He'd been off kilter before, his body not in perfect alignment with his spirit. Now, he felt perfectly calibrated, positioned one on top of the other. This was a new Mark. A changed Mark.

She was about to comment on it when the surgeon, still donning scrubs, entered the room.

In the flurry of activity that followed as everyone perked to attention and asked for news, Karma heard only two words. "He's stable."

Thank God!

Her dad was stable. He'd survived the heart attack, the surgery,

and was now in recovery.
     She breathed for what felt like the first time all night.
     He was going to make it.
     Her dad was going to make it.

Chapter 37

Forgiving does not erase the bitter past. A healed memory is not a deleted memory. Instead, forgiving what we cannot forget creates a new way to remember. We change the memory of our past in a hope for our future.
-Lewis B. Smedes

At almost three in the morning, she and Mark arrived home. The doctors had assured everyone her dad was doing well after surgery and that they would notify them immediately if anything changed. He was going to be sleeping for a while, so the best thing they could do was try and get some rest. Mom had stayed at the hospital, though.

"I'll draw you a bath," Mark said, trailing barely a step behind her on the stairs. He hadn't stopped holding her hand since they left the hospital, not even in the car during the drive home.

She was exhausted, but a bath sounded good. She caught his eye over her shoulder. "I'd like that."

They turned the corner and entered their bedroom.

As he disappeared in the bathroom and started her bath, she went to the closet and changed out of her clothes, pulling her pink and cream robe around her.

The scent of lavender greeted her as she stepped into the bathroom. Mark hadn't just started her a bath, but a bubble bath. And the foam covering the water's surface was as thick as insulation. Talk about an indulgence.

He caressed her fingers without taking hold of her hand. "I'll go make you some chamomile tea."

Before she could form a coherent response, he slipped out of the bathroom.

She wasn't sure what to make of this new Mark. He didn't appear to be afraid anymore. She couldn't pinpoint exactly what it was that made her think that, but it was . . . *something*. His energy, maybe. The crisp, clear focus of his eyes. The way he held his shoulders, taller, prouder, more self-assured. As if he had a purpose and was transforming back into the Mark who had sat down beside her at the blackjack table two years ago, brimming with confidence.

Only this time, it wasn't a façade.

She eased into the large, oval Jacuzzi tub and sank into the foamy water with a sigh, closing her eyes as she leaned her head back on the rim. The water was the perfect temperature. Hot, but not scalding. Warmth seeped deep into her muscles.

Mark returned a few minutes later, and she dragged her eyelids open as he set her cup of tea on the tub's deck.

"Mind if I join you?" His expression wasn't sexual or suggestive. He simply looked as though he didn't like being so far away from her, even if it was only a few feet.

"No, I don't mind." She didn't like being so far away from him, either.

He undressed, tossed his clothes in the hamper around the corner from the vanity, then slipped in behind her as she scooted forward.

The water sloshed and burbled around them as they got situated, and then his arms enveloped her. She relaxed into the cradle of his body.

"Are you doing okay?" He rested the side of his head against hers.

"I'm better now."

He was her haven. Her safe place.

"It sounds like your dad's going to be okay."

She nodded. "I was so scared I was going to lose him." Strangely, her words held double meaning. Not only had she been scared she was going to lose her dad, but Mark, too. She'd almost lost the two most important men in her life in one day.

His arms coiled more securely around her. "You won't lose him."

Did his words hold double meaning, too?

For a while, they remained silent, holding each other, breathing together, finding their way back to one another.

"I'm sorry for how I behaved last week," he said softly. "It wasn't you. None of it was you."

The corners of her mouth lifted, but she didn't say anything. Just nestled more firmly against him.

He caressed her arm under the water. "When I saw Carol and Antonio last weekend, it threw me. I wasn't expecting to see them there. They weren't on the attendee list." His scruffy cheek rubbed against hers. "What I did to you after . . ."

"Mark, it's okay. I'm not mad, anymore."

"No, I need to say this, Karma." His embrace strengthened. "The way I was with you . . . the way we had sex . . . that never should have happened. I wanted to make love to you, not fuck you. Not *use* you." He shook his head. "I never want to use you."

"Sometimes you just need that release," she said. "And I'm okay with that."

"Well, I'm not." He brushed his lips against her temple. "You're too precious to be treated like that. And you are not a conduit to connect me to my past. Okay? At no time during having sex with you did I ever see Carol instead of you. I never once imagined that you were her. I knew exactly who I was having sex with, which was why I reacted so badly. I hated myself for letting that happen. For letting myself take without giving. That's why I got sick. That's why I couldn't sleep. That's why I couldn't look you in the eye. Because I was ashamed. And then I was afraid I was going to lose you, which just made me feel even guiltier, and then I spiraled out of control." He squeezed her. "I'm sorry for hurting you. I'm sorry for making you think you were just a connection to Carol and that I wanted her, not you. Because I don't want her, Karma. From the moment we met, you became the only woman I could ever want for the rest of my life, and I hate that my actions upset you."

Mark was nothing if not an eloquent apologizer.

She rolled her head on his chest, angling her face toward his. "And I'm sorry for blowing up at you the way I did. I hadn't been sleeping, and all the insecurity from my past came back, and the combination sent me off the deep end. Lisa helped give me some much-needed perspective, and then when my dad . . ." She closed her eyes as the image of her dad clutching his chest on the kitchen floor slammed into her mind.

"Ssshhh." He rocked her.

But just as he'd needed to get all of his apology out, so did she. "Thinking he might die made me realize what was really important, Mark." She lifted her head and looked at him. "After praying he would be okay, all I could think about was you. I just wanted you. You're my rock."

"And you're mine." He gently kissed her.

Then she settled against him once more, letting the warm water and lavender bubbles seep into her skin, her mind flickering over the events of the past two days. Mark had left for Chicago on Friday as one man and had returned home as another.

"You're different," she said.

"Different?"

She turned her head so they were looking at each other again. "Yes."

"Different how?"

"I don't know. It just feels like something's changed."

His expression softened into one of pure love. "Something *has* changed."

* * *

Her delicate eyebrows twisted in confusion. "What do you mean?"

He glanced down at the layer of bubbles and shifted beneath the water so his legs wrapped around the top of hers as if he were shackling her. Then he met her gaze again.

By now, she had to know why he'd gone to Chicago. She was too smart not to. Even so, he needed to tell her.

"I went to see Carol."

As expected, she didn't seem surprised.

"And . . . ?"

"I gave her the rings and the necklace. I don't want them, anymore. I don't *need* them. I have everything I need right here. And I won't let anything take you away from me, not even my own fears."

The jewelry had been like a talisman, holding him in the past, influencing him through fear, its presence a constant force working against him. No more. By ridding himself of the rings and necklace, he'd rid himself of what they symbolized. Failure, fear, and heartache.

"You know what's so amazing?" He touched the side of his forehead to hers.

"What?" She turned slightly toward him.

"I spent two hours with Carol and Antonio. Two hours getting to know them and their adorable little girl, Krissy. And she *is* adorable." He smiled, and Karma smiled with him. "But in two hours, we released so much leftover . . ." He paused, searching for the right word. "Guilt," he said a moment later. "Guilt and regret and shame." He sighed. "If only we'd talked years ago. If only she and I had faced all this a long time ago, maybe you and I wouldn't have gone through so much hell."

She pulled away and turned to face him. "Mark, I wouldn't trade a moment of what we've shared."

He frowned. How could she say that about the roller coaster ride of their relationship? He hadn't made things easy for her. He'd hurt her, left her, made her feel inferior.

"Karma—"

"Sshh." She pushed her way onto his lap, placing her warm, wet hand on his cheek. "We wouldn't be who we are today—as a couple, I mean—if any one thing about our time together had been different."

"But I almost lost you. Twice. I let you go after falling in love with you." The backs of his eyes prickled. He wasn't used to showing his feelings, but the last twenty-four hours had tapped out his emotional stamina. "It's only by the grace of God I got you back. And then Friday . . . I thought you were gone. I thought I'd lost you for good. I—"

She placed her wet, lavender-scented fingertips over his lips. "You never lost me."

He blinked several times, searching her eyes. He'd won the lottery when he'd found Karma. She was the most remarkable, most understanding, most forgiving woman he'd ever known aside from his mom.

"I love you," she said. "I've never stopped loving you. In the year you were gone, I tried to, but I couldn't. You were everywhere I looked. You were in my every thought. Even when I was with Brad, it was you I saw when I kissed him. You I felt when he touched me. It was *always* you." She rested her forehead against his, closing her eyes. The gesture made his heart swell, full of love and honor . . . peace. "And Friday . . ." He wanted to put Friday behind them, probably as much as she did. "Friday's in the past." She slid her arms around his shoulders as he wrapped his around the small of her back. "We don't have to have a big, fancy wedding. I just want you, Mark. However I can have you. We can go to the Justice of the Peace. We can go to Vegas. We can wear jeans and T-shirts for all I care. If that makes it easier for you, then let's do that. Let's not make this a big deal, because all that matters is that I love you. Who cares about a big fancy wedding with a big expensive cake and — "

"I do."

She abruptly halted and pushed away. "What?" Her eyebrows furrowed, wrinkling the skin over the bridge of her nose.

He brushed his palms up her arms. "I care, Karma." He had no interest in diminishing their wedding ... or putting it off any longer. "I *want* the big wedding. I *want* the big, expensive, overly flamboyant cake. I want the church. I want a dozen bridesmaids and a dozen groomsmen if that's what you want. I want to stand at the head of the aisle, in front of God and everyone, as I wait to become your husband. I want to lose my breath when I see you in your wedding dress for the first time. I want to see you smile under your veil in that way you do that makes my heart beat just a little harder. And I want to say vows with you and dance with you at our reception. With *you*, Karma. I want to dance with you and cherish you for the rest of our lives. Will you let me do that?"

As he revealed his heart, Karma's eyes misted over, her tears balancing on her lower rims as she covered her mouth with one hand and nodded.

"Is that a yes, Miss Mason?"

She let out a tender sob and threw her arms around his shoulders. "Yes."

He held her for what felt like a very long time but not nearly long enough. Then he pushed her back, helped her from the tub, and dried her off before wrapping her robe around her.

In the bedroom, after changing into their pajamas, he eased her down to sit on the edge of the bed, fished the ring from the pocket of his jeans, then got down on one knee in front of her.

"Officially this time," he said, ready to make their love forever. "I have a question for you, Miss Mason."

She trembled, holding her breath as she bit her bottom lip.

"Will you marry me? Will you be mine forever and let me be yours? No more fear? No more walls between us?"

She nodded, obviously too emotional to speak as he slipped her engagement ring back on her finger.

Back where it belonged.

And this time, he was ready. This time nothing held him back.

This time really was forever.

Chapter 38

To be trusted is a greater compliment than being loved.
-George MacDonald

The diamond caught what little light filtered into the bedroom through the window, sparkling like her own personal star. She couldn't stop staring at it, her hand resting on his chest.

"I can't sleep," she whispered.

Too much had happened in the last twenty-four hours to allow sleep, even though exhaustion pulled at her body, as well as her mind. Her dad, Mark's return, her re-engagement. Her brain wanted her to fall into dream land, but her spirit wanted to dance.

"Neither can I." He shifted and turned on the light on his nightstand then secured her in his arms again.

"I'm too happy to sleep." She snuggled against him. "My dad's going to be fine. You're back. What more could I want?"

If she'd been happy before, she was practically ecstatic now. She'd forgotten all about the very thing that had upset her so much to begin with.

"Well, there *is* one thing left for us to discuss." He reached behind him and grabbed his phone from his nightstand. "Might as well make use of our insomnia and do it now."

"What's that?"

He rolled his head toward her and kissed her forehead then pressed his lips to hers. "Set our wedding date."

She smiled against his mouth. "Okay, Mr. Strong." She kissed him again. "I've been thinking about this already. How about September? That gives us plenty of time to plan and —"

He shook his head. "September's not soon enough."

A shiver rattled up and down her spine at the decisive glint in his eye. "Well then . . ." Her voice whispered between her lips. "What did you have in mind?"

He grinned. Tiny laugh lines broke around his eyes. "June, Miss Mason. I want June."

"June?" Her mouth fell open. "That's, like, only a month away!"

"Not if we shoot for the end of the month."

"Still, that's barely only two months. How are we going to pull off a big wedding in two months?"

"Anything's possible when you throw enough money at it."

She smirked. "And I suppose that's what you plan on doing?"

He rolled onto his side, facing her. "I do." His eyes opened wide as he sucked in his breath, making an O with his mouth. "See what I did there? I said, 'I do.' I'm practicing."

Mark had never spoken so lightheartedly about getting married.

"Are you okay?" She pressed her palm to his forehead.

He laughed then pulled her against him, sighing as he buried his nose in her hair. "I'm not sick." He kissed the top of her head. "I'm just ready to marry you, Karma."

She smiled against his chest. "That must have been *some* two-hour conversation you had with Carol and Antonio."

"You could say that."

"It feels like you've let go of a burden."

"I have. One I've been carrying far too long." His hold tightened. "Now it's just you and me. No more Carol. No more fear. No more panic." He patted her rump. "And I want to get married. The sooner the better. So, let's set that date." He released her and rolled to his back, lifting his phone and opening his calendar to June.

She shimmied up against him and rested her head on his shoulder as he scanned through the weeks to the end of the month.

"If you want a Saturday, we're looking at either the twenty-second or the twenty-ninth," he said.

She shrugged. "If we can get a Saturday in June, either day works for me."

His index finger pointed back and forth between the two days as if he were playing eenie-meenie-miney-moe in his head. "How about the twenty-ninth, but we keep the date open? That way, if we find a venue that's available on the twenty-second, we can grab it."

She lifted her head and set her chin on his chest. "I think we have a date, Mr. Strong."

His gaze drove deep into hers. So deep she could feel the love pour from his soul into hers. "I can't wait to be your husband, Karma. To start a new journey together as husband and wife."

She swirled her fingertips over his chest. "This new you is going to take some getting used to."

"Well, get used to it, because I'm not afraid anymore."

This was the Mark she'd fallen in love with, with one exception. He was all hers. And his confidence was real, not a mask hiding a secret fear.

Carol no longer haunted his memories. Her shadow no longer fell over his face. She was gone for good.

"What did you and Carol say to one another that brought about such a drastic change?"

He reclined once more against his pillows. "It was simple, really." He shook his head as though he couldn't believe how simple it had been. "We both just . . ." He blew out a cleansing exhale. "Apologized." He set his phone back on his nightstand. "She had been holding on to guilt, and I'd been holding on to resentment. Once we both apologized and forgave the other, the smoke cleared." He frowned as he turned his gaze to the ceiling. "Actually, that's not entirely true. The moment I realized she'd been living in her own self-imposed hell the same way I had, even if hers manifested differently than mine, all the resentment I'd been carrying all these years just sort of evaporated." He met her gaze again. "The reality was that we were both too young to get married. We started dating and, after a while, thought we *had* to get married. Like we couldn't possibly have grown apart and were only meant to be temporary stops in our journey to find *The One*. Instead of seeing that neither of us was right for the other, we tried to force it. And then she was too afraid of telling me she didn't love me, anymore, and really . . ." He rolled his eyes at himself. "I was too one-track-minded to have listened. I wasn't a good listener in those days and probably would have convinced her to still marry me, and then we both would have been miserable, because she still would have loved Antonio and would have been seeing him in secret." He shifted so he faced her again. "You know, the three of us had dinner while I was there, and it was actually . . ."

"Nice?"

"Yeah. It was nice. I kind of like Antonio."

She burrowed closer. "You do, huh?"

"Yeah. He's a good guy. All this time, I've blamed him for his part in what happened. But it wasn't his fault. It wasn't anyone's fault. It was just what had to happen to make me see."

"See what?"

He inched closer. "You."

She frowned. "Me?"

He nodded. "If I'd ended up with Carol—even if we'd gotten divorced later—my eyes wouldn't have been open the night I met you. I might have seen you—I mean, who didn't in that incredible red dress you were wearing?" He brushed her hair out of her eyes then rested his palm against her cheek. "But I wouldn't have *seen* you. My eyes would have landed on you for a few seconds. I would have admired the pretty girl in the red dress. And then I would have returned to Carol. I would have missed out on the most wonderful woman in the world, because I would have been blind to reality and the truth."

"And the truth is . . . ?"

"That I never belonged with Carol. As much as I thought I did, she wasn't my destiny. You are. Everything that has happened in my life was leading me to you." He smiled. "And I almost blew it so many times."

"Just goes to show that when something's meant to be, it *will* be, no matter how badly you try to fuck it up."

He laughed at her choice of words. "And I'm an overachiever when it comes to fucking things up in matters of the heart, aren't I?"

"I didn't say that."

"You didn't have to. I know it's true. But not anymore. I think I've finally gotten my shit together."

"Just as long as you don't get boring. I'd hate it if you became too predictable."

His eyelids slid halfway closed as a roguish smile curled his lips. "You *did* hear my previous confessions about the, how should I say, extracurricular sexual activities I fantasize about, right?"

She hid her face against his chest. "Yes."

"Then I think you already know I have no intention of ever getting boring."

"Good." She giggled. "I like being kept on my toes."

"And what pretty toes they are."

"I was wondering when we'd get back around to that."

He brushed his foot against hers, chuckling. "I do love your sexy feet."

Comfortable intimacy settled over them as they drifted silently with one another for a few seconds.

Then Mark sighed. "I'd marry you next weekend if I could."

"You can, you know. We could just go to Vegas."

He shook his head. "No. I want to do this right. The church. The reception. You on your dad's arm in a dress that takes my breath away."

"No pressure, of course."

He grinned. "None at all." He winked. "Baby, you could wear a burlap sack and be gorgeous." He grew more serious and searched her face. "But I want the big wedding. The cake, the flowers, the food. All our friends and family there."

"Okay, so no Vegas."

"June twenty-ninth gives us plenty of time to pull this off. And it gives your dad enough time to recover so he can walk you down the aisle. But given how he feels about me—that might send him right back to the hospital."

She shook her head. "Actually, I think my dad might have finally come around."

"How did you pull that off?"

"We had a long conversation, and I made him see how much we love each other. And then he told me a story about how my mom's dad didn't like him at first, either, so I think he sees his story in ours."

"Wait. You mean your dad went through with your mom's dad what he's been putting me through?"

She shrugged and stifled a yawn. "So it would seem."

He chuckled. "Well, I'm glad he's finally coming around. I didn't like the idea that I was getting between the two of you." He gave her a squeeze. "Come on, we should probably get some sleep. You look exhausted.

He clicked off the light and rolled toward her as she turned onto her side. It was the same dance they did every night when they went to bed. They got settled in then shifted position until he was spooning her, arm slung over her body so that his hand closed over hers.

She felt protected, even in sleep.

"I only have one question," she said.

"Mmm, what's that?" His breath warmed the back of her neck and shoulder.

"What exactly did you mean by saying you want to dance again?"

His arms briefly squeezed her as he snuggled closer and kissed her neck. "Trust."

"Trust?" Of all the possibilities she and Lisa had conjured up, trust hadn't been one of them.

"Dancing with a partner takes unconditional trust," he said, his voice quiet. "And, at least for me, dancing is a metaphor for life."

This actually sounded more ominous than his tender tone suggested. "Are you saying you didn't trust me?"

He shook his head and squeezed her even harder. "No, baby. I always trusted you. I've trusted you since the moment we met." He paused. "It's *me* I didn't trust."

"And you do now?"

"Yes."

"Okay, so you don't really want to dance with me then. You know, like *dance*-dancing."

He chuckled softly. "Oh, I definitely want to dance with you." His lips brushed her skin as he spoke. "I want to teach you the rumba and the Argentine tango and so much more." His body flexed as he burrowed closer under the covers. "And I think I can finally do that now without having a massive panic attack."

She tipped her head back. "Seriously? The thought of dancing gave you a panic attack before?"

"Dancing, weddings . . . " He uttered a soft, breathy chuckle. "I was fucked up, Karma."

"But you're not anymore?"

"No, not anymore. Because of you. You saw what no other woman saw. You loved me in a way no other woman ever has or ever could." He made a gentle, introspective noise deep in his throat. "For me, dancing is more than just steps. It's more than just leading a partner through choreography. It's personal and intimate. A union of souls with music, with trust at its core." He paused. "After what happened with Carol, I lost that. And it wasn't just the trust I lost, but the joy dancing gave me, too. And where there's no joy, there's no life. And without trust, there is no dancing. Just two people going through the motions." He softly shook his head, rustling the pillow. "Without that connection, I didn't want to dance anymore." He pulled her more snugly against him. "And then you came along and woke me up. Do you realize that the night we met was the first time I'd danced in six years? I never told you that, did I?"

She exhaled a tender gasp. "No."

"It was." He nodded and briefly pressed his lips against the back of her shoulder. "I didn't even realize that until recently. But leading you onto that dance floor that night felt so right." He kissed her shoulder again then went quiet for several seconds before he pulled back and rolled her so she faced him. He cupped her cheek in his palm, brushing his thumb back and forth. His eyes sparkled in the darkness as he gazed at her face. "So, you see, Karma, you made me want to dance again. You're the reason why I put that item on my list. Because I wanted to dance with *you*. In every way imaginable. And not just dance, but *live*. You've made me want to live again. You are my life partner in every way. My heart, my breath, my reason for living. And even if you and I never set foot on a professional dance floor, I still want to dance with you . . . and *only* you . . . for the rest of my life."

She stared wordlessly at him. As he'd done so many times before, he'd rendered her speechless. And when there were no words to express how he'd made her feel, all that remained were actions.

She pushed forward and claimed his mouth with her own. As she was his life, he was hers. And as she was his heart, his breath, and his reason for living, he was all those things and more to her.

He rolled to his back, and she slid onto his body.

"I love you." She pushed her hands under his shirt and curled her fingers against his firm, ribbed abdomen.

"God, I love you, too." The way he said it as he pushed her hair back from her face sounded like a prayer or a proclamation of gratitude.

Despite exhaustion's tug on both her body and her emotions, she had to feel him inside her. She needed that vital connection more than ever. To make her feel cherished and safe, reassured that everything was okay.

"Love me," she whispered against his lips. "Love me now."

His eyebrows pinched inward as his gaze searched her face. A moment later, he rolled her to her back and situated his hips between her legs. "I'll do you one better." He brushed his fingers down the side of her face and stared into her eyes. "I'll love you forever."

His lips met hers in a blazing promise as he slammed her hands against the mattress and rolled against her body.

Yes. This was the man she'd missed for the last week. The man she longed for and dreamed about and desired. So full of confidence. So virile. A force of nature who decimated her body in such a pleasant, mind-altering way.

He released her hands, kissing her to within an inch of delirious. Within seconds, he'd stripped her bare.

She tugged at his T-shirt, and he rose to his knees and bent forward so she could yank it over his head as he shoved his flannel pants down his legs and kicked them off.

He snagged a condom from the nightstand and hastily rolled it on.

And then he was on her again, skin against skin, his chest pressed against her breasts, his hips rocking forward and back, sliding his hard cock against her.

His forearms stretched under her armpits toward the headboard, and she felt the mattress bunch up beneath her as if he'd gripped the edge.

Leverage.

A fevered chill raced down her spine as Mark used his hold on the mattress to drag himself more forcefully up her body, making his shoulders and biceps flex and bunch. He was going to fuck her hard tonight. Fast and forceful. Like a man determined to stake his claim.

A hungry growl rumbled in his throat as she reached between them and guided the head of his cock to her entrance. Then she hitched her feet on the insides of his knees and locked her arms around his back. She instinctively knew she needed to hold on tight.

His chest pumped hard against hers, even though he was pressed so firmly against her it was a wonder he could breathe at all. His intense gaze burned into hers, making her belly clench. His mouth hovered barely an inch from hers. The moment stretched as if he were torn. Did he go on staring at her, or did he fuck her brains out?

She panted and rolled her hips, enticing him to do the latter. He was barely an inch inside her, but the pressure was incredible. If only she could shimmy down a bit, she could feel more of him. She squirmed and tilted her pelvis, managing to engulf another inch or two of his shaft.

One side of his mouth lifted in a sexy smirk. "Are we impatient?"

Her body needed his. Heat consumed her core. The muscles in her lower belly were already tight as a drum and ready to let go.

"I want you." God, she sounded like she was begging.

His smirk deepened, revealing his lone dimple in his right cheek. "How badly do you want me? Hmm?" He ever-so-slightly angled his hips forward, giving her a little bit more as she wriggled beneath him. She didn't want a little more, she wanted the whole enchilada. All of it. Now.

"Mark . . . please." She'd gone one step beyond begging, closing in on desperation now.

"Please what?" A tiny bead of sweat rolled down his temple, giving away how much his restraint was taxing him, too.

His body trembled as he tilted his hips even more and slid halfway home.

But Karma wanted him flush against her, pubic bone against pubic bone. And she wanted it now!

"Damn it, Mark. Fuck me. God, please, just *fuck me*."

With an animalistic growl, he plunged into her to the hilt, making them both gasp. His eyes popped open wide for a split second as if he'd just felt an explosion inside his body, and then God in Heaven above, he gave her exactly what she'd asked for.

With her breasts mashed against his chest, his hips slapped hard and loud against her flesh in a merciless rhythm. He used the leverage his death grip on the mattress gave him to his advantage, surging ferociously against her, building momentum. Under his breath, he uttered groan-like profanities that sounded more like reverent murmurings of disbelief. As if he'd never felt anything so pleasurable and never wanted it to stop even though he knew it would. And from the way it sounded, the end would come sooner rather than later. This wasn't the kind of fucking that burned hot and long like a dying star. This was supernova-at-the-moment-of-detonation sex. Blinding, powerful, all-consuming, and void-creating.

Each forward thrust pounded him deep into her body, striking her G-spot with relentless brutality. Her orgasm was already shooting to the surface, her body coiling, her fingernails digging into his back, the desperation rising to a deafening level.

But through the physical and sensual chaos, he never tore his gaze from hers. The last time they'd had sex, he hadn't looked her in the eye at all. This time, he seemed hell-bent on making up for that.

"Mark . . . oh God, Mark . . ." Her feet were still snared around his knees, and she levered them to the sides, wanting him closer, deeper.

And now he had another weapon in his sexual arsenal.

Digging his knees into the mattress, he pushed forward even as his arms pulled.

She saw stars.

The bed rocked like a tossed rowboat in a hurricane. The headboard thumped against the wall.

And Karma was about to explode.

"Fuck . . . fuck . . . oh, fuck!" Mark's eyes flared wide as he stared down at her. "Tight . . . " He gasped and sucked in his breath. "You're so fucking tight."

Yeah, because she was about to splinter into a million pieces as the supernova destroyed her body.

Usually, she came first, and she came multiple times. Not today. This time, they were getting there together for one massive, glorious sharing of nirvana. Karma could tell by the way his shoulders tightened and the way the skin around his eyes grew taut that he was on the same course she was. That they were approaching the edge and about to leap together.

"Oh my God, Mark . . . don't stop, don't stop, don't stop." Each demand rose in pitch, escalating as her throat tightened.

And just as she crested, crying out and clutching him close, he thrust his hips into her and briefly stilled as a bone-vibrating groan rolled from his throat and into her waiting mouth as she took his lips with hers.

As he continued pumping his hips against her, she swallowed every moan, every gasp, every muttered curse, reveling in her own body's euphoria.

This was what loving him and being loved by him did. Their emotions fed one another, strengthening both, delivering greater pleasure than either could find alone.

And now he was all hers. From this day forward, she no longer had to share him with anyone. The last remaining door in his heart that led to the past was finally closed and locked.

Let the future begin.

Chapter 39

Life isn't about finding yourself. It's about creating yourself.
-George Bernard Shaw

The next week breezed by in a flurry of activity as they set their wedding into motion between trips to the hospital to visit her dad. Daniel and Zach took on the task of finding a venue for both the ceremony and the reception, a florist, and a hair stylist and makeup artist to primp everyone on the big day. Lisa worked on invitations and the rehearsal dinner. Johnny found a photographer and videographer, as well as a DJ. Giada used her pastry chef connection in Chicago to find someone local to bake their cake. And Rob and Holly helped coordinate travel arrangements for family and friends from Chicago. She and Mark handled everything else and paid all the bills.

Their wedding became a massive group effort. Everyone was involved and received marching orders to throw as much money as necessary at any problem that presented itself.

Meanwhile, her dad's progress after heart surgery was good. He was sitting up in bed the next day even though he was still groggy. The day after that, he was able to walk himself to the bathroom a couple of times. The doctors said he was recovering as expected, and by the following Friday, he was discharged and sent home with orders to rest for six to eight weeks. He would fully recover just in time for the wedding.

It seemed the only thing left to do was to find a dress, something Mark's mom insisted on helping with.

Which was why Karma, Lisa, Daniel, and Zach had piled in to Zach's Escalade Friday afternoon and trekked up to Chicago.

Joined by Giada, Holly, and Daniel's sister Sonya, who lived just outside Chicago, on Saturday morning, they drove to a bridal store named Jasmine west of the city. Jasmine was a high-end salon/boutique with what felt like miles of white satin and a section for bridesmaids dresses that was bigger than a small country, where the dresses were organized and grouped by the colors of the rainbow. Jasmine saw clients by appointment only, but Giada was friends with the owner, so she'd been able to get them in on short notice.

Karma had been shopping and trying on dresses for two hours when she turned around in dress number six and stared at her reflection in the three-way fitting room mirror.

Exhale.

Two years ago, on the night she met Mark, she'd felt like Cinderella. Now she looked like her.

"Let's go show your friends and family," the attendant said, unable to hide her smile.

Forcing herself to look away from the mirror, she followed the attendant from the massive fitting room, out to the couches where everyone was sitting around a circular riser placed in front of another tri-fold mirror.

The gasps that rose from the group as she swept the long, flowing skirt around the corner confirmed she'd found her wedding dress.

She took her place on the platform, turned a slow three sixty, then lifted her arms.

"What do you think?

"It's . . ." Lisa's mouth hung open.

"Perfect." Daniel stepped onto the raised platform and pulled back her hair. "You look like a princess."

The strapless sweetheart bodice hugged her torso over a full skirt that fell around her legs like an Elizabethan gown. The shell was made of silky satin covered with a layer of shimmering tulle.

From a distance, the color appeared ivory, but looking closer, you could tell it was actually an extremely pale peach, with just a hint of rose. Beaded, ivory lace overlaid the bodice and cascaded in decorative tails over the top of the skirt. The same lace extended about a foot-and-a-half from the hem, dispersing to appear like a filigreed flower garden all around the bottom of the dress.

"It's exquisite, dear," Giada said, stepping behind her and placing a simple, jeweled tiara on her head.

Her gaze shifted to her reflection. "I love it."

"All we need is a strand of pearls, some matching earrings . . ." Giada's slender fingers grazed her neck and earlobes. "And an ivory veil. Then you'll be perfect."

When all the fussing was done and the accent pieces chosen, Jasmine's owner gathered her dress with those of the bridesmaids and promised to oversee all the alterations and adjustments herself. Then they grabbed a late lunch downtown, thoroughly exhausted but thrilled to have the most important part of any wedding taken care of.

* * *

Mark sat on the couch, his feet propped on the coffee table, his laptop in his lap as he scrolled through his e-mail. The sun had set an hour ago, and the TV was tuned to some extreme sports competition, the volume low.

With Karma in Chicago, the house was quiet. Too quiet. He liked hearing the gentle patter of her bare feet across the hardwood entryway. Loved the sound of her laughter and her voice. She wasn't overly talkative like some women. She enjoyed the silent spaces as much as he did, and sometimes just sitting together to watch a movie was more intimate than making love.

He'd never been so comfortable with a woman, which was just one more shred of evidence reinforcing his belief they'd been created for one another, to reach this moment and embark on a journey as a unified force rather than two separate elements simply sharing space. Any couple could live together, but when you really loved someone to your marrow, just living together wasn't enough. You wanted that piece of paper that said you were legally bound to one another under God and in front of witnesses.

That's how Mark felt about Karma, and now that he'd finally shed the painful leftovers from his past, he couldn't marry her fast enough. If only they'd agreed to visiting a Justice of the Peace the day after his return from Chicago. They could have gotten married right away then held a more public ceremony for friends and family. If he'd suggested it, he was sure Karma would have agreed, but now they were fully committed to the end of June. In just a little more than six weeks, he would finally have everything he'd ever wanted.

The garage door whirred. Ah, finally, his lovely bride-to-be was home.

A couple minutes later, she appeared carrying a handful of shopping bags she dropped by the foot of the stairs.

"Well?" he asked expectantly, glancing over the back of the couch as she approached. Her hair was pulled in a high ponytail, making her luminescent eyes pop against her fair skin.

"I'm wiped." She joined him on the couch and settled her cheek on his shoulder.

He kissed the top of her head. She smelled faintly of the vanilla body lotion he'd bought her a couple months ago.

"Does this mean you found your dress?"

She smiled and scrunched closer as she slid her arms around his waist. "Yes."

"And . . . ?"

"It's amaaaaazing."

"I saw the charge come through on my account. That must be some dress."

She laughed. "You're not having second thoughts about giving me *carte blanche* with your credit card, are you?"

He chuckled, kissed her hair again, then said, "I think I can afford it."

"It'll be worth it when you see the dress."

"You're that confident I'll like it?"

She nodded. "It will definitely take your breath away. It did mine."

"Mmm, I can't wait to see it then."

They fell into a comfortable silence as he returned to his e-mail.

The quiet comfort was nice. Easy. He liked her cuddled against him like this. In a way that didn't demand his attention but resonated with relaxed contentment. Six months ago, things had been so different. They'd been preparing to move in together, and she'd been so worried she wouldn't fit into his world, worried he would take over everything and not let her pay her own way.

He smiled, clicking through another e-mail as he leaned his cheek against the top of her head. "Remember when you found out about my money? Remember how you reacted?"

Her shoulders curled inward as she burrowed shyly against him and giggled. "Yes."

"Most women would have had dollar signs dancing in their eyes, but not you." He chuckled as she snuggled closer and hid her face. How adorable. "You were more worried about fitting in, and you were intent on making sure you would never have to rely on my money." He closed his laptop and set it beside him. "Do you still feel that way?"

She lifted her head and shrugged, her face pink, her mouth curved into an endearing smile. "Sometimes things still seem a bit surreal, but for the most part, I've adjusted, don't you think?"

"Yes, you have." He kissed the tip of her nose. "Money isn't everything, Karma. I mean, sure, I like nice things, and I can afford them. But I've never wanted to spend my money on things like extravagant vacations and houses and tubs full of diamonds until I met you."

She laughed. "Tubs full of diamonds? Really?" She glanced toward the stairs. "Maybe I should head upstairs and take a bath then."

He chuckled and wrapped his forearm around her thigh. "Okay, so maybe that was a slight exaggeration."

"Damn. I was really looking forward to that bath." She snapped her fingers then sobered. "But seriously, are you saying I'm bad for your inheritance?"

He cocked his head to the side and shook it. "On the contrary. You're good for my desire to live."

Her elegant brows bunched together, creasing her forehead as her pretty lips twisted into a dubious grin. "What do you mean?"

"What I mean is that spending money on myself isn't nearly as fun as spending it on you. On *us*. On things like those extravagant vacations. And on big, flamboyant weddings." He emphasized the last with a sly turn of his head and an arched eyebrow.

"And yachts and private jets and villas." She waved her arm in an arc toward the ceiling. "And a gigantic home big enough for an entire tribe?"

An entire tribe. He liked the sound of that. He wanted kids. At least three. Three was a good number.

He swept her into his arms, kissing her cheek. "Mmm, a tribe? Is that a hint?"

He could tell by the way she briefly frowned then grinned knowingly a second later that she hadn't intended it to be, but that her mind was now working over the idea. "Do you want it to be?"

"Definitely." He dipped his head down, forcing hers to the side so he could nuzzle her neck.

* * *

She giggled as he pushed her to her back and rolled her shirt up, exposing her stomach as he bent over her.

"Mark!" She squealed and squirmed her way out of his grasp then stood before he could nibble her torso.

It had been a long day and a long drive back to Indy. She hadn't been joking when she'd said she wanted to take a bath. She desperately needed to clean up after sweating in and out of wedding dresses all afternoon. And she needed food. The late lunch they'd grabbed in Chicago had ceased filling her belly a while ago.

But damn, he looked good with that sexy smirk on his face.

He sighed and settled dejectedly against the back of the couch, his eyes twinkling in a way that told her he wanted nothing more than to spend the next hour carnally welcoming her home.

"I really do need a shower," she said, bending forward until her face was only inches from his. "And I'm hungry."

His gaze dropped to her mouth. "I'm hungry, too. And I've missed you."

With her hands pressed against the plush cushion on either side of his hips, she pushed forward and pecked him on the mouth. "Why do I feel like we're talking about two different kinds of hungry here?"

His hooded eyes reminded her of smoke. And where there was smoke, fire wasn't far away. "Because you know me so well."

She let out an amused puff of breath. "I do, and I've missed you, too, but I feel dirty."

"Mmm, but I like it when you're dirty." He skimmed his palms up the outside of her arms.

She shook her head. "Once again, I think we're talking about two different definitions here, honey." She pecked his lips again, lingering for a long moment before pulling away and whispering, "I'm referring to the literal kind of dirty, and I'd feel a lot more comfortable showering before you put your mouth all over me."

One of his eyebrows arched as he made a noise deep in his throat that expressed his interest. "I do like the sound of having my mouth all over you." He curled his fingers around her triceps and gave he a gentle tug until his lips brushed hers. "Go ahead and get cleaned up," he whispered. "I'll make you something to eat. And then that whole mouth-all-over-you thing? Yeah, that's so going to happen."

Warmth kicked up inside her belly from the intensity in his eyes. She licked her lips then licked his. "I'll hurry."

He shook his head. "Huh-uh. Take your time. I'll make it worth your wait."

"What about *your* wait?"

"Oh, I'll make it worth my wait, too. Don't you worry." He reached around and gave her rump a gentle slap. "Now go."

She gave him one last kiss then pulled away, darting toward the stairs with a glance over her shoulder as he pulled himself off the couch and blazed her with one of his trademark sexy stares, head tipped forward, the corners of his mouth curled upward, shadows darkening his eyes under his heavy brow.

It was *The Look* only better. A look that said "I'm going to fuck you so hard when you get back you won't be able to remember your name." And it nearly made her dismiss the idea of a shower just so she could jump on and forget her name now.

Instead, she forced herself to turn around and head up the stairs. The sooner she showered, the sooner she could experience the force of nature known as Mark Strong.

Besides, a little planning for what was to come couldn't hurt.

So much for her lectures on spontaneity.

Thirty minutes later, with her hair still damp on the ends after a cursory blow-dry, she leaned forward at her vanity table and dabbed on some strawberry-flavored lip gloss. It was a junior high thing to do, but she didn't care. She loved how the gloss made her lips shimmer, and Mark had mentioned once that he liked when she wore it. He'd said that it reminded him of when he kissed her after feeding her strawberries.

She set the tube of lip gloss on her vanity, fluffed her hair, and stood. She'd decided to wear one of the kaftans she often wore when she was lounging around the house. It was short, flowing, and sheer. The pattern was mostly light grey with abstract, symmetrical black lines running through it. A black border lined the side hems, which hit just above the knee, while the shorter front and back hems reached just past her hips, barely covering her white panties. Her matching bra was clearly evident through the sheer, billowy fabric.

All the better to seduce Mark with.

Barefoot, she descended the stairs, the kaftan breezing around her body, caressing her skin with luxurious softness.

Mark had turned off the TV, and slow, sultry mood music piped through the home's first-floor sound system. There was a definite Latin flavor to the beat, and it filled her mind with images of humid nights, sweat-soaked skin, and bodies pressed together in the darkness.

Nice.

When she turned the corner and entered the kitchen, his back was to her. He was carefully spooning a tomato mixture onto toasted slices of baguette. From the way he wiggled his fingers every time he set a piece down on the plate beside him, she could tell it was hot, fresh out of the oven.

But the bruschetta wasn't what made her stop in her tracks and breathe in a long, appreciative inhale as her gaze drank him up and down.

Mark was dancing. Not *dancing*-dancing. More like dancing in place. His shoulders gently rocked and swayed side to side. His torso lightly twisted as he rolled his hips. And my, oh my, could he ever roll his hips.

She'd once heard that a man who was a good dancer was a man who was good in bed.

Mark was very good in bed. And the way he was moving his hips in a slow, rolling, side-to-side motion proved the adage was spot on.

For several seconds, she remained rooted in place. She'd never seen him dance like that and was getting a kick out of him kapowing her heart with his Latin lover moves, even if he wasn't Latin. But Italians were notorious lovers, too, so whatever.

Then her smile eased as the weight of what she was witnessing hit her full-on.

I want to dance again.

The last item on his list. He was finally living it. Finally seeing it through.

The significance of the moment warmed something inside her. A piece of her soul that dwelled deep within her belly bloomed, expanded, and made the backs of her eyes sting ever-so-slightly.

Until now, Mark had forgone his love of Latin-style dance. The only dancing she'd seen him do was generic slow dancing where all they did was sway side to side and maybe turn in a circle. And, yet, he was capable of so much more, as he was proving this very moment.

He'd been raised within competitive ballroom dancing. He'd studied it. He'd competed at the junior level. And from what he'd said, he'd even instructed other dancers.

Pushing away from the wall, she quietly approached as he sidestepped to the left, rolling his hips as he did, and grabbed a bottle of wine.

"Hey," she said, lightly touching his arm as she stepped up beside him.

He turned his head toward her and smiled the kind of smile only someone joyously happy could wear. It stretched all the way into the depths of his eyes.

"Hey." His gaze dropped for a quick scan of her outfit before meeting hers again as his eyes narrowed suspiciously but playfully. "Nice outfit."

"Thanks. I wore it for you." She took the glass of White Zinfandel he held toward her.

"How thoughtful." He raised his own glass.

"I try." She tapped his glass with hers. "So, I've never seen you move like that." She sipped her wine.

"Like what?" He appeared completely oblivious as he placed his hand on her hip.

She lowered her glass and cocked her head to the side. "Mark, you were dancing just now."

"I was?"

"Yeah. You were. It was kind of sexy." She took another sip of wine, watching him over the rim of her glass.

He paused and blinked several times as his strong brow scrunched downward. "I didn't even realize . . ." He let out a staccato exhale through his nose. "But, yeah, I guess I was." His face relaxed again as he grinned and met her gaze in a way that reminded her of a horny high school boy taking advantage of the fact his parents were out of town. "You thought it was sexy?"

Was he joking? Panting here. Heavily. Even if only on the inside.

"Uh, yeah. What dance was that anyway?"

"The rumba."

"Rumba." She rolled the word over her tongue. "You mentioned that before. When you returned from Chicago. You said you wanted to teach me the rumba." She dipped her chin and lifted her gaze expectantly to his.

"Yes, I did."

She set her glass down and stepped closer until the front of her body brushed against his. "Well, no better time than the present."

His hands settled on her hips. "What? Now?"

"Sure. Why not?" She ran her palms up his arms to his shoulders.

He stared at her for a long moment. Then he took a slow, measured step back as he raised his arms.

"Okay, Miss Mason. The rumba. First, the frame. Raise your arms like this." He briefly tensed his own arms to demonstrate.

She did as he said, and then he took hold of her right hand with his left and tucked his right hand under her left arm. His fingertips pressed into her back, just beneath her shoulder blade.

"This is closed position," he said.

She nodded, and a flash of excitement shot down her back and legs. He was teaching her how to dance. How to rumba. He was welcoming her into the last secret place within his soul, and she couldn't stop smiling.

"Listen to the music," he said. "Close your eyes and listen." She did. "Now, feel it. Anticipate the next beat. Become part of the music." He began swaying her side to side. Tiny movements, in a slow-quick-quick-slow pattern. "When we dance, we become the physical representation of the music. We give an image to something that can only otherwise be heard."

God, he made it sound so poetic. So ethereal. So . . . sensual.

After thirty seconds or so, he said, "Now, open your eyes and watch my feet."

She did and looked down as he took one slow step to the side, then drew the other foot in for two quicker steps side-by-side. Then he took another slow step in the opposite direction, followed by two more quick steps.

He did that a couple more times then said, "See, I step out with my left foot for two counts then close my right foot in for one then shift my weight back to my left for one. Then I'll repeat to the right. See?" He flicked his eyes downward and performed the footwork as she continued swaying in front of him and watched. "Slow . . . quick, quick, slow . . . quick, quick, slow . . . " He followed the tempo of his feet. "Now, join me."

She did, falling into the sequence with him, stuttering at first but quickly adjusting until their movements synced up with one another.

"This is the rumba's basic side-to-side step." He smoothly flowed with her, turning her as they continued repeating the series a few times.

"This is pretty easy." She smiled up at him.

"Wanna try the box step?"

She beamed and nodded. "Sure."

"It's the same slow, quick, quick step but instead of stepping to the side first, you step to the front as I step backward, then follow with two quick steps like this." He showed her then led her through the steps. The only tricky part was making sure when she made her first quick step, she didn't move straight forward but more at a diagonal. After a few times through, though, she'd mastered it.

Mark applied pressure against her back, securing his hand farther around her so they inched closer to one another.

"And this is what I meant by wanting to dance again," he whispered, pulling her even closer until they were almost cheek-to-cheek. He sighed. "God, I've missed this. This closeness. This incredible feeling of intimacy and trust. Not that we don't have that off the dance floor, but this . . . this love in motion . . . it just feels like I'm whole again. Like there'd still been one tiny piece of me missing until this very moment, because you and I had never danced together . . . like this." He turned his face into the side of hers and kissed just below her ear. "God, I've wanted to hold you like this for so long."

She knew what he meant, because sometime during the last five minutes, the last pebbles of the wall he'd kept erected around his heart for so long finally disintegrated. She'd actually felt the energy shift around them.

As close as they'd come in the last few months, she felt even closer to him now. Probably because she'd never seen this side of him. And now, she wasn't just seeing it, she was experiencing it *with* him. Bearing witness as a participant rather than just an observer in his reawakening.

She smiled and kissed his cheek before whispering, "You can hold me like this any time you want for the rest of our lives, Mark. I'm marrying you. That entitles you to covet my body any time you want to, any way you wish."

He pulled her closer as the music changed to a song just as slow, just as sultry, but with a different beat. He stopped leading her through the rumba and instead fell into more of a dirty dancing style. Lots of hips. Lots of slow thrusting. And lots of his arms holding on tight and the front of his body making love to the front of hers.

If she'd thought the rumba was hot, this was even hotter, and smoldering cinders kindled into flames between her legs as the top of his thigh rubbed her right where it mattered.

She was wearing barely anything, and it was forty degrees outside, yet the temperature inside had just spiked to balmy. Mark pressed her backside against the island in the center of the kitchen, did some Magic Mike Chippendales Channing Tatum hip roll thing between her legs that sent a bolt of fuck-me through her thighs, and then he tugged her kaftan down her shoulder and laved the tender stretch of skin at the base of her neck.

She closed her eyes and let her head fall back. God, he was giving her her own private all-male review in their kitchen. She made a mental note to add strip shows to her list of fantasies she wanted Mark to act out.

"I want to dance the rumba with you at our reception." He spoke against the side of her neck and sounded as sidetracked as she was.

She nodded. She could rumba. She could soooo rumba at their wedding. Absolutely.

No, wait. Huh? Rumba what? When?

Her eyes snapped open, and she brought her head back up.

"I don't . . . I'm not . . . at our reception?" Shit. She couldn't even talk right now.

"I'll teach you." *Kiss.* "Every night." *Lick.* "Lessons." He lifted her then set her on the counter before easing her knees apart and filling the empty space with his body. "You'll be fine." He peppered tiny kisses all around her mouth before claiming her lips in a fiery blaze.

He could be very persuasive when he got like this.

So, okay. Lessons. Rumba at the reception. Got it.

Right now, there was only one thing she wanted to think about, and as he dragged his tongue down her body, sank to a crouch between her thighs, and pulled her panties to the side, she knew she was going to get it.

And, later, when he put those dancing Italian hips to work while she was still in the throes of the orgasm he'd given her with his mouth, she knew sex would never be the same again.

Praise the dance.

Chapter 40

The best times in life are usually random, unplanned, and completely spontaneous.
-Author Unknown

Three weeks before the wedding, Karma returned to Chicago for her final fitting, leaving Mark alone for the weekend.

Two stacks of pale-pink RSVPs lay on the dining room table, alongside cartons of tiny Belgian chocolates wrapped in blush-colored foil. A stack of decorative, coral boxes with dark-brown trim were stacked beside them. That had been last night's job. He and Karma had spent three hours folding those boxes from the flat sheets they'd arrived as. And now it was his job to fill each with the prewrapped chocolates to set on the tables at the reception as party favors.

Karma had settled on blush with chocolate accents as the colors for the wedding, which was fitting, given how chocolate had figured into their relationship from day one. The two colors created a stunning palette.

Rolling up his sleeves, he sat down at the table and had just begun to fill the first box when his phone rang.

"Hello?"

"Uh, Mark." Karma's dad cleared his throat. He sounded much stronger than he had a few weeks ago. "This is John Mason. Karma's dad. Uh . . ."

He was surprised that her dad had called him, but he smiled at John's hesitant formality. "Yes, I know."

"Of course you do," John muttered. "Well, yes, I was wondering if you had dinner plans. I know Karma is in Chicago this weekend with her mother, and you and I haven't had much opportunity to talk, so, uh . . ."

"No, I don't have any plans, Mr. Mason."

Mark had hoped to speak to John before the wedding, but he'd wanted to give him a chance to recover from his heart attack first. Dinner was a great opportunity for them to spend some time together.

"Well, what say you come on over for some baked chicken and steamed vegetables. They say I need to eat healthier, so I can't promise you much in the way of taste, but this'll give us a chance to get to know one another, being that you're about to become my son-in-law."

Mark pushed away from the table and headed for the stairs. "I'd be happy to join you for dinner. But how about you leave the cooking to me. You should be resting, anyway."

"Uh, well, there's really nothing to it." He sounded surprised at the offer. "Just throw the chicken in the oven, and steam the broccoli."

"All the same, I'd be honored if you let me cook for you." A little schmoozing could go a long way toward smoothing things over, but, more importantly, John needed to take it easy for a few more weeks. "I'll pick you up and bring you over to our house. Give you the tour and let you relax."

John still wasn't allowed to drive, so he had to be going stir crazy being cooped up in the house.

"That's not—"

"I insist." Mark entered the walk-in closet and flipped on the light. "Please, Mr. Mason, let me do this for you."

Silence stretched across the connection for several seconds.

"Well, okay." John still sounded wary, but at least he was willing to let Mark wait on him.

"Great. I'll pick you up in forty-five minutes."

He changed out of his sweats into a nice pair of jeans and a dark-grey pullover. It was a chilly evening, so the long sleeves were a good choice. Then he shut off the dining room light, vowing to fill the boxes tomorrow, and then headed out.

As he drove, he built a spur-of-the-moment menu then swung by the store to grab everything he needed before picking up Karma's dad.

"You really didn't have to do this," John said, buckling into the passenger seat.

Mark backed out of the driveway.

"I know, but I want to."

They drove in silence for a couple of minutes then John said, "This is a nice car."

"Thank you."

"Karma tells me you've done pretty well for yourself."

He shrugged. "I get by."

John gave a dubious snort. "I'd say you do more than just get by. This is a damn fine automobile." He scanned the dash and tan, leather accents.

"I spend a lot of time in my car, so I wanted something comfortable."

John made another derisive noise, but it packed little punch, sounding more like he was forcing himself to be standoffish when he really didn't want to be.

Small talk was in short supply for the remainder of the drive, but when Mark pulled into their neighborhood, John whistled.

"*This* is where you live?"

"Yes."

"I didn't, uh . . . I didn't know that." John gaped at each large, custom home they passed, but when he noticed Mark glance at him, he sat back in his seat and tried to look less impressed, which lasted all of thirty seconds until Mark pulled into their driveway.

"Wow." John unbuckled and climbed out, staring up at the three-story home he shared with Karma.

Mark retrieved the groceries from the trunk and led him inside through the garage.

"We would have had you over sooner, but with things the way they've been . . ."

John waved him off, shaking his head. "It's okay. I know I haven't been your biggest fan."

Mark chuckled. "That's putting it mildly." He held the door open with his elbow since his hands were busy clutching grocery-filled plastic bags. "Come on in. I'll give you the tour."

After setting the groceries in the kitchen, he led John through the downstairs, then to the basement, which he and Karma were waiting until after the wedding to finish furnishing, and then upstairs before returning to the kitchen.

John took a seat at the breakfast bar across the immense center island while Mark set out preparing more of what he referred to as a sampler than a meal. He wanted to show John that healthy food didn't have to be tasteless.

"Would you like to watch the game while I prepare dinner?" Mark asked after a couple minutes of silence. "Karma tells me you enjoy sports."

He got the feeling John was trying to take everything in and figure out how to talk to him. Maybe giving him a reprieve and distracting him with sports would help.

"Okay . . . yeah, sure," John said distractedly. He followed Mark through the open floorplan to the recessed living room on the other side of the room from the kitchen.

Mark clicked on the flat screen. "Can I get you something to drink? Water? Iced tea? Coffee?"

"Iced tea would be nice if it's decaf."

"It is."

Mark returned to the kitchen and poured two glasses, taking one into the living room and setting it on a coaster.

"Karma always has a pitcher of iced tea in the fridge," he said as he walked back to the kitchen. "I have a feeling she gets that from you," he called over his shoulder.

"She does." John sipped his tea.

Mark sprayed nonstick spray in a skillet that had been heating on the stove. "She's told me that you two go fishing a couple times every summer and that you always bring iced tea in Ball jars."

"Yep." John set his glass back on the coaster. "Although we might not make it to the lake this summer."

"Why not?"

"My heart attack for one thing. Her marrying you for another." That sounded a bit like resentment.

"Oh, I don't know. She's pretty fond of those fishing trips." He tossed diced chicken in the skillet. Steam hissed from the pan as the meat sizzled.

John nodded but didn't say anything further. Just kept his eyes on the TV while Mark cooked.

A little while later, John surprised him by coming back to the kitchen and taking a seat on one of the barstools.

Mark was slicing a zucchini for the last dish.

"Okay, so what's on the menu?" John lifted his nose and sniffed, eyeing the skillets and dishes of food.

Mark tossed the zucchini in a bowl with diced red onion and a quarter cup of low-fat feta cheese. "I've created a bit of a sampler platter for you. He squeezed lemon juice into the bowl of zucchini and tossed in some fresh dill. "This is a zucchini salad, and that . . ." He pointed to a casserole dish filled with rice, chicken, and red and green bell pepper. Turmeric had turned the chicken and rice vibrant yellow. "That's chicken paella." He pointed to a platter of chicken-filled lettuce cups. "Those are Asian salad cups, and this is Thai chicken broccoli salad with peanut dressing." He lifted a rectangular platter filled with chicken, broccoli, and mandarin oranges. A bowl of peanut dressing sat on the corner.

John stared in wonder at the spread as Mark put the finishing touches on the zucchini salad. "You did all this in . . . what?" He checked his watch. "A little over thirty minutes?"

"They're all pretty quick dishes to make." He checked to make sure the burners were all turned off.

"And all these recipes are heart healthy?"

Mark gave him a sideways nod. "Every single one." He grabbed two plates. "The zucchini salad will taste better after a couple hours in the fridge, but I figured you could at least try it. I'll send the rest home with you." He spooned some onto a plate. "And I made these lettuce cups a bit on the mild side, but you can make them spicier if you want." He put one on John's plate then added some of the paella and chicken broccoli salad.

"Thank you." John appeared lost for words as Mark set the plate in front of him.

"You're welcome. I wanted to give you some tastier options to replace bland chicken and steamed vegetables."

John smiled appreciatively then took a bite of the paella. His eyes opened wide. "I think you've succeeded. This is good."

Mark filled his plate and sat beside him. "The trick is to use other seasonings to replace the salt." He dipped a piece of chicken in the peanut sauce. "You can come up with some fabulous flavor profiles with a little experimenting."

"Karma mentioned that you like to cook." He ate a forkful of the chicken and broccoli. "But this is far and away above anything I expected."

Mark speared an orange segment. "Thank you. That means a lot coming from you."

John took another bite then set down his fork, studying Mark for a long moment. Then he sighed and bowed his head. "I've terribly underestimated you, Mark." He looked up, remorse in his eyes. "I'm sorry I didn't give you a chance before."

Mark dabbed his napkin on his lips then set it back in his lap. "The situation didn't exactly lend itself to chances. I'm sure you know by now how our relationship started."

John uncomfortably cleared his throat and picked his fork back up. "Karma's told me enough. *And* I remember how she was after you left. I can only imagine—now that I know what I know—that things weren't any easier for you."

"No, they weren't. I was pretty devastated without her. Your daughter's a very special woman, Mr. Mason. I was an idiot to walk away."

John stabbed a piece of broccoli and dipped it in his peanut sauce. "It's clear you two love each other."

"Yes."

"And you've obviously taken excellent care of her." He gestured to the food and the house.

"I'm trying."

John gave him a stern glance. "You're *succeeding*, Mark. You've made Karma very happy." He ate another bite of chicken.

A few seconds later, a troubled expression fell over John's face. "When she was a little girl, she would cry in her room after school." He frowned and looked like he was recalling old, painful memories. "She would come home, shut herself in her room, and cry. She didn't know I knew, and I never told her. But I could hear her quiet sobs through the door." He glanced down at his plate. "She had this notebook she wrote poetry in, and one day she left it sitting on the kitchen table. I opened it and read some of what she'd written. Beautiful stuff, but sad. Really sad. I actually worried about her quite a bit, which was one reason I devoted so much time to doing things with her, trying to make her happy. And being that my son was part of what upset her, I tended to take my frustration out on him." He shrugged. "Something I'm trying to rectify now." He straightened as if getting his thoughts back on track. "At any rate, I remember this one poem Karma wrote where she was wondering if she would ever meet her Prince Charming. I can't remember the exact words, but she wrote about being carried away on the wind to a magical land where she wasn't this gangly, long-haired girl who got made fun of every day and was instead a beautiful maiden who captured the eye of a handsome prince." He met Mark's eye and gave him a knowing smile. "She finally got her wish."

Karma had never told him that about her past, but in light of everything else she'd told him, this certainly sounded like her.

"I'm no prince, Mr. Mason. I'm not perfect."

"You don't have to be perfect, Mark. Karma doesn't need perfect. She just needs someone who loves her. And clearly, you do. Oh, and uh . . . call me John."

Mark inhaled thickly, cleared his throat, and then lifted his glass of iced tea. "Okay, John. Here's to being Karma's prince. But not even a prince can replace a girl's father. So, here's to dads, too."

"I can toast to that." John clinked his glass to Mark's. "Welcome to the family, son."

Chapter 41

When I attained a certain advanced intimacy with a man — and I don't just mean sex — I married him.
-Hedy Lamarr

Karma took a deep breath and glanced around the table at all their friends and family. Rob and Holly were there. And Daniel's sister, Sonya. Their parents. Everyone who was anyone in her and Mark's life were with them for their rehearsal dinner.

In less than two months, they'd pulled it off. Everything was done. Everyone had pitched in to make their wedding possible, but Daniel and Zach had outdone themselves. The flowers, which she'd gotten a sneak peek at earlier, were beyond gorgeous. And the cakes—yes, cakes . . . plural—were amazing. She'd only seen pictures, but words couldn't do justice to the masterpieces she and Mark would be cutting into in less than twenty-four hours. The wedding cake was five tiers, each of varying height, with pale-peach roses wrapped in a strand around the cake. The groom's cake was three layers of chocolate upon chocolate, with pale-peach roses made of icing spilling down one side.

But Daniel and Zach hadn't stopped there. They'd gone all out, ordering a variety of confections in shades of blush and chocolate. Chocolate cake pops dipped in ganache and decorated with pale-pink and white ruffles made of icing. A miniature cupcake tower with a pink and white peony and cream-colored hydrangea topper. Chocolate macaroons filled with strawberry filling.

The guests would go into sugar shock just looking at all the treats.

And flowers, flowers everywhere. Daniel was a flower whore and had spent over a thousand dollars on the centerpieces alone. It was all a bit overwhelming, but in a fairy tale princess kind of way.

"Don't worry," he'd said. "I'll be at the reception hall in the morning, making sure everything is set up just right. You won't have to worry about a thing."

When she'd seen the bridal bouquet, she'd fallen speechless. It was beautiful. Every pink and peach flower known to man was bundled into the bouquet with enough white to make the arrangement pop but not take away from her dress.

After all, a wedding was all about the dress.

As dinner wound up, she lightly tapped her spoon on the side of her glass. Mark joined her as they stood, holding hands.

"I want to thank everyone for helping us for the past two months," she said. "None of this would be possible without all of you stepping in and lending a hand." She met Mark's eyes and smiled. Tomorrow he would be her husband. "We're just blown away and so grateful."

Mark lifted his glass in his free hand. "More grateful than words can express," he added with a chuckle, exchanging glances with her. "Two months ago, we had no idea just how much we'd bitten off when we chose tomorrow to get married, but with each and every one of you coming to our rescue when napkins were delivered in the wrong color, or when invitations needed to be addressed, or when tiny boxes needed to be filled with chocolate " — everyone laughed — "Karma and I owe you each a special thanks."

She smiled at him then let go of his hand as she reached under the table for the bag of gifts they'd bought for everyone. Mikimoto pearl bracelets for the ladies and gold, engraved money clips for the men.

Spirits were high as they passed out presents and expressed their appreciation.

Everyone finished dessert, and then it was time to head home.

Mark pulled her aside, eyes filled with love.

"I'm not going to sleep a wink tonight," he said, brushing his fingers down her cheek.

"Are you nervous?"

"No. I'm excited. And you're not going to be home to distract me." He pulled her closer.

They'd agreed she would spend the night at her parents' and he, Rob, Daniel, and Zach would stay at their house.

"It was your idea that we not spend the night together before the wedding," she reminded him.

He uttered a soft, frustrated growl.

"And," she added, "to abstain."

They hadn't made love for two weeks, and it was damn near

driving them both mad.

"Don't remind me," he said softly, nuzzling her neck. Then he whispered, "I've been hard for days."

"Have you now?"

He nodded, kissing the tender skin below her ear.

"Well, your wait is almost over. Twenty-four more hours."

He growled again. "I don't know if I can make it."

"I'll make it worth your wait." And she meant it. She had one extra special wedding present to give him tomorrow night.

He pulled away, a devilish grin revealing his thoughts.

As for tomorrow, everything was set. All the arrangements made. The only thing left was to say, "I do."

Rob eased up beside them. "You about ready to go, groom-to-be?"

"Yeah, just give me one more minute with my fiancée."

Rob nodded and joined the others by the door.

When they were alone again, Mark said, "Just think, the next time we see each other, you'll be walking down that aisle for real, and we'll be getting married."

"And you're okay? You're not nervous or — "

"Panicking?"

He'd taken the word right out of her mouth.

"Yes."

He shook his head. "My heart's racing, but it's not because I'm panicking." He leaned forward and kissed her ear then whispered, "It's because I know that tomorrow night I'll be making love to my wife for the first time. And I can't wait to know what that feels like. I can't wait to be your husband."

She smiled and dipped the side of her head against his cheek, knowing that the night would be even more special than he realized since she'd started on birth control over a month ago. What would it feel like to have sex without a condom separating them?

"And I can't wait to be your wife."

He hugged her, kissed her, and then sighed as he released her. "Good night, Miss Mason." A sparkle lit in his eyes, and she didn't need him to tell her what he was thinking.

This was the last time he would call her Miss Mason.

Because tomorrow she would be Mrs. Strong.

Chapter 42

I'm looking forward to the future, and feeling grateful for the past.
-Mike Rowe

Mark applied the last chocolate petal to the chocolate-covered strawberry rose he was making then carefully set it in the vase with the other five. Six down, six more to go.

"Hey, what are you still doing up?" Rob shuffled into the kitchen, rubbing his eyes.

"Couldn't sleep. What about you? Why are you up?"

Rob plopped onto one of the barstools. "I never sleep well when Holly's not with me."

Mark rolled a small ball of chocolate between his palms and placed it on a piece of parchment paper. "I know the feeling." He rolled out another small ball then puffed out a derisive breath. "Look at us. Two years ago, we were both contentedly single. Now, neither of us can sleep without the women we love next to us in bed."

Rob snorted and peeled himself off the barstool to head to the fridge. "Yeah, I never saw this day coming. But, you know . . ." He grabbed the milk and set it on the counter. "I wouldn't trade it for anything."

Mark placed a second sheet of parchment over his five chocolate balls and one chocolate snake then grabbed the rolling pin. "Neither would I." He flattened the chocolate then carefully peeled away the top sheet of parchment while Rob poured a glass of milk then grabbed a bag of Chips Ahoy cookies from the cabinet and returned to his seat.

"Are these for tomorrow?" Rob pointed at the vase of chocolate roses with his pinky as he bit into a cookie.

"Yep." He dipped a cake pop stick in melted white chocolate, pushed it into the center of the strawberry from the bottom, rolled the strawberry in the white chocolate, and then set it aside so he could roll his flattened milk chocolate snake in a coil around the top of the berry.

Rob dipped his cookie in his milk and quietly watched him mold the round discs of milk chocolate into petals around the strawberry, turning out the tops to make it seem like the rosebud was beginning to open.

Mark smirked as Rob dipped another cookie.

"What?" Rob said innocently.

"You still dip your cookies in milk? Really? What are you, nine?"

Rob flipped him off, his mouth full.

Mark chuckled, finishing the chocolate rose then carefully adding it to the vase with the others.

"You know," Rob said, chugging a swallow of milk, "maybe you should open a restaurant."

"A restaurant?" Mark stole a cookie for himself.

Rob's hand dove into the bag and dragged out another. "Yeah. You've been trying to figure out for years what you want to be when you grow up." He chomped half the cookie in one bite. "You've been guarding your inheritance like a dragon guards its hoard of gold, saying that someday you'll start your own business and use the money to fund it."

"Yeah, but a restaurant?" Mark dusted off his hands and started on rose number eight. "I don't know the first thing about running a restaurant."

Rob pushed the bag of cookies aside. "You learn, man. I mean, Mark, you've got to admit, you know food. You love cooking. I've eaten your homemade spaghetti and meatballs, which is better than any spaghetti and meatballs I've eaten *anywhere*, whether in a restaurant or out of a can. And, dude, most people simply use spaghetti from a box. But you? Noooo, you have to make your own. You could make a killing if you opened an Italian bistro."

Mark contemplated Rob's words as he flattened his chocolate petals for the next flower. He did love cooking. And how did that saying go? *If you do what you love, you'll never work another day in your life.* Maybe Rob was onto something.

"Good idea, huh?" Rob said, obviously seeing Mark's wheels turning.

"It's got potential." Mark dipped another cake pop stick in the white chocolate. "I'll look into it, but right now, my mind's focused on tomorrow."

"You nervous?"

"No."

"You sure? I know how you get with churches and weddings."

Mark pushed the stick into the bottom of a strawberry. "That was before Carol and I talked. Now, though? Everything's different now." He rolled the strawberry in the melted white chocolate. "All that shit from before is gone."

"I told you it would work. You just needed to bury the hatchet with Carol. You two never did that before."

"What can I say? You're always right."

"Damn straight I am." Rob drained his glass of milk and plunked it back on the counter. "So . . . you're okay? No panic attacks? I don't need to bring the Valium?"

Mark chuckled, his fingers busily coiling a chocolate snake on top of the berry. "No, buddy. I'm good."

Rob closed the bag of cookies and hopped off the barstool. "Well, I'm going to head back up and try to get some sleep." He put the cookies away then rinsed his glass and set it beside the sink. "You should try to do the same."

"I will. I've got to make four more of these, and then I'll head up." If he slept at all, he'd be grateful. As excited as he was about tomorrow, though, he'd be lucky if he slept more than a couple hours.

"Night." Rob headed out of the kitchen toward the stairs.

Alone again, Mark continued making his dozen special roses for his very special bride. The last time he'd made these for her, he was getting ready to whisk her away to Saint Lucia. Just like now. She didn't know it, yet, but that was where he was taking her for their honeymoon.

And this time, no secrets stood between them. His slate was clean.

For the first time ever, he felt whole.

And he couldn't stop smiling.

*   *   *

Karma sat in the living room of her parents' house, watching some cheesy late-night movie. The rest of the house was dark and quiet, but she couldn't sleep. She imagined Mark was suffering the same fate. Maybe even watching the same movie in their bedroom.

"Hey, pumpkin."

She jumped at the sound of her dad's voice then settled back, laughing at herself. "Dad, you startled me. I thought you were asleep."

"Sorry." He pulled his robe more securely around him then clicked on the lamp on the end table before taking a seat in his chair. "Just thought I'd check on you. You all right?"

"Yeah, I'm fine. I just can't sleep."

"You nervous?"

She smiled as she recalled how Mark had answered that same question just a few hours ago. "I'm excited. Too excited to sleep."

"I can see that. You *are* pretty smitten with that boy."

"He's not a boy, Dad. He's—"

"I know, he's a man. I remember you telling me that a time or two." He grinned.

"Yeah, once or twice." She smiled. "You know, I'm still getting used to you being so nice to him."

He sat back and gently rocked his chair a couple of times. "Well, he's a good man. Any fool can see that."

"Are you calling yourself a fool?" She folded her forearms over the arm of the couch and laid her chin on her hand.

"Never." He grinned and gave her a wink.

They held each other's gazes for a few seconds.

"Are you ready for tomorrow?" she said. "It's a big day for you, too."

"Don't remind me. I'm already worried I'll mess up my line."

She laughed. "All you have to do is say 'I do' when the minister asks who's giving me away."

"I know. Can you see why I'm worried?"

They laughed together then Karma said, "You'll do fine, Dad."

"You know, when I had my heart attack, I was afraid I wouldn't make it to this day."

"Is that why you changed your mind about Mark?"

He shook his head. "I'd already started to change my mind about him. The heart attack just helped hurry me along."

"I'm glad. And I'm glad you and Johnny are getting along better, too."

"Me, too. It seems my heart attack woke us both up."

A lot had changed in the last two years, especially in the last couple months. She felt closer to her brother than she ever had, and for the first time, the three of them had discussed taking a fishing trip together later this summer. It would be nice to spend time with her dad and her brother and not feel like she was in the middle of a war zone.

"Well, honey . . ." Her dad rose. "I'm heading back to bed. And you need to try and get some sleep, too. We'll be getting up in less than seven hours to get ready."

"I know. Maybe I'll get lucky and fall asleep on the couch." If she tried to sleep in her bedroom, her mind would just fire back to life with a million random thoughts about tomorrow. Or today. After all, it was after midnight. First would be a trip to the salon to get her hair and makeup done, and then back to her parents' house to get dressed. Then off to the park in the limo they'd rented to get pictures taken after Mark and the groomsmen finished with theirs.

And then . . . the wedding.

Finally.

It had been a long time in the making — over two years, in fact — but their big day had finally come.

Chapter 43

Every love story is beautiful, but ours is my favorite.
-Xuan Ta

Mark stood at the front of the church, hands clasped in front of him, as Sonya, Holly, and Lisa slowly walked up the aisle in their pale-pink dresses.

"You doing okay?" Rob whispered beside him.

Mark nodded without taking his eyes off the back of the church. "Yes. Stop distracting me." If he turned away for only a second and missed his first glimpse of Karma in her dress, he would never forgive his best friend, who seemed intent on checking on him every ten seconds.

"Just making sure you're not going to pass out."

"I told you, I'm fine." He was better than fine. He was about to see his bride in her wedding dress for the first time. Not a shred of fear remained in his heart, which held nothing but love and hope for their future.

What they'd been able to pull off in only two months was nothing short of a miracle. His first attempt at a wedding had taken over eight months to plan, and it had been nothing like the extravagance he and Karma had managed with the help of their friends. The church was a beautiful display of flowers, ribbons, and candles. Daniel and Zach had done well.

If the reception hall looked anything like the church, they were in for a fairytale evening.

The wedding march started, and all the guests rose. He squared his shoulders and straightened his back, gaze locked on the back of the church. In the vestibule, just outside his line of sight, she was waiting with her dad. He could see their shadows moving on the floor.

"You still doing okay?" Rob whispered.

"I'm fine, Rob. Stop asking."

He'd taken such a long, hard journey to get here. For so long, he'd had no interest in falling in love, and then he met Karma. She had changed everything. She'd made him want to love again, take chances, break free from his fear.

He couldn't imagine two people could love each other more than they did. After tonight, they would finally be one. His name would be hers, her heart his.

The shadows crossed the floor beyond the entryway, and he fought not to crane his neck to see her.

And then she was there, and Mark could hardly breathe.

"My God . . ." he whispered.

"You okay?" Rob said.

He couldn't take his eyes off her as she began the long, agonizingly slow walk toward him. "I'm perfect," he whispered.

Beneath the veil, she smiled shyly, and he knew she was blushing. He smiled back, their gazes locked one to the other. It was as if those in attendance disappeared. This was their day. His and Karma's.

Finally, her dad led her up the shallow steps and stopped in front of him. Karma's mom joined him, as did his parents, all standing a step behind.

Mark exchanged a glance of understanding with her dad. He was assuming responsibility for Karma's life today. The passing of the guard was about to take place. From this point forward, he would be responsible for Karma's happiness, her health, her everything. It wasn't a fact he took lightly.

The music stopped, and he gazed in awe at the woman who was about to become his wife. Almost a decade ago, he'd stood at the head of another church, waiting for another woman to join him. Only, that woman hadn't been meant for him. The one standing before him now had always been the one he'd been made for. It had taken meeting Karma to bring him full circle, right back to the very place that had sent him on a journey of despair. This time, he'd chosen right. This time, he'd found happily ever after.

Lisa took Karma's bouquet then stepped back into place alongside the other bridesmaids.

The minister stepped forward and addressed the room, welcoming the guests, but Mark hardly heard a word he said. All he could do was stare at the beauty in front of him as the minister asked her if she took him to be her husband, to love, comfort, honor, and keep, forsaking all others, and to be faithful to him for the rest of their lives.

"I will," she said.

"Mark," the minister said, turning toward him, "will you have this woman to be your wife, to live together with her in the covenant of marriage? Will you love her, comfort her, honor and keep her, in sickness and in health, and, forsaking all others, be faithful unto her as long as you both shall live?"

He gazed into her pale-green eyes, moist with tears, and said, "I will."

Then the minister glanced toward their parents. "Who blesses this union?"

"We do," all four parents said in unison.

"And who presents this woman to be married to this man?"

"I do." Her dad stepped forward and placed Karma's hand in his. Then he lowered his voice and said, "Take care of her." His eyes glistened as if he were on the verge of tears.

"I will," Mark whispered back.

Karma's hands trembled inside his. Or maybe it was his hands that were trembling. He wasn't sure. He was just so unbelievably happy.

"Repeat after me," the minister said to Mark.

Gladly, he did as he was told. "I, Mark Strong, take you, Karma Mason, to be my wife, to have and to hold from this day forward, for better, for worse, for richer, for poorer, in sickness and in health, to love and to cherish, until death do us part. This is my solemn vow."

His mom sobbed quietly behind him.

Then it was Karma's turn to repeat the same vow he'd just given, her voice gentle yet firm. "I, Karma Mason, take you, Mark Strong, to be my husband . . ." His heart swelled at the word. "To have and to hold from this day forward, for better, for worse . . ." Her grin widened as if she knew they'd already been through the worst. "For richer, for poorer, in sickness and in health, to love and to cherish, until death do us part. This is my solemn vow."

Rob stepped forward with the rings, handing them to the minister.

Mark took Karma's left hand with his and held the ring in front of her finger. "I give you this ring as a symbol of my love, and with all that I am, and all that I have, I honor you, in the name of the Father, the Son, and the Holy Spirit." He slid it on her trembling finger.

Then she did the same to him, repeating the vow as she slid on his ring. He had never had the chance to wear his first wedding band, but he would never take this one off.

The minister's voice rose confidently as he addressed the congregation. "Now that Karma Mason and Mark Strong have given themselves to each other by solemn vows, with the joining of hands and the giving and receiving of rings, I pronounce that they are now husband and wife, in the name of the Father, the Son, and the Holy Spirit." He looked at Mark. "You may now kiss your bride."

With a deep breath, he lifted her veil and tenderly folded it back.

"I love you."

"I love you, too."

And then he kissed her. He kissed his wife for the first time.

And his heart sang.

Chapter 44

Karma had never seen Mark so happy. Throughout the ceremony, he never stopped smiling. His hands had shaken a tiny bit when he took hers and slipped on her wedding band, but he'd kept himself together. When he kissed her to seal their vows, he'd done so with pride and without hesitation.

After another hour of wedding photographs, she stood arm-in-arm with him outside the reception hall as the bridal party began filtering in ahead of them.

"Have I told you how beautiful you are tonight?" he said.

She smiled up at him. "Only about a hundred times."

He beamed as his gaze swept over her face and down to her dress again. "Well, let me say it again. You're unbelievably beautiful. And this dress is truly breathtaking."

"And I'll tell *you* again that you're incredibly handsome. We need to go to more events where you have to wear a tux with tails."

"I'll start working on that right after we get back from our honeymoon."

"You still haven't told me where we're going."

He grinned mischievously. "It's a secret."

"At least give me a hint."

"Nope. No hints. You'll just have to be patient. Now, ssshhh. They're about to announce us, and I've been waiting for this my whole life."

She fought back a giggle at the way he straightened and lifted his chin as he placed his hand over hers, which was wrapped around the crook of his elbow. Who would have thought that the man who'd cowered at the idea of setting a wedding date barely three months ago would now hold himself with more regency than the King of England at the moment they were to be officially presented as husband and wife.

The doors opened, and he led her into a glittering, awe-inspiring ballroom. The round tables were dressed with blush-colored tablecloths, adorned with elaborate flower arrangements of peach, cream, and pale pink. Matching arrangements and satin ribbons draped the head table, as well as what Daniel had proudly called the confection table, where an array of treats tempted the guests. As Mark paraded her through the center of the room like they were royalty, even the wait-staff stopped filling water glasses to watch them.

Then she spotted the vase of chocolate roses in the center of the head table.

"Did you . . . ?" She looked up at him.

He grinned. "I couldn't sleep last night, so I made you a dozen chocolate covered strawberries." They passed the parents' table. Tears glistened in her mom's and Giada's eyes, and her dad and Adler smiled proudly at them.

She smiled back and tucked herself closer into Mark's side. "And since chocolate has been so pivotal to our entire relationship, they're more than fitting, aren't they?"

"And they go with our colors. Chocolate on the outside, blush-pink inside."

"You do think of everything, don't you?"

"You know I do." With a wink, he led her around the table to their seats and faced the room. The regal couple meeting the public for the first time.

Once seated, the guests immediately began clanging their silverware against their glasses. He leaned over and kissed her, making everyone cheer.

"Get used to that," he said.

"What? Kissing you?" She rolled her eyes and smirked. "I hope I never get used to that."

He grinned against her mouth. "Well, when you put it that way" He kissed her again.

Dinner was served, and the evening pressed on, sprinkled with more kisses and a never-ending stream of congratulations and laughter.

When Rob stood to make his toast, Mark wrapped his hand around hers and leaned into her, his expression both expectant and anxious.

"I have a feeling he's going to zing me," he whispered.

She angled her head toward his. "Why?"

"Because . . . that's how he is." He shrugged. "And I got him pretty good at his wedding, so . . ."

"Payback."

Mark's gaze locked on hers. "Precisely."

Rob took a moment as the room quieted. "When I got married last year" — he looked down at Holly — "Mark said he could only hope that someday he would know the happiness I was feeling that night." He smiled and met Mark's gaze. "Well, tonight I'm sure he knows exactly how I felt."

Mark exchanged meaningful glances with her then nodded back at Rob. "And you would be right."

Rob grinned and lifted his champagne glass a little higher. "Mark and I have been friends forever. I've seen him hit his highest highs and his lowest lows, sometimes at the same time." Laughter rang out from the guests. "Mark has always been stubborn, willful, and intensely focused. So much so there were times he couldn't see his nose to spite his face." More laughter. Karma glanced toward Mark's mom, who was nodding slowly, in total agreement.

Mark chuckled. "Are you toasting me or roasting me, Rob?"

Rob opened his fingers, indicating for Mark to hang tight. "I'm getting there, buddy. Just give me my moment in the sun. You haven't made this easy for me."

Karma snuggled against Mark's arm as he squeezed her hand and laughed. He knew he'd brought this on himself.

Rob swept his gaze around the room. "One of the things you have to know about Mark is that he gets in his own way. *A lot.*"

The laughter grew louder, and Mark bowed his head, his cheeks coloring pink as he met her gaze out of the corners of his eyes. She almost laughed at his expression, which was somewhere between *shoot me* and *I told you he was going to zing me.*

Rob continued, growing more serious. "The night he met Karma, I knew something was different this time. There was a spark in his eyes. I didn't tell him that at the time, but I noticed it." Rob met Karma's gaze. "You affected him that night more than he was willing to admit."

She curled her arm more tightly around Mark's.

Rob faced the room again. "Over the months, as he and Karma spent more time with one another, Mark continued to change. He was usually so put together . . . so sure of himself. When he met Karma, I saw the cracks form in his façade. He'd grown so used to putting on a front to the world, only letting people see the person he wanted them to see. But Karma chipped away at the veneer until the real Mark came back to us." He paused, and all the unspoken moments of their long friendship passed between them. "I've never seen Mark so happy as he is tonight." Rob hesitated, obviously keeping his emotions in check. Then he lifted his glass and cleared his throat. "I love you, my friend. You deserve to be happy." To Karma he said, "And thank you for bringing happiness back to my best friend. Here's to both of you and a long life together."

"Here, here." The guests all voiced their agreement, raising their glasses of champagne.

Mark leaned in and kissed her, holding his lips to hers for the duration as the room cheered.

Then he pushed back his chair, grabbed one of the chocolate roses from the vase, and stood.

Once the room quieted again, he cleared his throat and glanced down at her. In that moment, it looked like all the love in his heart shone through his eyes.

"Thank you for that *colorful* toast, Rob."

A few chuckles rose from the guests.

Rob saluted with his champagne glass. Then Mark faced the room again.

"Rob's right, though. The night I met Karma . . ." He looked at her again. "Everything changed for me. The moment I laid eyes on her, something inside me woke up. Something that had been dead for long, long time. Suddenly, I felt alive again." He grinned and turned back toward the room and lifted the rose. "She was like this treat. It looks like a chocolate rose." He set it on a small white plate and cut it in half with his dinner knife, revealing the strawberry inside. "But once you see inside, you realize it's so much more than just chocolate.

"That's how I felt the first time I met Karma. She was in Chicago, and she was wearing this incredible red dress and looked like a movie star. Even then, I knew there was so much more to her than what I saw on the outside. I could tell she was special." They exchanged intimate smiles. "And then I met her again here in Indianapolis, and that was it for me. I was hooked. And the more I learned about her, the more layers she revealed. I couldn't get enough, and even though we've known each other for almost two years, she still surprises me, and I've become unexpectedly addicted to the anticipation of what she'll surprise me with next." An amused yet appreciative murmur rose from their friends and family as he turned adoring eyes on her. "It was all those layers and the knowledge of what she held on the inside that captured my heart. I couldn't stop thinking about her, even when I returned to Chicago. I was lost without her, and the only way to find myself again was to come back and win her heart as she'd won mine."

A chorus of awes broke through the room.

She tilted her head to the side and placed her hand over the center of her chest, moved close to tears by his words.

Then a thoughtful expression overtook his face as he set the remainder of the rose on the table and stiffly squared his shoulders. "Many of you know I used to dance." He tipped his head toward his parents. "I wasn't as good as my mom and dad, but I could hold my own. And I enjoyed it. And then . . . I stopped enjoying it. And I stopped dancing." He turned back to her. "But Karma has shown me how to dance again, and tonight, for the first time in over eight years, I'm going to dance. Truly dance. With her." He held out his hand. "My lovely bride, may I?"

Her cheeks burned in such a pleasant way as she placed her fingers in his, rose from her chair, and let him lead her away from the table toward the center of the dance floor.

"Are you ready?" he said quietly.

She smiled. "Yes."

"Are you nervous?"

"A little."

He slowed, stopped in the center of the room, then faced her. "Just pretend we're in our living room. Just the two of us. And this is just another lesson."

Just another lesson.

Ironic how their whole relationship revolved around lessons. And chocolate. Chocolate had definitely played a role in their

418

relationship. But in one way or another, they'd been teaching each other through lessons from the beginning. He had taught her about sex. She had taught him about life. He had taught her how to make truffles. She had taught him how to trust and let go. And over the last several weeks, he had begun to teach her how to dance.

And the culmination of all those lessons was for this moment. Their first dance as husband and wife.

The music began.

His gaze locked to hers.

And then they took their first synchronized step.

Two months ago, she never would have thought she could dance like this, and while she was nowhere near an expert, she loved how it felt dancing with Mark. Their nightly rumba lessons had become her favorite part of the day. The closeness, the sensuality, the intimate sharing of trust and passion for something they could enjoy together.

And, honestly, dancing had become her favorite kind of foreplay. It had unlocked a whole new element in their sex life.

Most importantly, though, she finally understood exactly why he'd stopped dancing eight years ago and why he'd written *I want to dance again* on his confession list. There *was* something magical and special about dancing with someone you loved. Someone you trusted. And not the kind of trust where you know the other person wouldn't drop you or fail to grasp your hand during a spin. This was the kind of trust that only two people who loved one another unconditionally could understand. Trust that there were no lies or secrets between them. The kind of trust that shattered walls, banished fear, and opened souls.

No way could she dance with anyone else the way she danced with Mark. It just wouldn't have felt right.

And now he was her life partner, and she was his. Life partners in the dance. Dance partners for life.

As he guided her expertly through the simple yet elegant rumba he'd choreographed, she briefly glanced toward the pockets of guests bordering the dance floor. Those who knew Mark's history appeared moved close to tears. They knew what he'd gone through to get to this moment, and many of them had probably thought they would never see him dance again.

But it was his mother who was most affected. Tears streaked her cheeks, and she held her delicate fingers over her mouth as if stifling a sob. Even so, her shoulders shook. Seeing Mark find his way back to the dance floor had clearly overwhelmed her.

"I think you've made your mom's whole decade." She lifted her gaze to his.

"I think you've made *mine*." His own eyes glistened with unshed tears.

"Well, you've made my entire life."

He led her through a spin then pulled her back against his body, his hips moving like they had a mind of their own. Watching the way his body moved was almost as much of a turn-on as when he spoke Italian.

"It's *our* life now, Karma." He blinked, and a single tear dropped from his lashes to the apple of his cheek as he pulled her even closer and tipped the side of his forehead to hers. "To honor . . ." He kissed her. "To love . . ." He kissed her again. "To have and to hold, forsaking all others, I do solemnly vow to cherish you until my heart expends its final beat . . . *Mrs. Strong*."

A delighted shiver raced through her body. Mrs. Strong. It was the first time he'd called her that.

"Until death do us part then?" She smiled up at him as they gently returned to basic side-to-side steps.

He kissed the tip of her nose. "Absolutely. And I plan on living a very long time."

"Is that so?"

He nodded. "You're stuck with me now."

She placed her cheek on the front of his shoulder. "There's no place I'd rather be."

He angled his head so it lay over hers. "I completely agree."

They had been destined for this night from the moment he'd sat down beside her at that blackjack table. Actually, their path had been set even before he sat down beside her. The way Mark told it, their journey had begun the moment he laid eyes on her from across the room. He'd known then that he would have her. He had just thought it would be for the night, not the rest of their lives.

How wrong he'd been.

Chapter 45

Most guys want to be a girl's first. Smart guys want to be her last. Lucky guys get to be both.
-Xuan Ta

Karma faced the mirror in the white marble and glass bathroom in their suite at the Canterbury in downtown Indianapolis. She was wearing the lacy negligee she'd worn the first time she and Mark made love. How fitting that she should wear it again for their first time to make love as husband and wife.

She checked the timer on the counter. Only twenty seconds remained. Mark had drawn her a bath, laid the negligee on the marble countertop next to the sink, set the timer, and told her not to come out until it went off.

That was so Mark. Even on their wedding night, he couldn't just let things unfold naturally. He had to have a plan.

She smiled at her reflection. Okay, so a plan was fine. It meant he wanted to make the night even more special than it already was. A night she would never forget.

She couldn't hear anything from the other side of the door. No music. No sounds coming from the TV.

Ten seconds left.

How would he react when he found out she'd been on birth control for the last month and he no longer needed to wear a condom? For that matter, how would *she* react when she felt him slip inside her for the first time, skin-to-skin?

Five seconds.

She took a deep breath and stepped toward the door.

The timer beeped once before she shut it off. Turning off the light, she slowly opened the door.

Candlelight from a half-dozen white candles scattered throughout the room greeted her. The curtains were open, letting in the light from the city.

Mark lay on the bed, on his side, propped on his elbow, wearing a pair of white linen drawstring pants. His gaze raked her body as she approached. Then he slowly sat up, reached behind him, pulled out two boxes wrapped in gold and white paper, and set them in front of him on the comforter.

"What's this?" She shyly bit her bottom lip, eyeing the boxes.

"My wedding gifts to you." He took her hand and guided her onto the bed.

"Don't you think marrying me is enough of a gift?" She kissed him then sat cross-legged in front of him on the plush white comforter.

Shaking his head, he picked up the longer and flatter of the two boxes. "Open this one first."

Trying not to rip the paper like an overly excited five-year-old, she sliced it with her recently manicured fingernail and peeled it back from the edge. Inside was a blue box. She immediately recognized the color as Tiffany's. When she pulled it free from the wrapping, the black lettering that spelled "Tiffany & Co." confirmed her suspicion.

"Mark . . ."

"Go ahead . . . open it."

She untied the bow then lifted the top to reveal a black jewelry box. When she opened the lid, she sucked in her breath, covering her mouth with her fingers. The diamond and ruby necklace and matching earrings were beyond anything she'd ever seen. For the necklace, rubies of graduating sizes were surrounded by diamonds and strung together to look like dozens of flower heads lined up side by side.

"When I saw this necklace, it reminded me of you the night we met," he said, lifting it from the box with both hands and extending it toward her.

Speechless, she leaned forward as he fastened the clasp behind her neck.

"When did you . . . ? How . . . ?"

A pleased grin spread over his lips. "I have my ways of getting what I want without you knowing, my lovely bride."

Her fingertips danced delicately across the priceless gems collaring her neck. "It's beautiful."

He pinned the earrings in her ears then set the empty box and wrapping paper aside. "When I make love to you tonight, you'll wear nothing but this." He caressed her skin around the necklace.

"But first . . ." He leaned back again and picked up the other box. "Your other gift."

He handed it to her, and she shook her head, not being as careful this time as her trembling fingers tore away the paper. "Mark, you've already given me too mu—" She cut off with a laugh as she pulled their old Truth or Dare game from inside the paper. "What is this?" She held it up in front of her.

"It's been a while since we played. I thought it would be fun to see how much we've changed."

She set the box on the bed and opened it. "Oh, we've changed. I can already tell you that."

"Well then, let's just see." He pulled the cards out and fanned them on the comforter as if he were a card dealer in Vegas.

"Silly me for thinking I would come out of the bathroom and you'd simply ravish me."

He plucked a card from the deck. "Oh, I'll ravish you." He gave her a roguish smile. "But I want to seduce you first."

"That's sweet of you, honey, but I'll let you in a little secret. I'm a sure thing."

Chuckling, he flipped the card over so he could read it. "I never take anything for granted. Now, truth or dare?"

She bit her bottom lip. This wasn't what she'd expected tonight, but given how hot and bothered this game had made her the other two times they'd played, she could only imagine how intense the sex would be later. After all, as the wedding was all about the dress, the honeymoon *was* all about the sex, and Mark more than understood that.

"Truth."

His coy smile sparked mischief into his features. "What's the kinkiest thing we've ever done together? Describe in detail what you liked about it."

She thought back over all the kinky things they'd done, as well as all the kinky things they still had yet to do. "How do I narrow it down to just one?"

He looked like he was reminiscing on some of their greatest hits himself. "You can do it. I have faith."

She smirked at him, then, after thinking it over a few more seconds, she said, "I think the kinkiest thing we've done is when you took me into that stairwell during the benefit."

"Mmmm, yes. Nice choice." He nodded shallowly. "But something tells me our kinkiest moments are still to come."

"And something tells me you might be right." He'd teased her about taking her to a sex party—just to observe, he'd said—but had yet to follow through.

She picked up a card. He said "dare" before she could even ask.

She turned the card around and read, "Whisper something in another language to me. Make it sound as sultry as possible."

What a perfect dare for Mark.

He leaned toward her, eyes hooded, lips curved in a sexy grin. *"Quando stasera faro l'amore con te, ho intenzione di farti urlare il mio nome e farti andare in pezzi, fino a quando non ti tremeranno le gambe e non potrai respirare senza lodare il giorno in cui ci siamo incontrati."*

She had no idea what he'd just said, but it sounded hot. A delicious ache pulsed between her legs. "What did you just say?"

He licked his lips and leaned closer so his mouth brushed over her cheek toward her ear. "I said that when I make love to you tonight, I'm going to make you scream my name and come undone until your legs quiver and you can't breathe without praising the day we met." His tongue flicked her earlobe before he closed his lips around it in a gentle, suckling kiss.

"Oh." The temperature between her legs continued to climb.

As he sat back and picked up a card, his self-satisfied expression oozed confidence that he would do exactly as he claimed once the game ended, which caused a shiver to race down her spine.

"Truth or dare?" he said, his voice smug yet husky.

"Truth." She didn't think she could handle a dare right now.

He read the card to himself then laughed and dropped his head back.

"What? What does it say?"

With a shake of his head and still laughing, he turned it around so she could read it.

"Have you ever had multiple orgasms?" She giggled.

He tossed the card aside. "I already know the answer to that one."

She'd been having multiple orgasms with him since their sex life had begun.

He picked another card and read it to himself first. "Ah, this one's much better. Do you think make-up sex is better than everyday sex?"

She thought about it a second then said, "We don't fight enough for me to be able to effectively answer that one."

"We've had a couple of big arguments."

She regarded him with a one-shouldered shrug. "Yes, but I can't say the sex afterward was any better than everyday sex. I mean, Mark, your everyday sex is pretty hot." She leaned toward him, running the tip of her finger down the center of his chest and torso. "Of course, if you ever want to role play a pretend argument followed with pretend makeup sex, I'm completely fine with that."

He closed his fingers around her hand and lifted it to his lips. "Noted." He kissed each knuckle. "Although faking an argument with you could be pretty difficult."

"I'm sure you'll manage." She grabbed the next card. "Truth or dare?"

"Truth," he said, releasing her hand.

"Tell me the dirty phrase you most love to hear in bed."

"That's easy. My name."

She gave him an admonishing glare. "Your name isn't a dirty phrase."

He rolled his eyes. "Fine. 'Fuck me, *Mark*,' or 'Oh God, *Mark*, I'm about to come.'" He did his best to imitate her voice while emphasizing his name. "It's how you say it that makes it sound so dirty." He narrowed his eyes lasciviously, if not a tad mockingly.

"I do not sound like that."

"Yes you do. You're just too busy coming to hear yourself."

"And you're not?"

He winked and gave her a lopsided grin. "Good point. But . . ." He held up his index finger. "Do I get brownie points for setting up a good pretend argument for later?"

She blew out a puff of breath. "You're impossible."

He pressed forward so his lips were barely an inch from hers. "And you love it."

She closed the distance and gave him a sweet, heated peck. "More than you know."

"Thought so. By the way, dare."

"It's your turn."

"I want you to go again."

She fought not to smile and stared into his eyes for a long moment. "Okay, fine. I'll go again." She reached down blindly, pulling a card from the pile. He sat back.

When she read the card to herself, she shook her head. "No way."

"What?"

"It says for you to imitate what I sound and look like when I orgasm."

He laughed. "Didn't we just discuss this? We're both too busy coming to actually know what we're hearing and seeing from the other, right?"

"Exactly. I'm picking again." She tossed the card aside and grabbed another. "Sit on my lap or let me sit on yours for the next three cards."

"This could be dangerous." He inched backward then patted his lap.

"Or severely shorten how long we continue playing." She crawled over the cards and straddled his crossed legs then wound her own behind his back.

"This is all just foreplay anyway." He cradled her exposed rump in his hands.

"Ah, so the truth comes out."

"You know I never do anything without ulterior motives." His fingers tapped her bare cheeks then squeezed.

"True."

One hand left her bottom, and she heard the soft whisper of the cards sliding over each other before he selected one and glanced to the side to read it. "Truth or dare, Mrs. Strong."

She couldn't get enough of him calling her that.

"Truth." She draped her arms over his shoulders.

He met her gaze. "When I'm on top of you, what's your favorite part of me to watch?"

"Ooohhh, that's a good one." She closed her eyes and imagined them having sex. He moved more like a powerful ocean wave than a human body, every muscle rippling as he surged into her then retreated only to flow against her again with even greater force. But it was the little details about his movements that she enjoyed the most.

"I love looking into your eyes, but . . ." She slowly swept her hands along the backs of his shoulders and down his biceps. "I think my favorite part to watch are your shoulders and your arms. And your chest. The muscles bunch and flex and kind of roll and twitch really hard when you're about to come. It's really sexy."

His eyebrows lifted as if he hadn't expected that answer. "I never knew that."

"I never thought to tell you before."

"Mmm, this game has allowed me to learn something new tonight. Maybe I can return the favor. Do you want to know what my favorite part of you is to watch when you're on top of me?"

She nodded, snuggling closer, feeling his erection beneath his smooth linen pants.

"Your hips." He gripped them and rolled them forward. "I don't know if it's all your yoga training or if it's just the way you naturally move, but you move your hips in the most incredibly sexy way. You hold the rest of your body almost completely still, but your hips . . . God, it drives me wild watching you fuck me."

"Really?"

"Yes."

She had no frame of reference. Before Mark, she'd slept with only two other guys, and neither had taught her much about sex. Then, last year, she'd been with Brad, but he was nowhere near as imaginative and attentive in the bedroom as Mark.

"Are you saying that most women don't . . . you know . . . use their hips the way I do?"

"I'll just put it this way. You are unique in every way, Karma. You truly were made for me."

That sounded like a thoughtful way of saying he wasn't going to talk about other women on their wedding night.

He reached behind her, snagged a card, and slipped it into her hand. "Truth."

Feeling like the luckiest woman in the world, she read, "Which is your favorite kind of sex: soft and sweet or aggressive and feisty?"

"Both," he said without hesitation. "You and I have done both, and, as you know by now, I have a dark side that likes to come out and play occasionally. So . . . I like both equally, depending on our mood. I love the intense feeling of connection when we *make love*. But when we *fuck* . . ." He emphasized the word to indicate that he considered feisty sex fucking and sweet sex making love, "I love the way we lose ourselves. It's as if we become different people when we're fucking. There's something extremely exciting about that, especially given my enjoyment of role-play sex."

"I feel the same way. I like both, too, for the same reasons." She was normally so conservative and straight-laced, but Mark had a way of pulling out a different side of her. One that was her polar opposite. Conservative became daring. Straight-laced became wanton. He was able to persuade her good girl persona into the shadows while coaxing out her inner vixen.

His grip tightened at the small of her back. "I think this is something we need to explore further now that we're married."

"What did you have in mind?"

He gave her one of his looks that said he wouldn't divulge anything tonight, but that she should expect the topic to come up again sooner rather than later. "We'll see." He picked another card. "Truth or dare?"

"Truth."

"What is the strangest thing that has ever turned you on?"

This was a no-brainer. "When you speak Italian."

"I didn't know that."

"Then you aren't paying attention. Haven't you noticed how hot I get when go all *Italian Mark* on me? I mean, I practically had an orgasm back there." She hooked her thumb over her shoulder, indicating five minutes ago.

"Mmmm, I have to remember that."

"Yes, please do, because that is damn near the sexiest thing ever."

"I thought *I* was the sexiest thing ever."

She slid her hands up his chest to his shoulders. "You're a given."

"Aren't you sweet." He pushed a card into her hand. "Dare."

"You sure enjoy the dares." She flipped the card around to read it.

"No risk, no reward."

"Then you'll love this." She cleared her throat. "For the next sixty seconds, touch yourself like you'd like me to touch you."

The way his eyelids fell and the corners of his mouth lifted, he clearly liked this dare. Leaning back on one arm, he rubbed his large hand across his chest then played with the sparse, dark trail of hair down his sternum, plucking with his thumb and forefinger. "You do this thing I really love."

What was he talking about?

Her confusion must have shown on her face, because he said, "You like to pluck my chest hair."

"I do?" She hadn't even realized she did that.

He nodded. "I love it. After we have sex, when you're lying next to me, your fingers play over my chest." He brushed his fingers back and forth to illustrate. "And every so often, you pull the hair. Not hard. You're very gentle." He tugged at a couple of tufts then grew more serious as his hand trailed south. "But what I really love . . ." He untied the drawstring on his pants then pushed the waist down to expose his ruddy erection. "Is when you wrap your hand around my cock." He did, and seeing his fist engulf his girth made her draw in an abrupt breath. "Your hand is smooth and gentle, yet firm." He stroked upward then back down. "And you never rush. You seem to enjoy holding me right at the edge, keeping me balanced between getting there and going over." He stroked a few more times then let go of himself without covering back up. "And . . . I think that's sixty seconds."

Why did time fly when she was enjoying watching him masturbate?

She reached behind her, snagged the first card she found, then handed it to him. "Dare."

"Mmm, a dare. You've been mostly about truth until now." He scanned the card.

"No risk, no reward, right?"

His hooded eyes met hers. "Now you're getting the hang of it." He read her dare. "Slowly trace my lips with your tongue." He flipped the card away so that it lifted on an invisible draft then tumbled and rolled to the opposite corner of the bed.

He was still reclined and supported on his arms, so she had to unwrap her legs from around his waist and shift forward so she draped along his body. His erection rubbed against the wisp of a thong that only just barely covered her privates.

"Like this?" She ran the tip of her tongue along the seam of his mouth.

His lips parted as he moaned. "That's nice."

Tracing around his mouth with tiny flicks, as if she were teasing an ice cream cone, she ran from one side to the other and back again. He rolled his head as she did, challenging her to stay on course as he sought her tongue with his.

Giving him a playful swat, she nipped his bottom lip. "Quit moving. I'm supposed to be the one licking you, not the other way around. You're just supposed to sit—"

She let out an abrupt, high-pitched moan—a startled squeak, really—as he swallowed her words, blistering her mouth with a searing kiss that curled her toes and made her roll her hips involuntarily against his cock.

The game had taken a fiery turn. He pushed forward and snared her in his arms, assaulting her mouth with his, claiming her breath.

When he broke away a moment later and shoved a card in her hand, snarling the word "dare" before attacking her neck and shoulders with the same intensity as he'd taken her mouth, she fought to focus. How did he expect her to read when he was kissing her with such fervency?

"Using your mouth"—he was already using his mouth to exceptional effect—"make your way from my wrist to my ear." She tossed the card over his shoulder as she dropped her head back, opening her neck to him. "Take your time."

He chuckled low and deep then dragged his mouth between her breasts as he lifted her arm. His tongue leaped from her sternum to her wrist and swirled a long, heated circle on her tender skin, sending a ripple of pleasure up her arm.

This was her husband. She was making love to her husband for the first time.

His lips blazed a trail up her arm, stopping briefly in the crease of her elbow so he could stroke his tongue side to side. Then he nipped his way along her upper arm, across the slope of her shoulder, up the side of her neck, finally reaching her ear, where the tip of his tongue circled all the way around before he whispered,

"I'm done playing." He gently thrust his hips between her legs.

She almost came on the spot, her whole body shuddering. Licking her lips, she nodded, gripping him like he was her life raft in the middle of the ocean. "Me, too."

He rolled her to her back, rose to his knees, gathered the cards in a haphazard pile, and dropped them to the floor beside the bed. Then he pushed his pants down his thighs and slowly peeled them off one leg at a time while she watched.

As always, the body that greeted her was perfection. Strong, powerful, dominant.

Sinking on his haunches, he pushed against her legs, raising her feet off the mattress so he could take hold of them and lift them to his chest. He pressed her soles against him, held them there, then let go as he leaned forward and seized the thin straps of her G-string on either side of her hips.

Like a man opening a treasured gift, he peeled the wisp of fabric away, exposing her, and dragged the G-string up her thighs, over her knees, to her ankles, where he wrapped the swatch of satin around her feet and caressed her ankles with his free hand.

"Take that off." He nodded toward her negligee, his voice husky, gruff, and commanding.

He refused to release her feet, making it harder for her to comply. As she wriggled out of the cotton and lace babydoll, he began kissing her toes and the top of her foot, burrowing his nose into the satin thong.

"You're glistening." His heady gaze drilled her between the legs, and he released her feet so he could slide his fingers between her labia.

She moaned, rotating her hips as he played his fingers up and down, lowering his head.

"Fuck." He pushed her legs apart and knelt between them. "I don't think I've ever seen you this wet." His fingers sank into her, followed immediately by the flick of his tongue on her clit.

She arched her back, crying out, already on the verge of coming.

"Let go. Come for me." He swirled his tongue around her swollen nub again.

She squirmed. So close. "But ... don't you ... ?" Didn't he want to be inside her when she came?

Following her train of thought, he paused long enough to say, "We have all night, Karma, and I'm going to make you come every way imaginable by morning," before feasting on her overly sensitive core once more.

He'd forced abstinence on them two weeks ago, telling her he wanted to build anticipation for what was happening this very moment. With that much of a celibate stretch between them, no doubt they would both come every way imaginable tonight, especially once he learned he could go bare.

Letting herself go, she succumbed to his tongue violating her clit, his fingers stroking her G-spot. Her body rose on a crescendo, her cries grew louder, and in less than twenty seconds, she blew apart as he pressed the pads of his fingers hard against the front of her vagina, deepening her orgasm, prolonging it.

"Mark! Oh God!" She thrust into his mouth as the vibrations in her core strengthened.

She was still coming as he tore himself away and reached for a condom.

"No." She grabbed his wrist. "You don't need one." She needed him in her. Now!

"But . . ." Confusion gave way to realization, which gave way to lust as he figured out what she was telling him.

She grabbed at his hips, pulling him, needing him. Another orgasm was already clamoring for release.

If what she felt tearing her body apart from the inside out was any indication, Mark was going to make good on his earlier promise. He'd have to carry her out of the hotel in the morning, because her legs might not function properly for the next twenty-four hours.

With more gusto than he'd ever shown, Mark pushed her legs open, panting hard as if he were on the verge of exploding, and drove into her.

Almost immediately, she came again.

She didn't know how it felt for him, but for her, having him inside her without a layer of latex between them felt . . . smooth. Hot. Slippery. He glided more easily in and out as he thrust harder, faster.

"Fuck, but that feels good." He was a piston in a high-performance engine, and all she could do was let him accelerate, push harder, drive faster, and speed toward the finish line.

"God, I need to slow down." He shivered, stopped, and let out a ragged exhale. "If I don't, I won't last ten more seconds."

She combed her fingers through his hair, which had fallen over his eyes. A film of sweat had erupted over his forehead.

Her muscles still quivered from her second orgasm, her thighs still tingling.

"Do you like my wedding gift?" she asking, smiling.

He arched one eyebrow appreciatively. "Like? Try fucking love it." He rolled against her for emphasis. "How did you keep this from me?"

She pulled her legs up, hooking one over his shoulder, making him groan. With a syrupy smirk, she said, "You're not the only one who knows how to get what you want and keep it a secret. I've been planning this for two months."

"You actually planned this?" He gave her one of his trademark crooked grins. "Someone's been taking notes."

"Someone's had a very good teacher. One who's taught me that a little planning *can* occasionally be a good thing."

"A teacher who's going to reward you for being such a good student." He thrust into her, making her gasp. Then he did it again. "A teacher who has a primal urge to fuck you senseless right now."

Their flesh slapped together as he plunged inside her to the hilt.

"Oh God!" Her blunt nails dug into his back as he awakened a third orgasm. "Don't stop, don't stop!"

Gritting his teeth and wrapping his arm around her thigh so he could maneuver her at will, he levered himself on his free arm, half-kneeling between her legs, thrusting into her at a breakneck pace.

She was helpless to do more than hang on. He was a man possessed, as taken by her special wedding gift as she was.

His shoulders bunched, his biceps flexed, and she knew he was close.

The moment his gaze met hers, her soul split open as her third orgasm shattered her body.

One continuous, keening moan drew out of his chest, growing as he took what was now his by law. To have and to hold — and give leg-numbing pleasure to — till death do they part.

With one final thrust that translated into a series of stiff-bodied shudders, he emptied inside her, spilling warmth through her core.

She'd never felt that before. That feeling of life pouring into her, from his body into hers.

Overcome, she cried out and clutched him close, holding his quivering body to hers, feeling the ceaseless pulses of his cock as he continued pumping into her.

It had been a long time since she'd felt him come so hard.

His arms gave out, but instead of collapsing on top of her, he rolled to his side and scooped her into his arms, pulling her against him.

Her cheek lay on his chest. She could hear the hard, rapid pounding of his heart.

It took him a moment to catch his breath enough to speak. "That was . . ."

She grinned at his speechlessness. "Good?"

His fingers combed through her hair. "I was thinking more along the lines of fucking incredible." He kissed the top of her head. "You've always been able to surprise me. Just when I think I know what you'll do, you throw me a curve and prove me wrong. I hope you never stop surprising me, Karma."

It was the same thing he'd said during his speech at the reception.

"I'll try not to."

He uttered a weak chuckle and nuzzled her hair. "You know, there's a lot I can still teach you. A lot of *lessons* we never got to before."

She recalled their four months of lessons two summers ago with fondness. She had enjoyed being his student, especially when he made her feel the way she felt right now.

"Are you thinking about reopening your classroom?"

His arms tightened around her, drawing her more firmly against his body. "Give me ten minutes to recover from your gift, and you'll find out."

"What? Here? Now?" Her body responded at just the thought of engaging in Mark's idea of lessons again.

"Can you think of a better time?"

She lifted her head so she could look him in the eye. "Absolutely not." She drank in the strong angles of his face, his solid jaw, his straight, regal nose . . . his firm lips. She kissed him. "I love you, Mr. Strong. I'm ready for you to teach me all that you know . . . so that I can please you for the rest of our lives."

One side of his mouth curled upward. "You've already pleased me for the rest of my life by marrying me."

"Then let me rephrase." She trailed her fingertips down his chest and abdomen, to his rebounding erection. "So that I can *give you pleasure* for the rest of our lives."

"I like the sound of that." He closed his hand around hers as she teased him. "But are you ready?"

"Ready for what?"

"Another journey, Mrs. Strong." He reached under the pillow and pulled out a red scarf, slowly twirling the fabric around his fingers.

She grinned at the twinkle in his eyes. Then she rolled to her back, making a deliberate show of opening her arms and laying them on the comforter in surrender, submitting herself.

"Lead the way, Mr. Strong."

As he placed the soft fabric over her closed eyes, she felt all the love in his heart. He would take care of her, cherish her, and keep her safe. He would more than live up to his vows.

"There's no one else I'd rather take this journey with," she whispered.

His lips brushed over hers as his fingers caressed her nipple to attention. "I feel the same way. It's you for me, Karma." He kissed her again. "It's always been you."

She bit her lip as he shifted his weight and linked his fingers around hers, pressing her arms against the bed, holding her down.

"I only have one question," she said as he kissed the side of her neck.

"What's that?" He spoke softly, his mouth beside her ear.

"Is there even anything left to teach me?" She already knew the answer, but teasing Mark was fun.

His dark, sexy chuckle sent a thrill through her body. Heat bloomed between her legs once more.

He flipped her abruptly to her stomach and smoothed his palm over her derriere, letting the tips of his fingers graze along the crease. "Oh, you really shouldn't have asked me that, baby."

Oh, yes she should have, because his reaction was exactly what she'd hoped for.

Let their new journey begin. She had a feeling it would be a good one.

Epilogue

Every story has an ending, but in life, every ending is a new beginning.
-Author Unknown

Friday, July 5
Cupid Loves Psyche
Mark and Karma's Blog

There once was a virgin named Psyche who was so beautiful she roused jealousy from the goddess Venus herself. Furious that her subjects doted their affection on Psyche rather than her, Venus ordered her son Cupid to make Psyche fall in love with a hideous, unworthy creature and thus punish her with mortification for all eternity. But when Cupid saw Psyche, he was so stunned, he wounded himself with his own arrow and fell deeply in love with her.

Obviously, this infuriated Venus, but Cupid was determined to have Psyche, no matter the cost.

Many trials and tribulations followed. They battled trust, battled Venus, and damn near battled the universe to be with one another. They were together, then they weren't, and then finally they found each other again. Ultimately, they were united by the gods in a glorious wedding and banquet in the heavens. Psyche later gave birth to a child they name Pleasure.

Their story is the inspiration for this blog. My Cupid and I have been through our own trials and tribulations. We met and fell in love against all odds, then were separated, and finally found one another again because our love refused to die. We've just come from our own glorious wedding, and even though it didn't take place in the heavens, it definitely felt divined by the gods. And through it all, we've discovered our own brand of pleasure.

Now we will share our journey and resulting pleasure with you as we continue forth in this magical thing called life, which refuses to make falling in love easy, which many of you probably already know. But my Cupid and I wouldn't have it any other way, and neither should you, because it was through fighting for one another that Cupid and I learned who we are and gained a level of intimacy and trust that is almost supernatural.

Isn't it through the flames that the phoenix arises reborn? So it is with love and intimacy. The harder you fight for it, the better it is once you find it.

My Cupid has opened my eyes to the woman I am and could potentially become. He has struck me with his arrow, and I anticipate he will never stop teaching me all the ways of pleasure. And I hope I can forever do the same for him, because he is my heart, my soul, and my life. Ours isn't a perfect story, and our journey has endured its share of bumps, but we are perfect together.

There are so many journeys we have yet to take and so many stories yet to tell. And we plan on sharing them with you so that many more Cupids and Psyches can find their way to each other through our example.

For now, Cupid and I have some honeymooning to do in Saint Lucia—a place for lovers like us—as we plan the next adventure in our ongoing story. So, until next time, live hard, laugh often, and love completely. Where there's possibility, there's hope. And where there's hope, anything's possible.

Forever in love,
Psyche & Cupid

Thank you for reading Full Circle, the final book of the Strong Karma Trilogy. However, this isn't the last you'll see of Mark and Karma. Make sure to subscribe to my newsletter and follow me on Facebook for more information about the upcoming books that will continue their story.

If you enjoyed this book, please consider leaving a review at the site where you purchased it. Reviews make a difference and matter more than you might realize in this reader-driven business called publishing.

About the Author

Donya Lynne is the author of the award winning All the King's Men Series. Making her home in a wooded suburb north of Indianapolis with her husband, Donya has lived in Indiana most of her life and knew at a young age that she was destined to be a writer. She started writing poetry in grade school and won her first short story contest in fourth grade. In junior high, she began writing romantic stories for her friends, and by her sophomore year, they had dubbed her *Most Likely to Become a Romance Novelist*. In 2012, she made that dream come true by publishing her first two novels and two novellas. Donya has many more novels and novellas planned for years to come.

For more information on Donya's books or just to say hello, visit her on Facebook or swing by her website.

https://www.facebook.com/DonyaLynne

www.donyalynne.com

www.ingramcontent.com/pod-product-compliance
Lightning Source LLC
Chambersburg PA
CBHW020500260626
47156CB00006B/1804